They Don't Know

By

Patricia Dixon

For Elfie and Sumaira
'If I had a flower for every time I thought of you...I could walk through my garden forever.'

– *Alfred Tennyson*

Foreword

The book you are about to read was inspired by the words of a song, They Don't Know by Kirsty MacColl. Perhaps before you begin you might take a moment to listen, it is the soundtrack to the lives of Daisy and Adam and the essence of a very different kind of love.

Prologue

France
December 2017

Daisy snapped shut the cover on her iPad and placed it on the table beside the radiator, sighing as she rubbed her tired eyes and plumped the cushions, which supported her aching body. Once the adjustments were made she poured tea from the Thermos before relaxing back into the armchair. To her relief, the tension she had felt for that and much of the previous week had receded slightly, those unrelenting vibrations of anxiety that flooded her heart before heading north to splash around, crashing and thrashing inside her brain, had eased. This partial release wasn't due to any resolution; it was merely because she was giving up, losing hope. Yet despite having one less emotion to battle, a murmuring persisted, refusing to give her the thing she lacked and craved most – peace of mind, and only an audience with the culprit responsible would remedy it.

Still, amidst the anxious mutterings, faint whispers of anticipation could be heard, which at first brought flickers of hope but were soon drowned out by the subsequent cries of despair each time she checked her empty inbox. The waiting was literally driving her mad. Until there was a reply to the messages she'd sent in the early hours, several days ago, following a long and sleepless night of deliberation, there would be no respite from the torment. Daisy accepted that.

Once again her eyes were drawn to the bedroom window where, outside, a row of hardy pine trees lined the driveway. Each was marked by a white spotlight that illuminated the quivering branches and shed light onto the lane, which wound gently to the entrance of the campsite. The proud guardians of her home were swaying in the harsh wind that had blown in from the Atlantic, remorselessly battering anything in its path. At least the incessant rain had stopped. The pounding on the roof tiles and banging of the loose, storeroom door had become unbearable and only added to the irritants in her head, tap-tapping away like a jackhammer. Despite its ferocity, Daisy was grateful that the wind had blown away the black storm clouds and now, the downpour had made way for Jack Frost who was busy airbrushing everything in a silvery sheen. He was aided in his task by an almost-full moon, which glowed benevolently on the fields and valleys of the Loire while crystal gems shone from the midnight blue, star-studded sky.

For as long as she could remember, her bedroom lookout post was one of Daisy's favourite places to be. From here, she could watch the new arrivals as they trundled up the drive, adhering to the 5mph speed limit before checking in at the office below. She had always found it intriguing, wondering who they were and where they were from, the only clue being the number plate on their cars or motor home, the weary cyclists with their backpacks and tanned legs more curious, their origins a mystery. Spying from above gave Daisy a thrill, catching a glimpse of the passengers who pressed their faces against the windows, eager to glimpse the pool or glean more about their holiday location. And in her teenage years, when she and her friends had spotted a handsome newcomer or two, it instigated a flurry of excitement and a mad dash downstairs to get a closer look.

Tonight, on this cold and blustery winter's evening, there was only one face Daisy wanted to see through the windscreen of his car. She had been sure he would come, or at least ring once he read the carefully composed email and duplicate text, each word agonised over, deleted then retyped. She had even sent a message via Facebook, restoring her dormant account before quickly logging out, unwilling to look on images from the past or acknowledge attempts at contact from old friends. Anything had been worth a try. Daisy knew she hadn't been deleted or completely blocked by him, and that in itself was a symbol of hope she could and would cling to.

After re-reading the message, Daisy worried it was too short; maybe she should've composed an essay, told him everything in words because Lord knows it would have been easier. But then again she knew him too well and the mood he was in, he would likely delete it, so the best way to get through was face to face, in the flesh – it always had been.

Daisy had no idea where he was currently living, or working, or anything about him really, a seemingly insurmountable problem made solvable by technology. His disappearance had been expected, or was it running away? The notion that he may have been driven to this excess had caused her great distress and tempered only by the knowledge that no matter where he was in the world, he still knew his way here, to France.

Ever since she'd pressed the send button, unless otherwise occupied, Daisy was resolved to sitting right there in her armchair, waiting for as long as it took, religiously checking her inbox and watching for headlights to appear at the top of the drive. She could just about see the ranch-style gates, which were closed but not locked, she had made sure. It was out of season and the pitches and rental caravans stood empty, so apart from a few guests over the Christmas period – those hardy travellers who used the site as a halfway house en-route to Spain – Daisy knew it was unlikely that they'd have visitors, especially this late at night. Yet still she persevered.

Pam, Daisy's mother, said she was being foolish and couldn't just will him to appear. And she would only make herself ill, going back to her obsessive ways and trawling over the past, and anyway, staring into the darkness made her look a bit deranged. If anyone looked up they'd think a mad-person lived there, the creepy woman in the window, like in a horror film.

She had been slightly relenting when she came in earlier bearing a tray laden with sandwiches and cake, a Thermos tucked under her arm and a gentler tone in her voice. As Pam bustled about the room, feeling the radiator to check it was warm, she once again reminded Daisy that all this moping wasn't healthy, especially in her condition. And it could be days or months before she got a reply, if one came at all.

Daisy tolerated her mum's fussing, especially when she had been forgiving of his behaviour, but it had taken a while and only because of how much he was hurting was he so angry and heartbreakingly sad. They all were. So until he was ready to talk (and only then would it be on his terms) Pam advised it was better that Daisy put him out of her mind – there were more important things to focus on. She knew her mum was only trying to soften the blow and toughen her up all at once, but it hadn't worked, although she was right about one thing.

As his personality dictated, he would be alone, festering, overthinking, maybe in some back of beyond place with a rubbish phone signal or purposely out of reach, a virtual Do Not Disturb sign hovering overhead, ignoring her plea and determined to make her suffer. Daisy just wanted a chance to explain, which he had denied her at the first asking, and now she berated herself over and over again for leaving it so long. Yes, she had been a coward but who wouldn't be after being utterly scalded by harsh and cruel words? His rage had prevented her from speaking out, numbed by shock, rendered weak and confused before being consumed by grief and loss.

Now, time was running out and it was so important that she told him everything and eased the hurt that a secret and two promises, one made to her soul mate and one made to his brother, sworn such a long time ago, had inflicted on them both.

They had shared such a colourful and at times confusing history yet despite everything that had passed between them, the good and the bad, she still loved him. And even though he was probably on the other side of the earth right now, one thing bound them together and would do forever, and for that reason she had to find a way to get through.

But there was something else. Daisy needed him by her side. She admitted it to anyone who would listen but just saying the words made it even more real and for now, for a little while longer, she could pretend it wasn't going to happen. Daisy was so scared, simply terrified of the pain she knew was coming and while her mum would be there for her throughout, it was his hand she wanted to hold, his face she needed to see. If he understood why she did what she did, then he'd forgive her and then everything would be okay, Daisy was convinced of it.

Pulling the duvet over her legs, which rested on the cushion and stool, Daisy settled in for the night. It was too uncomfortable to lie down so she would remain there, the uneaten food and flask of tea by her side, keeping an eye on the driveway and the red numerals of the alarm clock, which she'd placed strategically, directly in her line of vision, marking the hours.

Daisy had also invested every last ounce of faith in her guardian angel who she was relying on to deliver her repeated prayers to the relevant heavenly department, and then insist they were answered immediately. And failing that, Daisy had pinned every ounce of remaining hope on just one thing. That the man she loved all those years ago, who had been around for such a long time, who'd made her laugh and probably cry as many tears, who was deeply ingrained in the most precious memories, would remember how they once felt and what they had shared. They had missed out too because fate always had its own ideas for them but now, it was time to set their own agenda and give destiny a run for its money.

It was 3am and Daisy's eyes were weary from staring into the moonlit distance and being burnt by hot, stinging tears, so giving up the fight, they began to close. The heat from the radiator warmed her cheeks while the rhythmic clicking of air trapped inside the pipes kept time, accompanied from outside the window by a chill wind, humming nature's lullaby. Both worked together to aid much needed sleep and abet an escape from her woes. As she yawned and leant her head against the wing of the armchair, slowly drifting off, floating away on a cloud of memories, Daisy's mind headed in one direction only – into the past where Adam and Ryan were waiting, a happier place and time.

Chapter 1

Daisy met Adam on their first drizzly day in Manchester as they queued up to enrol for their university courses, and as it turned out, both were thinking exactly the same thing – they wanted to go home. The problem was that Daisy's home was in France, ironically a place from which she'd been desperate to escape and therefore had no intention of returning, cap in hand or otherwise.

Adam was in a slightly worse predicament owing to the fact that he didn't actually have a proper home to go to, unless you counted the floor of your brother's room at an air force base, so after weighing up his options, for now, regardless of the spartan furnishings and peach coloured walls, the halls of residence were his best bet.

Daisy had never felt so out of place and with every passing hour regretted more and more her decision to study in England, along with her stubborn refusal to bend to her parent's will or consider their advice. Maybe they had been right after all and she was unprepared for city life, a country girl at heart who would struggle being away from home amongst the hubbub of campus dwellers.

When she dared to look up from the leaflet she was pretending to read, Daisy took in the swarm of young men and women before her and cringed, knowing that even the way she dressed set her apart, never mind her accent. Hers was a moveable feast of dialects, her parent's lingering Manchester twang merged with her own bilingual lilt, making it hard for most people to place her true origins.

Daisy was also sorely regretting her choice of outfit. She had always gone her own way where fashion was concerned and never

1

followed the crowd, preferring to make her clothes or alter and embellish the ones she bought from the markets and charity stores in France. The students milling about or resting against the walls as they waited in line looked so different and at ease with themselves, dressed in baggy denim jeans and sweatshirts emblazoned with the names of American colleges, or in contrast, gothic characters, eyes lined with black kohl, their spiky, ink-coloured hair tinted with gaudy hues.

She told herself that it was all in her mind and they probably felt as nervous as she did, yet even the less garish students, those studious looking creatures who blended naturally into the crowd (like they were born to this life), all looked so much more at ease. How could it be that in the space of forty-eight hours, the girl who exuded confidence and joie de vivre, who was always the leader of the pack and breezed through life, felt like her flame had been snuffed out? How could she have got it so wrong?

Daisy wasn't afraid of the city, not in the least, and had rammed this fact home to her parents, pointing out that if she'd remained in France to study, her relocation would still involve facing the big bad world. Maybe they'd have felt happier if she'd chosen Nantes, Angers or Rennes, so much closer to home, or would they have reacted in the same way had she searched further afield and picked Marseilles or Toulouse?

Feeling a lump forming in her throat and the threat of tears brought on by a simple truth, Daisy sucked in air and blinked back any eye leakage. Had she been sensible and less headstrong then maybe right now she'd be standing in a never-ending queue at a French université, with one of her friends by her side. And if not, at least home wouldn't have felt so far away. Oh how she missed Cassandre and Inès, her closest friends, sharers of teenage secrets and childhood adventures. They had been inseparable since école maternelle where Cassandre had adopted Daisy on the first day, fussing over the shy little English girl before reluctantly sharing her with the other classmates.

*

After selling up and leaving their life in Manchester behind, Bill and Pamela (Daisy's parents) had taken the bold step of starting a new one in France where they had bought a thirty-acre campsite with a fishing lake in the village of La Forêt. It was situated right on the edge of the parc naturel and a stone's throw from la Loire, an idyllic place for a young child to grow.

At the age of four, Daisy's transition had been quite painless, owing largely to her patient teachers and having everything a child could wish for right on the doorstep. On site there was a heated swimming pool and a lake in which to frolic during the summer months, along with an endless supply of extra friends, courtesy of the campers and caravanners who pitched up year after year.

Daisy's favourite classmates also benefitted from the many facilities at Campanule Campings. Here they would while away their school holidays under the watchful eyes of Bill and Pamela, who in the boring winter months would open up the sports shed so their daughter and her friends could play ping pong and bar football, or dance the night away, singing along to the karaoke machine. Out of season, Daisy and her little gang refocused on flirting with the boys from the village school, mere substitutes until the start of spring. As far as they were concerned, country boys had nothing on the trendy city dwellers who would soon be rolling into the village.

Yes, Daisy would be the first to admit that her formative years were more or less perfect, cycling along quiet country lanes, rowing on the lake or picnicking in the woods with the girls. They would camp out and talk for hours, watching stars shoot across an ebony sky, just far enough from Bill and Pamela to make it an adventure but close enough in case the night time noises sent them fleeing to the sanctuary of Daisy's bedroom.

The arrival of raging hormones was followed closely by innocent romances that blossomed with each holiday season. The expectation of the summer months and new arrivals of the male species was almost as thrilling as the real thing. Daisy broke hearts and had hers bruised too, waved goodbye to forlorn faces who had sworn to keep in touch, shedding tears for boys with whom she was in love, until another happy camper arrived.

For Daisy and her friends their early teens involved harmless fun, holding hands and chaste kisses, all emboldened by the bottles of cider they hid in the woods. There had never been anything serious until at the age of seventeen and three quarters, just before she left home for university, Daisy lost her virginity to Jansen, a fair-haired, athletic, freckle-faced boy from Germany. There was nothing calculated about the event, yet when the opportunity arose and after being a good girl for so many previous summers, and lagging behind Cassandre, Daisy decided that perhaps it was time to get it over and done with, just one less thing to worry about when she ventured into the big, bad city.

Their time together was fleeting and remembered through a perfect summer haze where the searing heat of August lent itself to swimming naked in the lake, just the two of them. Afterwards, they lay together on a bed of campanulas, beautiful bellflowers whose heady scent infused the humid air. Daisy could still recall every second of that night, the sounds of the frogs and crickets, the saucer moon reflecting on the water, distorted by the ripples as they swam. The feel of grass beneath her body as the worldly Jansen lay above, their skin on fire, set alight by a simple touch. As first times go, and after hearing less romantic versions from her friends, Daisy saw hers as a rather wonderful experience and ever since, whenever she caught the scent of bellflowers on the breeze, would think of her fair-haired lover, her golden German boy.

After such a blissful and carefree existence, when Daisy announced her intention to study in England, Bill and Pamela were naturally confused and terribly shocked, unable to comprehend why their daughter would seek out a life in a faraway city, and an English one at that. They had always assumed she would remain there, in the heart of the Loire, with them.

Daisy swore it was simply the desire to strike out alone, experience something new, to compare, and then she would know for sure the direction her life should take. Did she want to expand their family business or gain experience within a career of her own choosing? Daisy was English yet could remember nothing of her country of origin, or the city where she and her parents were born. She wanted to walk the streets that they once had, reconnect with her heritage and find her own identity, and in order to do this she needed to leave the sanctuary of home. It was like an experiment and she had a three-year segment of her life in which to conduct it. They had taken a chance, thrown caution to the wind and set off on an adventure and now, Daisy wanted hers, but in reverse.

She would never have said as much, not unless she'd been backed right into a corner, but sometimes, on those days when the silence and isolation of the countryside became restrictive, Daisy suffered moments of resentment. At four years old she hadn't been given a choice or say in the matter, her parents had upped sticks and moved to France so now, maybe they owed her a free pass, or at least a taste of what it feels like to do something unexpected and a teeny bit reckless.

Thankfully, Pamela and Bill knew when they were defeated so after they'd tried every trick in the book to change Daisy's mind, they gave in gracefully and set her free. The knowledge that Bill's brother still lived on the outskirts of Manchester and could be called in an emergency eased their minds. And so in the autumn of 2002, Daisy bade a tearful farewell to her similarly distraught parents and for the first time in her life found herself completely alone, in Manchester, the sprawling city where she was sure her destiny lay.

Chapter 2

Adam and Ryan
Manchester 2002

From the moment Adam spotted Daisy in the queue he was drawn to her like the proverbial moth to the flame, which is why he tried to move further along, taking advantage of the chaos and noise of the corridor. Most of the excitable students were deep in conversation and couldn't care less if someone snuck in front of them. They were in no rush and didn't notice the tall boy in a leather jacket as he pushed in, his stealth and determination egged on by curiosity.

There was something different about the bohemian girl with the long, strawberry blonde hair that hung in waves, with sun-kissed arms and a riot of freckles covering her gently tanned face. Maybe it was her clothes, the tasselled, multi-coloured sparkly scarf and the way the folds of chiffon were wound stylishly around her neck, or the tie-dye t-shirt teamed with patched up jeans, slung low on her hips, revealing her pierced navel and taught stomach. Her bag was made of velvet, or maybe a piece of old carpet, with long, fringed handles and it hung low by her side, casually, with ease. She was cool.

Adam thought she resembled a throwback from the seventies, or maybe she was a ghost, caught in another dimension, a misty vision that only he could see. That she looked nervous and shy was in contrast to her garb, and she appeared to be alone which made him feel sad because Adam too was hating this creeping feeling of dislocation, floundering in a new world amongst so many strangers.

During his surreptitious observance Adam had gleaned much useful information, like the fact that she had green eyes and was pretending to read the leaflet she was holding, a map of the campus and not that interesting. If he hadn't spotted the vision he would most likely be doing the same thing because in his imagination, the first day at uni hadn't been like this and so far it had fallen short of his expectations. In his desperation to strike out and gain independence, Adam hadn't considered whether or not he possessed the necessary skills to survive in an alien environment and assumed it would be just like his first day at college in his home town of Chorley. There, he'd had back-up from a handful of school friends who'd also made the leap from school to student life but it was an adventure they'd embarked on together; here he was quite alone.

The most important factors of all that he'd omitted from this flawed equation were his gran, Olive and older brother, Ryan. It had hit him with a wallop that once lectures were over they wouldn't be there to listen to his news as they sat around her kitchen table and ate their tea. He had assumed that he could languish there forever and would have been content, mapping his life around them, not straying too far, coming home each night to roost. But when the centre of gravity in his very small world disappeared after life dealt him another bitter blow, Adam was forced to rethink. So after much deliberation he decided to head for the city and what he saw as his spiritual home but really, when it came down to it, university life in Manchester was his only viable option.

*

Adam and Ryan, since the age of ten and fifteen, respectively, had been cared for by Olive who, despite having struggled all her life, not just making ends meet but coping with her feckless daughter, had taken in her grandsons when they needed her the most.

Ernie, their father, had being incarcerated for much of his adult years, the brief spells when he was released into society never lasting long, much to the relief of the whole family. Their mother, Miriam, didn't cope well with life in general, be it as a mother, the wife of a convict or during the interminable periods when Ernie wasn't banged up. In all instances she turned to the bottle for comfort and oblivion, leaving her sons to suffer the wrath of their father or in a state of neglect, teetering on the verge of intervention by the care system.

In most cases Ryan took on the responsibility for Adam, especially at school where he was relentlessly picked on for having a smelly uniform and tatty shoes. Nobody dared make fun of Ryan because he could defend himself whereas Adam was an easy target, laughed at for being a scruff, the odd one out, the kid who got rubbish Christmas presents and free school meals.

When Adam was seven, Ernie was killed during a prison scuffle and despite their father's gruesome death at the hands of a disgruntled lifer wielding a DIY knife, both boys shared a sense of gratitude for his departure from their lives and hoped it was a turning point. They were disappointed.

Miriam reacted in much the same way as she did to any crisis and sought solace in gin and the arms of other men – any old low-life, especially those with access to happy pills, would do. One loser after another found their way into her bed, although there were a couple of candidates who showed promise, raising the hopes of her sons who hankered after just a hint of stability in their lives. Eventually Adam and Ryan accepted the inevitable. Not only would Miriam never find true love, she was beyond redemption where motherhood was concerned and well on her way to killing herself through drink and drugs.

When their mum overdosed on a cocktail of Valium and Blue Nun, the coroner recording her death as accidental, both boys moved in with their gran. It wasn't ideal, two growing teenage lads squashed into the box room of her council flat, but they managed. Ryan hung around for as long as he could, taking labouring jobs to help pay their way while accepting that his dream to join the air force would have to wait until his younger brother was old enough to manage without him.

Once Adam left school and embarked on his A levels, Ryan knew it was now or never and after receiving the blessing of his only two family members, joined the RAF, but not before making a solemn promise to always be there for Adam, no matter where his job took him.

Ryan slipped easily into military life. It offered almost everything he had lacked whilst growing up and it felt like salvation. There was order and routine, a solid framework and a pathway that he could follow. Here he could actually envisage his future, make plans.

Once his training period was over Ryan soon began to travel the world, and surrounded by a steadfast group of friends he embraced service life and its advantages. He was free, unencumbered, waged and happy, a potent combination that Ryan thrived on. Ever conscious of becoming too selfish, he made a concerted effort to keep in touch with home, visiting when work commitments allowed, mainly to show his face and reassure Adam, but the pull just wasn't as strong. The desire to return to a place that held dark memories lessened with each visit. His departure felt more like another escape, a thought that left him racked with shame and guilt.

And it wasn't just the abandonment that unsettled him, it was his younger brother's gentle nature and increasingly peculiar ways, along with his precarious predicament owing solely to their gran's deteriorating health. Adam wasn't a burden, not yet, but unless he found his feet in the big bad world, Ryan expected that eventually he would be.

Adam did his best and more or less looked after himself. He had a part time job at B&Q and took on all of the household chores, but it was becoming clear that he couldn't care for his gran – some things were best left to the professionals. Ryan had arranged for a home help and set up a direct debit to help towards the bills. Despite all their best efforts nobody could prevent the inevitable and one month before Adam sat his final exams, Olive suffered a stroke then contracted pneumonia. After hovering at death's door for weeks she slowly recovered, but only to partial mobility. Social services intervened and pronounced their judgement, and regardless of Adam's protests, Olive was moved to a local nursing home.

Now rendered homeless, Adam needed a safe haven until he could take up his place at university in Manchester, a city that as far as he was concerned, ticked all the boxes. Taking full advantage of a student loan, he'd chosen a media studies course, which was broad enough to leave his career options wide open while resolving to worry about repaying his debt when the time came. The lure of Madchester, the home of Oasis (Adam's all-time favourite band), was irresistible and along with the music and club scene, there were ample opportunities in the city to find part-time work and perhaps one day, put down roots.

There was no way the rules could be bent so that Adam could remain in Olive's flat; council accommodation was in short supply and they were given two weeks to vacate the property. Thanks to the kindness of Adam's college friend whose parents took pity, he was offered shelter until he'd completed his last exam. One day later, Adam filled a holdall with his belongings and then a box containing his second-hand record player and vinyl discs. Boarding a coach was soon heading east to an air force base and a blow-up air bed on the floor of the block where Ryan lived.

Until his course began in September, Adam bedded down with his brother for the summer. The months he spent with Ryan in Norfolk would always be remembered as one of the happiest times of his life, tempered by trips to see their gran who now spent their visits sleeping. When she did awaken, Olive was lost in another world where her grandsons' faces resembled those from her past, a time and place in which she seemed happy to reside.

Back on the base, as jets flew overhead, Adam spent the days reading, immersed in books on pop culture, world history, memoirs, travel adventures, anything which kept his mind stimulated, searching for knowledge and inspiration. Just like his brother, Adam was determined not to squander one single moment of his life and although they'd chosen different paths, both vowed to avoid at all costs an existence that involved crime or being dependent on the contents of a bottle containing pills or alcohol.

They packed as much fun and laughter into those summer months as they could, binding tightly their bonds of brotherhood, recording days by the sea and listening to music that in the future would always transport them back in time.

When Ryan turned his attention to practicalities and their impending separation, he bought Adam a leather jacket, James Dean style, and enough clothes and home comforts to see him through the first year at university. The jacket was Adam's pride and joy, something precious, a temporary replacement for his brother's real-life protection and warmth. Every time he slipped his arms inside and wrapped the tough leather around his body he was reminded that with Ryan in his life, he would always be safe.

Both were about to take different directions, parting them for long periods, but no matter where the road took them, however far apart, they would always have each other, and nothing could ever change that.

*

It was a drizzly September day when Ryan dropped Adam off at the halls of residence. After lingering as long as possible, doing his best to appear casual while battling the urge to stay one more night or a few more hours at least, just to ensure Adam was settled, the time came when they had to say goodbye. Both were stoical, jokey. One stressed about the other's long haul journey back across the Pennines then onwards to Norfolk, the older elicited promises that the younger would eat regularly and ring if there was anything at all he needed. The parting was swift and man-like when in fact both felt more like children, desperate to cling on, the past coming back to haunt them.

Ryan's resolve crumbled the minute he turned the corner and was out of sight, forcing him to pull alongside the road where for the first time in years he sobbed unashamedly, trembling palms covering his face, crying bitter tears laced with sorrow, regret and resentment. Memories resurfaced of the day three years ago when a young, eager man stepped off a train, alone and bewildered.

It all came flooding back. Ryan had boarded a military coach that transported him and similar looking new recruits to RAF Halton where he would begin basic training. The difference between him and them was having nobody to wave tearful goodbyes. His eyes were staring downward as the coach pulled off, not out of the window thus avoiding scenes of parental love.

That first night amongst strangers, sleeping in a room lined with steel beds, lying beneath cold sheets, surrounded by unfamiliar sounds and smells, that memory was ingrained in him. Yes, he cried silently, for what he wasn't too sure. Maybe it had been a test, all part of the experience. Once you'd resisted the urge to change your mind and run came the gradual stripping back of who you were, and then they built someone new. And Ryan would do it all again, even the 4.30am starts followed by a five-mile run, marching in the sleet and rain, a sergeant bellowing orders in your ear. It had all made him the man he was now, capable, prepared and proud to have endured and triumphed.

Ryan's passing out parade was one of the greatest achievements of his life and the only downside was that their gran had been too frail to make the journey to Buckinghamshire, meaning that such a hard-earned moment of glory was witnessed only by Adam. Their whole life seemed to be captured in snapshots where either one of them experienced momentous occasions alone in a crowd or without a family embrace. So many silly, small things that actually mean so much, like swimming your first length at the baths, being a wise man in the nativity, getting a certificate in assembly for Reading Star of The Month, coming first in the sack race, passing your driving test, collecting your exam results, joining up to the RAF. All those shiny beacons along the path of life they had navigated alone.

On a good day, Ryan told himself that maybe it had made him stronger, more determined to succeed and got him to where he was today, but on a bad day he was swamped by such loathing it clouded his mind and hardened his heart.

It was precisely that sobering thought, the image of his solitary brother who'd reached another unmarked milestone, that had undone him. Ryan knew Adam was different, made of gentler stuff, and what had made him strong had left his brother vulnerable, unsure.

Adam was one of life's easy-going dreamers, deeply intense, slightly OCD, his thirst for knowledge and the desire to broaden his horizons another borderline obsession. He was overly sensitive and easily hurt, mainly because he gave too much of himself in friendship and his loyalty was often abused or never repaid. As a small child this had led to disappointment and confusion, tears in the playground after trying to join in and being pushed to one side. Adam was always the boy who ended up stuck in goal and sent over the fence to retrieve the ball regardless of whether he'd been the one to kick it there in the first place.

Thankfully he'd fared better at secondary school when his cheeky personality began to emerge. Adam was a joker, deflecting jibes and teasing with humour, leaving fist fights and petty arguments to the rougher boys. Popular with the girls, Adam had his fare share of admirers but relationships never seemed to last long. He preferred his own company, cocooned in their tiny bedroom listening to music, lost in lyrics and a world of his own.

While Ryan enjoyed many a romantic liaison, Adam remained unattached and seemed disinterested in the girls who rang the house phone or hung around on the corner. It had never been a big issue yet selfishly Ryan wished his brother would find himself a nice girlfriend, or even a boyfriend if that was his thing. Then at least he wouldn't have felt so guilty when he went on a date and now, with opportunities further afield, he could leave Adam behind knowing he had someone to turn to, love or lean on in his absence.

This was another reason why Ryan worked so hard. He was desperate to lay some foundations and prepare for the future, just in case Adam ever needed a safety net if life treated him cruelly. Ryan couldn't bear the thought of a return to the instability and poverty of their childhood. The trade-off was having to spend time apart yet Ryan told himself it would be worth it, a sensible sacrifice. But leaving his brother behind in Manchester brought back so much, triggering buried emotions.

Ryan knew how it felt to embark on a new life when the one you had left behind had given you only crumbling blocks on which to build. They'd had little in the way of guidance, nurture or support yet he'd been lucky to find himself a new and more reliable family. The military had given Ryan that stability, a goal and purpose, he only hoped that his brother would find the same and somewhere amongst the sea of people who had come to study in Manchester, some decent friends of his own and a temporary replacement for family.

*

Adam had waved like crazy as Ryan drove away, determined not to let his brother pick up on even a hint of what was going on inside his head and heart. A sense of such abandonment, borderline panic and an overwhelming desire to chase after the car had swamped him. Never before in his life had he felt adrift, made a hundred times worse because in two days' time, Ryan would be boarding a plane to Oman. The location of the air force base was marked firmly with a red dot on the map in Adam's mind. He knew exactly how far away his brother would be – 4,894 miles to be precise – and had plotted the route the military plane would take, crossing mountain ranges and sea, taking Ryan so far away.

Turning to face the halls that were teaming with excited students unloading cars stuffed with their belongings, Adam inhaled and blinked the tears from his eyes. Skirting around a family group who were piled up with boxes he hurried past and flung open the doors to the halls, acknowledging the unfamiliar smell of fresh paint. Taking the stairs two at a time he assured himself he'd become accustomed to the noise and find friends amongst the blur of strange faces. He could do this. He *would* do it, for himself and for Ryan – keep his part of the bargain and stay true to their oath. Today was the start of a brand new life and no matter what, he had to grab the opportunity with both hands.

Chapter 3

Daisy and Adam
Manchester 2002

He only needed to jump two more places before he was standing by her side. Determined not to spend another twenty-four hours riddled with regrets or give in to the growing urge to pack up and hot foot it to the coach station where he would buy a ticket for the first destination on the departure board, Adam took a deep breath and spoke to ghost girl. She was definitely real because her floppy bag touched his leg and he'd caught the scent of patchouli, or something very similar. His nerves almost got the better of him when instead of making some smart and interesting comment, he asked a rather stupid question: "How long do you think this will take?" Those eight tentative words changed Adam's life.

Daisy was so relieved to have someone to talk to she barely noticed the flushed cheeks and nervous expression of the boy who seemed to have appeared from nowhere. Once they'd discussed the banalities of the queue situation and agreed that it might take forever, Adam, as he'd introduced himself, asked about her course and then told Daisy all about his. She was studying Travel Management; he was studying Media Studies. Daisy hoped her degree would be useful in expanding her parent's business that she would someday inherit, or perhaps she might go her own way and work for a commercial holiday company. Adam wanted to keep his options open but quite fancied working in television or maybe the record industry, anything as long as it involved fun and travel, but most of all his love of music and the telly.

As they shuffled along, Adam also learned that her home was in France, that they were going to be living in the same block and both of them were starving, prompting him to suggest going for a bite to eat once they were signed up. After eagerly accepting his proposal, Daisy admired Adam's leather jacket, presuming it was a family heirloom, which forced him to confess that the distressed look was due entirely to a sheet of sandpaper, not the passing of time. Daisy, now feeling less shy and mightily impressed by her new friend's creative streak, then explained that she'd made the patches on her jeans after saving fabric from her old clothes – it was a way of recycling her favourite things and also making the denim last longer.

By the time they finally made it to the row of tables behind which sat fatigued administrators, both Daisy and Adam felt somewhat buoyant, eager to fill in the forms and head off for lunch. As the woman opposite silently shuffled and stapled a multitude of paperwork, Daisy stole glances at her new friend who was seated at the next table, chatting away.

Adam was fair of complexion with a handsome face made more masculine by the firm set of his jaw, which was covered by the hint of a shadow, like a rock star whose shoulder-length and unruly, dark brown hair she suspected had been styled to look exactly so. Daisy looked away quickly, just before his pale brown eyes, previously focused on the task at hand, sought hers.

Later in the cafeteria over baked potatoes and mugs of tea, they discovered they had the same warped sense of humour, hated horror films about witchcraft but had nothing at all in common on the music front. Daisy was a huge fan of Kirsty MacColl and Adam was an Oasis devotee. She was a vegetarian and he certainly wasn't, and although it seemed like a great idea at the time to move to a huge city where they could go mental and party till they dropped, both had no idea of where to begin, never mind find their way back to the halls.

It was Adam who eventually posed the 'relationship' question by asking Daisy if she had a boyfriend back home in France. Yet there was something about the way he said it that told her he was asking out of genuine interest and not as one would expect – to ascertain her status for his own benefit.

"Nope! I'm totally single and have been for a while now – what about you? Have you left someone behind in Chorley?" Daisy expected him to describe a loyal lass who was pining away at home so was somewhat taken aback by his forthright answer.

"Nah…that's the last thing on my mind. I haven't got time for relationships and intend to stay single for as long as possible. There's plenty to occupy myself with at the moment but I'm surprised you've not got someone waiting for you. You'll be beating them off with a stick soon, especially at the Freshers' Ball – are you going?" When Daisy shrugged, attempting to swallow a mouthful of potato, Adam carried on, looking quite pleased.

"We could go together. It's a rite of passage so it'd be a sin to miss out. I'll be your chaperone if you like and make sure you don't get mauled by a third-year sex-pest. You do know what they call the first week of uni, don't you?" Adam was scraping his plate and had already gleaned that he was in the company of someone who may benefit from the shelter of one of his wings and sure enough, when he looked up noted Daisy's bemused expression. He helped her out by leaning forward, whispering dramatically.

"It's Fuck a Fresher week!"

Daisy's eyes widened. "Is that what they call it, seriously?"

"Yep! This place is crammed with randy kids who have escaped their cages and intend to live the student dream in all its glory. There's not a parent in sight so they can go totally wild and celebrate their freedom by taking their pick of the crop, which is why looking at this lot I'm more than happy to keep my legs crossed." Adam nodded sideways to a table teaming with giddy girls, one of whom caught his eye and smiled.

"See what I mean? To coin a very well-known phrase, they'll all be mad for it!" Adam winked at Daisy who had reverted back to feeling provincial and unprepared but forced a laugh at his joke, not quite sure if it all sounded thrilling or bloody terrifying.

"Well I might just follow your lead and occupy myself elsewhere. I've got three years to find myself a boyfriend so for now I accept your offer and you can protect me from whatever evils are out there, is that a deal?" Daisy hoped that romance would be on the cards during her time at university but had no intention of whipping her knickers off in the first week.

"Yeah, it's a deal, and you can protect me too – believe it or not, I'm a chick magnet." Adam winked at his dumbfounded new friend then spared her from having to respond. "Come on, let's go for a wander, and we need to sort our bus passes then we can have a mooch around town. I've got a list of all the places I want to see, starting with the Haçienda. It's not actually there anymore but there's a plaque on the wall, which is better than nothing I suppose!" Adam was fastening the straps on his rucksack, oblivious at first to Daisy's second vague look of the day. "You have no idea what I'm talking about, do you?"

Daisy shook her head, laughing when he put his head in his hands before looking up and feigning hurt.

"I cannot believe you have never heard of it. This is the centre of the Brit-pop universe and The Haçienda was a huge part of one of the most brilliant eras in music history! And then there's Morrissey and The Smiths, Joy Division, New Order – they are all total legends from right here in Manchester, and don't even get me started on Oasis. I'm going to top up my record collection with all the greats, do you like vinyl? I love it. The sound is just something else." Adam had come alive during his mini-homage to Manchester, eager now to drag his new companion along on the adventure of a lifetime, or at least a bus ride into the city centre.

"Right, passes first, and then I can start to educate you properly. Never mind your Travel degree, this is much more important. Come on, drink your brew, we need to go." Adam tugged her arm and pointed to the door, sighing dramatically for effect.

Glad to have a funny companion and an easy-going and very good-looking one at that, Daisy did as she was told and shuffled along the bench before following Adam onto Oxford Road. The drizzle had stopped and the sun was peeping from behind a greyish cloud. As they headed off, merging into the crowd of students, Daisy had the strangest feeling that this was meant to be, that meeting Adam on the corridor had been pre-ordained and just maybe, despite her earlier concerns about Madchester, she really had made the right decision after all.

Later that day, despite terribly aching feet, they somehow navigated the route to their halls and after buying two pot noodles and a packet of chocolate chip muffins from the corner shop, both plucked up the courage to enter the communal kitchen and boil the kettle, then scurried back to the sanctuary of Adam's room to enjoy their feast. While outside the rain poured down and wind battered the windows, inside they listened to album after album on Adam's treasured record player and here, Daisy's musical odyssey began. That first night together was one they would never forget. It was the beginning of them.

Without thinking too much about it Daisy and Adam's life soon took on a companionable pattern. In the mornings she would descend one floor and call for her sleepy friend who stayed up far too late and hated early starts, before walking to their lectures. After splitting up for a few hours and where timetables permitted, they'd meet for lunch or make the return journey together at the end of the day. Almost inseparable amongst their slowly growing group of new acquaintances, they occupied themselves with their studies, listening to music, eating toast topped with something from a tin and in between mouthfuls watched Coronation Street in the communal lounge, or laughing at everything and nothing in particular.

It was clear from Adam's general demeanour that he had no romantic intentions whatsoever towards Daisy. There was a distinct absence of gooey-eyed looks, electrically charged vibes when they accidentally touched, or veiled romantic hints and cheesy chat-up lines. They would sit side by side on her bed while they scribbled notes onto A4 pads and on a number of occasions had fallen asleep mid-conversation, both exhausted after staying up late to finish an assignment. Yet despite their close proximity, Daisy felt more comfortable around Adam than she had ever been with a member of the opposite sex. Maybe it was his determined statement about remaining single or that despite there being a honey pot of students who regularly gave him the eye, Adam appeared to be oblivious or completely disinterested.

Daisy knew something of how his admirers felt because when she spotted him in a crowd her heart lifted, but only because she was glad to see his gorgeous smiley face, the one that seemed to light up when he saw her across the cafeteria. They would link arms as they walked and when the sole of her boot began letting in water, Adam gave Daisy a piggy back all the way home. Physical contact was the norm, familiar and comforting. As was the smell of the shampoo and deodorant he used and the washing powder they shared during weekly visits to the launderette, another companionable ritual, like buying dreadfully unhealthy food that would have made Daisy's mum weep.

The best night of the week was Friday because they always had a chippy tea. These were the things her mum and dad used to talk about, the missing links in her heritage and something as simple as this somehow brought them close. One of Daisy's favourites had to be chips and gravy, or a chip barm, or pudding and chips with Manchester caviar – mushy peas. Her indecisiveness drove Adam completely mad so he invented the rule that she had to make up her mind on the way, otherwise everyone in the queue would starve to death. And then there was Vimto, the best cordial in the world served either boiling hot on a winter's day or ice cold in the summer. The cake shop in the precinct sold the best meat and potato pie ever, as well as Daisy's favourite discovery – Manchester tart. Their list of culinary delights was endless.

Adam was like a cultural gold mine of information and soon educated Daisy on the ways of her Mancunian ancestors, explaining the ins and outs of a Northern way of life. For a start, nobody ate dinner in the evening; in Manchester and where he came from you had your tea, which occurred roughly between the hours of five and seven. At midday you had your dinner, *not* lunch, because that's why the women who worked in the school canteen were called dinner ladies.

And then there was the mysterious language that Daisy heard everywhere, frequently translated by her personal tour guide and Manc Guru. The alleyway that led behind the shops to the housing estate was called a ginnel, if something or someone was truly awful you would describe them as mingin' and if you were really happy this was translated to buzzin'. The list went on and on and Daisy loved adding new words to her expanding vocabulary, one that made her parents howl with laughter when she phoned home.

While Pamela and Bill were amused by their daughter's cultural excursions and the sampling of Mancunian delights, they were also intrigued about her new companion, hinting that love might be in the air, only to be summarily assured that there was absolutely nothing going on, end of story! And while her parents may have been curious and slightly incredulous, Daisy wasn't offended in the slightest that Adam didn't find her sexually attractive, for two simple reasons. Number one: despite his undeniable good looks, in a scruffy, stick-thin, rock-star kind of way he wasn't actually her type (she'd always been drawn to tanned and preferably muscular boys); and the second was that after giving it much thought as she yawned through her more boring lectures or lay in bed at night, Daisy suspected that Adam might be gay.

It was a conversation that she had no intention of starting, simply because she didn't care and anyway it was Adam's business. Not only that, Daisy was sure that when he wanted to talk about it he would and knew without a doubt he would confide in her. When he was ready to come out she would be there to support him – that was a given.

As the weeks and months rolled by, both made new friends from within their respective courses and amongst the students who lived along the corridors of the halls, swelling their social circle and expanding their knowledge, not necessarily in an academic sense, fun was always high on the agenda.

Their group of friends included Jimmy the Ted, a six-foot-two Geordie who had jet black, Bryl-creamed hair and wore blue suede shoes, and was utterly convinced he'd been reincarnated from the soul of a departed Teddy boy. Then there was Kiki and Carol. The former was the daughter of an Evangelical preacher and the latter hailed from an intolerant family who were best left ignorant to many things. They met at the Fresher's Ball and had remained together ever since, quite clearly madly in love and embracing the freedom to be themselves. Tommy was the Romeo of the gang and would float in and out of the group, disappearing for days on end before popping back to his room for a well-earned rest. Everyone loved Lester the Posh One who'd ended up in Manchester after failing to achieve the grades for Cambridge, something that he seemed overjoyed about, that and escaping his over-bearing parents and their stately home in Berkshire. Shalini was the really clever one, determined to become a doctor and make her parents proud. She lived at home so brought them amazing food in Tupperware, made by her mother and gratefully received by all of her mates. The other thing she brought to the table was a semblance of calm and wisdom. Shalini saw the good and beautiful in everyone and everything and made you think twice about putting washing-up liquid in the toilet systems because the poor caretaker would have to clean up all the bubbles.

Once the giddy stage wore off it soon became clear to everyone (apart from Lester) that they needed to fund their big-city lifestyle. For Daisy and Adam this meant becoming twenty-four-hour party people, attending gigs, adding to their record collections (Daisy's new hobby) and buying clothes from Afflecks Palace, one of the coolest places in Manchester. And so after a day spent trawling the city centre, they both found work waiting tables in a restaurant, a job that had the added advantage of a free meal and end-of-shift leftovers. And to make life just perfect, whilst citing the inconvenience and hardship of having to climb the stairs to visit his best friend, Adam swapped rooms with the boy who resided next door to Daisy. A carton of beers and a doner kebab sealed the deal, which was worth it to have her on the other side of the wall, reminding him of having Ryan close by, and those scary times at home.

*

When the shouting and crashing noises began downstairs, their mum screaming abuse and their dad retaliating with his fists, Ryan would knock on the wall – a signal that Adam should scarper just in case Ernie decided to take whatever had pissed him off out on his kids. Not needing to be told twice, Adam would leap from his cold bed and run barefoot on the floorboards to Ryan's room, and there in the dark they'd hide under the blankets until it was all over. Ryan truly hated their Dad and as he grew became more and more scathing of their mum. Every now and then his anger and despair would bubble to the surface, causing tears to pump from tired eyes. He was so fed up of being cold and hungry, the bleakness of their situation exacerbated by the sobbing of his frightened little brother who was sweaty from fear, clinging on tight.

"When I get older I'm going to cave his head in, I mean it! One day I'll be bigger than him and he's gonna get it. As soon as I get some money I'll be down that gym and get a six-pack and muscles like Mr T then I'll smack shit out of him. I swear, Adam, I'll make him sorry. I hate him so much I wish he was dead." Ryan held his skinny brother close, both huddled under the blankets trying to keep warm and somehow drown out the noise from downstairs as Ernie launched the contents of the kitchen against the walls.

And even amidst the chaos of Miriam screaming and the neighbours banging on the wall, nothing could smother the sound of Adam's pleading. "No Ryan, please don't hit him cos the coppers will lock you up too and then I'll be on my own, I don't wanna be on my own with Mum, promise you won't Ryan, swear on the bible." Adam's heart pounded in his chest. He was scared of his dad but even more terrified of losing Ryan, so the idea of a dead dad or being left with his mother gave him not a shred of comfort.

Wiping away his own tears, Ryan was forced to back down. "Okay, I promise I won't leave you mate, but I will find a way to get us away from here. Try not to worry, just close your eyes and go to sleep, shush now, I'll be right here." Hot rivers ran down pinched cheeks, but his tears were borne not of sadness or fear, more from a burning resentment at the unfairness of it all.

Maybe it was the start, a shifting point at which both brothers changed, the elder sensing the growing weight of responsibility for the younger, whose fragility was a burden just as heavy. Ryan tried to be brave in front of Adam when their dad got angry and began lashing out after losing money on the horses or running out of cigarettes. It didn't take much to rile Ernie, especially the resentful face of his eldest son who, as he got older, was becoming more challenging, a look in his eye that questioned authority and tested his patience.

The truth was that Ryan goaded Ernie to distract him from Adam who, according to their dad, whimpered like a soft tart, but it was better that he took the beating. And while Ryan did his best to protect his younger brother and bridge the gap left by inadequate parents, Adam continued to watch life through wide, worried eyes. As children do, he blew their situation out of proportion, tormenting himself with images of children's homes and foster parents, his fears repeatedly fuelled by Ernie and Miriam's behaviour. The thought of being alone horrified Adam. It was a fear that had never left.

If the police came, which they frequently did, Adam and Ryan would creep out of bed and listen at the top of the stairs as their mum swapped allegiances, screaming abuse at the coppers as they locked Ernie in the back of the van. Both boys prayed that Miriam would drink herself into the next morning, quietly if possible, and their dad would remain in a cell for the night, longer if they were lucky. Adam clung onto Ryan for comfort and in restraint, so much so that the tiny grasping hands and fingers left their mark on his skin while life stained Ryan's heart, causing his sense of duty to become ingrained, a mission.

*

Now, despite the thin wall of breeze block and plasterboard that separated them, when Adam felt homesick for his gran and brother or began to dwell on the past and fret about the future, he would tap on the wall and Daisy would tap back. It was all he needed, just to know she was there.

It was inevitable that owing to their closeness, other students and friends would start to ask questions about them, and when they did, both Daisy and Adam deflected any curiosity or insinuations about the nature of their friendship with the truth: they were best mates, nothing more. Maybe they did send out the wrong signals to confused onlookers. Like when Adam made Daisy laugh, sometimes to the point of hysteria at something nobody else understood. Perhaps it was the way she took care of him, banging on his door in the morning to wake him up and making sure he ate properly, not just crisps and chocolate. They would disappear for hours behind closed doors or share unreadable looks that excluded others, but whatever it was outsiders imagined, this relationship that somehow required a name, a title, they all missed the most obvious thing.

Daisy and Adam just fitted together, harmoniously blending at the seams, merging in thought and deed. They were non-identical, biologically unrelated twins, yin and yang, positive and negative, opposites attracting before being drawn together by the invisible force of destiny. So if their friends didn't get it and boys hated Adam and girls despised Daisy, if people thought they were weird, or gay, or aliens, so what!

In the beginning, they embraced their youth and were possessed by the spirit of the adventurous. Both emboldened by the other, they felt less inclined to contemplate the future, preferring to live in the moment. Inevitably as they evolved, together as friends or separately as man and woman, outside elements would interfere with the order of things. Where affairs of the heart were concerned, their bond would cause the odd ripple, testing loyalty and restricting relationships outside the one they shared. But for now Daisy thought she had it all and as long as she was on the other side of the wall, or the cafeteria, or Manchester, or even the world, then nothing would faze or hinder him Adam. He had a best friend, his safety blanket, a magnet, someone to orbit. It was just one of those unfathomable things but with Daisy, Adam knew right from the start that he had found his soul mate and for him, she was enough.

Chapter 4

Valentine's
Manchester 2003

Adam had messed up. Big time. He hadn't meant to upset Daisy, in actual fact this whole shitty mess had arisen because he was trying to do a nice thing but instead, she was holed up next door, sulking. And that bloody Fliss was becoming a right royal pain in the backside and her constant hounding of him wasn't helping matters one bit. She was like an obsessed sex-pest and her presence was suffocating. In fact he wished that Barry the caretaker had something in his cupboard that he could sprinkle all over her and watch her disintegrate, like a slug.

Pushing thoughts of Fliss away, Adam was forced to accept that had he thought it through and just told the truth, two situations could've been avoided in one go, but he'd become complacent, too used to living a lie. Until now, smoke and mirrors had provided the best solution to what he regarded as a problem, not so much to him, but that's how other people would see it. And even though subterfuge was the easier option and he'd done well to get away with it for so long, where Daisy was concerned it was time to give her an explanation – Adam owed her that.

*

The 'problem' arose shortly after the Christmas break with the arrival of Fliss. She'd had a falling out with the other girls in her shared accommodation so requested a move and unfortunately had landed on their corridor. Adam had missed Daisy like crazy over the festive period but was kept occupied by Ryan who, on returning from Oman, took his very excited brother on a skiing holiday to Italy. Despite having a wonderful time, when he returned to Manchester the only person Adam wanted to see was his best friend. He was supposed to meet Daisy off the coach on Chorlton Street but had been roped into helping the new girl and by the time he'd helped Fliss move all her stuff upstairs he was running late so decided to wait at the halls, just in case they missed each other en route.

The jubilation of being reunited was soon ruined by the flash of suspicion on Daisy's face when she spotted Fliss, who was loitering outside Adam's room and seemed incapable of taking a hint. From that day on, war was declared. Nothing physical or verbal, more a sullen battle as jealousy radiated from every pore of Fliss's body, bouncing straight off the invisible force field that Daisy had erected to deflect any attempts at infiltration. While Daisy protected her territory, Fliss did her utmost to prise Adam away, using all of her womanly wiles in the process.

Around the same time, it had come to Adam's attention that Daisy also had an admirer – a nice enough lad named Greg who was on the periphery of their group, yet recently, his presence was more noticeable. As much as he dreaded the prospect, Adam knew it would happen sooner or later, that someone would come along and catch Daisy's eye, and he was prepared for it, sort of.

In the past when female college friends had found boyfriends, Adam accepted that he was surplus to requirements and occupied himself elsewhere; however, with Daisy it was different. This time it was going to hurt. He told himself over and over that loving someone meant setting them free – annoying and cringey, but true. He had repeatedly assured his anxious heart that they would still be close, best friends, because their bond was unbreakable, yet when it came to the crunch it seemed so hard to let her go and deep down, he didn't want to share.

By the night of the Valentine's Dance, Adam had bravely resolved to step aside and allow Greg a look in, and so that Daisy didn't feel awkward in any way he had a cunning contingency plan that would hopefully put her at ease. They arrived as a group and as the evening wore on, Greg eventually sidled up beside Daisy.

Adam in return made a conscious effort not to liken Greg to a snake and to appear engrossed in conversation with posh Lester. He also forced himself not to look in their direction while they danced or acknowledge they were holding hands under the table. It almost killed him but he had to give her space while missing her already, selfishly envisioning nights of separation once Daisy became Greg's.

As the evening drew to a close Adam sensed that Daisy was floundering, just as he expected she would, torn between bringing him into the conversation with Greg and wanting time alone. It was easy enough to pick a willing dance partner just before the smoochy songs were played so avoiding Fliss like the Black Death, Adam grabbed the hand of a lively girl name Nell and whisked her onto the dance floor. Soon after, he spotted Daisy waving coyly as she departed. Adam waved back with hands that felt like lead while wearing the best fake smile he could muster, his heart sinking further when he realised she didn't look back, not once.

Meanwhile, over on the wallflower side of the room, Fliss hadn't taken her eyes off Daisy and Adam – working them out was her one true mission in life. And now Greg was on the scene she hawkishly monitored every single nuance, waiting for her chance to pounce. Knowing he was under surveillance by his stalker prompted Adam to take things one stage further and during the last dance, accepted the amorous kisses offered by Nell. Still aware of beady eyes burning holes in his back he then offered to walk her home. It was the least he could do and anyway, he was in grave danger of his jacket being set aflame by Fliss who, when he dared to peep, was clearly furious.

Snubbing Fliss was one part of his big mistake; not being honest with his best friend was the other. Adam was made aware of his aberration following a very terse and upsetting conversation with Daisy, who he found in the kitchen and where for the first time ever, she let him pour his own water into the Pot Noodle – a sure sign she was pissed off with him.

As he stirred the gloopy yellow concoction, Adam waited in silence for Daisy to speak and when she did his heart plummeted on hearing the question, let alone the sarcasm in her voice.

"So, how's Nelly?"

"No idea, how's Greg?" At this Daisy blushed crimson and Adam felt like a complete and utter dickhead, prompting the exact reaction he'd contrived so hard to avoid.

Daisy indicated towards the brimming Pot Noodle. "He's fine, thanks. And you've put too much water in and stirred too soon, so now it's going to taste like shite." Then, after fixing him with a cold stare she continued. "Have you seen Fliss this morning?"

"No, I've been saved the trauma, why?"

"Because *Romeo*, she was in my room until three this morning where *I* had to listen to her wail like a banshee over you! I've had no sleep, she ate all my digestive biscuits and my bin is overflowing with snotty tissues."

Adam ceased stirring his noodles and gave Daisy his full attention. "What do you mean, over me, and what happened to Greg?"

"He went home when we realised there was no getting rid of her...she caught up with us and ranted the whole way back here! She's taken this Nelly thing really badly you know? She reckons you've rejected her and can't understand why."

"But...I haven't rejected her. I don't even like her and I've been doing my damned hardest to keep her at bay since she arrived, and I've given her no encouragement whatsoever. You know that Daise!" Adam was pissed off and hungry, not a great combination. "And you know what? If I want to snog someone, I flaming well will. It's got sod all to do with her, the fucking psycho!" Adam was seriously wishing he'd avoided the stupid dance altogether and gone to the cinema, on his own.

"Well, that may be but she's confused and feels rejected, and the *really* bad news is you're not off the hook entirely, not now she knows you're straight. To be honest I think it's given her more hope and made her extra determined to have her wicked way with you." Adam saw the corners of Daisy's eyes crinkle as she sipped her tea but it didn't ease the pounding that had begun in his heart.

Abandoning his task he pulled out a chair and seated himself at the table. "Did she think I was gay, is that what she really said?"

Daisy merely nodded, recognising shock when she saw it. Adam, however, was furious.

"The cheeky cow! That's so typical…just because I've not jumped into bed with her, or you, or anyone who gives me the 'come on' means I prefer men…so are you considered to be a lesbian because you've been a good girl and kept your legs crossed since September?" The shrug of Daisy's shoulders did nothing for his temper. "No, I thought not. Talk about being hypocritical." Adam was livid but rattled.

Noticing the two red spots on Adam's otherwise pale and angry face, along with his fingers which were drumming on the table, Daisy realised she'd hit a nerve so tried to reassure him. It didn't go too well.

"I think that's probably where the confusion started if I'm honest…with you and me. You know everyone gossips and jokes about how close we are especially cos we've stayed together overnight, and she's asked me countless times if we're having sex but I assured her nothing has ever happened, I told you that!"

"Ah, so she's going down the friend with benefits route, is she? How very predictable."

"Yep! But my denial just caused Fliss and a few others to presume you were gay, not that they've ever said it to my face because I'd have told you. People gossip, Adam, it's unfair and nasty but that's how it is. Just ignore them."

Adam folded his arms across his chest, his heart thumping through his t-shirt, haphazard brainwaves playing havoc because the next question was a biggy. "And while we're on the subject and loads more important than that nutter, did *you* think I was gay?" Adam prepared for Daisy's reply, expecting her allegiance then mistaking truthfulness for betrayal.

"It crossed my mind. But it's your business and if I'm honest I was sort of waiting for you to discuss it with me, or come out if that's the case." When she heard Adam's gasp and took in wide eyes that were swimming with hurt, Daisy slid her hand over his and squeezed tightly. "Look Adam, I don't give a toss about any of that stuff, really I don't, all I care about is that you are happy and we don't fall out over other people, like Greg and Fliss. And I'm sorry if I've offended you, and from the look on your face I think I have."

"Why the hell didn't you just ask me? You're my best friend, we talk about everything. You shouldn't have judged me Daise, you're the last person I thought would do that."

"I'm not judging you, not at all. I'm sorry, I really didn't mean to upset you but some things are just too personal and I respect your right to privacy no matter how close we are. I've talked about growing up in France and you know all about my old boyfriends but when it comes to your turn you always change the subject or clam up so I didn't pry. I was simply following the signals that told me to wait. You were really vague when you told me about that girl Lara from your old college but I got the impression she was nobody special, or maybe she hurt you. I just thought being tactful is what being a good friend is about. I'd never want to make you feel uncomfortable or put you on the spot. But it looks like I got that wrong so once again, I apologise." While Daisy's voice was soft and sincere, when Adam spoke his was hard and accusatory; the tone alone made Daisy recoil.

"No, it's my fault, I see that now. I've made an error of judgement and I've only myself to blame. I should've known I'd lose you over another bloke or because of how I am. I've been kidding myself all along, ever since we met, so perhaps we should cool it for a while, you know, not hang out together so much, especially now you've got Greg. It's probably for the best." When he snatched his hand away Daisy was doubly stung.

"Adam, please don't be like that, we can sort this out and there's no need for our friendship to change, and what do you mean, how you are? I've told you, I don't care…Adam please speak to me, don't be like this." Daisy reached over and hoped he would take her hand again, so when he ignored the gesture it felt like she'd been slapped, and it hurt.

Silence enveloped them. Adam didn't dare speak, in fact he couldn't because a huge ball of despair was lodged in his throat. Avoiding Daisy's eyes he stared at his hands, which were rapidly blurring out of focus until the interminable quiet was shattered by two pyjama-clad bodies entering the kitchen, laughing raucously, oblivious to the presence of others and the tension that hung in the air.

Unable to bear it any longer Adam stood abruptly and pushed back his chair, creating a wince-inducing screech as metal scraped across tiles. Daisy remained seated and watched aghast as he stormed from the kitchen, racing along the corridor before slamming his door shut, a sound that was repeated seconds later when she too locked herself inside her room. They remained secluded all afternoon, lying on their beds, separated by a wall, both ignoring knocks at the door and texts on their phones, lost in a world of hurt and confusion, neither knowing what to do next.

Daisy was distraught, confused, angry and ashamed. She had let Adam down, not only by sloping off with Greg but also by harbouring ridiculous judgemental thoughts about her closest friend. And Adam was right. She should've asked him why he never talked much about ex-girlfriends or maybe hinted in a jokey way about his sexuality. There had been a few occasions when she could have brought it up but chickened out. And anyway, why should she ask a question that he might not even know the answer to, one that could embarrass or offend? Now it was out there and just like she'd suspected, Adam was hurting inside.

She was so pissed off with everyone gossiping behind their backs, and sick to death of insinuations from people like Fliss, sticking their noses in and ruining things. '*You're like peas in a pod,*' everyone said, and probably thought that one day they'd wake up and admit how perfect they were for each other. Until now they'd both laughed off nosy questions and shook their heads at the odd sarky comment, carrying on regardless because when they were together it was perfect, easy.

Daisy was bereft, assuming the worse and blaming her own stupidity, which just made her angry, followed closely by annoyance, both at herself and Adam because if they were playing the blame game then he would have to take some responsibility for his reticence in opening up about personal stuff. Not only that, he'd made it seem like she was doing something wrong being with Greg and even more bloody irritating, it wasn't a decision she'd taken likely. Daisy had played it cool for ages after worrying herself stupid over Adam, pondering the dynamics of having two men in her life. Was it possible to share her time and avoid jealousy, not lose Adam or put Greg off?

Sometimes, Daisy likened Adam to having a brother but after the things she'd heard from her friends, real-life siblings were never as much fun and more likely to dob you in to the parents. Taking that step away from Adam and their closeness had been so hard. She'd felt very strange the previous night, self-conscious about holding hands in front of him and thank goodness Greg hadn't kissed her because it really would've felt, ugh, just too weird!

Daisy's head was mashed, in fact it was pureed. Everything in her life was becoming infuriatingly intense; it had been so simple before. And spending the evening listening to Fliss feeling sorry for herself hadn't helped. 'Crying girl' hadn't batted an eyelid when Greg cleared off after ten minutes of listening to her hiccupping and swearing undying love for Adam. Any normal person would have admitted defeat but no, not Fliss.

She swung from being jubilant that her obsession wasn't gay to dismay that he had failed to fall for her apparently superior womanly wiles. In between eating Daisy's bar of Galaxy and the last of her Waggon Wheels, whilst casting Nell as a disease-ridden hooker, Fliss had vowed to soldier on and win Adam over, no matter how long it took. When Daisy started to fall asleep still sitting up, her chin resting on her chest and dribbling, Fliss finally took the hint and buggered off, leaving her counsellor surrounded by paper wrappers and very short on loo paper.

*

It was dark when Daisy woke up after eventually crying herself to sleep. Her room was chilly and she was hungry so after nipping to the loo she splashed her face with warm water and brushed her hair before pressing her ear against the wall, listening for signs of Adam. How they were supposed to 'cool it' was beyond Daisy as she was missing him already. Anger flared again, igniting the stubborn rebel within her soul that decided his sexual orientation and a wall wasn't going to separate them and neither was Greg, Fliss, Nell or anyone else for that matter. Resolving there and then to make peace, Daisy hopped off the bed and made her way to the door, flinging it open to find Adam on the other side, hand raised and about to knock.

"I missed you." Adam lowered his hand.

"I missed you too." Daisy smiled before rushing into his arms where she was met by a comforting embrace.

After kissing the top of her head, Adam released her from his grasp and picked something up from the floor. "Get your coat, we need to talk and I don't want any interruptions, especially from my stalker who I've just spotted going into Kiki's room. I've made us a flask and some sarnies so come on, hurry up before anyone sees us, I've got a surprise." Adam held up a white carrier bag and surreptitiously glanced both ways along the corridor.

Doing as she was told, Daisy shoved her feet inside her trainers then grabbed her coat and woolly hat before following Adam, who took her by the hand and led her to the stairwell, wordlessly continuing upwards one more flight until they reached the door that opened onto the roof. Signalling for her to remain quiet, Adam removed a key from his pocket, unlocked the metal door then swiftly ushered Daisy through, locking it behind him.

"Adam! We shouldn't be up here. We'll be in deep shit if we get caught and where did you get that key?" Daisy hissed her fears.

"Don't worry, nobody will know we're here, just talk quietly and stop stressing. I got a spare one cut when I looked after Barry's cat, remember before Christmas, he had to stay in hospital overnight and asked me to feed it. I was going to surprise you on your birthday and bring you up here to watch the stars, like you said you do in France, but I can't wait until then. Now shush, come on, follow me."

Daisy was too touched to speak, blown away by Adam's gesture albeit months in advance of his intended surprise. Just knowing he'd wanted to do something special, unique and thoughtful only reminded her of just how precious he was. When they rounded the corner Daisy spotted the blanket on the concrete floor, along with Adam's duvet and pillow.

The night was still and the sky jet black, obscured in places by streaks of clouds that partially covered the moon, helping to conceal them both in the shadows. The lights from the taller buildings across the street provided a warm glow, radiating outwards, peeping above the perimeter walls of the roof. Daisy leant against what she presumed was the electricity generator, which was humming gently as Adam covered her with his duvet and then poured a mug of tea, unfolding the tin foil around the cheese sandwiches as she blew steam from her cup.

They ate in companionable silence, listening to voices on the street down below, delighting in the fact that nobody knew they were there as they watched planes on approach to the airport, their lights flickering as they banked and descended. There weren't as many stars as Adam had hoped for but Daisy said it didn't matter, smiling when he promised to order a clear night and a champagne supernova for her birthday in June. He was clever like that, his mind quick to connect life with lyrics, his head full of words that probably meant little to others but the world to him.

Once they'd finished eating, Adam scrunched up the tin foil and tucked the duvet around their legs before resting his head backwards, staring silently upwards. A moment or two passed and then he sighed before turning to Daisy, regarding her carefully as though deciding what to say, or how to say it. Her eyes looked straight into his.

In those green eyes he knew so well, which changed colour with her mood to brown with a splash of hazel, deep green and a hint of blue, Adam saw only kindness. She was waiting for him to speak; this was the time so before the moment was lost he grabbed her hand and turned to face the stars.

"I'm going to explain something to you and once I've finished you can ask me whatever you want, and I mean anything, okay? I've never told anyone, not even my brother, so I want you to promise this will be our secret, just between the two of us. I feel I can trust you with my life but I need to hear you say it. Do you promise?" Adam turned back to Daisy, scrutinising her reaction, waiting.

"I promise." Daisy saw him nod before turning away, and then he began.

Chapter 5

Up on the roof
February 2003

Adam wasn't too sure where to begin so he started with Daisy's comment that he never spoke about ex-girlfriends, or boyfriends for that matter. It was as good a place as any. "You know like you said that I clam up when you talk about ex-boyfriends? Well the reason I don't join in the conversation is because I've only ever had one proper girlfriend, I told you about her, Lara. Anyway, when it came down to it I didn't come up to scratch and the person I dated after that got bored with me too, so in the end I just gave up. It's not like I was horrible to them or anything. We got on fine when the relationship was platonic but when it came to being intimate, kissing or to put it bluntly, sex, I couldn't give Lara or anyone else what they wanted. Actually that's not true. I am quite capable of having a sexual relationship but I just don't want to, not in the slightest." Adam glanced at Daisy who had turned to the side and was listening intently, letting him talk.

Another deep breath in, then out through the nose. "The thing is, I don't have the same urges as other people, like Tommy for example, but then again who does? I doubt anyone can match him in the bedroom department." Daisy laughed at Adam's comment – they'd already lost count of their sex-mad friend's encounters.

Daisy used the ease in tension to speak. "I don't understand, do you mean you are celibate?"

Adam shook his head vigorously. "No, that's a totally different thing altogether…there's actually a name for people like me – asexual. How about that for a conversation stopper?"

"Asexual, I've never even heard of it, are you sure, how do you know?"

Adam smiled. "Yes I'm sure and believe me after wandering around in the wilderness for years, I was so relieved to find out that there are other people like me out there and I'm not the only one who feels like this."

"Right, so an asexual person just doesn't like having sex with anyone, men or women?"

"It depends on the individual, but from what I read it can vary from one person to the other and everyone has their own needs and desires. All I can describe is how I feel."

"I'm still confused, so do you fancy people in general but just not the sex bit?" Daisy's brow was furrowed, concentrating fully on Adam, desperate to understand, and when he sighed she hoped it wasn't because she was annoying him by being dumb.

"Okay, here's a different way to explain it. I am attracted to people, you for example. I see and recognise beauty, physical perfection, great personalities, kindness, eccentricity, intellect, all the things that may draw one person to another, but I only want to get to know them in a way that doesn't require intimacy. I don't have the urge to act out my feelings of closeness or love in a sexual way. And just so we are clear, I feel exactly the same way about men as I do women, believe me, I've been there and got the t-shirt. I have tried to be normal, if there is such a thing, but I'm just not. Being like this has plagued me for years and I've dealt with it by myself. Like I said, I've never told a soul, until now." Adam was exhausted, the strain of being so honest after all this time was causing his body to tense and there was something else – he felt a familiar anger building inside but directed at who or what, he wasn't sure.

Daisy remained silent for a moment or two, gathering her thoughts. "I think I get it and I'm so glad and totally honoured that you chose to tell me, but it's not right that you've had to bottle all this up for so long. But now I know, so many things are starting to make sense. I just wish you'd said something earlier then I could've stuck up for you, especially with Fliss."

"Christ! She's the last person I want to find out…can you imagine? Anyway, I'm used to the sly digs and misconceptions.

I've got a thick skin and learned to laugh off jibes and insinuations a long time ago. It's easier to make a joke about it or leave people guessing whether I'm gay or bi, or just plain boring. It is getting harder though and I am so flaming weary of it, this secret and feeling different. It's totally crap to be honest." Adam stole a glance at Daisy who was listening intently but as promised, trying hard not to interrupt.

"You know what the worse thing is? Sometimes I feel isolated and now and then it hits me that I might not ever have the things other people take for granted, like a wife and kids. And I can deal with it when I'm having fun or part of a group, you know, just hanging out, but eventually my mates pair up and then drift off. And I just know that sooner or later you'll do the same and I have to be prepared for that. I'm only telling you this because for the first time in my life I've found someone who I don't want to fade away, so I thought if I was honest then maybe you'd stick around for a bit longer and not lose patience with me like everyone else does." A lone tear leaked from Adam's eye, which he swiped away quickly but Daisy had spotted it, along with the nerve in the side of his taut face, pulsing angrily as he spoke.

And there was something else – a creeping feeling of dread, an atmosphere, because for the first time ever Daisy felt very detached from Adam. This new person he was telling her about was like a stranger, someone he'd hidden away. Maybe he was ashamed, quite obviously scared, and she didn't want him to feel like that; she wanted him back and had to reconnect with him, try to reassure him. Threading her arm through his, Daisy pulled Adam closer, locking him in with her other hand, feeling the tension of his body as she held on tight.

"Adam, look at me."

He turned to face her, their bodies resting at the same angle, eyes locked.

"I can tell that getting this off your chest has been a massive thing and I am truly touched and so so glad that you chose to share it with me. But before you go on or I ask you anything, you have to believe me when I say that it changes nothing about the way I feel about you, okay?" Adam nodded. "You are my mate, my best friend forever, the best boy I have ever met in my entire life and I don't give a shit about Lara or anything from your past. It's now that matters, you and me, right here on this bloody freezing roof. Do you understand?" Daisy was squeezing his arm, forcing the words to permeate his leather jacket, be absorbed by his skin then flow through his blood before infiltrating his brain. When she saw the flicker of a smile and his eyes crinkle at the corners, the tension began to ebb.

Throwing his head back Adam exhaled then let out a stifled groan as the weight of his secret began tumbling away. "You don't know how relieved I am to hear you say that but I still feel so angry and I don't know why. I think I'm just scared of losing you, especially because of this. It makes me so mad and it's so unfair that I get to be this way. I've lived with it for years, questions going over and over in my mind. It's like a battle raging inside. One minute I'm fine, totally cool with who and what I am and then wham! Someone or something comes along, like a situation where I'm forced to behave in a certain way to avoid the truth or stop people asking questions. Everyone expects me to be one thing or another when all I want is to be me. Is that too much to ask?"

Daisy shook his arm gently. "No it's not, and from now on I'm going to help you, but I have to admit that I'm still a bit confused so can I ask you some stuff? You said I could but I don't want to make you feel uncomfortable. It's just hard to get my head around, that's all."

"Ask away, I swear it'll be fine. I want you to understand, I need you to."

"Okay, I'll try to be as tactful as possible and not say the wrong thing or make you squirm. And if I cross the line, just slap me." Daisy saw Adam smile and nod, encouraging her to continue.

"So, when did you start to feel different, you know, realise that you didn't fancy girls, or boys?"

"At high school, probably when I was about fourteen and the other lads were more interested in copping off than playing football on the field. I joined in with their conversations but it was fake because I didn't fantasise about kissing or having sex with anyone. I did have crushes though. I thought my history teacher Miss Hennessey was amazing. She had long, black hair and it was so straight it looked like it had been ironed and really glossy, like one of those sleek racehorses. And she never wore stuffy clothes like the other teachers. Hers were flowery and floaty and her perfume lingered in the air when she passed by. She was clever and funny and made us laugh in lessons. I couldn't wait for double history on a Thursday because everything about her was wonderful. But not once did I ever think about doing anything I'd get expelled for, or her sacked. Then at college my friends suddenly became sexually active and talked about it all the time. Christ, it was like they never shut up. That's when I began to suspect that a piece of the jigsaw was missing. I just didn't experience what they did and it started to bother me, more so because I was worried there was something wrong and if I thought that, then others might think the same."

"So is that when you met Lara, at college?"

"Yeah, she was in my maths group. I got on with everyone, but Lara wanted more than friendship and I was tired of putting up barriers so I thought, why not give it a go, what was there to lose?"

"So did you sleep with her…I mean, does everything work, you know, down there?" Daisy could feel herself blushing, especially when Adam started to laugh.

"Yes of course it works, quite well as a matter of fact, especially first thing in the morning."

"But I don't understand, how can it work if you don't have sexual urges? I thought one thing led to the other. Are you sure that it's not something that can be fixed? Perhaps you've got a hormone imbalance and if you spoke to a doctor they could sort it out." Daisy was really confused now, especially because Adam was laughing hard.

"It's not a medical thing but if it was I assure you I'd be down at the med centre first thing Monday morning. And I didn't get it either, the whole bloody thing, especially the physiology. I wanted to know how my mind and body worked, or in this case wasn't functioning in harmony, so I had a gander in the library."

"Is there really a book about it?"

"Yes there is and if you ever bothered to use your library card you'd know there's a book on everything Daise…some have big letters for numpties like you!" Adam winced when Daisy punched him in the arm.

"Anyway, back to my specialist subject…it seems that arousal is a physical response and it doesn't require attraction. In lots of cases it's just your body parts letting you know they're working properly. Little boys get erections for no reason, in fact, I remember our Ryan getting told off all the time for playing with his willy, so did I. It's just something that happens and I for one thought it was really funny when I was a kid, just something else to play with I suppose…does that help?" When Adam saw Daisy nod he felt it safe to continue.

"The kissing stuff was easy. I think I'm quite a good kisser actually and I even managed to perform when it came to having sex with Lara, but I didn't particularly want to do it again. I saw it more as an experiment, something I thought I should experience and at the same time prove to myself I could do, and check everything was in working order. I suppose it was one less thing to worry about."

"Well that's good news! You know, just in case you ever need it." Daisy was glad that she was making Adam smile even though she was actually being serious.

"Yes, Daisy, I suppose it is but I doubt the situation will ever arise."

"Is that a joke?"

"No it's not. Now will you shut it! I've lost my thread. Oh yes, back to Lara. Well she soon picked up on my lack of interest and presumed I was going off her, which I was because the whole thing was a sham and I was sick of feeling pressured so I finished with her. She wasn't pleased and started rumours, making sarky comments whenever she saw me, hinting that I was gay and telling her mates I was crap in bed – the usual spurned lover shite, which is why I found myself another girlfriend as soon as possible, so I could prove Lara wrong."

"But you already knew it would turn out the same way so why did you bother? It sounds like you were punishing yourself in order to fit in. Just the thought of it makes me angry because it's not your fault." Daisy wanted so much to travel back in time and rescue him from Lara. She wanted to rescue him from everyone.

"I know, but it is also shit being gossiped about and I really liked college so was desperate not to look stupid in front of my mates or make enemies. But I got a lucky break with Debbie – she was the next one, by the way. Not long after we started dating she dropped out of college and went to work in a call centre, and then to my utter delight she dumped me for one of her colleagues. It was the best outcome because I got to play the injured party when in reality I was *so* relieved. I managed to avoid women for the rest of my course and hoped that when I came here I'd be able to blend in and my peculiarities might remain undetected, but it's clear now that I was kidding myself."

"The thing is you shouldn't have to lie. Don't you think it's time to stop hiding who you are? Perhaps there's a group you could join, you know, to discuss it, and our friends will support and respect you, I know they will."

Adam turned sharply to face Daisy, determined in his response. "No! I'm not ready to talk about it with anyone else and I can't deal with being laughed at or whispered about – it was bad enough at primary school. I hated being the odd one out, the kid who nobody wanted to sit next to or play with, and this can't be solved by our Ryan giving somebody a good hiding. This is my mess and I'll sort it out."

"Is that what you're scared of, Adam, being talked about?"

"Bloody hell Daise, sometimes I think I've spent my whole life being scared of everything and everyone. I'm frightened of being labelled or asked the same questions over and over, and talking about it won't solve the wider issue, the one that's waiting for me in the big bad world because once I leave here it'll start over again. I'll have to meet new people with the same expectations and prejudice. It's like being a sodding gerbil on one of those wheel things. If I was gay or bisexual then I know for sure most people wouldn't bat an eyelid but the complexities of me, of how I feel, or more to the point don't feel, are just too…weird. There, I've said it. That's how I feel sometimes, like a weirdo."

"Well you're not! So don't ever say that again, do you hear me? Nobody has the right to judge you and you're right, your feelings are personal and not up for discussion unless you decide. Your privacy is non-negotiable and I will always back you up, okay?" Daisy had nudged closer to Adam, squashed together almost face to face and both had eyes awash with tears.

"Okay." Adam allowed himself a small smile.

"Here's another question…why haven't you confided in Ryan? You are so close and he's never off the phone, and from what you told me about your childhood he's always been there for you, surely he would have understood."

"Because I felt ashamed, it's as simple as that. I just can't imagine ever saying the word asexual to him. I'm scared of how he would react and even if he said he was okay with it, deep down he might not be. Our parents were both flawed, one hundred percent crapsville and we always wanted to be different, and by that I mean normal and not resemble them in any way. I've always looked up to Ryan, he's like my hero. When you meet him you'll know what I mean."

"He sounds lovely, like the perfect brother, which is why I think he'd understand."

"To me he is perfect, physically and mentally. He's tough and brave, fit and healthy, loyal, honest and straight down the line. But our Ryan sees everything in black and white, there are no grey areas. I think it's how he coped with our parents and was able to look after me. He saw it as his duty. Mum and Dad were a waste of space but instead of crying, Ryan's attitude was to just deal with it, move on and make the best of life. He likes to keep things ordered and uncomplicated. I suppose that's why military life suits him so well. I knew I could never be like him, not that he expects that but I owe him. I want to make him proud, repay him for putting his life on hold and sticking by me, and if that means getting my degree and being able to stand on my own two feet, I will do everything I can to achieve it. Ryan deserves his freedom too and to not be worried about me or how I'll manage in life, so that's why I don't want him to know. And I couldn't bear it if he thought I was weird or looked at me differently, if he was ashamed or confused. I just want us to be the same as we've always been, brothers and mates, no complications." Adam laid his head on Daisy's shoulder, his words hanging in the air while they both contemplated silently.

Daisy didn't know the man yet had the urge to defend Ryan in his absence because she was convinced the person she'd heard so much about would feel none of the things Adam feared, but maybe that was something she could work on in the future. For now she had to get her head around everything and it wasn't easy.

"Alright, I get it and I respect your decision because it *is* a hard concept to grasp, so maybe Ryan would find it all a bit full on – you blokes can be funny things when it comes to personal stuff." Daisy kissed the side of Adam's head as she heard him tut. "So let's get this straight once and for all – you are not celibate or abstaining from sex forever out of choice or some theological or personal belief?"

"Yep, that's right. It's nothing to do with behaviour, it's more to do with the connection between sexual attraction and being platonically attracted to someone you like, or even love. Somewhere in between there is a flat line, maybe you could call it a missing link."

Daisy's heart hurt for Adam so in an attempt to lighten the load and maybe switch focus, she made a confession of her own, not that it would balance the books.

"This will probably make you laugh but seeing as you've been so honest with me I'm going to return the compliment. This morning when I heard about you and Nell, for a moment I was *so* jealous, and hurt I suppose. I was happy to believe you didn't fancy me cos you're gay, so the Nell thing was like a slap and I felt rejected, like I'm a minger or something. There, permission granted to laugh your head off. Go on, I totally deserve it."

"No you don't! But I sort of suspected you'd feel like that. I went round in circles thinking of a way to set you free but at the same time not feel rejected if I used my plan B and copped off with some unsuspecting girl, and look where that's got me."

"So, if you don't fancy me, which is fine by the way because I don't fancy you…God that sounds awful but I mean it in the nicest possible way, can you explain why you picked me out of all the girls here?"

"Ah, that's easy. When I spotted you on our first day you looked so nervous and lost. If I close my eyes I picture exactly what you were wearing, your bag, your hair, everything. I thought you were cool, like a girl from a seventies photo or an album cover, you just stood out in the crowd. And I remember thinking that you looked how I felt. I hated the sense of isolation I'd had since Ryan dropped me off so I just decided there and then that I wanted to talk to you." Adam took Daisy's cold hand in his.

"I know, you just popped up out of nowhere and you're right, I felt exactly the same, in fact I wanted to go home and was dreading the rest of the day. I was so relieved when you spoke to me, it was like a huge weight had lifted and I swear the sun came out – it hadn't stopped raining since I arrived." Daisy shivered as she spoke, it was really nippy now so she pulled the furry hood up over her head and then realised that Adam must be freezing. "By the way, you need to get a proper winter coat, you'll perish in that jacket. It might look cool but it's not very practical. We should hit the charity shops next week and find you a warm one…but before that, you haven't told me the truth about how you feel about me. What you want out of us."

"I think you are beautiful Daisy, in every way possible. And if I was going to choose someone to be with for the rest of my life it would be you, I swear. This will sound mental but the only way I can describe myself is by using you as an example."

"Go on."

"You're drawn physically to guys who are the total opposite of me, therefore you don't find me sexually attractive and have no feelings of that kind for me, yet you are my closest friend. We more or less live in each other's pockets, think and laugh about the same stuff, miss each other when we are apart. So imagine having to kiss me, or worse, sleep with me. There's a huge divide between the two very separate relationships and for me, the bit in between that would normally join the two together just doesn't exist."

"Right, I get it now, I really do, but what does that mean for us?"

"That's what has been troubling me for a while. I missed you so much over Christmas. It was like my arm had been chopped off. I couldn't get over not having you around and when Greg started to show an interest I knew we were in jeopardy, but at the same time I had to let you go. You see, I love hugs, and holding your hand and cuddling up to you at night when we watch telly, you're like my very own real-life teddy bear. When I'm with you everything is perfect, it's just so easy and natural, not tense and fake. If I had one wish it would be that I could have a normal relationship but I'd never expect anyone, especially you, to give up that part of their life for me, it's just selfish."

"Will you feel jealous or hurt if I go out with Greg?"

"Yes, I will. But not like an ex-boyfriend would, craving the intimacy they'd lost. I suppose it's the same feeling a girl gets when her female best friend is in love, sort of redundant and excluded. The only difference with us is that I'm the guy who's found his soul mate and has no idea how to deal with sharing you with another bloke, Greg or anyone who comes along in the future. Does that make sense?" Daisy nodded, lost in thought.

Information overload caused ideas to zap through her head, a long twisty road spreading out before her. Hazy images were distorted by undulating waves of the unknown, all the places yet to see, faces she would one day meet, blurry figures and shapes, intimidating shadows threatening what she had with Adam. There'd be fun and laughter, and no doubt somewhere along the line sorrow and pain. They were so young. How could either of them know what the future held, where their lives would take them or who they would love or maybe marry, make a family with? Or in Adam's case, have to stand alone on the edge of everything, watching as others joined the dots and discovered their missing link before getting on with their lives.

Daisy knew right there and then that they had to find a way, some formula for them both, because no matter how much she fancied Greg or anyone for that matter, Adam was going to remain part of her life. When she looked beyond the shadows, his face was in full focus, clear and bright, constant. She wasn't going to let him down by moving on and leaving him behind. He needed her, it was as simple as that.

Rubbing his hands in hers, Daisy tried to bring fire and strength into what Adam saw as a cold and bleak future; if she believed then he might too. "I know what we're going to do. We are going to find a way to have it all. It's not going to be easy and it will take a shed load of trust and honesty and understanding, but I reckon if we put our heads together and take it one step at a time we can do this. I don't have all the answers right now, maybe we will have to make it up as we go along, but one way or another it's going to be okay, I promise."

"Do you think so…but how will you juggle being my friend and Greg's girlfriend? He won't like me being in the way and I don't want to spoil things for you. If I had the guts I'd step aside and get out of your life but if there's a way we can stay like this, I'll take it. I'll do anything not to lose you. I love you so much Daisy, I've known it for months. It sounds totally crazy, but it's true."

"And I love you too Adam and no, it's not crazy, it's just a different kind of love, that's all." Daisy pecked him on the cheek and then held him close. She knew he was crying.

"So what shall we do now…do we make rules or a proper plan. For a start I think you should be in charge." Adam swiped away tears and then wiped his nose, which was running and very red.

"Well in that case my first big decision is that you can give me a hug. I'm bloody freezing and someone has stolen my toes, I can't feel them anymore. Then we are going downstairs to get some warm food and a brew and thaw out. And after that we'll just get on with our lives, you and me. Let's see how it goes and play it by ear, that's if we've got any left. And whose bloody stupid idea was it to come up here anyway?" Daisy was trembling now, the cold infiltrating her bones.

"That'd be me. Guilty as charged and sorry as hell for freezing our bottoms off! Come on, we'd best put this duvet on the radiator, I think its gone stiff like my bloody legs."

As they gathered their things and tried to stand, Adam's heart felt light and unburdened for the first time in years, and Daisy? Hers was aching slightly for the beautiful young man by her side who she knew was facing an uncertain and maybe turbulent future, which was why she would do her damndest to keep her promise and be there for him, always.

Chapter 6

The fine art of misdirection
Manchester 2003

In the end the plan turned out to be that there was no plan. Both Daisy and Adam realised that they couldn't anticipate how their lives would pan out so the best thing to do was carry on and see how it went. They did make a couple of bold decisions and the first to be brave of heart was Adam, who took it upon himself to let Fliss down as lightly but firmly as possible while similarly and independently, Daisy told Greg exactly how it was going to be.

Adam's heart-to-heart was somewhat more trying than Daisy's, mainly because Fliss was involved and she wasn't the type to take rejection well, although in the end it turned out far better than expected, well, sort of. After Adam assured her that she was drop-dead gorgeous and any bloke would be lucky to get a look in, he then went on to explain that despite her baby-blue eyes and flowing blonde hair, petite yet perfectly formed body and being one heck of a great girl, there was no getting away from the fact that she just wasn't his type. When asked the obvious, Adam described his perfect girl as a six-foot-tall brunette with the physique of an Olympian, lots of body piercings and a penchant for tattoos, and preferably Spanish – apparently he had a thing about the accent.

Once she was over the shock of rejection, Fliss scathingly commented that he was being selective and borderline picky, a point which Adam conceded so agreed to accept someone with three out of the five attributes, insisting for good measure that everyone was entitled to their own little fantasy, and a Hispanic, tattooed Olympian was his. When Adam related this to Daisy she literally cried laughing and actually wished that one day the figment of his vivid imagination would morph into reality, just to see the look of horror on his face.

The down side was that once Fliss realised Daisy was no threat romantically, she changed tack and laid down the gauntlet in the battle of the perfect friend. The truly worrying part as far as Daisy was concerned was that Fliss appeared to include her in the prize fund and now seemed determined to be the best buddy anyone could wish for, to both of them.

It was Adam that nailed the psychoanalysis with an old yet very erudite saying. Fliss was keeping her friend close, but her enemy closer still. If Adam didn't fancy Daisy *or* Fliss, then that was fine, it was nil-nil, but in the friendship stakes he was still there for the taking and consequently, Fliss turned the pursuit into an art form. Secure in their feelings for one another, Daisy and Adam just let Fliss get on with it, putting her peculiar and often manic behaviour down to being completely and utterly bonkers!

Daisy's dilemma was far easier to deal with because even as she said the words, she realised she didn't actually care if Greg agreed or not. She was nineteen and a half years old, far too young to settle and unlike some they knew, sound of mind and admitted – if only to herself – that while she'd enjoyed the giddy flirtation stage, Greg wasn't a keeper.

She was gentle yet forthright whilst laying down the terms of their prospective relationship, which meant that in between their separate social commitments – for him, five-a-side football and the debating society and for Daisy, sewing costumes for the drama group – she couldn't devote more than three nights per week to being a couple. The remainder of the time she wanted to study and socialise with her own friends, or one in particular – Adam.

Greg accepted the terms willingly. He too had no intention of settling on the first girl he got the hots for and after all, the option to plunder the campus remained. And he preferred it if Daisy hung out with her own friends separately, especially Adam. There was something about him that gave Greg the creeps. He couldn't put his finger on it but the guy was just odd, hanging around Daisy all the time and even if he was gay (as suspected), he needed to butt out now and then.

The arrangements suited everyone well. Fliss was now the unelected leader of their group, keeping her flock tightly corralled and under beady eyes. She was their mother hen, always on hand to offer advice, a shoulder to cry on and willing to lend anything you required, even Daddy's money. Adam put her antics down to having rich parents and being freakily insecure. Daisy simply chose to ignore her controlling tendencies while every now and then a niggling voice whispered a warning, that Fliss was just waiting for an opportunity to snatch Adam away.

On the subterfuge front, occasionally Adam would accompany Posh Lester into Manchester for an evening of clubbing where they would head to Canal Street. The bars that ran along the narrow streets and the waterway, acting like a magnet for the gay community and revellers of all persuasions, and a place where Lester felt particularly at home and happy. Adam enjoyed the vibrancy and atmosphere of the clubs and the easy-going nature of Lester's friends, the only difference was that unlike his flamboyant buddy, at the end of the evening Adam returned to the halls alone. Apart from the social element, his night on the town served another purpose: it kept people guessing and off the scent.

There had been no more dalliances with girls like Nell, who now gave Adam a wide berth after being left on her doorstep on Valentine's Day. However, he did receive an unexpected letter from an ex-girlfriend who fancied hooking up when she came to a gig in Manchester. Daisy teased Adam mercilessly only to be told off by Fliss for not respecting his privacy. Supposedly shamefaced and chastened, Daisy half-heartedly apologised to Adam, knowing the envelope was empty and the ex-girlfriend a smoke screen, their illusion.

And to ease her own conscience as much as to spare Adam's feelings, on her 'Greg nights' Daisy always stayed over at the house he shared – it was too weird knowing Adam was on the other side of the wall. And when she was Greg-free, life carried on just as it always had, like accompanying Adam on his visits to the nursing home where Olive lived.

Adam had promised Ryan that he would keep an eye on their gran despite her not having a clue who he was, so when restaurant shifts and assignments allowed, they would take the coach to Chorley and spend Saturday afternoons with Olive who was now bed-bound, but only physically. Here, Daisy would read her a story, a different one each time because it didn't matter what they chose – Olive never remembered the plot or the characters. Otherwise they watched films, old classics like Gone with the Wind and Casablanca. Ever watchful, Daisy suspected Adam enjoyed them much more than faraway Olive.

Their afternoons always involved the odd chuckle and a trip back in time. Sometimes Olive told them she'd been on the bus to Wigan market and bought them all black pudding for tea, and often thought that Daisy was Adam's mum, or Rita Hayworth, and her grandson was the doctor, or the nice man who used to clean her windows.

Seeing his gran like that didn't upset Adam, not any more. He knew she was clinging onto life albeit in a strange world that she wandered in and out of, but he didn't care. Even though Olive hadn't a clue who he was, Adam knew her, the gran she had once been, and that's what mattered. He could still hold her liver-spotted hand while Daisy read or helped her sip tea, and when she thought he was Karen the hairdresser he would comb her wispy white hair and tell her all about uni. They ate lunch together, Daisy and Adam watching her chew slowly as she nibbled on morsels, just enough to feed a sparrow. They'd even shared a bottle of Babycham when Olive announced that she wanted some to toast the bride and groom because Lady Di had popped in earlier to show off her wedding dress. Adam ran all the way to the off-licence, praying as he swerved dawdling shoppers that they'd have some in stock and his gran would still be in party mode when he got back.

Daisy knew that Adam was also clinging on, not ready to let go of his gran just yet. Apart from Ryan, Olive was his last living relative, someone who had loved him unconditionally, just because he was her grandson, no strings attached. And even though she wasn't medically inclined, it was clear to Daisy that Olive's grip was loosening on the world and after a quiet but honest chat with the nurse, thought it prudent to increase their visits, just in case.

Thankfully Adam heeded her tactful advice and they got there just in time to say goodbye, one sunny morning in late May, a month before the end of term. Olive woke up just once during the hours they waited by her bed, listening to her shallow breaths and the weird rattling noise in her chest, both holding her bony hands that were covered with tissue-thin, velvet skin. When Olive finally opened her eyes she turned her head slowly to one side, her sleepy eyes resting on Adam. Reaching out she sighed, recognition and love casting a serene glow across her face as she stroked his cheek. Olive didn't manage to speak, for which Daisy was grateful, holding her breath and praying that the perfect moment would remain unbroken by confused words.

After she closed her eyes and fell back to sleep, they stayed by Olive's side during which time the sun set and the room took on an eerie greyness, forcing Daisy to switch on the lamp, warm yellow light softening the mood. It was close to midnight when Olive floated away, so quietly that they almost didn't notice she was going but when they did, the only sound in the room came from Adam as he sobbed into the pink bedspread, lost in his own grief. The sound of his sorrow broke Daisy's heart.

From the moment they left the nursing home Adam was of no use to anyone, burrowing down in his room, closing himself off, immersed in memories and music, too distraught to talk. It was Daisy who made the call to the RAF using the special number that Ryan had left, to be used if and when there was bad news from home. And it was she who spoke to Ryan when he called from Cyprus after his commanding officer had given him the sad news, and between them they made some kind of provisional plan.

Once his flights had been arranged by work he would book a hotel for him and Adam, being together might be of comfort, but in the meantime Ryan asked Daisy if she would hold the fort to which she naturally agreed. After thanking her profusely for everything, especially looking after his gran in those final hours, he suggested, well asked, if she could help co-ordinate the funeral as he had no idea what to do. When she got off the phone Daisy was struck by Ryan's sensible approach, softened by the warmth and gratitude in his voice and there was something else – he sounded so mature and confident, nothing at all like Adam. Most of all, because he'd insinuated that he wanted her to help with the funeral, Daisy felt included, almost family, and it was nice.

From then on, in between keeping Adam company and making sure he ate and functioned in general, Daisy found herself counting down the days and then hours until Ryan arrived; the burden of another's grief was heavy and she craved relief. After seeing plenty of photos, Daisy knew exactly who they were looking for as she waited with Adam in the arrivals lounge but when the doors slid apart and Ryan emerged from the crowd of passengers, she wasn't prepared for the man who strode towards them, or for her heart to perform a triple somersault.

Whereas Adam was fair of complexion, Ryan tended towards olive skin, an asset that enhanced his Mediterranean suntan. Their eyes were exactly the same, pale brown, the firm jaw was less angular than Adam's, as was his body, and apart from both standing at six foot two, Ryan carried a muscular physique, one which screamed dedication and commitment.

After he hugged his brother tightly, whispering words of strength and comfort into his ear, Ryan then turned to envelop Daisy in a gentler and friendly embrace. In the seconds she felt the shadowed skin of his cheek touch hers and inhaled the scent of the man whose strong arms wrapped around her tiny frame, Daisy's world flipped upside down and she was lost.

Chapter 7

Thorns
Manchester 2003

Olive's funeral was sparsely attended but nonetheless turned out to be a decent enough affair, and due to the eulogy written by Adam, which told the nurses and carers from the home just how much she was adored by her two grandsons, her send off was laced with dignity and love.

*

Along with managing to read out loud without breaking down, Adam had showed surprising grit when he point-blank refused to allow any of their friends to attend the funeral – an offer made by Fliss who assured him they all wanted to show support at such a sad time. And even though she knew it wasn't the time or the place to gloat or feel remotely superior, Daisy enjoyed every minute of Fliss's rejection.

Ryan stayed at The Britannia and insisted Adam join him there; it was either that or squashing into his room at the halls – their togetherness was non-negotiable. On the lead up to the funeral Ryan and Daisy succeeded in luring Adam from his all-consuming grief where, out of respect to their gran, they allowed themselves some moments of happiness, because that's what she would want.

The thorn in Daisy's side was Greg, whose existence in general was becoming a hindrance. She was needed elsewhere, by Adam. Had she been completely honest with Greg and herself, Ryan's name would've been tagged onto the reason for readily abandoning her frustrated boyfriend. And while it was clear that Ryan didn't need her to comfort or care for him, he appeared to enjoy her company.

Daisy wasn't actually required to do very much when it came down to arrangements, although her opinion was sought on most things, even the really morbid ones like choice of coffin and an outfit from Olive's wardrobe, which they delivered to the chapel of rest. There was no wake after the service, the people from the care home had to get back so instead, the three main mourners bought a feast from Greggs and had a picnic in the park across the road from Olive's old flat.

They sat by the children's playground, a place that Adam had mentioned in his eulogy, a happy memory of times spent with their gran who provided an escape from their warring parents. Here they ran free and let off steam, paddling in the fountain, being children, which is why Daisy suggested they head there. It was a much cheerier place than the musty, old pub on the corner; the park was somewhere that if they closed their eyes, might transport them back to happy days with Olive.

Once they'd eaten, all three relaxed on the grass, soaking up the sun, lost in a few moments of quiet contemplation. Daisy's head was turned skywards but when her neck began to ache she changed position, opening her eyes to catch Ryan watching her, not in a creepy way but one that made her feel funny, especially when he smiled, amused at being caught in the act.

It was Adam who broke the silence and altered the mood, announcing that he felt like letting his hair down. There was a band on at the Students' Union Bar so assuming the role of grown-ups pandering to the whims of the youngster in the group, both Daisy and Ryan agreed they should set off back to Manchester before rush hour. On the drive down the M62 while Adam fiddled with the radio and Ryan told him off for being distracting, Daisy became aware of a strange atmosphere. Perhaps it was Ryan's laughing eyes that caught hers in the rear view mirror, holding her gaze for a second longer than necessary, or the touch of his skin when he passed her the Polos that caused an undercurrent of expectancy, something thrilling in the air.

Later, after ripping clothes from hangers in an attempt to find something more appealing and colourful than her funeral outfit, Daisy emerged from her room, flushed yet resplendent only to bump straight into another thorn – Fliss. Willing her to disappear before Adam and Ryan appeared she felt her heart sag when the next door opened and both stepped into the corridor. After introductions were made and feeling like he had to make up for shunning his friends, Adam suggested that Fliss tagged along too, roping in Lester and Jimmy the Ted who was currently burning toast in the kitchen.

Despite being irked by the inclusion of Fliss et al, Daisy was kind of glad they'd been duly summoned as now, amidst the music and trips to the bar, everyone was doing their utmost to maintain Adam's buoyant mood, leaving her time to talk to Ryan alone. It was quite hard to hear owing to the noise from the band so naturally, Daisy had to sit very close in order to communicate. Being squashed up against his muscular arms, their skin touching, his athletic thighs pressed into hers while looking into those pale brown eyes was almost unbearable, forcing Daisy to banish the urge to kiss him. But best of all, she sensed he felt the same.

"Look, do you want to go outside? I can hardly hear what you're saying and it's too hot in here. I'll get us a drink and then we can find somewhere quieter." Ryan glanced over towards Adam who was laughing at something Lester was saying, before nodding in his brother's direction. "I think he'll be fine on his own for a while, he seems to be okay. It's nice to see him smiling again." When Daisy's eyes wandered towards Adam her heart lifted. He was indeed in the throes of hysterical laughter as were Lester and Jimmy, so taking this as a cue to slip away, Daisy stood and beckoned Ryan.

Drinks in hand they made their way out of the Union and onto the steps at Oxford Road. The cool evening air was refreshing and mildly sobering, and in Daisy's case quite necessary. No matter how attracted she was to Ryan, doing something reckless, today of all days, would be foolish on so many levels, the least of them throwing her best friend's rather fragile heart into further turmoil. And then, even more sobering than that, Daisy remembered she had a boyfriend. The change of scene also appeared to have cooled Ryan's ardour and there was at least an inch of space between them now, less intense and slightly easier to deal with but when Ryan began to speak, Daisy knew exactly where his questions were heading and why.

"I'm glad Adam has you in his life, he's told me all about you and how you met. In fact most of his emails prominently feature your name. When I dropped him off last year I was worried sick about how he'd manage by himself but I can see he's fine now he has you."

"Aw, thanks, but the feelings entirely mutual. I was almost ready for doing a moonlight flit and running home to France but Adam appeared in the nick of time, and he's very special to me, much to the annoyance of my boyfriend." Daisy had no idea why she mentioned Greg; maybe it was a subconscious safety valve reminding her to be good even though that was the last thing on her mind.

"So, how does he deal with Adam being around? I bet he thinks it's odd, you two spending so much time together. I don't know if I'd be so understanding. I bet the poor bloke feels like a spare part."

Daisy felt nothing but irritation at the mere thought of Greg. "Oh, don't feel sorry for him and to be honest it's not looking like we'll be an item for much longer. I've known for a while now we're not meant for each other and with the summer holidays coming up I think it might be the perfect time to take a break, and the fact that Adam will be coming to France with me won't go down well either. So I can safely say we are doomed." Daisy surprised herself by verbalising the truth she'd been avoiding for the past few weeks.

Ryan grimaced. "So does he know this yet or are you saving it for an end of term surprise?"

"I think he might have guessed and anyway there's a chance he'll dump me first after all the time I've been spending with you and Adam. He's had a right face on him." Again annoyance swelled – she really needed to give Greg the chop.

"Yeah, it definitely sounds like its run its course to me, but back to you and our Adam. I must admit to being a bit confused after the way he goes on about you. For ages I've been expecting a text saying you are together properly, so if *I'm* wondering what's going on I can see why what's-his-name feels like a spare part."

"Yeah, it has been tricky but I can assure you that my relationship with Adam is purely platonic even though we are joined at the hip most of the time. We just get each other and even though it's a bit of a cliché, we are like twins, brother and sister, but without the sibling rivalry and fights. I know everyone gossips about us and I think a few girls on his course hate me. He's quite a catch but very picky. I'm like his faithful bag carrier, you know, the friend who tags along and cheers from the sidelines while he gets on with being Adam." Daisy was mindful of saying too much or telling a fib, so she stuck to the script and Ryan seemed to buy it so she drove home the point.

"I don't know what I'd do without him really. He was the first person to say hello and be nice to me, and after that we just clicked so now he's my best friend, just that, I swear." Daisy held up the palm of her hand and hoped the tone of her voice told Ryan she spoke the truth.

"It's okay I believe you but I presumed he was just being shy and would eventually pluck up the courage to ask you out. He's always been like that where girls are concerned, a bit slow on the uptake. I used to wind him up when he was a kid because he was so self-conscious and really cagey when I asked if he had a girlfriend. The two I remember from college were nice enough but I hardly ever saw them. Has he got his eye on anyone at the moment?"

Spotting an ideal opportunity to stir, Daisy got her own back on her nemesis. "Not that I know of, that's if you don't count freaky Fliss who's got a mahoosive crush on him. She's like his twenty-four-seven stalker, just waiting to pounce if and when he gives her the nod." Daisy rolled her eyes, not caring if she sounded like a bitch; it was all true anyway.

"Yeah, I noticed she's very intense, a bit too eager and deffo a flirt. I bet she's a closet bunny boiler. I take it you're not her favourite person and vice-versa?" Ryan had been the recipient of a few flirty looks since they'd arrived.

"Yep, got it in one, she can't stand me so if I ever get pushed under a bus it was her that did it!" Daisy liked making Ryan laugh – his face was often set deep in thought and guarded.

"Still, no matter what you say I bet most people think you are a couple, I know I would if I saw you and our Adam together, so it might put them off."

"I think it did at first but since I met Greg, Adam's been a bit more independent. There was a girl called Nell a while back, and he's always out on the town with Lester or Jimmy so who knows what they all get up to when I'm not there, but privately he's still the same as you remember and I swear his OCD is getting worse – he's even started organising my room. I nipped to the corner shop and when I came back all my toiletries were in alphabetical order!"

They both cracked up laughing, Ryan shaking his head at the thought of his brother. "I swear I love him to bits but sometimes he's a bloody weirdo. You know at Gran's he rearranged the food cupboard in size order? And God help you if the labels on the tins didn't face outwards. I wanted to sellotape his hands together because it used to drive me flamin' mad!"

Daisy was completely unfazed by this revelation. "Aw, bless him. But that's what makes him unique, his funny little ways. I love him to bits too, just the way he is. Anyway, enough about me and Adam, have you got anyone special in your life or do you keep a woman in every port, or would you say air base?"

"Nah, there's nobody on the scene at the moment, we'll be in Cyprus for a few more weeks then I'm off to America – Las Vegas would you believe? Not the casino area by the way, there's an air base in the desert. I'm really looking forward to the posting. One of the bonuses of my job is that I get to visit some amazing places."

Ryan was staring into the middle distance, maybe imagining his next adventure, but Daisy wasn't ready to let him go just yet.

"Do you get lonely though, I bet you miss being with Adam?"

"Yeah, I suppose that's the biggest down side, working away so much does limit our time together and it's the same if I meet anyone, I suppose. I'm not a monk or anything but I am careful not to get attached. It's unfair to expect anyone to hang about for me and I admit to being a selfish sod who has a habit of volunteering for anything that looks exciting and involves a trip abroad, so I definitely don't think I'm relationship material."

"That's putting it mildly! You sound really happy though and it must be nice to enjoy your job so much, but maybe you need to give yourself a bit of a break now and then, come back and see us a bit more often if you can. I know Adam would like that, and me too." Daisy couldn't believe the last bit had slipped out but when Ryan's face lit up, she was glad it had.

"I promise I'll try, and I'd like to keep in touch with you while I'm away if that's okay. It'd be nice having someone to talk to other than the lads, and you can tell me how Adam is getting on, you know…if he's coping after losing Gran or been banned from the library for rearranging their shelves." Ryan took a swig from his bottle, laughing along with Daisy at the image of Adam being ejected from the building by an irate librarian.

"Of course, I'd love that, we can get to know each other better and if you need me to send you anything while you're away, just ask. I bet you miss stuff from home. I know I do. And I'm quite excited about keeping in touch because it's years since I've had a pen friend. It'll be just like at school but more grown up." Daisy nudged him and winked in an effort to assure him she didn't expect anything more than a friendly chat.

"I was thinking more on the lines of texting, I can't remember the last time I wrote a letter, but you never know it might be fun, using old-fashioned pen and paper. I know, I'll send you a Bluey… that's what we call Forces mail by the way. It's nothing weird and refers to the colour of the paper so don't look so worried.

You should see your face!" Ryan was laughing his head off because when he saw Daisy's wide-eyed look he realised she'd got the wrong end of the stick.

Daisy held her hand to her heart. "Thank God for that! I was just about to leg it and tell Adam his brother is a perv! Stop laughing, it's not my fault I didn't know what a Bluey meant." Daisy slapped his arm in mock anger. "But on a serious note, please don't worry about Adam, I'll keep an eye on him when you leave and he's going to love it in France. It'll do him good and I'll make sure he has some fun. All my friends are dying to meet him and my parents will keep us both busy, and my mum will see it as her personal mission to pamper him. He'll be a right fatty when he gets back here."

"I know he'll be okay with you, and thanks Daisy, not just for looking out for Adam but for being around the last few days. I was dreading it all being too heavy but having you with us made everything so much easier. I really don't know if I'd have coped on my own. You've been a star." It was just a natural reaction, Ryan's gratitude mixed with relief at hearing his brother would be in good hands, along with an irresistible urge to kiss the life out of the gorgeous creature sitting beside him that caused him to wrap his arm around her shoulders and pull her close for a hug. Managing to be respectful of her status and not wanting to ruin what could be the start of a long distance friendship before it began, Ryan steeled himself and kissed the side of her head, lingering a while longer than necessary before letting her go, relaxing his hold enough for her to look up, which is when he saw the look. It was just fleeting, the softness in her hazel eyes as she held his stare, a silent yet thrilling moment that he could have acted on, made his move, until they were rudely interrupted by a familiar voice. It belonged to a thorn much bigger and spikier than Greg. It was of course, Fliss.

"Hey, Adam's been looking everywhere for you. We're going to get some food in town. The band's speaker blew up so the show's over. Are you coming or not?" Fliss had her hands on her hips and was eyeing them suspiciously.

"Yeah, we're on our way, stop stressing." Daisy rolled her eyes at Ryan who just smiled and then stood, offering her his hand before heaving her upwards. Whatever had passed between them was lost, thanks to Gob Almighty, yet Daisy still felt reluctant to let go of Ryan's hand. It was weird but it felt the same as when she held Adam's, that sense of belonging, safe and natural with a spark of something hot and fizzy added to the mix.

As their hands dropped and they made their way inside, Daisy felt sad that their time together had ended. She would have loved to spend the rest of the evening alone with Ryan, just chatting and finding out more about him, his job and his friends. Shaking off a sense of disappointment she consoled herself with the fact that he wanted to keep in touch and she had every intention of doing so. Better still, because Adam was in her life then Ryan would be too, so it was all fine. There was no rush, she could wait.

Ignorance they say is bliss and she had no idea of knowing it at the time, but Daisy had just made a huge mistake, unwittingly showing her hand to someone who had been waiting eagerly to score a point. Fliss still hoped to manoeuvre herself closer to Adam, or failing that, punish Daisy for being a barrier to any kind of relationship with him, and now, she had been handed both things on one plate.

After watching them all night, it was clear as day that Ryan had the hots for Daisy and, surprise surprise, little Miss Perfect felt the same way. After toying with the idea of texting Greg, Fliss thought better of it because there was a simpler way to punish the enemy and once they were back inside the bar, wasted no time in making her move. While covertly watching Daisy and Ryan from the top of the steps, acutely aware of their body language, seethingly envious of the hug and chaste kiss, Fliss had already decided that if she couldn't have Adam, she would take Ryan instead.

Chapter 8

The triangle
Manchester 2003

After they'd left the Student Union Bar everyone headed into Manchester and at some point during the evening the main group became separated from Fliss and Ryan. Adam didn't notice he was missing at first; it was only when he found Daisy sitting alone in the booth that he became concerned, noting from her downcast look that something was up. Within minutes he understood why.

Fliss had moved in on Ryan at Pizza Hut and continued her onslaught in the club, culminating in them both sloping off without even saying goodbye. It was fair to say that Ryan was completely smashed and the following day, when he finally turned up to be interrogated by Adam, seemed to have little recollection of how he got back to the hotel or what happened inside his room at The Britannia. It didn't matter though because Fliss made sure she filled in all the blanks by informing Kiki and Carol – in great detail – about her night of passion with Ryan. The news of which filtered back to Daisy.

Adam found Daisy in her room, pretending to write up notes when in fact she was staring out of the window, pen in hand and looking lost. He closed the door before throwing himself backwards onto the mattress, silently opening his Mars Bar.

"You're going to break the bed jumping on it like that! And where's *my* chocolate?"

Adam rummaged in his pocket and pulled out a Twix then threw it to Daisy, hoping her smacked bottom face wasn't down to him, unless you counted being sick in the grid outside the halls the night before. But there hadn't been splash-back so on reflection it was more likely to do with Chinese whispers passed on by Jimmy and Lester. Adam waited until she'd demolished her chocolate before asking the obvious.

"So, why the mard face, has somebody upset you?" Adam unwrapped a tube of Rolos and offered Daisy the first one, stretching out and catching her eye as she plucked it from the pack, receiving a stern look in return.

"I'm going to tell Greg that we're finished. There's no point in dragging it out and anyway I don't think he's even that interested, and neither am I to be honest. I think it's best to make the break before we head off for the summer cos I really can't be arsed faking interest when I get home. It's bad enough when I'm here." Daisy had spun around, watching Adam intently, gauging his reaction to her harsh decision and challenging tone. She really was on one but knew before he even spoke that Adam wouldn't care; he'd more than likely be pleased.

"Ouch...that's all very clinical, I hope you're going to soften the blow and not be that brutal? Perhaps leave the guy with a tiny shred of confidence and dignity if you can."

"I'm all out of soft and I'm sick of being nice to people who don't deserve it. You can play piggy in the middle all you want but from now on people who push their luck like Fliss can just piss off! I mean it Adam. I'm done with her, and Greg. End of!"

Adam flicked the ring pull on his can; the fizzing noise made him think of Daisy. "Ah, now we're getting to it. This is more to do with the bit of juicy gossip I've just heard than you splitting up with Greg, and don't turn away, you know I'm right."

Daisy swung around to face Adam. "I'm just sick of her sticking her oar into everything. She's a pain in the arse Adam and you know it! And I'm not in the least bit bothered about Greg or his ego, as far as I'm concerned he's history and just a waste of time and space." Daisy was twisting her hair around her finger as she stared Adam out, openly defying him to contradict her, which he did.

"Well, I'm not going to argue with you about Greg but you're playing it all wrong with Fliss and you can't let her see how upset you are. And surely you're used to her butting in by now. It's who she is and what she does so don't give her the satisfaction. Look, is it this business with our Ryan that's got you all fired up? Come on, spill. You know you can tell me anything so don't bottle it up. It won't help and I can't be doing with this narky attitude, it doesn't suit you."

Daisy didn't answer straight away, crossing her arms defensively over her chest, which along with the sulky expression told Adam he was correct.

"Sort of...but it's not like anything happened between us. I'm not a two-timer and he probably doesn't even like me in that way, but it was just nice being with him and she ruined it *as usual*. All I wanted was to spend some time with him and then she turned up and boom, game over. I really felt like we had a connection and he's so different from anyone I've met here, more grown up I suppose. I just felt drawn to him. Aargh...I feel so stupid saying all this, especially to you, so let's forget it, I'm fine. Pretend it never happened." Daisy was working herself up into a temper, twisting her swivel chair back and forth as she spoke, restless fingers tapping tense arms, pent up irritation about to explode.

"Daisy chill out, I get it, I really do. And you don't have to apologise. I can see why you'd fancy our Ryan...and don't look at me like that, I'm not stupid *or* naive so give me some flamin' credit! And I also understand why you like being around him. He has a way that's reassuring – it's how he makes me feel, sort of safe and relaxed. I'm glad you two hit it off, I really am."

"Really?" Daisy looked up shyly and saw that Adam was grinning.

"Yes, really, I swear." Adam made a cross sign on his chess.

"He asked if we could keep in touch and I said yes. He's really easy to talk to and interesting, not like my crappy boyfriend. I just wanted the night to go on forever and get to know him a bit more and have a laugh, but then Greg's annoying face kept popping into my head and then Fliss stuck the knife in. And not only that, she knew Ryan was going back today and more or less pinched him when he should've been with you. That is so out of order because your time together is precious. I thought they were going to the loo but they never came back, the sly cow! I could slap her, I really could!"

"Yeah, she's one to watch that's for sure."

"I reckon she was slipping double vodkas in his coke. There's only her and Lester that can afford spirits and she did go to the bar a few times."

"I bet he's sick as a dog this morning but it serves him right. He drinks far too much and I've bollocked him about it before *and* he knows why." Adam checked his phone. The lack of messages from Ryan more or less proved his point.

Daisy went over and flopped onto the bed then slipped her arm through Adam's.

"I just wish he'd picked anyone but her for a one-night stand because she'll never shut up about it now. I hope you're going to tell Ryan what he's let himself in for. I did hint that she was a snidey cow, which is why I'm so shocked. Perhaps he just fancied a quick leg-over before he went back to base." Daisy was trying hard to bring some levity to the situation when all she really wanted to do was cry.

Adam tutted his disapproval. "Well I'm going to make sure he knows exactly what Fliss is like and nip whatever she thinks this is in the bud."

"Do you think he'll listen because he obviously took no notice of me?" Daisy rested her head on his shoulder.

"Yeah, I'll find a way to get through to him, and you! I feel like a broken record saying this but will you take some advice where she's concerned? Just don't let her bug you. Fliss is insanely jealous of everything Daisy, we know that. But we can take revenge in loads of ways so let's start by meeting Ryan for lunch, come and say goodbye with me. And no matter how fed up you are, you should keep in touch with him like he asked. You just have to forget about Fliss because when it comes down to it, Ryan's made a ten-pints gorgeous mistake with the local loony!"

When Daisy started laughing the tension in the room eased, agreeing with Adam that Fliss had taken her pound of flesh and wouldn't get an ounce more. Still, nothing would persuade Daisy to go for lunch. She was adamant that it was Adam's time with Ryan and anyway, she had an appointment with her soon-to-be ex-boyfriend. They did make a point of leaving the halls together and telling Lester that they were going to meet Ryan in town, smug in the knowledge that eventually Fliss would hear about it.

When Adam arrived at the hotel Ryan was expecting Daisy too, and registered the disappointment he felt at her absence along with the huffy attitude of his brother. Over a giant fry-up interrupted by incessant texts from Fliss, Adam admonished Ryan for sloping off then explained all about Fliss and her obsessive ways, especially where Daisy was concerned.

"Mate, nothing happened, I swear! She asked me to walk her to the cash point and there was a cocktail bar right next door so she treated me as a thank you, then before I knew it we were back at the club and you'd all disappeared. She said she'd missed the night bus so we shared a cab, but when we got to the hotel she desperately needed the loo and asked if she could use my bathroom. What could I say? Yeah, I hold my hands up to getting pissed but I can assure you that I did not end up in bed with Fliss! And I did take on board what Daisy said but hey, I'm a chick magnet, kill me now!" Ryan drunk some of his tea and wished Adam would give it a rest, not wanting to talk about what really happened in the hotel – it was history.

After hearing his brother's sincere and regretful apology and noting that he was in the throes of a self-inflicted injury, Adam forgave him and moved on. It would be the last time they'd be together for a while and there were other things to discuss, like what to do with Olive's meagre possessions. They amounted to nothing more than a faded wedding photo in a worn frame, a tatty album containing images of family members they preferred to forget, and their grandad's pocket watch and service medals. Olive's rings were inside a small, velvet-covered box – engagement, wedding and eternity – along with a fine gold chain that held a tiny crucifix. Any other belongings that remained in her room at the nursing home had gone to charity.

Ryan insisted that Adam kept all of Olive's trinkets, knowing how much his brother coveted such keepsakes. And it was unlikely that he'd have use for the jewellery, having no intention of tying the knot anytime soon, then joked with Adam that he'd probably be the first to fall in love and produce an heir. Although he was rather pleased and more than willing to be the custodian of their family heirlooms, Adam refrained from voicing his true thoughts on the matter of marriage and procreation. No matter how much Daisy insisted that nobody could predict the future, he was still of the opinion that for him, the likelihood of happy ever after was slim.

Next on the agenda were Olive's ashes. They quickly agreed that Adam would do the honours. He didn't think it was at all morbid having his gran as a roommate until they could decide where to scatter them so, glad to have that matter sorted, Ryan swiftly changed the subject.

He had always been fastidious in his care for Adam and now he was earning a decent wage could afford to treat him, hence the envelope containing a cheque that he slid across the table. After it had been pushed back and forth a few times, Adam got the message and placed it in his pocket, the mood lifting now that financial and depressing issues had been dealt with. It seemed that Ryan's hangover was also dissipating and over their third cup of tea he asked Adam to convey a message on his behalf: tell Daisy he was sorry if he'd upset her by disappearing with her arch enemy and if she was still okay with it, he would like to keep in touch.

"You don't mind, do you...if I send an email or the odd text? I know you two are just mates but if you've got any unrequited feelings for her just say. You always keep stuff bottled up so I never know what the hell you're thinking but I'd rather you tell me – the last thing I want to do is get in the way of true love or have to look at your mardy face." Ryan grinned as he waited for

Adam to answer, hoping so hard that he didn't object. The fact alone surprised him.

"Do I heck! I've been over all this with Daisy this morning because she was worried I'd take the huff if you kept in touch. I think she may have a bit of a crush on my big stupid brother, though I can't think why looking at the state of you. Seriously mate, you need to pack the boozing in, and anyway, I thought your body was a temple? There's no point in looking like a killing machine on the outside when your vital organs are knackered." Adam saw Ryan hold up the palm of his hand and nod repeatedly; the message was obviously getting through to his beer-haggled brain so he left it there, moving swiftly on.

"So, back to our Daisy. I assure you there's nothing going on between us so you have my permission to keep in touch. We can adopt her, then she'll be part of our family circle, or maybe cos there's just three of us it's more like a triangle."

"What *are* you going on about? You say the weirdest things sometimes. I swear you're from another bloody planet!" Ryan mopped up his egg with a slice of bread, too tired to fathom Adam's idiosyncrasies.

While Ryan ate, Adam took the opportunity to do some digging. "So, you do like her then, Daisy I mean, not Fliss the psycho?"

"Yeah, I do. To be honest it was nice meeting someone different. She's really natural and not all tarted up and caked in makeup like the girls I see in clubs, and she's interesting too, you know, has something to say for herself. We're a tight team on the squadron but every now and then I'd like to talk about something outside my box and see another name flash up on my phone. God, I sound like a right saddo. It must be the alcohol turning my brain soft. And what are you smirking at?" Ryan could tell that something was amusing Adam but then again he was off with the fairies most of the time, so who knew.

"Nothing, I'm just glad you two get along, that's all."

"So you don't mind? It'll be purely platonic. I don't have any expectations or romantic notions, especially when I'll be out of the country for ages, and she's got that Greg bloke in tow so even if I did, I have to respect that."

"Don't worry about him, he's a right dickhead and Daisy's not that into him. He'll be history soon so just keep it light and see how things go. But in the future and for a small fee payable on demand I'll exterminate any potential love rivals so the coast stays clear, believe me, it'll be my pleasure." Adam was actually being serious but in a jokey way.

"You're alright mate. Between you and me I like the single life – no strings attached suits me just fine. It's just that Daisy is a really nice girl and I think we bonded over all this stuff with Gran. We're just in the wrong place at the wrong time."

"With the wrong bloke and a freak-show stalker."

"Yeah, looks like that, and I'm sure she'll meet someone new soon enough. Maybe Daisy will just have to go down in history as the one that got away." Ryan drained his mug and made to stand.

Adam nodded at his brother's comment then fell into silence, deep in thought, watching Ryan as he paid at the counter, a cocktail of emotions swirling inside his head. Olive was at the epicentre, surrounded by the sinking feeling you get before you say farewell. And it was there again, that hint of being alone, like a mist hovering on the edge of his consciousness, a menacing figure lingering in the shadows, a silent threat. Not wanting to ruin their last minutes together Adam shrugged them away and applied his default setting – Daisy. She alone had the power to fend off the gloom, like a warrior princess with a magic sword and protective shield. Clinging onto this belief, her spell began to work, the fog cleared and his spirits lifted.

Adam watched as the taxi pulled away, his arm aching from the strain of waving, not wanting to stop until Ryan was out of sight, then turned reluctantly towards the campus. He did a lot of thinking as he watched his trainers pound the pavement below, content in his own company, formulating the brief outline of a plan that had taken seed in the cafe. He knew it could take years to complete and was a long shot but nevertheless of huge importance, the rather simple solution to two huge problems. At last there might be a way to banish the spectre of ending up a lonely old man, on the outside of everything, separated from his remaining family member or parted from Daisy by some unsuitable husband.

As he pushed open the doors of the lecture hall Adam felt buoyed even though the future was hindered by logistics and separation, a dusty desert and the streets of this city, and his final destination was still many years away. Whereas before it stretched endlessly into the distance, like Route 66, today Adam had glimpsed a sign, pointing directly to hope. Now, he had a map to follow. It was all so glaringly obvious and doable the minute he'd realised that his journey through life would be a much better place if it contained just three people – a simple triangle consisting of him, Ryan and Daisy.

Chapter 9

Olive, Elvis and the angels
France 2003

In June, the day after the end of term, Adam and Daisy packed up their belongings and moved out of the halls for good and began their journey to France. They would be sharing a house with Kiki and Carol when the new term began, and on Daisy's insistence, Fliss wasn't given a look in. Adam was in complete agreement knowing that she would be a nightmare to live with and after her stunt with Ryan, had little inclination to spend more time than necessary with her.

Adam absolutely loved being at Campanule Campings and slotted straight into Daisy's family; it was like Bill and Pam's long lost son had finally returned and they were complete. He was given one of the bedrooms that overlooked the pastures to the rear of the house where, to his delight, the door held a wooden plaque saying 'Adam's Room'. Over the summer months he put his own inimitable stamp on the interior, filling it with bits and bobs that he collected from markets and day trips out with Daisy. On the chest of drawers was his 'corner of curiosity' adorned with rocks from the local mine, shells from the beach and bits of wood that he'd attempted to carve, which looked nothing like arrowheads *or* animals.

Their summer was one of the happiest times of Adam's life where he experienced family as he'd always imagined it to be, not perfect and rose-tinted, even he knew that this vision was one of fantasy. Their days were marked by mealtimes around the table, breakfasts of croissants and freshly laid eggs from Pamela's chickens, long lunches eating the produce from Bill's garden and late dinners in the shade once their daily duties were complete.

Poor old Bill was always being told off for a variety of male misdemeanours: footprints on the kitchen floor, drinking too much wine at lunch, forgetting to write down messages on the office notepad, leaving imprints from his mug of tea on paperwork and more often than not, disappearing in the afternoon for a sneaky kip by the lake. But now, he had an accomplice. Adam was a willing sidekick who lapped up their one-to-one talks during excursions in the dusty pick-up truck or as they watered the vegetable garden. Bill had refined the art of looking busy, sleeping with one eye open, delegation and feigning innocence when he was caught out by Pam – a regular occurrence. He also knew everything about the area, especially where they sold the best farm cider and cheap local wine, and a well-trod short cut to the English chippy.

Adam had his first driving lesson with Bill, something that he'd previously shied away from despite Ryan's offer of lessons. They had been on an errand for Pam so took a detour along the bumpy track to the hill where the windmills were stationed, five towering grey monuments that looked out across the valley and once they were at the peak, Bill told Adam to swap places and drive them back down again. Noticing Adam's hesitation and wide-eyed stare, Bill pointed out that they could see all the way to the bottom – there were no other vehicles and nothing to bump into, just fields of corn and the odd herd of cows and sheep.

"But I haven't got a licence. Won't we get in trouble if the coppers see us?" Adam was trying hard to get out of it as he slid across the seats, reluctantly placing his hands on the steering wheel, his mouth bone dry.

"We're in France lad, there's not a gendarme for miles and if we saw one up here it'd be a bloody miracle, now stop buggering about and start her up, come on, chop chop. Our Pam's made a steak pie so let's see if you can get us back in one piece and in time for dinner. We can stick to the farm tracks all the way home so just do what I say and you'll be fine." Bill looked straight ahead and waited, fully aware that Adam was nervous but just needed a push in the right direction, or maybe a kick up the arse.

It was baking outside. The midday sun bore down onto the battered old truck that had never known the luxury of air conditioning and whose faded interior was strewn with grass and mud. Adam thought he was going to internally combust from heatstroke and fear but didn't want to let Bill down or have him think he was a wimp, so doing as he was told he started the engine, took a deep breath and then followed his instructor's every word.

By the time they'd reached the foot of the hill Adam had managed fourth gear and they were trundling along at a steady pace. Plumes of brown dust and spatters of stone followed in their wake, as did the sound of Bill giving encouragement.

"Well done lad, just keep her steady and put your foot down a bit. I can smell that pie from here...I'll make a rally driver out of you yet, just don't let on to our Pam what we've been up to, you know how she goes on." Bill relaxed in his seat and took in the scenery, ignoring his rumbling stomach and allowing himself a smug smile as he caught a glimpse of the young man by his side who was now beaming from ear to ear.

Adam was elated, free. The wind that blew through the cab tousled his hair as the truck bounced over potholes along the deserted single track. Why had he not done this before? He should've listened to Ryan and taken lessons when they were offered but manually dexterous challenges made him nervous. Maybe Bill would give him a few more so when they got back to Manchester he'd be confident enough to tackle the city roads and traffic. Adam sneaked a look at his passenger who gave him a cheeky wink then indicated they should take the track on the left before resting sun-weathered arms on his huge pot belly.

Adam felt buoyant and for the first time ever, unburdened. Maybe it was the sun and the fresh air, or the peace and quiet of a place where you could lose yourself amongst the fields and woods, avoiding the stresses and demands of the outside world. Here Adam could hide away; he was safe. Had he believed in God, he would've thanked him for sending Daisy into his life and for everything that came after, like Bill. He was a top bloke, his new mate, someone to look up to and maybe ask for advice when Ryan wasn't around. But along with joy came the usual tensing of heart muscles when a fail-safe mantra reminded him that all of this had to be guarded. Adam wasn't going to give any of it up, not now he'd found his utopia.

"Right lad, you'd best pull over by that gate and I'll drive us home from here, don't want our Pam giving us grief. I'll let you have another go tomorrow, we can drive over to see my mate Dominique, he's got his still going and I think it's time you sampled some eau de vie. It'll put hairs on your chest I'll tell you that for nowt." Bill waited as Adam tentatively pulled onto the back field of the campsite before changing places, giving his student a firm slap on the back before setting off in search of steak pie.

On other days, while Bill was 'busy' elsewhere, Daisy and Adam helped with various jobs around the campsite, which was sectioned into four areas. The largest field was reserved for touring caravans and camping cars, the second was for six static caravans, which they rented out, while the tents were situated in the field adjacent to the forest. The fourth, the large fishing lake, was dotted along the edge with hides for bird watching or budding anglers, but eventually Bill hoped to build a row of log cabins, an idea that due to lack of funds remained a pipedream.

On site, along with the heated swimming pool and its adjacent small bar and cafe, other facilities included the games room and the quaint cobbled terrace where from Thursday to Sunday you could dine under the stars and sample traditional French cuisine prepared by Enzo, the chef from the village bar.

By nature he was a bit of a charmer, his mass of dread-locked blond hair seemed an extension of his effervescent character, and only when he tied it in a man bun and began to cook did the calmer more serious chef emerge. After he'd fed the locals and passing tourists with his lunchtime plat du jour, during the holiday season Enzo worked at Campanule, grateful for the extra money whilst enjoying the very convivial surroundings, especially the bevy of bikini-clad ladies who lounged by the pool. In the evening, bronzed and dressed in their holiday finest, they allowed him to flirt and flatter whilst he served his rustic fayre cooked on a huge outdoor grille, the smell of roast boar turning on the spit luring hungry campers from the four corners of the site. Daisy was impervious to Enzo's charms, although it didn't prevent him from giving it a go, year after year, much to her amusement and the displeasure of a watchful Adam.

Each morning Franc and his bread van would arrive, followed by a swarm of hungry campers who would purchase freshly made loaves and batons, and on a Wednesday, everyone flocked towards Amine's pastel pink Citroen van from where he'd sell freshly made crêpes. Once a fortnight they were treated to an evening of music when solo artists and bands would perform on the makeshift mini stage, which was festooned with multi-coloured lights. Bill and Pamela booked the same acts each year, hardy musicians who travelled France on the holiday centre circuit and while they weren't necessarily A-list celebrities, the guests loved them.

There was plenty for Daisy and Adam to do despite it being fully staffed by cleaners from the village, plus Dorian, Cassandre's brother who worked in the pool and bar area. And not forgetting their loyal groundsmen, twins Sasha and Rémi, who looked as ancient as the trees in the forest. They were identical yet kindly aided the locals and site owners alike by wearing different hats. Sasha was never seen without his cloth cap whilst Rémi sported a similarly immovable woollen affair but apart from that, their baggy pants, pulled high at the waist, were secured by a thin belt, teamed with hobnail boots, a faded but nicely pressed shirt in summer and in winter, accessorised with a knitted tank top and tweedy jacket. While the two hardy gentlemen looked more rumpled and weather beaten as each season changed, their uniform remained the same year on year, despite Pamela's charitable donations amidst fears they'd die of heatstroke in the summer or freeze to death in winter.

Adam and Daisy mucked in when needed, maybe to man the reception or show a new arrival to their pitch or caravan.

Adam particularly liked working in the bar serving ice creams and hot dogs, chatting to the little kids and their parents, but his top job was driving the huge mower and trailer. He would literally hover by a departing guest then hop on his machine and tend the vacated pitch while Daisy watched on with amusement at his sudden attraction to all things motorised, suspecting her wily dad had something to do with it.

Another of Adam's favourite things was a hidden gem shown to him by Daisy on their very first day in France, the sight of which had blown him away and being there, just as she said it would, made you feel at one with nature, part of an ancient ethereal experience.

*

Well away from the tracks used by campers, deep inside the forest stood an old beech tree. It was huge with a myriad of sturdy silvery boughs spreading outwards, casting a long shadow on the soil below, their shade inhibiting the growth of ground fauna so at its feet lay a velvety carpet of earth. It was the King of trees, an ancient grandfather guarding the younger oaks and silver birch that had gathered around him, his subjects. The other amazing thing about the beech was the hollow in its trunk, tall and wide like a yawning, gaping mouth, large enough for three or four adults to sit comfortably inside.

Bill found it soon after they arrived and couldn't wait to show Daisy. He'd told her the tale of Robin Hood and his hiding place in Sherwood Forest as they made their way through the forest then explained that their very own giant was probably 400 years old. Daisy soaked up every word and once she saw the mighty beech with her own eyes, named it the Grandad Tree and insisted that her parents took her there as often as possible. The forest was dense in places and unchartered territory so Bill had made secret carvings on the bark to help find their way, something that thrilled Daisy at the time yet caused great distress when she was older.

When she hit her teens, Daisy became increasingly aware of her natural surroundings and developed a heightened sensitivity, especially where saving the earth and the animals that lived upon it were concerned. It was during a science class discussing photosynthesis, their teacher focusing attention on the life cycle of trees, that the light dawned. The feeling she got when huddled inside the Grandad Tree or each time she touched his companions' silvery bark all made sense.

After rushing down her lunch, Daisy spent the rest of her free time in the school library, lost amongst pages of nature, flicking through photo after photo, eager to learn more. The magic of the trees entranced her. Reading about their intertwined roots that were covered with thousands of hairs, connecting to their neighbours and creating an extended nervous system that soaked up water and nutrients from the soil gave Daisy goosebumps. Deep inside the trunk consisting of four layers of tissue, a network of tubes acted like a plumbing system carrying minerals up from the roots to the leaves and in reverse, sugar down from the foliage via the branches, trunk and roots. The heartwood (Daisy loved that name) supported the tree and was filled with sugar, oil and dyes and most importantly, the thing that made her gasp when she read the words, dead cells of the old nutrient givers, the ghosts of the tree, their spirits contained within. And while the elders languished in the heartwood, the cambium grew on, adding layer on layer to the tree, giving life. This meant the Grandad Tree's legacy lived on – it was alive.

This new-found knowledge blew Daisy away and she spent the rest of the day willing the bell to ring. As soon as she arrived home, rejecting her usual snack, she ran through the forest stopping at each tree on which they'd carved a symbol, wrapping her arms around the trunk then saying sorry to the spirits sleeping inside. On reaching the Grandad Tree Daisy stood beneath his bows and placed her hands on the rough, knobbly bark then told him face to face that she would never again harm one of his friends by marking a cross or carving a name and for the rest of her life would protect them as best she could. Daisy then asked for forgiveness.

As the warm breeze rustled through his leaves Daisy closed her eyes and waited, resting her head against the trunk, the ridges beneath leaving marks on her cheek and despite her tears, inside her head a picture emerged. It was the face of a wise old man staring kindly down on a repentant young girl. His arms were made from branches, tenderly wrapped around her body and the leaves that adorned them caressed her face, soothing away her anguish. In that moment Daisy knew she was forgiven.

It had remained her most sacred and special place ever since, where on hot days, either alone or with friends, Daisy would sit inside the cavern or under the leafy boughs. It was a meeting place to share secrets, a place of refuge, an escape, which is why when the time came Daisy had to share it with Adam.

*

As they walked along the track towards the Grandad Tree, Daisy explained the science behind what she described as magic, which as far as she was concerned was an undeniable connection between the spiritual and the physical. It was 6am and the scent of the forest filled the air, the mulch of damp soil, moss and rotting bark that was trampled underfoot mingled with the wild floral perfume of campanules and honeysuckle, woken by soft rays from the sun.

They sat inside the mouth of the Grandad Tree and allowed the silence of the forest to envelop them, interrupted only by the cry from a kite soaring above the treetops or the chatter of the redstart and chaffinch, hidden somewhere amongst the leaves.

They stayed there for hours lying beneath the boughs of the almighty tree and it was here that Adam converted. The soil between his fingers, the dew on his jeans, the layers of earth on which he lay and the twisted labyrinth of roots below had a strange effect because here, he could touch and smell nature, immersed in the cycle of life, the ritual of rebirth. Adam didn't believe in God, aliens or the supernatural, nothing. He needed proof before he would give himself over to the notion that there was something more, yet right there, as he lay next to Daisy and watched the rays from the sun streak through the highest of the trees, spreading a bright light onto the ground below, for the first time in his life he felt something, a connection.

Now, Adam went there to think, nestled inside the trunk. After reading more about the special power of the trees he agreed with Daisy that here, alone with the spirits of the forest, you could really find peace. But it wasn't nature that made him feel whole. For Adam, that summer in France introduced him to another life and he was as perplexed as Bill and Pamela that Daisy chose to leave it behind because if he had a choice, he would have stayed there forever.

Pamela was the glue that held them together. Not just a mum, she ran the site, and while trying to keep Bill in order found time to make a huge fuss of everyone, checking they were fed, comfortable and happy. Bill was ace, down to earth and hen-pecked and had taught Adam allsorts, like how to fish and drive, or disappear for a few hours without being rumbled. They talked for hours as they wandered through the forest, supposedly checking for litter and wild campers, Bill naming flowers and herbs along the way, telling tales of his youth at The Ritz Ballroom in Manchester and the speedway at Belle Vue.

On a humid August evening following a scorching day serving hot dogs and melting ice cream, Daisy and Adam were lying on the pontoon that floated on the lake, singing along to their favourite music and sharing a bottle of wine as they watched for comets. They'd just murdered 'There's A Guy Works Down The Chip Shop Swears He's Elvis', Daisy's favourite karaoke song, and as she changed tracks, she glanced at Adam, his arms folded behind his head. He was lost in contemplation and gazing at the sky.

"Hey, are you okay? Penny for your thoughts." Daisy settled back down and sensing the need for quiet turned off the music.

"I was just thinking about Gran. She'd have loved it here. D'you know something? I can't remember her ever going on holiday. When she told us stories about the past she never mentioned going abroad, or anywhere really. Apart from the odd trip to Blackpool to see the lights, I don't even think she went much further than Chorley. How sad is that?"

"I think that's just the era they lived in, you know, poorer families had it hard and you said she worked in the cotton mill and her dad went down the mines – it was probably a real struggle to make ends meet, never mind go on holiday. My grandparents were the same. Dad's never mentioned going on holiday as a kid but you're right, it's really sad and flipping unfair."

"Our Gran worked until her late sixties in a factory sewing overalls and then she got a cleaning job when she took me and Ryan in. She should've been putting her feet up not looking after us. I wish I could turn back time and do something nice for her, like bringing her here. You two would've got on like a house on fire. She was ace before she got sick and lost her memory but it's all too late now, she'll never meet you or go on holiday, nothing." Adam's voice caught on the last word causing Daisy to move closer and lay her head on his chest, knowing instinctively that he'd fold his arms around her.

"Hey, Olive wouldn't want you to be sad. She did everything she could for you while she was alive so you've got to honour her memory by being happy, and anyway, how do you know she's not here right now and been watching you driving around on a tractor like a pro? She's probably up there, on one of those stars trying to tell you to cheer up." Daisy pointed to the sky. "See the one that's twinkling? I reckon it's heavenly Morse code for I love you." Daisy felt Adam's arm move as he wiped away a tear before replacing it around her shoulders.

"Daisy, that's a satellite not a star, but I wish I had your faith, I really do. It would make loads of things more bearable. I want to believe she's okay and happy, not picture her working her fingers to the bone or scrimping and saving."

"Well I believe enough for both of us." Daisy was floundering, sensing the onset of gloom.

Adam exhaled, trying to curb the swell of sadness that washed over him, but it was so hard to banish painful images. "I keep seeing her in that room at the home, confused and fragile, she was so helpless wasn't she?"

"Yes she was but never in pain so that's a good thing so Adam please, don't focus on the bad bits, you have to try and remember her before she was poorly, making your favourite tea and telling you off for drinking all the juice out of the tin of peaches. Or when Ryan got into a fight on the street and she bashed the other lad's mum, funny stuff like that. You should picture Olive when she was full of fire and quick-witted because that's what she will be like in heaven, all fixed up and back on form."

"Do you *really* think it's true? I just wish she'd send me a sign so I'd know for sure. I think things would make more sense if all the suffering and hurt gets wiped away once you float up to heaven and everyone is waiting for you in the arrivals hall. I just don't believe it Daise, it all seems a bit too good to be true."

Daisy turned on her stomach so she could see his face. "I get that it's hard for you but why not just go with the idea and try to feel the same connection with God as you do those trees over there? It makes me so happy you know, I wish I could pass that on to you. When I was growing up I used to feel left out because I wasn't Catholic and my friends went to mass in the village church so to stop me from sulking, Cassandre took me there on Sundays. I loved it there, still do. It's just so serene and peaceful. I'd listen to the songs and the priest giving his sermon and even though I wasn't Catholic he encouraged me to go up and be blessed – I really looked forward to that bit. He'd make the sign of the cross with oil on my forehead and I swear I could feel the mark all day, like a tattoo on my skin that made me glow inside. There are beautiful pictures on the stained glass windows and during the service my mind would wander off, sort of hypnotised by the bible stories they tell. One of them shows a host of angels; it's my favourite and I swear their faces move in the sunlight. I've read loads about them and I truly believe that your angel stays with you from the moment you're conceived and then, when you die, they carry you gently in their arms and deliver you to God. It's like their final mission."

"Hmm, I just think you are far too trusting Daisy, hypnotists call it suggestible. Just because someone tells you a magical story doesn't mean it's true. How do you know angels even exist, you've never seen one, never mind anyone actually having cast-iron proof about God or spirits?"

"I just do! I *want* to believe it Adam. I can feel it, like a presence. I imagine my angel wearing a pale pink dress that's covered in millions of twinkling diamonds, like stars, and when her wings unfold, multi-coloured glitter sprinkles everywhere like a sparkly mist. Your gran will have had an angel with her when she went up to heaven, making sure she was okay, I believe it with all my heart."

"I know you do…and I'm envious of that belief. And trust you to have a Barbie angel. I thought they wore white dresses made of old sheets and tinsel halos."

"Nah, mine likes to be different, and she gets in trouble a lot for leaving glitter on the carpet, apparently St Peter is a bit OCD when it comes to cleaning, he goes through tons of Mr Sheen shining his pearly gates." Daisy was relieved to see Adam finally laughing.

While Adam quite liked Daisy's version of heaven, as usual he had to push his luck and put his own spin on it. "So my spiritual friend, do you think that once you land in heaven you get to mingle with dearly departed celebs? There are a few people I'd rather avoid but once I've had a chat with Gran I'm going to hook up with John Lennon, oh yeah, and I'd like to know once and for all if Elvis did peg-it or as the song says, works in a chip shop, or wherever else he's been sighted."

Both Adam and Daisy were laughing now; the sombre mood had lifted.

"Well, we'll never know. Not until it's our turn but I reckon it will be an eye opener and if Elvis is up there, I hope he looks hot, like in that film we watched, not chubby and sweaty and wearing white leather. What *was* he thinking?"

"It must have been all those burgers, and it was Jailhouse Rock, that film we watched."

"Oh yeah, I remember now." Daisy nodded at Adam who had turned on his side to face her.

"But seriously, I wouldn't mind having a look in the church before we go back, I'm intrigued and you never know, maybe the magic will rub off on me."

Daisy's elbows were hurting so flipped over onto her back. "Really? I'd love to show you inside, we can go during the week. It's still lovely and atmospheric even without the singing. Or we could go to mass on Sunday with Inès. Cassandre gave up being Catholic ages ago because it interferes with her hangovers and she can't deal with confession. Apparently fibbing to the priest about her sins is another sin, but if she told the truth would still be saying Hail Marys at midnight."

"That's hilarious, but she does get about a bit so maybe it's not worth the risk."

"Yeah, true. And we can light a candle for your gran while we're there and even one for John Lennon if you like."

"I'd like that…but I'll have to write a list before we go of all my departed heroes. I don't want to miss anyone out, and I'll light the candles, you always burn your fingers." Daisy smiled as Adam kissed the top of her head and then she had an idea, a divine message from her sparkly angel.

"Adam, you know you said Olive would love it here, well why don't we bring her ashes and sprinkle them in the forest? No matter what you say that casket in your room is really depressing and unless you and Ryan think of somewhere else, Olive's going to be stuck on the shelf next to your football trophies…so perhaps she'd like to come here, what do you think?" Daisy saw Adam's silence as an opportunity to push the point. "And it'll be like bringing her on holiday. She'll be in a lovely place where you can visit forever. My home is yours now, Mum and Dad love you to bits and they've already said you're welcome anytime, so Olive will always be here, waiting for you to come back. You will come back with me, won't you?" Daisy knew Adam was gathering himself and for a second, thought she'd gone too far, smothering him or being insensitive, but then she felt him squeeze her hand, hearing emotion in his voice.

"Course I will. I love it here Daisy, it already feels like home. These past few weeks have been the best so if your mum and dad don't mind I'll be here like a shot. And that's a brilliant idea about Gran but I don't fancy scattering the ashes. I wouldn't like to think of people trampling all over her."

"Oh yeah, I never thought of that."

"I know, maybe we could bury them and make a little memorial, then whenever we come back we can put flowers down and have a chat with her."

"I know the perfect place – under the Grandad Tree. And when we come back at Christmas, Olive can come too." Daisy smiled, silently congratulating herself while Adam remained silent, still deep in thought, and Daisy was just about to suggest they called it a night when he surprised her with a final question.

"Daise, can we make a deal? I know you'll think I'm being all morbid but it's sort of important, to both of us."

"Go on…but let me hear what it is first before I say yes."

"Let's make a pact that whoever goes first, when we're old and knackered, if there really is an afterlife, we'll get a message back to earth and let the other one know we're okay. I don't think I could bear it if I lost you and had to deal with never seeing you again. At least I'd have something to cling on to, a bit of hope that there was more to us than flesh and bones."

It was Daisy's turn to wipe away a tear before she answered, Adam's words reminding her of how much he needed her.

"You mean like going to a séance?"

"Nah, I really do think that's a load of mumbo jumbo. I was thinking like a sign or a message that only you and I will understand, so there's no mistake or con artists involved."

"Right, I get you. Like a spy code. That's right up your street and mysterious! But I'll do my best to let you know I'm okay, I swear." Daisy held up her hand, offering her little finger, which Adam entwined around hers.

"You promise not to forget?" Adam squeezed a little tighter. Daisy squeezed back. "I promise."

The pact was sealed and rather than head off through the woods, they remained a while on the pontoon, listening to the sound of a fox calling his mate and the hum of mosquitoes as they flickered around their heads. And while fireflies danced by the shore and space hardware traversed the skies above, both were lost in their thoughts of Olive, Elvis and the angels.

Chapter 10

Christmases at Campanule
Daisy, Adam and Ryan

When Daisy went home for Christmas at the end of their first term at uni, she left Adam behind. With a lump in her throat and a leaden heart her upset was intensified by a sense of shame and abandonment as she pictured his face, trying hard to be brave as he waved her off at the coach station. Adam assured her he'd be fine, working at the restaurant up until Christmas then heading off to stay with Ryan at the air force base. As the coach zoomed down a grey and storm-bashed M6 on its way to Portsmouth, Daisy stared solemnly out of the rain-splattered windows, worrying herself sick about the man-puppy she had left behind.

Only two things cheered her up. The first was that Adam looked warm in the green Parka she'd bought him for Christmas. Daisy spent ages searching for it and the retro woven patches that she lovingly stitched onto the outside so it resembled those that Mods wore in the sixties. Adam loved it, not just for the CND and Beatles motifs but because Daisy had spent time and effort on his gift, vowing to keep the coat forever, another prized possession to go with his leather jacket and record collection.

The second was seeing her parents after four long months apart. Daisy's Noël in France whizzed by and during that time she reconnected with her childhood home, breathing in the cold and misty morning air as she collected eggs or rode her bike into the village to fetch bread and pastries. Or simply sitting in the kitchen while her mum baked and the windows misted over, obscuring the line of trees that bordered the woods and the campsite beyond. They still had the odd crazy guests, old-school campers who embraced the outdoors and didn't require any of the high-season facilities. Autumn and winter was a time to take stock, make repairs, prepare for spring and relax a little. Daisy's parents had never made a fortune on the campsite but they made ends meet and had a good life in their own little piece of France.

The following Christmas, Daisy's second at uni, she was thankfully spared the guilt of leaving Adam behind. Due to Ryan's job, he had to spend all of December and the New Year overseas, which meant Adam went home with Daisy and experienced a wintry Noël in the Loire.

*

Adam blew warm air into clasped hands and stamped his feet, not in temper but in an attempt to keep warm while he waited for Daisy to lock the door of the house they rented. While he experienced a bubbling of excitement and anticipation at their forthcoming journey, it was tempered by the fear of missing the coach because Daisy was holding them up, as usual. They were heading south to catch the evening ferry from Portsmouth. It was a trip they'd made during the summer and Adam had loved every second of their voyage and therefore eager and impatient for another to begin.

Adam hadn't slept a wink, repeatedly checking his clock, scared to death of missing the coach and now, Daisy was driving him mad with her dithering.

"Bloody hell Daise hurry up…the bus will be here any minute and we're going to be late for the coach. I want to get a window seat like last time…oh shit, it's here. I'll go to the stop and make him wait, come on. Run, woman, run!" Picking up the giant carrier bag containing their Christmas presents and a wooden casket, Adam shot off leaving Daisy on the doorstep.

Following on behind, trying to hook the strap of her rucksack over her shoulder as she made towards the bus stop, she chuckled at Adam, his arms flapping away in an attempt to slow down the driver. But she loved seeing him so happy and spent much of the previous evening teasing him as he ticked off his list and repacked his rucksack, fretting that her washing was still in the dryer then telling her off because she hadn't put her passport with the tickets and ferry booking.

After they climbed onto the bus and flashed their passes, Adam stacked their rucksacks onto the baggage area then plonked himself down beside Daisy, puffing and panting after his mad and rather unnecessary dash to the bus stop.

"Well, looks like we're on our way…are you excited, I am? I hope we don't get held up on the Mancunian Way. If we do I think we should get off and walk, it's not far, that way we won't be late for the coach." Adam checked his watch again as Daisy smiled and ignored him.

Although he drove her potty with his pedantic ways, she didn't begrudge him one second of his happiness because for Adam, Christmases past had been dismal affairs, but one thing was for sure, this one would be different.

Once aboard the coach Daisy slept, her head lolling from side to side, dribbling on Adam's shoulder while he occupied himself by peering into cars and lorries as he ate his packed lunch, wondering where they were all going or why they looked so miserable, voyeurism at its most innocent.

Portsmouth also presented a fascinating hive of activity and looked so different in winter compared to the sunny holiday vibe in June. The white floodlights perched on top of cranes shone down onto the jet black Solent and in the distance, the forts at the mouth of the estuary stood guard, like monsters in the sea. Their sailing turned out to be really rocky but it added to the fun, as did the atmosphere on board where passengers heading to France for the holidays created a Christmassy buzz. Adam insisted they sat on deck so he could breathe in sea air but after nearly freezing to death they made their way inside and slept side by side on reclining seats, oblivious to the waves that rocked the ship as it headed towards France.

In the early hours both Daisy and Adam stood at the helm, huddled together in the dark, watching the coastline appear and then the yellow port lights of St Malo welcoming them home. Bill was there to meet them and as they set off across land, Adam marvelled at how different everything looked. Trees laden with mistletoe and pale green fields slowly emerged from a wintry mist, the temperature outside the car just about hovering above freezing.

Waking up in his bedroom underneath a winter duvet and a layer of blankets, feet protected by woolly socks, came as a shock compared to the sweltering summer months when nights were humid, the window left wide open welcoming in the merest hint of a breeze. As opposed to baring his chest and skinny legs, Adam wrapped up warm as he crunched through the woods with Daisy or brought in logs for the fire. But he wouldn't have cared if the temperatures dropped to minus because for Adam every moment was bliss, especially being with Pamela and Bill. Yet despite the glow inside and out he was unable to prevent memories of harder times from coming back to haunt him, and he missed his brother and his gran.

*

Olive had always done her best for her grandsons and tried to make Christmas a happy time, a big ask considering they lived with constantly warring parents who used their meagre benefits selfishly. Knowing that it would fall flat without her input, Olive took over and steered her alcoholic daughter and short-tempered son-in-law through the day. Adam remembered there was always tension in the air, nervous members of a cast trying to remember their lines and not put a foot wrong otherwise the whole play would be ruined. At Daisy's house, Adam felt he could breathe normally and during that Christmas, the first of many, he often thought of Ryan and wished he was there too.

Daisy hadn't seen Ryan since Olive's funeral, although they had kept in touch with emails and texts, always jokey and fun, informative and relaxed while underneath the platonic words they quizzed and searched for clues as to the other's status, Daisy passing on information as to the well-being of Adam.

Keeping her promise, Daisy never divulged the intricacies of her friend and as time ticked by her concerns over his welfare had diminished and she began to see him and his life as less and less of a conundrum. Adam wasn't complicated or confused, in many ways he lived up to the general perception of normal. Between them, Daisy and Adam had further developed their system of misdirection by which he could avoid suspicion or innuendo and yes, it was like living a lie, but only a white one.

For all intents, Adam was what you'd call a fly-by-night as opposed to Tommy who had been labelled a full-on Romeo. Adam on the other hand became notorious for one-night stands, preferably with an out-of-towner who couldn't give him evil stares across the refectory once rejected. Every now and then their group would notice Adam with a lovely lass who was enjoying a big night out, then watch them leave, presuming whatever they liked. Only Daisy knew that he never slept with his dancing partner. Instead, after seeing her safely home Adam would sneak back to the flat they both shared, his door would click shut and within minutes he was snoring away in his own bed.

So when Ryan enquired after his brother's health, studies and love life, Daisy related exactly what she had seen. And whenever he hinted about her own romantic status she was semi-honest, because apart from the odd flirtation and a disastrous week-long affair with a two-timing member of the rugby team, Daisy's heart always beat fastest when she thought of Ryan.

*

Since Adam's very first summer visit to France and his return trip for Christmas, it had been clear to Pam that there was absolutely nothing going on between Adam and Daisy, despite Bill being less convinced and listening out for creaking floorboards in the night.

During emails and telephone conversations when she first heard about Daisy's new best friend, Pam was proud of her daughter, opening her generous heart to someone lonely and in need. Which is why, when Daisy rang late one November evening (all of a fluster) to ask if this Christmas, Adam's brother could come and stay too, Pamela naturally agreed.

Daisy did a grand job of selling her mother the idea that it would be brilliant if they could all hang out together, especially as Adam had expressed the desire to include Ryan in a proper family Christmas and at the time, Pam thought nothing of it, putting the request down to Daisy having a kind heart and anyway, the more the merrier. Little did she know as she replaced the receiver and went off to tell Bill the news that within a few weeks her take on Daisy's motives would alter, her daughter's golden halo seeming slightly off kilter.

On a chilly December morning just a few days before Christmas, Pamela welcomed into her home a strappingly handsome man and very quickly realised that in the case of Ryan, platonic was not a word she would have used to describe his friendship with Daisy. It was clear as the ice on the window ledge that her daughter was besotted and Pamela suspected that the feeling, if allowed to flourish, was more or less mutual. Yet despite Daisy's increased blood pressure and fanatical attention to her appearance, nothing happened between her and Ryan during that wonderful Christmas week.

It was nigh on impossible to get a minute alone when you had an over-excited man-puppy in tow, overjoyed that everyone he loved was under one roof, and your mother watched you like a bloody hawk. Then there was Bill. He revelled in recruiting another co-conspirator with whom to escape into the depths of his cave, a candle-lit cellar where the men-folk could sample his homemade and very potent beer. Poor Daisy just floated on the periphery, looking gorgeous and perplexed as she waited patiently for her chance.

On his first full day at Campanule Adam showed Ryan around the site, talking of Bill's plans for the future like they were his own before expertly weaving his way through the woods to the Grandad Tree. Here, they stopped by the memorial to Olive, a simple tribute consisting of a heart made from shells and pebbles, set firmly into the earth. Between the crests of the heart stood a wooden cross and nameplate carved by Bill, marking Olive's final resting place.

It was somewhere Adam left trinkets, small mementos from days out, curious objects that only he understood the meaning of; a place to sit and think beneath the boughs of the ancient tree that protected his gran, watching over her while he was away.

Ryan laid a wreath made from holly, entwined with red ribbon and decorated by tiny Christmas baubles and sprayed with white frosting – the handiwork of Daisy. The evening before while he played cards with Adam and Bill, Ryan stole glances in her direction, watching her sew golden stars onto the greenery as she sat on the rug by the fire, lost in concentration, glasses perched on the end of her nose, a stray strawberry curl escaping from behind her ear.

It was as he looked around the room and took in the sight of normal, a glimpse of what could be, that Ryan was forced to take a breath. For a second, the preconceived idea of the impossible had become a reality. And this simple notion was something that troubled him, unused to soft edges, misty-eyed images and fuzzy feelings. His life had always seemed angular, obtuse and often hard. The whole package was alien, to be amongst people who gave and seemed to want nothing back, who cared for a stranger and his brother like it was the most natural thing in the world. Ryan told himself he didn't belong here but from what he'd seen and heard, his brother clearly did. Even Daisy's childhood friends had become Adam's. Listening to him laughing and joking with them caused such a surge of pride. And witnessing this acceptance into the fold was accompanied by immense relief because now, whenever he was sent overseas, Ryan could rest assured that his brother was cared for.

But mangled up amongst this postcard-perfect scene were unhelpful thoughts, which left unguarded began to surface: vibrations from the past, unsettling snapshots borne from years of self-preservation. It was best not to get too settled or attached. Avoid disappointment. So while the inviting world of Daisy encouraged him to stay, his instinct told him to run. And there was something else on Ryan's mind: his weakening defences and growing feelings for the strawberry-blonde seamstress.

This unfamiliar feeling of contentment, complicated by lust, wasn't helped in the slightest by the Christmas-card ambience of her childhood home where the combination of roaring logs fires and stunning wintry scenery chipped away at the most protected of hearts. Amidst all this, adding to his confusion and just as Ryan's carefully constructed barriers began tumbling down, seriously considering the possibility of a long-distance relationship, an annoying and disruptive conversation from the past returned to unsettle him. As much as he tried to push it away, a radar blipped away inside his head, refusing to let the memory pass unnoticed. At the time, the spiteful and clearly jealous words were easy to brush aside yet now, a bitter warning came back to haunt him, cautioning his eager heart.

*

After Olive's funeral on the journey back to his base in Norfolk, the last thing on Ryan's mind was Fliss because Olive, Adam and Daisy kept him fully occupied during the four-hour drive. Eventually, maybe a day later, after fobbing her off with texts and hiding behind voicemail, he finally succumbed to answering the phone, intending to nip Fliss in the bud before he returned to Cyprus. Needless to say the conversation didn't go too well and it became clear that this one was going to be hard to shake off and didn't take kindly to rejection, no matter how kindly he put it.

Not wishing to drag things out, Ryan instantly threw cold water on her brazen flirting by insisting that while it was nothing personal, he was far too busy with work to have any kind of relationship, long-distance or otherwise. When she changed tack and offered a more casual arrangement, Ryan assured Fliss that he wouldn't be returning to Manchester anytime soon and it was equally unlikely that she could visit him. At this point her tone changed and recognising a brush off, no matter how polite, flirtation was swiftly replaced by retaliation. The green-eyed monster in Fliss returned, infuriated by her memory of the cosy scene she witnessed on the steps between him and Daisy, which, after all, had been the true point of her exercise with Ryan.

"So you won't be coming north to see your brother then, oh dear, what will poor little Adam do without you? But I suppose he's still got his precious Daisy to hold his hand and keep him company, especially at night." Fliss had unleashed her inner devil and Ryan could hear the bitterness in her voice.

Against his better judgement he was unable to ignore the jibe. "No, like I told you I'll be overseas and just so you know, there's nothing going on between my brother and Daisy, I can assure you of that."

"Ha, they might've pulled the wool over your eyes but they can't fool me, so if you fancy your chances with Daisy I can tell you right now you're barking up the wrong tree. Those two are a pair of sickos and Adam won't take kindly to sharing his shag buddy, not even with his big bro! We're all surprised he's put up with Greg but maybe that's what they're into, a bit of swapping." Her sing-song sarcasm really grated on Ryan, who took a breath and tried hard not to snap.

"Look Fliss, I get the impression Daisy isn't your favourite person but you can't go around spreading malicious rumours. They're just friends, that's all there is to it."

"Ha, you are so wrong!" The retort was high pitched, veering towards manic.

Warning bells told Ryan to disconnect the call before he heard anything that would taint the image of Daisy, or his brother, but curiosity and the desire for self-preservation won the war. "Really? Go on, amaze me."

Fliss didn't need to be asked twice. "Because those two are freaks! Everyone talks about them behind their backs and let's face it, no matter how much they fob us off with their 'just friends' routine, I've caught them sharing a bed on more than one occasion. For fuck's sake, it's just puke making. You might believe whatever crap they've told you but I certainly don't!" Fliss ended the sentence with a sarcastic snort, the sneer on her face transmitted down the line, but she'd lit the touch paper and Ryan had taken just about enough.

"Look Fliss, whatever Daisy and Adam get up to is their business and I've got no intention of discussing my brother with you or anyone, and I think he'd be really pissed off if he knew you were spreading lies about him so I'm going to hang up and leave it there. But before I do, I suggest you watch your mouth where he's concerned otherwise I might just tell everyone what an embarrassing slobbering mess you were the other night – talk about desperate!" Ryan heard a slight gasp so went in for the kill. "Let's put it this way, I'd rather pay for it than choose to sleep with a spiteful cow like you. Just shows how wasted I was to even let you in my room – is that how you get all your blokes into bed, by begging? Now, don't ever contact me again, and be nice to my brother, okay?"

The sound of the beeps as the call was disconnected told him that Fliss had got the message, loud and clear. As he sat on the side of his bed, sucking in air, he was unable to get her nasty insinuations out of his head, trying to balance the brother he knew with the person Fliss had described. She was wrong. Daisy and Adam wouldn't lie about something like that, especially not to his face. Why would they?

Things like this unsettled Ryan. Protecting himself had become second nature and the reason he stuck to one-night stands or flings, avoiding the opportunity for anyone to ruin his life by trapping him into marriage and parenthood. His philosophy was simple: if and when he put down roots, he'd be one hundred percent sure. There was no way he'd ever subject a child to an unhappy life because repeating history would be a sin. And although he'd taken a shine to Daisy, now really wasn't the time and therefore he had no reason to dwell on the words of a poisonous slapper like Fliss.

His head was clearing, calm almost restored. As he folded his uniform into his ops bag Ryan reassured himself that Fliss was a cow, and Daisy and Adam's friendship was strong and loyal yet purely platonic. Shaking away any straggling doubts, Ryan zipped up his bag and headed out the door, relegating thoughts of a strawberry-blonde beauty to a corner of his mind.

It was true to say that during the months that followed he experienced a mild fluttering of the heart and the odd ungentlemanly thought when it came to Daisy, during their sporadic emails and casual texts or more often than not when the tedium of twelve-hour night shifts kicked in. But now one year later, during his Christmas in France, all those suppressed urges and unhelpful comments returned with a vengeance and both were ready to bite him on the arse.

*

During his festive visit, with Slade and Wizard belting out from the radio and the aroma of mince pies baking in the oven, Ryan watched Daisy and Adam like a hawk (just as Pamela watched him). Both gave absolutely nothing away and no matter how hard Ryan scrutinised every nuance, sarcastic remark and playful hug or slap around the head when one or the other cheated at cards, he could see nothing suspicious in his brother's relationship with Daisy. And just as Bill had done, Ryan spent the moments before the home-cooked food and rich red wine sent him to sleep, listening out for tell-tale creaks on the landing outside. There were none.

There was something though, but it had nothing to do with Adam. Ryan could definitely feel it as he chopped wood, like her eyes burning holes into his back. And the teenage thrill when fingers touched as he passed her a log for the wheelbarrow, or when their shoulders rubbed together during a walk around the lake. It happened when they were huddled inside the Grandad Tree, waiting for the rain to stop before trudging back through the woods, Adam racing ahead collecting cones and kicking leaves.

Daisy joked that he was like a child trapped in an adult's body, her words playful while her eyes shone with laughter, hinting at love but not of a romantic nature. It was the kind Ryan associated with that of a mother to a son or sister to a brother, and the thought eased his worries.

When Adam went down with a bad cold the day before Ryan was due to fly out, Daisy offered to drive him to the airport as planned. His eight-day stay had sped by too quickly and Ryan was almost jubilant at the prospect of spending some time alone with her in the car until Bill overruled the decision, deeming the country roads too icy, so in the end, three was once more a crowd.

He wasn't too sure what he would have said or done during forty-five minutes of peace and quiet, three quarters of a clock's worth of opportunity to say something, anything that might set the wheels in motion or indicate that maybe, in the future, he could let down his guard and remove a section of barrier that surrounded his heart. Ryan could see that now was not the time, they both had things to do and it would complicate matters. But at least his observations had silenced that nagging voice, echoing words of a spiteful girl who'd spouted cruel insinuations he would never repeat.

All Ryan wanted was a hint, to be sure, but as it turned out he would have to wait for a while. Instead of a heart-to-heart they chatted about the weather and how hot it would be in Qatar– his next port of call. At the doors of the airport Ryan accepted a firm handshake from Bill and a long, shy hug from Daisy before they waved goodbye. Turning away quickly he headed for check-in, and doing what he did best Ryan sealed off the boundary and moved inside his perimeter fence, where it was safe.

Once the fairy lights had dimmed from his memory and the magic of Christmas began to rub off, his military life went on and Ryan continued to live it to the full, filling the months away on detachment as young single men do. Still, in quieter moments his mind would wander back to Manchester and once he'd paid due respect to thoughts of his brother, he would concentrate on Daisy. Ryan was loath to admit that his heart lifted when he received her letters – funny, interesting snippets of university life – but it did. And while keeping Ryan up to date on all matters concerning Adam, Daisy also made it quite clear that for now, there was nobody special in her life.

It was of no consequence though because Ryan knew full well what the future had in store for him, and it involved being overseas for longer periods than normal and in a far more dangerous place than he had travelled to before. If all went to plan he would be in the UK long enough to see Adam graduate and then soon after he would be flying out again with his jets. There was a war being fought in Iraq and his squadron was going to be part of it.

Ryan had decided to tell Adam face-to-face once he'd sat his finals and his degree was in the bag. And then there was Daisy. To declare his feelings now would be foolhardy and unfair so security would have to remain in place.

He had a job to do and being single was less hassle, it was as simple as that. There would be time in the future for settling down, or maybe not; Ryan remained untroubled by either scenario. Where Daisy was concerned he would just have to take a chance and if she met someone while he was away then so be it. Life could be cruel, a true fact that he'd dealt with before and anyway, he would always have Adam. Ryan told himself for now, that was enough.

Chapter 11

All grown up
Manchester 2005

It had arrived at last, graduation day, the end and the beginning, the final step onto the giant stage where they would take part in a grand performance before making brave strides into a real and scary world.

Daisy and Adam were amongst the black-caped graduates who swarmed like ants onto the pavement, ignoring the hubbub and jostling whilst they scanned the crowd for familiar faces, those of Ryan, Bill and Pamela. Somewhere out there were two proud parents and a slightly exhausted brother who had flown in from Al Minhad then drove overnight from Brize Norton, reaching Manchester just in time to attend the degree ceremony.

Once Daisy got over her stage fright and collected her scroll, she had clapped and cheered for all of her friends as they took to the stage, but her special boy got the loudest ovation. As Adam made his way up the step and towards the podium, her heart swelled with pride and love for her constant companion who had remained by her side for the past three years. It had all flashed by so quickly, that first day in the queue to now. All that had gone on in between was soft padding that filled up their lives, stuffed full of memories, tears, laughter, shitty bits, and along with the parties and dossing about, some proper hard work.

None of it would've been the same without Adam. Yes, Daisy would have reached this destination but the journey was made all the better by having him along for the ride and now they were set to move on, buy another ticket and explore the big, bad world of the employed, together. Daisy had secured a job with a holiday company at Manchester Airport and Adam would be working at the Evening News – nothing exciting just admin but he didn't care as long as he remained in the city. First though, they would be working at Campanule Campings, putting off a new life adhering to rules and four weeks' holiday a year. Bill had been unwell and after a scare with his heart was ordered to take things easier so both he and Pamela would be glad of the help.

Afterwards, Daisy and Adam still hoped to visit at Christmas. She couldn't imagine not being with her parents for the festivities, a time that had been made more special by the addition of Adam and Ryan as honorary family. It had been one of the best Christmases ever, made all the more thrilling by the spark of attraction, that zing of electricity she had experienced whenever Ryan looked in her direction or came into close proximity. Daisy had been in a quandary, both disappointed and relieved when he said goodbye, fearing she would explode with unrequited lust, yearning for one extra day in his company.

In the days before graduation, just thinking about walking onto the huge stage in front of all those people to accept her degree certificate left her sick with nerves, but what really kept her awake at night was the thought of seeing Ryan again, wondering whether amongst all the teasing e-mails and jokey conversations there was the merest possibility of something more than just words.

Her butterflies were startled then fluttered away when Adam dragged her back to reality, vivid imaginings and romantic notions smothered, the task of searching for faces in the crowd became uppermost. Ignoring amused stares from those around them, Adam began jumping up and down, waving his arms in the air, trying to attract their attention and stand out amongst hundreds of clones.

"There they are, Daise! Look, over there. I can see Ryan and your mum. Wave otherwise they'll wander off, oh it's okay, your dad's seen me." Adam grabbed Daisy's hand and wove through the hugging bodies, bumping into Fliss and her parents on the way, saying rushed hellos and goodbyes, stealthily avoiding being waylaid before making contact with their intended targets.

Once the hugs and congratulations were dispensed, photos were taken in a combination of poses and family members and then Adam asked a passerby if he would take one of the whole group. After repositioning themselves and squashing together, they all smiled for the camera. The flash made Daisy blink so she demanded a retake and then Adam's hat blew off in the wind and then some ignorant woman walked right in front of them just as they all said 'fromage'.

When they finally managed a shot that Daisy approved of, they headed off to the Midland for a joint family celebration. It was to be one of the happiest days of Adam's life and the group photo would take pride of place wherever he lived, in fact the same one stood on the mantelpiece at Pamela and Bill's, on the dresser in Daisy's bedroom, and was the screensaver on Ryan's laptop. It reminded them all of a proud day, one where they laughed and made plans for the future.

They were seated around a table in the corner of the hotel restaurant where, amidst the kerfuffle of ordering their food and drinks, Daisy was in a total flap ever since her dad made an impromptu suggestion. Ryan mentioned in passing that at the end of June he would be in the north-east of France – his squadron were taking part in a joint European training exercise. Daisy knew exactly what her dad was going to say before he opened his mouth but even if he hadn't, no doubt eager beaver Pamela would have jumped in anyway.

"Why don't you come and stay with us afterwards? It's Daisy and Adam's last summer at the site before they have to do some real work and it'd be grand to have all three of you there, won't it Pam?" Bill winked cheekily as he tore open a bread roll.

"Of course it will. But Ryan might not be able to get time off. You know he's always flying off somewhere, and Bill, don't eat all the bread, save some room for your meal." Pam tapped him on the hand with her knife, giving her husband a stern look before turning her attention to Ryan. "Would you be able to get time off love, there's always room for one more at ours?"

Her question was swiftly followed by a plea from Adam. "Go on mate, come and stay, we'll have a right laugh, won't we Daise?"

Daisy didn't realise but she was holding her breath, hanging onto every word and afraid to speak in case her voice gave away how excited she was at the prospect, so instead, she just nodded and smiled like a fool as she took a sip of water.

Ryan already knew he'd have time off. Everyone got leave before they went to Iraq but he just couldn't bring himself to say it, not right now, so he swerved the truth. "I reckon I could swing it. I'll have to let you know once I'm in work, but if you're sure you don't mind I'd be made up to come back. Adam's told me how different it is in summer and I'd like to see your place when it's a bit warmer, and I don't mind helping out. I can turn my hand to most things."

Bill gave Ryan the thumbs up. "Correct answer! Now, let's get this man another pint, and where's that waiter gone off to, I'm bloody starving? I'm going to order some more bread and butter. I could eat a horse." Pam rolled her eyes as she passed her malnourished husband the last bread roll. "No you're not, you can wait for your meal like everyone else, and Ryan, we don't mind one bit. I'm sure the three of you will have a brilliant time and anyway, having you there will give Bill even more opportunities to delegate and slope off, won't it love?"

"Don't know what you're talking about. Ah, here's the food at last, I thought he'd gone to bloody New Zealand for that lamb. I might order my pudding now just in case they have to hand pick the apples for the crumble."

As Bill was told to be quiet by Pam and the waiter swiftly served his impatient diners, Daisy swallowed down the ball of volatile fizzy stuff that was bubbling away in her chest, and it looked like Adam had taken a swig of it too, already making rapid-fire plans with Ryan.

Tearing her eyes away from the brothers, Daisy looked up and caught the amused look on her mum's face, flushing slightly when Pamela winked and passed a knowing look. After mouthing the word '*what*', Daisy shook her head and concentrated on the plate of food before her, unable to hide a smile. Her canny mum was mostly to blame but the rest was down to the thrill and expectancy of the summer ahead, and spending part of it with Ryan.

Chapter 12

That last summer
France 2005

It was a typical situation where after looking forward to something so much, for so long, when it finally arrives the highly anticipated event doesn't live up to expectations or in Daisy's case, the very person she had been longing to see since June. After literally counting down the days, imagining allsorts and generally behaving like a moonstruck teenager, it wouldn't have taken a genius to notice that Ryan was playing it cool. Friendly, fun, helpful and a pleasure to be with in a brotherly, matey kind of way but the Christmas-time intensity and any sense of expectancy had definitely evaporated.

Ryan was staying for two weeks so Daisy and Adam planned days out and get-togethers in between mucking in on the site. Sometimes Ryan would work with Daisy in the snack bar where for a couple of hours they laughed and joked with the campers. Otherwise he would disappear with Adam who reluctantly relinquished control of the lawn mower and allowed his brother to cut the grass, pointing and tutting if he missed a bit.

Daisy felt flustered around Ryan yet outwardly did her utmost to appear casual and unconcerned by his presence, stepping back while Adam took centre stage and monopolised his brother. It was all part of her misguided strategy because pre-arrival, Daisy had advised herself to wait patiently for the right moment or let Ryan make his move. But it was clear by day three that something was different, as though he was carrying an invisible shield, which left her feeling foolish and confused, and by day five, pent up frustration was driving her mad.

In the evenings they would go down to the pontoon and listen to music, sometimes joined by their friends from the village, yet to Daisy's dismay, every romantic situation she had concocted in her head fell flat. Like the night they camped at the edge of the lake. It was the perfect setting – stars, the moon, wine, the scent of bellflowers and barbeque smoke filling the air, Adam leaving them alone while he dared Inès and her boyfriend to find to the Grandad Tree without a torch.

Ryan and Daisy lay beside the tranquil lake, their hands literally centimetres apart, listening to monster noises and the sound of Inès screaming in terror. He held onto his beer bottle whilst she plucked nervously at the grass by his side. Daisy could almost hear him breathe and caught the faint fragrance of after sun that lingered on his skin, already bronzed and stretched over his toned and muscular body. Not that she'd been staring while he skimmed the swimming pool for leaves or played football with Adam – well, not much. But he might as well have been a mile away or floating in the middle of the lake in a canoe, not in immediate snogging distance.

Daisy was left feeling stupid and rejected, especially later when she knew he was still awake, lying in between her and Adam who was snuggled inside his sleeping bag, snoring gently. Daisy had left hers unzipped, just in case. The light from the moon illuminated his face with soft silvery rays, his eyes were closed but twitchy, and although he was breathing steadily, Ryan wasn't fooling anyone.

It was blatantly clear that he'd gone off her, somewhere between Christmas and summer the fizz had worn off, either that or he was getting his excitement elsewhere. While she listened to Adam mutter in his sleep, laughing through his dreams and occasionally snorting like a pig (something he'd always done but vehemently denied), Daisy watched space hardware float across the night sky. As her resentment of Ryan became palpable, anger made her heart beat faster while her feet tapped bad temperedly to an impatient tune composed by her befuddled brain. She wanted to fill one of the discarded beer bottles with lake water and pour the lot over his pretend-sleeping face, or perhaps she should march off home so he'd worry when she disappeared onto the woodland track, swallowed up by the darkness to be eaten alive by a wild boar. Maybe he'd chase after her, then again maybe not.

Since December he'd occupied so much of her time and led her heart a merry dance, sending out mixed messages and false signals. Yet despite her dwindling self-respect, Daisy wasn't prepared to give in, not just yet. As her eyelids admitted defeat, a stubborn voice persuaded her to give it one more try, or at least find out where Ryan's head was at. It was so simple, all she had to do was reach out and whisper his name or hit him with her flip-flop but instead Daisy turned on her side, blocking out the very real image of his loveliness. It was easier that way.

On day six, amidst what could only be described (by Pam to Bill) as a faintly prickly atmosphere, the youngsters (as the elders called them) headed west for a day at the seaside. Daisy kept herself to herself in the back of the car, feigning tiredness and mild nausea whilst mentally restraining herself from punching Ryan in the back of the head every time she heard his carefree laugh or enquiry as to her current state of health.

Relaxing on the golden sands at Pornichet, Ryan topped up his perma-tan while Adam stressed about burning and melanomas so hid under a parasol, reading his book, earphones plugged in to Oasis. Daisy just seethed. She'd found it hard since their outdoor sleepover, being in the company of someone she still had the hots for and on whom she'd squandered hours of fantasy. Ever mindful of Adam's feelings and not wanting to spoil the outward, jolly-holiday mood in any way, she tried hard to mask how gutted she really was.

Back at Campanule, even Pam was feeling somewhat put out that she too had misread the signs, apart from the one of despondency on Daisy's face when she thought nobody was looking. Pam put it all down to gooseberries. After much thought she concluded that having the parents and the brother around 24/7 wasn't exactly helpful or conducive to a bit of hanky panky, so it was hardly surprising that Ryan had gone off the boil. Pondering the situation as she fed the chickens, Pam felt disappointed for her daughter and slightly miffed with Ryan, but then again, maybe there was something he wasn't telling them. Now and then she'd noticed he looked rather pensive and thoughtful so hoped for Daisy's sake it wasn't anything to do with another girl because in her experience, it usually was.

Although it had puzzled them at first how close yet romantically separate Adam and Daisy were, Bill and Pam had come to accept their genuinely platonic friendship. And even when she'd suggested to her husband that Adam might be gay, Bill was adamant that it wasn't the case – he was just a slow starter and in his opinion straight as a chip, whatever that meant. So really, when you thought about it there was no reason any of them should object to Ryan and Daisy getting together, especially Adam, which is when it occurred to Pam that for him, the situation would be perfect.

Ryan was amusing himself by throwing tiny pebbles at Adam's feet while Daisy tidied away the remains of their lunch in between reprimanding him for tormenting his brother.

"Stop winding him up! Look, that one's gone in his belly button, just leave him in peace. He's been trying to finish that book for ages…I was starting to think he'd forgotten how to read it's taken him that long."

"He loves it, don't you?" Ryan mouthed the words slowly to Adam who answered with the V sign. "Anyway, how can he read and listen to music? Look, he's definitely got it turned on, his feet are tapping away. Surely he can't concentrate on the words…look at him, he is *such* an odd bod." Ryan was lying on his stomach watching Adam who was lost in his book, oblivious to any scrutiny.

"He's always done that. I've seen him write an essay, listen to music and watch telly with the sound off *and* eat his tea at the same time. He reckons he can lip read but I think he's just mentally and physically dexterous."

"Nah, he's just weird!"

"Don't be tight." Daisy flicked Ryan with her beach hat. "I wish I could multi-task, I need complete silence while I write, don't you?" Daisy glanced over to Ryan and noticed he too was miles away, deep in thought and come to think of it, he looked sad.

Seeing him that way softened her heart slightly so closing the lid of the picnic box she shuffled over to where her beach towel lay next to his. Keeping her back to Adam (just in case he really could lip read) and without thinking too much about the outcome, Daisy asked Ryan the question that had been eating her up for days.

"Ryan, hey, earth to Ryan." When he looked up and smiled it was first time since he arrived she knew she'd caught him off guard because his face was open and yes, his eyes did look sad, and troubled, so before he slipped his mask back on she continued.

"Ryan, is there something bothering you, only you don't seem the same as you did at Christmas? You've been a bit uptight and miles away, like you've got something on your mind. I can't put my finger on it but I hope it's nothing I've done. Maybe if you share with the group we can sort it out?"

Without speaking Ryan pushed himself upright before turning away from Adam and shuffling closer to Daisy (the lip reading thing was on his mind too), but instead of answering, he asked Daisy a question instead.

"What makes you think you've done something wrong, have you got a guilty conscience? Perhaps there's something you want to get off your chest."

"No! Why would you ask me that? I don't understand. Why are you being like this Ryan, it's just not like you and to be honest I can do without your sarcasm and messing with my head? If you don't want to talk that's fine, sorry I asked, but don't take whatever is pissing you off out on me, okay?" Daisy had had enough and was looking for her flip-flops. There was no way she was sitting there for a minute longer, not with a sulker. She'd rather be on her own.

"Daisy, stop, please don't go. I'm sorry and you're right, there is something on my mind and it's put me in a weird mood. I just didn't know how or when to tell you and Adam."

"Tell me what? Oh I get it. I had a feeling this was coming... you've met someone haven't you? But what's that got to do with me or Adam? He won't care and neither do I. You're free to do what you want so why the big mystery?"

"No, it's nothing to do with meeting someone but at least I know where I stand with you! And you're wrong about Adam because he would mind. It may have escaped your attention but he's hell bent on getting the two of us together, he has been ever since that business with Fliss, which is why he's been sloping off and making excuses to leave us both alone. Surely you realised?"

Daisy looked sideways, incredulous. "What on earth are you going on about?"

"He's got it into his head that it's a way of keeping us all together, his idea of creating a perfect family...why are you looking so shocked? I told you he was weird!"

If Ryan felt foolish about being so open and then rejected he didn't show it, unlike Daisy who was beyond flustered and confused by his direct approach to a subject she'd been skirting around for days, months really. And Ryan was on the money where Adam was concerned. She'd suspected him of matchmaking and knowing of his fears for the future, it all made sense. But there was something else. Even though Ryan was joking and she was used to the laddish banter between him and his brother, that he had used the word 'weird', the one Adam feared the most, set off alarm bells.

An awkward silence hung in the air, both of them smarting from the other's comments and wondering how to remove the sting of harsh words. It was Ryan who found the solution.

"Come on, let's go for a walk. We can get Pale Boy an ice cream. I think you and I need to have a chat." Ryan didn't wait for her to reply. Instead he stood and held out his hand, which she took.

Once he'd hoisted Daisy upwards, Ryan turned to Adam who was lost in music. Popping his head under the parasol he mouthed a question very slowly, which made Daisy laugh and broke the ice.

"We're going to get some ice cream, do you want one?"

Adam gave him the thumbs up before going back to his book, seemingly disinterested in anything other than the words before him, yet as soon as they turned, watched intently as they set off across the sand.

The beach at Pornichet was packed – sounds of laughter from a group playing volleyball, the chatter of children splashing at the water's edge mingling with the low hum of voices, the strains from a radio adding to the holiday atmosphere. As they walked towards the harbour wall where the fishermen's boats were tied up, bobbing on the tide, Daisy tuned out the sound of 'happy', hearing only the silence that enveloped the two of them. And on the outside, as her shoulders burned from the heat of the sun, inside, a cool breeze of impending doom washed through her body.

They hadn't got far, maybe a few metres when Ryan just blurted it out, his words freezing the air before melting in the heat, evaporating and being carried off across the Atlantic.

"My squadron is being posted to Iraq. We are off to war and I'll be gone for four months at a time. That's what I wanted to tell you and Adam."

Daisy's heart lurched as images of a harsh desert landscape, cold-blooded snipers and lethal bombs flashed before eyes that only a second before had looked upon a peacetime summer scene. Her mind was scrambled, questions racing around her brain.

"When did you find out? Surely they can't just spring it on you like that, what about people with families, is it dangerous, will you be safe?" A torrent of questions poured from Daisy's mouth and they were only the more practical ones. Those concerned with her aching heart she kept to herself.

"Believe me they can send us where they want, when they want and our families aren't taken into consideration, but that's our job. It's what we signed up for."

"I get that, but it must be such a shock for those left behind, especially the wives and children. I bet they find it hard to be parted for so long. But is it different for you, being single, you know, sort of easier to say goodbye...aren't you scared, do you even want to go?" Daisy realised her torrent of questions were more a reflection of her own emotional state, a knee-jerk response.

"Truthfully, yes I do. It's not like I've wished for it but now it's happened I want to do my bit, see some action and put all my training to use. Some of my mates have families and I expect it will be hard to leave them for such a long time but that's life, our life really. And they will be telling their other halves and kids exactly what I'll tell you and Adam. I'll be safe so don't worry." Adam kept to the script.

Daisy asked the obvious question – she needed time, lots of it. "When are you going?"

Ryan knew the answer was going to sting. "Early September. I'm not supposed to say exactly when but I'll let you know nearer the time when it's definite."

"That's only weeks away! You have to tell Adam as soon as, he's going to miss you like mad and he'll worry himself to death, it's in his nature. All the other places you've been weren't like this and he's got a thing about being on his own...I don't know if he's ever mentioned it but it bothers him a lot and it's one of the reasons why we are so close. I promised I'd always be there for him, our friendship gives him a lot of comfort especially when you're not around so you'll have to reassure him that you'll be okay."

Daisy was experiencing what she could only describe as panic yet forced it down, determined to keep the conversation practical and let Ryan do the talking, which thankfully after his recent glut, he seemed willing to do.

"I will. And I know Adam worries about me so I'll try to soften the blow. I'm used to his funny ways even though I have no idea what goes on in that head of his. It sometimes feels like I've spent my life protecting him from reality. He was scared of everything, monsters, ghosts, the end of the world, aliens, internal combustion, bloody green fruit pastilles, you name it, Adam was terrified of it. With hindsight I think he lived in a permanent state of fear, mainly from our dad and when I picture Adam's face, I can see still his big wide eyes. They were always on alert, a jumpy nervous kid who hid behind me, clinging on to my jumper." Ryan was miles away, lost in the past, remembering things he'd rather forget but that never failed to pester him. Memories of a man he despised crawling to the surface.

Ryan's hate for the person he called Dad was palpable, as was the hurt in Daisy's heart when she too imagined Adam's little-boy face. "Adam never talks about what went on at home, not in great detail, he's told me the basics but maybe it's his way of wiping it out, by sticking to the bare bones. I filled in the gaps myself."

"That's exactly what he does. Adam stores it all up in his head then filters out what he's prepared to talk about. Anything that's too upsetting gets filed away, the stuff he can't deal with I suppose."

"That's why he needs you, his hero. It's like you're always the centre of the story, not your parents. He just focuses on the fact you never let him down. Adam's so lucky to have a brother like you. I hope you always remember that." Daisy was floundering now. Her desire to comfort Ryan was semi-selfish, yearning to connect with him as they waded through the mire of the past. And whilst attempting to keep Ryan afloat, her own heart remained heavy, knowing that very soon his brother would be in need of support.

"Thanks Daisy, I just wish it wasn't necessary, you know, the things we saw and heard, and in my case felt. Don't ever let on to Adam but I took quite a few good hidings on his behalf. I used to goad my dad on purpose, just to draw his attention away and save him from the belt. He was very handy with that, and his fists. It's not that I'm resentful of Adam or anything, just glad he had me to look after him. And even though he's a grown man I still feel responsible for him."

"It sounds awful, no wonder Adam blocks it out."

"I think it's scarred him, up here." Ryan tapped his forehead. "When he was little he would cry if Mum sent me to the corner shop. He thought I might get knocked down or pinched by a bad man so I used to run all the way there and back. I can see him now with his face squashed against the window, watching for me to come up the street. It was the same when I went on dates or away with the cadets, and when I passed my driving test he would obsess about the motorway. You can imagine how hard it was for me to join up and leave him behind so now, while I'm in a war zone, I get that he is going to be a nightmare. I'm really glad he's got you though. It will make a huge difference and ease my mind. I mean that." Ryan turned to face Daisy and saw that her eyes were swimming with tears, which she blinked away.

Linking his arm she pulled Ryan close. "Just imagining what it was like freaks me out never mind having to live it…and don't worry I won't say anything about what you did, but for a little boy I think it was really brave of you, taking a beating to save Adam." Daisy leant into Ryan and rubbed his arm before continuing, leaving her hand where it was, enjoying the feel of his skin next to hers. "And the last thing you need is to be worrying so just leave Adam to me. I'll make sure he's okay and anyway, we need to think positive. We can still keep in touch and send you stuff."

"That's the thing. We can't take our laptops or phones like when I'm in Cyprus or other bases; we have to use the military ones for security reasons. The Taliban can tap into our devices and it causes all types of shit, the last thing I want is for someone to ring you up and tell you I'm dead, or what they are going to do to me. That's what can happen if they hack your number."

Daisy stopped dead. "Oh my God, really? That's just sick!" She was aghast, more so when Ryan nodded confirmation.

"But we can still write and I'll ring when I can. They give us a phone card to use on the base that gets topped up each month so I will keep in touch, I promise."

"So is this why you've been acting weird, and don't say you haven't because I felt it from the moment you arrived, and what was all that before about me keeping secrets, what did you mean by that?"

"I'm sorry, I shouldn't have snapped like that. I've just got so much going on in my head...you, Adam, going away."

"So I do figure in all of this?"

"Yeah, course you do, which is another reason we need to talk. There are things I have to say and I don't think you're going to like them but I'd rather be honest than mess you about, you need to know where you stand."

Daisy was all for honesty but sometimes Ryan took it to another level. "Bloody hell, now I'm really worried, but you still haven't answered my first question, about the secrets – go on, tell me what you meant."

"Oh that...it was just something that Fliss said. It rattled me for a while but I know she's a liar and a bit unhinged where you are concerned so I took it with a pinch of salt, only every now and then it pisses me off, even though it shouldn't."

"Go on, amaze me." Daisy stopped in her tracks and faced Ryan, trying to be glib yet already fuming inside. Just the mention of that name lit a blowtorch.

"Basically she just insinuated that you and Adam have a friends-with-benefits kind of relationship and before you flip out, I put her right back in her box, which is why I haven't spoken to her since. She's the original bunny boiler and I can do without nutters like her in my life. I never mentioned it to Adam because she was really vile about him and he's too sensitive so it was best to forget about it."

Daisy was livid. "You know, one of these days she's going to push me too far...what is wrong with her? She needs a bloody good slap! I'm praying that when we get back to Manchester she's pissed off back to wherever she came from otherwise there may be a murder. But enough about her, me and Adam have had this big question mark hanging over us for years and I'd hate it if you were like the others."

Ryan nudged her and smiled. "Stop stressing, I do believe you, I swear. It's obvious that you two are just mates, I can tell the way you are together, but mud sticks and even though I know it's wrong I had to be sure. And I'm sorry for bringing Fliss up but take it from me, she's got a huge crush on Adam and you clearly irritate the shit out of her. Maybe she's just one of those girls who's used to getting everything she wants so can't deal with it when someone says no or in your case, takes the prize."

"Well that's a bit of a turnaround because you seemed keen enough before and from what I heard Fliss got exactly what she wanted from you – the way she described her night at the hotel it sounded like *she'*d hit the jackpot, not me!"

"Well, between you and me, Fliss is a liar. She was wasted that night. The cheeky cow emptied the mini-bar then threw up and passed out on the twin bed, I slept on the other one. Nothing happened...in fact I was so hungover I can't even remember her leaving. I was just glad she wasn't there when I woke up so whatever she told you, it's a lie. Don't get me wrong she tried her best and was gagging for it but I was in no fit state to take part in what sounds like her little fantasy." Ryan shook his head and laughed, as did Daisy who revelled in Fliss's shame.

"The flaming liar, her version of events was very different I can tell you. I'm just glad you didn't fall for her lies, or anything really." Daisy knew he was still tense, she could feel it through the skin of his taught arm but it seemed to be easing. Sick of hearing the name Fliss and while she was hearing some good news amongst the bad, Daisy pressed Ryan further.

"And what about me, where do I fit in? You said you wanted to tell me where I stand, which sounds a bit like I'm getting dumped before the event...I've not even had chance to chat you up yet!" Daisy nudged Ryan who saw the funny side of her comment and grinned, although saying the words had hurt like hell, humour allowing her to retain some pride.

They had reached the harbour wall and the small cabin that sold food was inundated with customers, a long line snaking along the promenade, so rather than bake in the queue, Ryan pointed to the base of the wall and a shady spot next to the wooden breakers.

"Come on, let's wait here until the queue has gone down, I don't want everyone listening in." Ryan sat down first and gazed out to sea, waiting for Daisy to join him and when she did, she made sure there was no gap between them. Some inner sense told her to maintain contact because he was about to slip away. She was right.

"I don't know how to put this without it coming out all wrong because then you'll think I'm a complete bastard, which I'm not, but I just need to keep things simple, okay?" Ryan turned to see Daisy nod.

"In a nutshell I think you are amazing and I've fancied you since the moment the doors opened at the airport. I guess it was one of those wow moments that I've heard about and never experienced, but I kept a lid on it owing to the shitty circumstances." Ryan, as usual, looked unabashed at his bold statement whereas Daisy's heart flipped, performing a small celebratory jig inside her chest.

"But the thing is, no matter how much I fancy you and want to take things further, it's wrong and unfair because where my job is concerned *I am* a selfish bastard – it always comes first. I love what I do and at this stage in my life I don't want to be tied down. I'm twenty-seven and it's too young for commitment and not just that, things are moving fast overseas so I can be sent anywhere at any time and be gone for months." Ryan was resting his arms on his bent knees, focusing on the palms of his hands, afraid to see any hurt or disappointment if he looked into Daisy's eyes.

Daisy could feel him drifting away, relying on a thin layer of practised excuses that as far as she was concerned were full of holes. "I don't think that's selfish at all. Lots of people focus on their career. It's not a crime and neither is being single or borderline relationship-phobic…which it sounds like you are. Isn't it possible to have both, lots of people do?"

"Oh I assure you I am selfish, right to the core and yes, it might be possible to have my cake and eat it but then I'd be worse than selfish, I'd be cruel and heartless and although I have my faults, I'm neither of those. This is how I see it: whenever I get back to the UK more often than not one of the lads arranges a jolly, and squadron activities take me all over the place, like when I went to Italy skiing or scuba diving in Greece. I can't expect you to wait for me or be cool about it when I want to shoot off to Scotland for a week of extreme sports. I wouldn't like it so it's wrong to expect it from you or anyone, not right now."

Daisy's heart was now running round in circles, panicking, desperate. "Bloody hell, Ryan! Don't you think you are taking life a bit too seriously? I mean, I understand everything you said but it sounds like you've put so much thought into what you want out of life, you've left no room for any grey areas. Do you have to live by some self-made rules? Why not go with the flow and see what happens because you never know, you might just be surprised?" Daisy remembered something Adam once said about Ryan seeing everything in black and white and preferring an orderly life, but surely there was room for manoeuvre now and then?

"I knew you'd think that, and now I've come across like some kind of control freak but I'm not, I swear, it's just my defence mechanism – I have a default setting that's hard to switch off. In a nutshell, growing up was crap, and while I have breath in my body I am never going to be like my parents. I can't afford to make mistakes Daisy. I want a decent life, nothing fancy just nice things, a bit of money in the bank and stability but what I want most of all is self-respect and to wipe out the past, especially that piece of shite we laughingly called a father. I don't blame Mum for everything but she did have a choice and could've left him, or tried harder to look after us, especially while he was in the nick, but she didn't and we suffered. The last thing I want is to ruin my life or someone else's and the worst thing of all, be a terrible father to a child I don't want. That scares me the most, getting someone pregnant and then having to do the right thing, because I would, just for all the wrong reasons. One day I imagine I will settle down but right now it's not on the agenda and yes, I am taking it all too seriously and no, I don't want any grey areas – it's as simple as that."

There was such anger in Ryan. It emanated from every pore along with an overpowering sense of determination borne from the need for self-preservation. Slipping her arm through his, Daisy laid her head on Ryan's shoulder. Feeling his head rest against hers, she smiled.

"I have no right to tell you how you should run your life, Ryan. We only get one shot so you have to do what you think is best. And I understand why you don't want commitment, I really do. I'm too young to settle down or get serious, not yet anyway. So you can rest assured that I've no intention of snaring you *or* pushing a pram around the precinct. If I'm honest I thought I'd misread the signals and felt a bit rejected, which hurt my feelings, more so because I thought you were special, not like the other guys I've met. I'd convinced myself we had a connection so when you started being cold with me I was really confused."

"I'm sorry Daisy. I should've said something sooner, do you forgive me? I hate the thought of upsetting you as much as I hate me for causing it."

"Of course I do, and I'm okay now, I promise." Sensing the doom was shifting, slowly being replaced by a warmer front, Daisy wrapped her fingers around his and felt him squeeze her hand. Deciding on the flip of a coin to keep things light, the hurt of Ryan's past still hanging in the air, Daisy had taken the understanding route, with added humour. "And the funny thing is, a few years ago I actually had a similar conversation with Adam. How's that for a saddo? In fact now I come to think of it, the pair of you do my head in!"

"What do you mean, has Adam rejected you?" Ryan pulled away slightly, confusion etched on his face causing Daisy to cling tightly to his hand; he wasn't shaking free, not now.

"No…but the first time he went off with a girl called Nell I had a mardy sulk, which was daft because I didn't even fancy him. I was just jealous that he thought she was prettier than me, Daisy the Rejected Minger. And we were so close that I panicked and presumed I was going to lose him as a friend. He still takes the piss, even now…so as long as you don't think I'm one of the ugly sisters, I can deal with it." Daisy saw Ryan laughing and silently exhaled. She had made him smile and kept Adam's secret into the bargain.

Ryan rolled his eyes. "What are you like? Perhaps I've misjudged Fliss and it's you that's the bunny boiler, but even if you are I promise you're not a minger and definitely my type."

"Just in the wrong place at the wrong time, again! We'll just have to blame it all on fate or destiny, who in my opinion are both evil twins with a sick sense of humour."

"Yep, looks like it. And I feel even worse now because you've been so understanding, this is like torture and you're right, the evil twins need a rocket up their arse. I might be able to arrange that. But are you really okay, you do understand where I'm coming from?"

And as much as she wanted to scream, 'YES! You are killing me inside, and NO! I don't understand why we can't have everything right here and now', Daisy forced herself to be silent. Instead she smiled before kissing him softly on the cheek. And then, right on the back of her previous thought, something occurred to her. Moving in closer, their skin touching where exposed, Daisy softened her tone and turned up the heat.

"Yes, I get it, so stop stressing. That's the nicest let down I've ever had, but just so you know, you're not totally off the hook – let's just say you are still on the end of my line. I'll just have to be patient and wait until I can reel you in."

"Really, and what do you mean by that?" Ryan was grinning, his eyes had lost that faraway look and she had his full attention.

"Well, now you've shown your hand I might just have to cheat. And maybe between now and when you leave for Iraq I'll persuade you to take a vacation from your rules and regulations. I think you've had it all your own way for far too long so don't say you weren't warned." Daisy gave him a knowing look before winking.

"Who are you and what have you done with Daisy? I'm not sure if I should be scared or excited about the prospect, will I need my body armour? In fact, I might just let you have your wicked way with me after all. Should I surrender right now and suffer whatever you have in mind?"

Daisy shrugged her shoulders. "Stop being a spoilsport and wait and see."

They had both turned to face each other, centimetres apart. Daisy knew she'd flipped it around and taken the right tack, relieved him of guilt and burden and now they could have some harmless, no-strings-attached fun – the exact thought that crossed her mind as she kissed him. It was just a sample, nothing heavy, more of a hint.

Daisy couldn't let Ryan get away that easily. He was there, in France with her, and after waiting for so long she wasn't prepared to waste all those hours of letter writing and expectancy. No, life was for living in the here and now. The future could take care of itself, as could Ryan, whereas the present needed a bit of a nudge. Actually, Daisy was going to give it a good, firm push.

"And while you ponder over that little conundrum I suggest we join the queue otherwise Adam will starve or think we've got lost. Come on, don't just sit there looking all confused and handsome, chop, chop." Daisy stood and after brushing off the sand, offered her hand, which Ryan took but once he was on his feet she didn't let go, and as they climbed the steps, neither did he.

From his vantage point under the parasol Adam scanned the beach, watching for two familiar figures to appear. They'd been gone ages. He'd somehow resisted the urge to bang their heads together after hearing every word of their conversation earlier. His music wasn't switched on; his tapping foot just gave that appearance. Adam had a bad feeling because Daisy was right, Ryan was acting strange, a bit distant, which could possibly mean he was pining for some woman. If this were the case it would be a first because Adam had never known his brother to pine for anything, apart from a bike for his birthday, which like the cassette player he'd himself longed for, never materialised.

In truth, Adam was becoming exasperated and a teeny bit shattered from the effort required in being Daisy's BFF, not that she was demanding or anything, it was more the constant awareness that at any point some bloke would come along and ruin it all. Going forward, this would continue to be a worrying possibility unless she was with Ryan because then his life, their life, would be sorted.

Ryan would never push Adam out or make Daisy choose – they were brothers, a team, one that Daisy had to be a member of. Yes, Adam knew it might never happen and neither of them could be easily manipulated, but it was worth a shot.

He had succeeded so far by getting rid of Greg. Chinese whispers always worked wonders and had Daisy not ended their relationship, the knowledge that she had the hots for Ryan would've done the trick. And now they had graduated she was staying in Manchester, with him – another tick in Adam's box. He'd done a magnificent job of persuading Daisy of all the benefits of city living and even if that failed, he would've simply followed her back to France and kept an eye on her from here. Although he felt sad for Pam and Bill who expected her to return to home, for him it worked out well. They would be renting a flat, not student digs, a real home and in a nicer area and starting a new chapter together, meaning Daisy would be occupied with a new job and homemaking, so hopefully he could relax for a while.

Adam pondered on his earlier eavesdropping, which as always was done for a good cause. He didn't mind that Ryan called him a weirdo, not in the context of his conversation with Daisy. They'd called each other much worse when they were growing up and most of it was said in jest while they were arguing over who'd eaten all the Jaffa Cakes or used the hot water. They were lads, the near-the-knuckle banter and brotherly rows were just harmless spats and soon forgotten.

What mattered to Adam the most was that Ryan didn't ever look upon him in a way that distanced them or caused confusion and disdain, or called him cruel names in ignorance or anger using words that couldn't be erased. Adam couldn't bear that. It would kill him if Ryan really thought he was weird.

When something caught Adam's eye, his maudlin thoughts clambered out of their worry pit as he focused on two figures picking their way across the sand. The deep hole, littered with angst and uncertainty, was swiftly filled in then topped up with a smidgen of hope. The gap that had separated Daisy and Ryan was no longer there. Instead, their bodies were squashed together. Ryan's arm was slung around Daisy's shoulder, pulling her close while they laughed at the blob of ice cream on her nose. She was trying to rub it off at the same time as carrying two cones.

Adam smiled as he watched them from behind his sunglasses, remembering to tap his foot and lower his head as if reading the book that rested on his knee. Maybe it was going to be okay after all. If he played the long game and with a bit of tweaking here and there, his master plan could in fact work.

As they neared, Adam recognised the mischievous look on Daisy's face and surmised by the one on Ryan's that his mood had also lifted. So when his brother plonked himself down and signalled that he should remove his earphones, Adam obeyed. Daisy passed him a dribbling ice cream cone and then seated herself close by. Suspecting an announcement was on the cards, Adam closed his book and applied a vacant expression, waiting expectantly for what he hoped would be some good news. It turned out to be quite the opposite.

Chapter 13

Daisy and Ryan sitting in a tree
France 2005

Daisy's first choice had been one of the rental caravans but after a quick look at the bookings saw they were occupied, and she didn't have a tent, then again in the July heat it would've been unbearably hot, especially for what she had planned. There was no way anything was going to happen under her parents' roof, that was a passion killer from the word go and anyway, she wanted something much more romantic and memorable, a setting that Ryan would picture while he was away. It was turning out to be a logistical nightmare until her dad became an unwitting ally, just by asking Adam if he fancied a spot of night fishing at a rival lake on the other side of the village. Adam agreed instantly, followed by Ryan saying fishing wasn't his thing and Daisy saw her chance. Or maybe, Ryan handed it to her on a plate.

*

Once Ryan had told Adam that he was going to Iraq, the announcement was met by a similar reaction to Daisy's, followed by a multitude of intense questions and equally reassuring answers. The drive home from the beach had been subdued, Adam for once declining the wheel. Ryan tried to make conversation as he drove, while his companions submerged themselves in thought. Adam was no doubt worrying himself half to death while Daisy loitered on another planet entirely, one where only she and Ryan existed.

She understood Ryan's mindset and his honesty, for having the courage of his convictions, and knowing he wasn't easily won added to the appeal. That he possessed inner strength and determination to succeed made him even more of a prize. Ryan was the opposite of everyone Daisy had ever met – boys masquerading as men. He was the real deal, someone who made her feel wild, her body alive, every throbbing, tingly nerve cell in fact. Daisy wasn't prepared to waste all that, just turn away and shrug her shoulders *or* deny herself the opportunity to sample every muscle-bound, golden-tanned inch of him. She risked being punished after sampling previously forbidden fruits but it was better than the alternative. At least this way she'd have memories instead of regrets.

If Ryan thought he was being mature by doing what he thought was the right thing, holding back and setting her free, then Daisy was going to show him the true meaning of the word. She was a young, intelligent woman with a 2:1 to prove it and therefore quite capable of being independent and making her own choices, of mind, body and soul. So no, this time Ryan didn't get to call the shots.

Starting the very next morning, after a long and sleepless night, Daisy had ramped up the heat and made sure she looked gorgeous, even at 7am while she collected eggs. When they were together she ensured that regardless of necessity, a moment or two of bodily contact was made, delighting in the knowledge she saw in Ryan's eyes. Her teens had perfected the art of lingering looks from beneath long lashes, then a shy smile before turning away but now, Daisy put them to good use on Ryan and he was pliable putty in her hands. It was clear from his reaction that he was enjoying being played and flirted with, the anticipation that she was about to make her move palpable, after all, she had warned him.

*

Dusk approached and the stage was set as Daisy ran back through the woods and straight upstairs, breathlessly closing her bedroom door, giddy with anticipation. After taking a shower and spraying her body with whatever perfume came to hand first, she then threw on her lacy sundress, panicked when she couldn't find her sandals so headed barefoot towards the kitchen. Ryan was nowhere to be seen and after quelling panic and irritation she found him in the lounge with Pam, who was settling down to Pride and Prejudice. For a second the devil in Daisy was tempted to let him suffer Mr Darcy in the lake but when he turned and smiled her heart flipped. So, instead of leaving him blushing on the sofa, Daisy decided to make his cheeks flush in another way entirely.

"Mum, do you mind if I pinch Ryan for a while, I fancy going for a walk and it's too hot to sit indoors, will you be okay by yourself?" Pam would have eaten her own tongue rather than deny Daisy so wafted them both away, saying she was going to enjoy having the telly all to herself, and the bottle of wine Ryan had just uncorked.

Willingly following Daisy outside, Ryan inhaled her floral perfume, admiring from behind her tanned arms and very long legs, and the sheer backless sundress revealing the notches on her spine covered by silky smooth skin. As they emerged into the heady evening heat he was similarly overwhelmed by the sensation of being led astray, an alien notion that greatly appealed.

As much as he'd tried to put the thought out of his mind, Ryan had been expecting this since their chat on the beach and it had become clear that Daisy had an agenda. Whilst he enjoyed the thrill, Ryan stuck to his self-inflicted rules and made no attempt to take things further. As far as he was concerned, his conscience was appeased. If Daisy still wanted him that was precisely what she was going to get, and as far as he could tell, it would be anytime soon. He was only human, after all.

To his surprise, as they walked on nerves got the better of him so Ryan attempted conversation, mentioning the heat, Adam and Bill's impromptu fishing trip and Pamela's dreadful taste in films. By the time they'd reached the outskirts of the campsite, heading towards the lake, Ryan could take the suspense and Daisy's reticence no longer.

"What are you up to, where are we going? If you want to swim I'm wearing the wrong shorts, hey…stop messing about. Come on, Daise, what's going on?"

"Ryan, don't be a spoilsport, anyone would think you were nervous. I've got a surprise for you so just stop asking questions. And no, we're not going swimming and you definitely won't need your shorts for what I have in mind, okay?" When Daisy turned and gave him a cheeky smile he could hear the laughter in her voice and simultaneously his stomach swirled, blood rushed around his body, downwards mainly, eager expectation tempered by apprehension. It was a sensation he'd not experienced for such a long time, like a teenager on the brink of his greatest adventure.

Once they moved off the sandy track to the lake, they followed a less worn route, which was when Daisy took Ryan's hand and silently led him through the woods. He knew immediately where they were headed. The notches carved high in the bark of the trees gave away a secret code.

It was as their feet crunched on parched earth and fallen leaves, the scent of nature filling his nostrils, a potent sensory combination of earth and wild garlic, the breeze rustling through leaves and the temptress up ahead, that Ryan felt a swell deep inside. A surge of emotions, the build up of pressure, all-consuming excitement and raging adrenalin caused a reaction in Ryan that he feared the most – he was losing control and he couldn't have that. He needed to reclaim some ground, gather himself and show Daisy that he wasn't going to be played but he would take part in the game.

Ryan stopped dead in his tracks causing Daisy's body to jerk and halt. Turning to face him, quizzical yet remaining an arms stretch away, in the silence of the forest well away from prying eyes, disconnected from the outside world, Daisy waited for Ryan to make the next move. The oppressive, humid air clung to their skin, both enveloped in a ball of pressure, sealing them inside a leafy world where only they existed. When Ryan pulled Daisy towards him, holding on tightly with one hand until she was close enough to wrap his free arm around her back, the feel of her skin beneath his palm ignited the chemicals metabolising deep inside his blood, skin and bones, a toxic reaction about to combust. Only seconds occurred until their bodies touched, lips against lips, flesh pressed against flesh, and in that moment Ryan felt something he had never experienced before. It was more than desire or passion, it was the need to be close to someone, consume them, take more than he gave, give more than he took, absorb that moment, the thrill of Daisy, capture a piece of her heart and soul and make it his.

When she pulled away, breathless and wide eyed, as caught up in the moment as he, a smile played on their tingling lips. Daisy pushed away then turned quickly, leading him deeper into the forest, no need for childhood carvings, lust and the thirst for what lay ahead propelling her forward.

Dusk was turning into night, the transition always swift and graceful and Ryan knew that they had only minutes before the woods would be plunged into darkness, their pathway lit at the discretion of the moon. He spotted the soft glow moments before they reached the clearing where the Grandad Tree stood and as they made their way closer it occurred to Ryan that Daisy had timed it all perfectly. That she had been planning all this. Her deepest thoughts had been of him. A notion that served only to intensify the hunger that raged inside.

As they neared the foot of the tree, Ryan had only seconds to take in the small jars that held the tea lights, their flames flickering like moths captured inside the glass. On the ground, blankets lay in the hollow of the tree, entombed within the great gaping mouth of the birch, and whether it was the glowing yellow candle jars or the spirit of the forest, some magical force seemed to be beckoning them inside.

Daisy was almost breathless when she finally spoke. "Do you like it? I wanted it to be special, you and me, our first time and maybe our last, but it has to be perfect so I can always remember it like this." Daisy had placed her free hand on the bark of the tree, its ridges rough and brittle underneath her hand but energy, nature's force still ran through its heartwood, straight to her own.

Ryan felt odd, caught in an intense moment, like a dream. "It's perfect, you're perfect…"

Daisy smiled. "Tonight there's no need for plans and rules, just two people, right here, right now. But I do want to make you a promise, one I'll never break." Daisy took one step closer and placed her finger on his lips, sensing he might break the spell. "That I'll never ask more of you than you are prepared to give and after tonight I'll set you free, then wait for you to come back, but only if you want to, always on your terms."

Without giving him time to respond Daisy moved forward and kissed him slowly, her fingers entwined in his hair, her body melting into his. This time it was Ryan who pulled away, almost gasping for breath as he took both her hands in one of his, and led her silently inside.

Chapter 14

I'm only human
Basra Airport, Iraq 2007

The airport was loud and noisy, military personnel from every imaginable NATO country going about their business. So many variations of camouflage and strange accents merging with the sound of dusty boots marching across tiled floors as planes roared overhead, smothering the muffled announcements on the tannoy.

Ryan's eyes drooped and his back ached from a long journey on a noisy, bone-rattling troop carrier, their discomfort now prolonged by an unexpected delay due to a security alert. Until their flight sergeant told them otherwise, the terminal and the unforgiving stone slab of wall he leant against would be their resting place for the next few hours. Accepting that sleep wasn't an option, Ryan decided to use the time wisely, so dragging his rucksack closer he pulled out his notepad and pen then searched for a Bluey. Maybe amongst the relentless cacophony he would be able to find a way to explain himself, minimise any hurt and banish the searing pangs of guilt that tormented him.

Ryan was tired, in fact he was exhausted and not just by work – a combination of circumstances were taking their toll. The danger and intensity of their surroundings along with the monotony of long shifts and all that being on an operation entailed were major factors but his fatigue was also due to the emotional baggage of being in a new relationship. Something that he'd tried so hard to avoid yet more or less walked right into.

He'd been aware of Charlotte ever since she had joined their squadron, mainly because she was in the minority of women who looked good in overalls and stripped bare of make-up. Initially he regarded her as another team member, a colleague and occasional drinking buddy, yet after a while she began to grow on him. Charlotte was clever, funny and easy-going, and even more appealing, hidden underneath her military work wear, lurked a temptress. After rebuffing her many admirers one by one, Charlotte turned her attention to Ryan midway through a tour and not only was he delighted, he was sex-starved putty in her hands.

In his guilt-ridden moments, Ryan tried to load some of the blame onto Adam because had he not set Charlotte a challenge, maybe she would've focused her attention elsewhere but as it was, having Daisy's name rammed down her throat every five minutes really hadn't helped.

*

Adam had been staying with Ryan in Norfolk, a flying weekend visit arranged on the spur of the moment after Daisy had returned to France. Following a tearful conversation with Pamela, they'd learned that Bill had suffered a heart attack then undergone emergency surgery and although he was out of the woods and in recovery, Daisy insisted on seeing her dad. To add to her distress, Ryan was due to return to a battle zone but the choice when it came down to it was simple so she cancelled their plans to say farewell, which is why Adam went instead.

On the Saturday evening, whilst in the local pub enjoying a few drinks with some of Ryan's friends, a woman approached the table and joined their raucous group. At first Adam thought little of it especially when she was introduced as a colleague but as the night wore on he began to notice the way Charlie (as she preferred to be called) looked at Ryan, setting off clanging alarms bells.

Perhaps behaving like a jealous child who had been introduced to his potential stepmother for the first time wasn't the most mature way to behave but Adam couldn't help himself. After cutting her out of the conversation and purposely not laughing at her jokes it was clear that she wasn't going to get bored or, despite his fervent prayers, burst into flames. So, swiftly changing tack he decided to irritate the shit out of her instead. His weapon of choice was Daisy.

After finally deigning to engage Charlotte in conversation, Adam bombarded her with wondrous tales of happy family times where Ryan and Daisy were central to the plot, all of which were backed up with smiley loved-up photos, which he more or less rammed in her face. Fair play to the girl, she didn't bat an eyelid and frustrated Adam even more by showing great interest in and even admiring his beautiful best friend, much to the amusement of Ryan who presumed his brother was having some kind of chatty reaction to real ale.

When Charlotte became bored by images of Daisy and the sound of Adam's voice she made her excuses and left, but instead of scoring a point, Adam had unwittingly lain down the gauntlet. And while his hyper brother had been extolling the virtues of Daisy, Ryan had listened in silence, nodding and joining in when necessary, smiling at the photos that in his case were having their desired effect. He was secretly gutted that Daisy had rightly opted to see her dad because lately, in his solitary moments, thousands of miles and months away from home, Ryan was beginning to realise that he missed her. A lot.

Since his squadron had joined Op Telic they had been based in Qatar and done more than their fair share of tours where Ryan relished the opportunity to put hours of training into practice and uphold the oath he had attested to on his first day of basic training. And during these two years, whilst on leave in the UK, there had been a number of passionate liaisons with Daisy. After juggling rotas at the airport and in between Ryan's various excursions with his mates, they had snatched time away from Manchester and Adam.

Flashes of their woodland tryst in France still had a startling effect on Ryan, the heat of that night still burned deep within. Afterwards they had made no secret of their feelings for each other, both Daisy and Ryan had too much respect for Bill, Pamela and Adam to lie, but still they insisted that neither had made any promises and both intended to get on with their lives and leave the rest in the hands of destiny. For his part Ryan meant every word whereas unknown to him, Daisy's agenda was far less honest. In truth, had he said the word her heart would have sworn allegiance to him there and then. Instead she was forced to play the long game.

In his ignorance of Daisy's true feelings, Ryan was increasingly enamoured, entranced by her womanly wiles and admiring of her ability to let him go. She didn't cling or pine, neither did she hint at wanting more or press him into making advance arrangements. Had she not been equally content with their relationship then Ryan would have brought it to an end because whilst he was – according to Dan, his best friend – a cold-hearted, selfish bastard, he wasn't cruel and respected Daisy enough not to use her. If he wanted sex there were plenty of opportunities for one-night stands that required even less effort than he put into his long-distance, no-promises friendship with Daisy. Their mutual arrangement suited them both, simple as that.

The ironic and niggling factor that began to interfere with Ryan's carefully constructed equation for a happy and self-absorbed life was that over time, Dan's constant jibes had started to get under his skin. Maybe he should tweak the master plan and give it a go with Daisy, take a chance on a proper relationship. During many a long night as he lay on his bunk, listening to the sounds of war carrying on beyond the perimeter fence, Ryan faced up to the possibility that letting his guard down wouldn't be so bad. Daisy had proved she was loyal and supportive of his career and on top of that, a beautiful person inside and out. Her friendship with Adam proved the point.

Thoughts of his curious brother often made Ryan smile, remembering his ramblings about a triangle that included all three of them, a perfect happy family that existed only in Adam's imagination. And Ryan was just about coming round to the notion that it might not be a bad idea. So far he'd remained in control of his neat and tidy life and going forward, combining homecomings with both Daisy and Adam would certainly make it easier. And there were only so many lads holidays you could take before it all wore a bit thin. Dan would say he was still being a selfish bastard but it was a step in the right direction, taking down one of his barriers.

The future, however, has no respect for the private plans of the individual and in Ryan's case seemed hell bent on throwing a spanner in the workings of his mind. By simply altering the path of Charlotte and placing her directly in that of Ryan's, destiny got its own way as usual. Just as Daisy was about to be rewarded for her patience and guile, a more available and equally persevering young woman stepped boldly into the breach.

*

Ryan clicked the tip of his pen and placed the nib onto the paper, sighing in a resigned and semi-reluctant way, knowing he had two letters to compose and the recipients of both weren't going to like what they read, not one bit.

Regardless of his so-called best intentions, Ryan knew that Dan was on the money and he was guilty as charged. He'd kept Daisy on a string but now, after giving in to temptation had well and truly burnt his candle at both ends. To make matters worse, Ryan knew that Adam would be totally pissed off with him for scuppering his weird master plan for family unity, but what was done, was done. He would have to face the consequences and make the best of it and by that he meant keeping his promise to Charlotte and telling Daisy that it was over.

Leaning forward Ryan searched down the line. Seven sets of legs further along he spotted her, chatting with their corporal. Sensing she was being watched Charlotte looked in Ryan's direction, flashing him a smile then glancing at his pen and sheet of blue airmail, pausing slightly before turning away. In that precise second Ryan hesitated. Had he seen a hint of smugness on Charlotte's face, and was that resentment he felt or pressure? Did he really want to write those letters?

With the last remnants of battery power his sleep-deprived brain could muster, Ryan attempted to appease his conscience. His no-promises arrangement with Daisy was about to come to an end but the situation was sweetened by having a girlfriend in such close proximity. Yes, Charlotte had made rules, ones that ensured their relationship wouldn't interfere with work whilst avoiding the obvious pitfalls of being in each other's pockets, but Ryan was confident it would work. And as much as he was tempted, Ryan knew he couldn't have both.

Charlotte had slotted nicely into his life and whilst being fairly independent and ambitious, also understood the rigours of his job, and their mutual desire and attraction was a huge bonus.

Unfolding the Bluey, Ryan rested it on the back of his notepad and rucksack and before what remained of his conscience could intervene, he began to write. The letter began with: Dear Daisy…

Chapter 15

Adam
Manchester 2007

Adam was in a foul mood and so rare was his display of
sulky, belligerent behaviour that his wary colleagues
respected his need for complete isolation, fearing
disintegration should they step within the boundaries of his
workspace and fall under the gaze of his death-ray glare. As is
the norm, in hushed tones using hand gestures and exaggerated
eye movements everyone speculated as to the cause of Adam's
uncharacteristic mood swing. The possibilities ranged from
being given his notice (highly unlikely as he was popular and
hard-working) or spurned by the chatty courier Adam frequently
flirted with, losing his wallet, a raging hangover or getting a
parking ticket outside work (welcome to the club). More likely,
it was something to do with the blue airmail letter Jean had seen
him reading when she passed him a brew and a packet of custard
creams earlier that morning.

From within his partitioned walls Adam knew they were
whispering about him, and despite the tumult of emotions
sweeping through his brain he did have the grace to feel bad about
his mammoth sulk. He couldn't help it though. When he'd opened
the post box on the way out of the apartment that morning and
spotted the two Blueys that lay inside, Adam's heart lifted and
knew Daisy would feel the same. Now, he was kicking himself
for texting her to say the bloody letter had arrived otherwise he
could've burned it and then persuaded Ryan to change his mind.

The words he'd written on the flimsy sheet of paper were far
from uplifting and worse still, Daisy wouldn't open hers until that
evening, meaning Adam had eight whole hours in which to worry
about the fall out.

How could Ryan do this? As soon as he clapped eyes on her Adam bloody well knew that Charlotte girl was trouble and wished he'd tried harder to put her off, but what more could he do? He'd already behaved like a petulant teenager and despite his best efforts had hit a brick wall because she didn't take the hint, *and* his stupid brother obviously couldn't keep it in his pants.

Oh God! What if he'd actually made things worse by goading her and set Charlotte some kind of challenge that she had since risen to? The thing was, Adam couldn't help himself where matters of the heart were concerned and was guilty of behaving in much the same way with Daisy and her male acquaintances. Thus far he'd managed to get away with the 'peculiar and annoying flatmate' routine, mainly because Daisy was never that into whatever poor love-struck guy she'd dated. Furthermore, Adam was convinced she secretly pined for Ryan, which was probably why her rare dalliances came to nothing.

Placing his head in his hands Adam fumed inwardly, his fury and resentment reminiscent of teenage tantrums after being denied the most trivial of things, yet this wasn't remotely trite – it was more like his life's work had been ruined, his master plan had crashed and burned.

Adam put so much effort into preserving his unique existence with Daisy. She was key to everything; his happiness and future depended on her. All Ryan had to do was fall in love and then everything would slot into place but that fucking Charlotte had ruined everything. He was incandescent, piqued, outsmarted and fooled.

He'd spent two whole years feeling mildly smug, ever since that last summer they all spent together where it was abundantly clear to watchful bystanders that Ryan and Daisy were mad about each other. During Ryan's time in Iraq Adam had casually encouraged Daisy's infatuation with his brother whilst prowling in the shadows, preparing to pounce and fend off anyone who might interfere with the equilibrium of his own happy yet purely domestic existence. Adam sometimes wondered if he had a personality disorder of some kind so tried to keep a lid on his controlling tendencies, but then again, he quite enjoyed his alter egos.

He wavered between a jolly (presumed bi-sexual) workmate, the nutter who threw tomatoes at those dog walkers who allowed their pets to foul the towpath below his balcony, the most accommodating and loyal best friend in the world and, if anyone dared steal Daisy away, the serial killer lurking in the dark, wielding a machete. And there were even more curious personalities dwelling within Adam's head, all ready to come out to play when required.

Whilst he was quite prepared to dedicate his life to having Daisy in it, during those past two years the pursuance of this dream had required an immense amount of patience and fortitude. While he appeared accepting of her very liberal approach to whatever was going on with Ryan, the same degree of tolerance had to be applied to the odd eager chap who whisked Daisy off on dates. This was the thing that almost killed him, but not in the regular jealous kind of way. It was because the fear of losing her to one of the 'casuals' was like a knife in the heart. And there was yet another topic that caused Adam untold disquiet. His bond with Bill and Pamela was precious and he would've fought to the death to preserve it – they were the parents he'd always wished for so losing Daisy meant losing them too.

Sometimes though, Adam wished he could smother this all-consuming sense of jeopardy once and for all. He had tried hard to erase the portent of predestination that hovered in his subconscious, feeding the electric current inside his head, causing the jumble of panicky signals to multiply. If only he could pop the giant bubble of angst then maybe he could talk himself into believing that his future might actually be bright, and then he could do the honourable thing and really set Daisy free and allow Ryan to make his own mistakes.

But Adam didn't trust destiny. It had chosen this cowardly life for him, one that was based on illusion, smoke and mirrors, a lie. And yes, he still feared stepping out from behind the curtain and telling everyone who he really was, no matter how society progressed. By admitting his own weaknesses and being honest about his controlling tendencies, Adam also conned himself into believing that his auto-analysis allowed him a free pass, permission to self, confirmation that protection was required at all costs.

Yes, he pushed his luck, parading around the apartment wearing nothing more than a hand towel, emerging from the shower to ask Daisy to rub moisturiser into his back. Or behaving like an annoying kid brother who didn't take the hint and bugger off to bed while Daisy and some irritated guy watched a film. It was all too easy. It was like a sport, flaunting his superior knowledge of the inner workings of Daisy's mind – a sure fire way to wrong-foot a would-be lover boy. Adam knew what made her laugh, cry and rage, who and what she would go out to bat for, her dislikes, interests, foibles and even her monthly cycles, all of which was guaranteed to piss anyone off. And if they were hoping to snatch a point in any kind of contest, Adam always pipped them to the post.

He bought Daisy the best presents, knew when to have a hot water bottle and a packet of Feminax waiting when she got home, which toppings she liked on her pizza and where to take her on a day out. Whilst all this was part of his strategy, it was also done out of love because Adam truly adored Daisy and setting aside any hidden agenda, his feelings for her were honest and pure. Along with Ryan, he placed her happiness above everything else.

Unfolding the letter once more, Adam re-read the words, trying desperately to be pleased for his brother who seemed to have found a companion amidst the most unlikely of settings. There was no mention of love or adoration; professional compatibility seemed the only positive. After the fourth time of deciphering Ryan's very literal, black and white explanation of his fledgling relationship, Adam began to read between the slanted lines and was able to alter the plot. Instead of wading around in a pool of miserable sludge he saw a way to climb out of the mire, grabbing onto a glimmer of hope.

This was just Ryan being Ryan. He was making the best out of a monotonous and possibly ongoing situation – he said as much in the letter. Adam knew his brother had a way of seeing situations in a practical way, no complicated formulas or tangled webs. Just because Charlotte the Harlot had obviously laid herself at Ryan's feet and provided an easy solution in the short term, it certainly didn't mean she was 'the one' or forever. Chas (as Adam now sarcastically referred to her) was merely a stop-gap until the war was over and then he would come back home and settle down.

Folding the letter before slipping it inside his jacket pocket, Adam was filled with a renewed sense of purpose. He had to stop feeling sorry for himself and divert his attention to Daisy who would need his support once she read the contents of her letter. No matter how Ryan worded it (and Adam prayed that he'd at least attempted to soften the blow, not gone down the cruel-to-be-kind route) Daisy would be hurt and disappointed, to put it mildly.

His mission accepted, Adam promptly set off to convince his boss that he was suffering from some vague virus that had induced his man-mood and after a spot of amateur dramatics, emerged from his office building with a spring in his step. First stop was the supermarket to buy the ingredients for one of Daisy's favourite curries, and then the florist – gerberas always cheered her up, as did a giant bar of Galaxy, which had to be left in the fridge before consumption, it was the law. Adam intended to be there when Daisy came in from work and hover tactfully while she read the letter, after which he would assure her that Nasty Chas was just a passing fancy and until Ryan came to his senses, she would always have him.

The current was fizzing through Adam's brain once again, his mind clicking away, Morse code messages revising devious plans. His heart pumped as he strode through the city centre, oblivious to passersby, focused solely on the task ahead. Everything was going to be okay. Adam's orders were received and understood, the missile was firmly locked onto its target and hurtling with well-meant turbo-speed velocity towards his best friend, the love of his life – Daisy.

Chapter 16

Are you looking for another girl?
Manchester 2007

Sometimes we make promises we can't keep, even though at the time they were pledged in good faith and with every intention of following them through. Then, in the cold light of day, maybe when we've sobered up or thought things through, examined the consequences or sheer enormity of what our oath-taking entails, we wish we'd kept our big mouths shut.

When Daisy made her promise on that freezing cold evening, perched on top of a roof, at that moment in time her heart was true and her fledgling love for Adam had wings, there were no boundaries. Life was for living and her best friend was at the centre of her happiest times. They had laughed at mindless stupid things, played wicked pranks on their friends and stolen random, useless objects from a restaurant just for dares. Even the quiet times were perfect – pizza-eating, music-loving solitude. And whilst the purity of their bond had never become contaminated by resentment, the burden of her commitment – Daisy's self-inflicted responsibility for Adam – could sometimes be restrictive and on occasions suffocating.

Every now and then Daisy would have liked not to worry, second-guess or overthink a situation that involved the opposite sex or even her female friends because sometimes girls just want to have fun in their own, man-free world. And it wasn't even that Adam made it difficult, sulked or showed any outward signs of jealousy. It was more intrinsic and subtle, a silent force field that emanated waves of crackling static in her direction, like a spell that sometimes needed to be broken. Daisy was well aware of Adam's fears, both of being alone and of being discovered, and that he dreaded losing her to another, body and soul, permanently. This would mean having to find his own way in a society that might not understand as she did, and going solo simply terrified him.

In pursuit of Adam's happiness she had tried to steer him in the direction of others because society was evolving, more open-minded, curious even, and being Adam wasn't as dreadful as he once imagined. But no matter how much she encouraged him to seek the company of similar souls, perhaps embark on a relationship with another human being who had the same needs, or lack of them, Adam resisted. She couldn't quite decide whether it was out of fear or sheer bloody-mindedness. Maybe he was too lazy and had become complacent, settled in their life therefore had no need to seek out another.

It even crossed Daisy's mind that she had made it too easy for him and a serving of tough love was needed, a cutting of apron strings or a firm push from the nest, but how could she force upon him something that he swore he didn't desire?

And there was something else, a niggling sense or perhaps intuition on Daisy's part. It came hand in hand with knowing someone so well and society's increased awareness to the state of the mind, alerting her to an aspect of Adam's personality that caused moments of great concern. It had occurred to her that if allowed, he had the propensity to succumb to depression and if he was ever gripped by such a malaise, it could easily spiral out of control. Maybe subconsciously Adam had put safety procedures in place to prevent such an event, something that was made all the more real by his memories of a fickle mother who regularly descended into the depths of her own mind, serving as a vivid warning to both brothers.

Daisy concluded that this was one thing Adam and Ryan had in common. The elder was haunted by the past and strove not to repeat it whilst the younger was tormented by the future, and the added burden of their parent's inadequacies only intensified their anxieties.

Adam was a dreamer who empathised with the downtrodden, lonely and maligned, so much so that Daisy banned him from watching the late night news knowing he would take the troubles of the world to bed with him. She dreaded natural disasters, Comic Relief and Sport Aid because he would spend all evening in tears, despairing of the tragic tales before reading his credit card details to an enthusiastic call centre operative. She was also adept at steering him away from collection tins held forth by well-meaning charity workers at the entrance to stores, and binned the junk mail that she found in the postbox as he was a sucker for a desperate cause. Adam was too susceptible and took everything so seriously that it threatened to destabilise him if not fastidiously monitored.

By nature Daisy was kind and giving, slightly carefree and impetuous but not daring or brave so left the thrill-seeking to Adam and would allow him to cajole her into adventures if only to see him smile. Through practice and dedication she'd managed to find a life balance that whilst not capitulating entirely, enabled her to pull him out of his gloom when she spotted the blackness creeping in, etching shadows on his face.

Daisy suspected Adam's need to collect and store mementos was borne from his dread of an imagined destiny. To collate those things that marked the happiest periods in his life proved he was making progress, laying foundations, and these objects, records, photos, clothes, paintings all represented solid tangible evidence of good times. When he held them in his hands they gave him comfort, as did she.

Their bond had been forged in steel and it gave Adam strength and hope, and Daisy knew without a doubt that he regarded her as his most priceless object, a gift he was convinced could not be found elsewhere. This made him watchful and suspicious whilst trying so hard to appear casual and friendly. Daisy knew him too well; she could read him like a book. And the acknowledgment of these facts sometimes drained her, having a window into his heart and a free pass inside his head. Being privy to all of it made her his prisoner. She was locked into a contract, sealed by a heart that despite the hidden clauses and awkward addendum still loved

Adam unconditionally and now, couldn't bear or contemplate letting him down.

Maybe, by admitting to herself that she had been naive and far too willing to sacrifice her own happiness, or silly and immature in her belief that she could make everything right for Adam, be his fail safe, caused these unsettling flashes. Perhaps she was annoyed at herself, not her friend, because after all on the very night he bared his soul, Adam had also been prepared to walk away.

Yet in a hypocritical comparison, despite her misgivings, when Daisy was having a down day, if she was tired or pre-menstrual and ratty, had a shitty shift or a date she'd looked forward to turned out to be another belly-flop, Adam made everything okay.

His name was first on speed dial and just hearing one of his incredibly bad fake accents when he answered the phone immediately cheered Daisy up, as did the smell of curry when she opened the apartment door. Adam insisted that a dish of comfort food was the remedy for almost anything when in actual fact Daisy knew it was the chef, not the menu, which provided the miracle cure.

And on the subject of antidotes, Daisy knew full well she had succumbed to the drug that was Ryan, but in an attempt to dilute the dose was open to flirtations and the odd date from those she called her casuals. These deluded chaps served many purposes because after all there was no harm in going to the cinema, or the theatre, dining out (a girl has to eat) or inviting them round for coffee, but that's where it ended. Another advantage was that while she could hand-on-heart reassure Ryan that there was nobody serious *or* sharing her bed, it did no harm to make him wonder.

Maybe in some respects she overcomplicated her life but even the quizzical looks and intrusive questions from colleagues had become the norm and Daisy was now quite used to playing the part of Adam's on-off girlfriend at his work's functions. It was fun, an evening of role play, fancy food, a free bar and an opportunity for everyone in the office to have a gander at the woman Adam constantly talked about.

At home, Daisy had learnt to ignore the sarky comments from frustrated casuals as Adam walked around the apartment, eating cornflakes, resplendent in his rather tight boxer shorts. He was relaxed in his own skin and oblivious to their discomfort at his intrusion. But just as she had done with Greg, Daisy always made it quite clear that Adam was her best friend and flatmate, a non-negotiable part of her life so they could like it or lump it.

It also didn't help that their apartment had become an extension of their personalities, displaying either shared or individual interests, a museum of their own creation containing artefacts from every stage of their life together. When they began home-hunting Daisy wasn't keen on the spanking-new builds, pronouncing them clinical and soulless, so instead they chose to buy in the Northern Quarter. The converted Victorian mill instantly appealed to Daisy and her artistic tendencies. Set along the banks of the Ashton Canal, their home was in the heart of industrial Manchester and the long factory windows looked straight onto the waterway below. Here, narrow boats meandered by, as did joggers, commuters and tomato-splattered dog walkers. It was also within walking distance of the Etihad Stadium, the home of Adam's beloved Manchester City – a deal-sealer.

The interior that retained many of its original features such as exposed brickwork, iron beams and wooden floors was furnished with mainly retro furniture, Art Deco – one of Daisy's favourite eras being a dominant theme – along with iconic music posters adorning walls. Her eye for colour and fabric added warmth, as did the shelves stacked with books and records. But most important of all were photographs of the two of them, plus Pamela, Bill and Ryan, cataloguing their bond.

It wasn't just their possessions that added another link to the chain. It was how they came across them that produced another layer to their friendship that Daisy's casuals found hard to slip between. She loved everything historical and her favourite places on earth were stately homes, followed closely by antique markets and car boot sales. Adam was a willing and enthusiastic companion, not minding early starts so they could rummage through piles of other people's junk to unearth something unique – he'd even bagged himself a few rare records in the process. And neither did he complain as they wandered through the halls of Cheshire's finest homes, gazing upon portraits of pale ladies and portly gentlemen. To see the sparkle in Daisy's eyes as she gazed wistfully through the glass cabinets of the fashion museum was worth stifling a yawn and terribly achy feet.

There had been failures too. The one she teased Adam about the most was their trip to Glastonbury, which she hated every minute of. Slopping around in mud and being rained on for days, then abandoned by Adam who found a friend (real or imaginary, she never really knew) in Turnip, the eco-warrior with an abundance of magic mushrooms. And then there was their weekend stay in a haunted Scottish castle, their mission to witness the existence of the hereafter. While Adam snored beside her, Daisy had lain awake, terrified by the creaks and night noises of the castle while at the same time hoping for a glimpse of a roaming spirit so she could nudge sleeping boy awake and prove once and for all that the 'other side' existed.

These glaring testaments to their curious relationship was enough to turn off Daisy's most ardent of casuals, as was Adam's ability to usurp any man when it came to buying gifts. Due to his dedication and attention to detail, he knew exactly what made her happy and how to make her smile, like the annual subscription to the National Trust, a full set of crocheting tools and a giant bag of colourful wool, or an afternoon treat at the vintage tea rooms.

Daisy adored Adam's gifts regardless of the price tag; sometimes they'd cost pennies, like the paper bag containing a 10p mix that she found hidden in her lunch box, or the friendship bracelet made by one of the dinner ladies in his work's canteen. It was stuff like that that mattered, not flashy gifts in a shiny Selfridge's bag or ostentatious bouquets. And the words on their matching hand-painted mugs that hung from the hooks in the kitchen told their own story belonging to the Best Boy and Best Girl of the house.

In her honest moments of reflection, Daisy was forced to admit that she could be accused of being selfish and at times contrary, asking far too much of her casuals while giving no ground, treating them like a throw away commodity. Yet at the same time, she sometimes wished that Adam would take a mini-break and give her space but when he did, she found herself wishing he'd come home. In short, Daisy wanted it all.

And there was something else, the gut-wrenching truth that was hidden deep within her heart, the one thing that could bring her to tears and even Adam's bowl of homemade vegetable Madras was incapable of curing. While Daisy was quite prepared to sacrifice anyone for Adam because she loved him so much, there was another reason she didn't cling on too tightly to unsuitable men, and that was Ryan.

He had captured her heart and soul, the torch she held for him still burning strong and bright while she waited and waited for him to come back, praying for the day he'd be ready to give love a chance. Ryan was the one and only man that she knew Adam would stand aside for and given the opportunity, Daisy wouldn't let go of ever him again.

Daisy had made promises to each brother. One she had sworn to protect and keep close, the other she had vowed to set free. She would never let Adam down or ask more of Ryan than he was prepared to give, accepting his need for freedom in the same way that she accepted his brother's need for attachment.

So, in her contrary, moody, self-centred moments when Daisy felt wronged and hard done by, she reminded herself that a promise was a promise and whilst the situation may not be perfect, there was still hope, there had been glimmers of it. During their weekend trysts she'd caught Ryan watching her, deep in thought, as though he was waging some kind of battle deep within. Their time together was beyond perfect, infused with passion, laughter, lust and that tangible essence of belonging. Maybe she was finally getting through, taking down his wall brick by brick, and Lord knows she had tried so hard to assure him of her worth by not clinging on or being needy, bravely letting him go and stepping onto the train with the driest of eyes and cheeriest wave goodbye.

While her heart cried out for him to let her in, she remained patient, steadfast, hopeful that such tenacity would eventually pay off. In the meantime the three of them were still bound together – their very own innocent yet bizarre love triangle. And as much as she erred on the side of caution, Daisy told herself that they just hadn't joined up the dots, not yet.

As she drove into the underground car park of their apartment block Daisy was eager to get upstairs and read her letter from Ryan. During the day she'd been thinking of things to put in her reply, some funny anecdotes, news from France perhaps, and the obligatory update of the goings on in Coronation Street – he seemed to enjoy that. Just writing to Ryan made Daisy feel closer to him. It strengthened their connection and above all, putting her wants and dreams aside, she felt duty-bound to support him while he was so far away from home.

Maybe the letter was thanking them for the box of goodies she and Adam had put together. It had become a regular thing while he was away and they both loved buying bits and bobs, Manchester foodie delights, magazines and sweets, simple things to make him smile.

The lift seemed to take ages, which added to her impatience but on opening the door Daisy relaxed, greeted by the pungent smell of madras and the colourful vase of flowers on the coffee table. After hanging her coat on the stand she called out to Adam, noticing the bottle of wine and wondering what she'd done to deserve the special treatment. It was when she came face to face with Adam and recognised the look in his eyes as he glanced nervously towards the unopened blue airmail letter on the counter that alarm bells started to ring and instantly she knew. He wasn't dishing up a treat; Adam was serving comfort food.

Chapter 17

Besotted
Manchester 2009

When he first heard the news, many years later, Adam was sad that Daisy's relationship with Jamie had come to an end. Not because he liked the bloke or thought he was good for his best friend, because in truth Adam thought Jamie was an arsehole and totally wrong for Daisy. It was because he hated to hear her cry and had he not been thousands of miles away when he took her hysterical call, he would've cheerfully smashed Jamie's face in. What riled Adam even more was that due to his enemy's appalling and cruel behaviour, Daisy was selling up and going home to France, and ironically, it was bloody Jamie who had been the main reason for Adam leaving Manchester in the first place.

The year 2009 was Adam's very own annus horribilis, when everything he'd worked so hard at crashed and burned. And as painful as it had been at the time, it was made somewhat easier by finding what he considered to be the perfect job and a way to escape.

*

Once they graduated, Daisy and Adam had decided to remain in Manchester for a trial period, enough time to pay off their debts whilst enjoying life and earning a wage, as opposed to being impoverished students. Daisy endured her job working for an airline based at the airport while Adam put his Media degree to no use whatsoever at the newspaper. Neither felt particularly fulfilled in their roles but their respective employment allowed them to rent a flat and have some fun. It was Adam who'd suggested they both invest in property after spotting an advertisement for new build apartments that were springing up all over the city. Without further ado and while one hundred percent mortgages weren't a fantasy, they'd both obtained a loan and bought an apartment each, next door, just like always. Adam lived in Daisy's and rented out his – an arrangement that worked well, for a while.

Their busy lives were interspersed with regular trips across the channel to see Daisy's parents, and at home in Manchester they made the most of city living and their group of friends, including some from uni who had remained solid since their university days.

The day before graduation everyone vowed to stay in touch and reunite once a year, something that despite the odd missing face due to work commitments and the like, they managed to honour. The person still responsible for rounding them up was Fliss, who also found time to lasso a rich lawyer, more or less straight after uni, and then made damn sure he never got away. The birth of her first unexpected child was preceded by a huge white wedding, well before a bump could spoil the fit of the gown.

During the lavish bash the old gang made the most of their salubrious surroundings, chuckling to themselves that Bridezilla had orchestrated the wedding of the year. Daisy attended mainly out of curiosity. Relieved at not being enlisted as a bridesmaid, she respected Fliss's blatant snub for what it was and found herself cheered immensely by the sight of poor Shalini, miserable as sin in her vile powder-puff dress.

Following her wedding bonanza, Fliss concentrated on home-building and motherhood, which for a while distracted her from shit-stirring, instead expanding her brood with regularity and ease. But she still clung on, like a cartoon animal whose fingertips strained on the edge of a skyscraper, and as much as she annoyed the hell out of Daisy and Adam, neither had the guts to stamp on her fingers so she'd let go.

So, all in all Daisy and Adam's lives were full and in his case having a female flatmate remained invaluable. Daisy could be passed off as his girlfriend whenever a colleague or someone at five-a-side or the gym started to show interest, a ruse that she was still happy to go along with. On other matters though, she was less than content.

Although Daisy would rather implode than admit it out loud, Adam knew she still pined after his brother. Ryan's insistence (or maybe it was Charlotte the Harlot) on a total state of transparency had broken Daisy's heart and abruptly curtailed their snatched liaisons. Holding a torch for Ryan hindered any chance of romance blossoming, secretly raising him up as a standard that couldn't be matched. It was a situation that continued to suit the selfish side of Adam while the other half wanted her to be happy, which for the most part (disastrous dates aside) she was.

Maybe it was because they'd perfected their symbiotic relationship, falling easily into a lifestyle that included each other, but not exclusively. For Adam, his mantra had remained ingrained: as long as Daisy was in his life he would ask for no more. As for Daisy, she had kept her promise to find a way and never ever abandon him, remaining Adam's camouflage, his invisible cloak, comfort blanket and safety net. And it wasn't entirely a one-way street because Daisy had long since accepted that Adam was her soul mate and even if she never found true love (increasingly likely), what they had was as close to perfect as you could get.

They sometimes joked that they were probably the happiest unmarried couple in the world, arguing about what they watched on telly, whose turn it was to take out the bins and choice of take away, and nothing Daisy tried could induce Adam to become a vegetarian *or* put the toilet seat down. They were rarely apart and the only ripple in an otherwise tranquil existence was caused by Adam when he visited his brother.

Since Charlotte had arrived on the scene, Ryan had been notable by his absence and in order to maintain their bond and spare Daisy's feelings, Adam would travel eastwards alone. Here, he suffered Chas – that name irritated her like hell – and respected his brother's relationship, which from an outsider's perspective seemed more and more like one of convenience, on both their parts. Following each trip to Norfolk Adam would report back in his own honest and forthright way, one Daisy described as being as subtle as a ton of bricks. He insisted it was only a matter of time before Ryan got tired of his mundane situation and then Chas would be history. Adam was utterly convinced that Ryan chose her to compliment his lifestyle, the same way he had chosen his car and a career – compartmentalising every aspect of his life.

Daisy always took Adam's pronouncements with a pinch of salt, rolling her eyes as she listened to Dr Freud psychoanalyse his brother. Deep down though, her heart hoped he was correct while her head told her to get a grip and not waste any more time on Ryan.

Apart from Charlotte the Harlot neither Adam nor Daisy had any reason to contemplate the future, and the present was a great place to be until one fateful Friday evening when Daisy bounded in from work, cheeks flushed, her eyes twinkling. Over a chippy tea she told Adam in great detail all about the cute guy she'd met at the wine bar – his name was Jamie and he'd asked her out. She was meeting him in town the very next day.

In that instant, just from her body language and the way her eyes shone, hands flapping away as she described how they met and what he said, Adam sensed a portent of doom settling above his head. It caused his heart to tense and their familiar equilibrium juddered. His Daisy had moved one step away, he actually felt it. As the vibrations in his brain sent out panicked signals and his face struggled to remain impassive, Adam saw life as he knew it tumbling away, falling out of balance and later, as he lay in bed and tried to quell his fears, they refused to be banished. Within a matter of weeks his prophecy was fulfilled and Adam had to face facts. He had failed and it was all over. His Daisy was in love and the annus horribilis had begun.

All too soon it became abundantly clear to those concerned that the flat-sharing arrangement was no longer viable and just as his premonition had insinuated, Adam and Daisy's perfect bubble was about to be popped. Jamie couldn't abide Adam, and vice versa. For Daisy's sake, Adam tried to get on with him, find some common ground or see through the shiny veneer of the man who was stealing the heart of his best girl. The gesture wasn't reciprocated in any way and soon Adam felt like a stranger in his own home, or Daisy's – a situation and fact that irked Jamie, something he made no secret of.

When in close proximity the atmosphere between them eventually became intolerable and despite Daisy's futile attempts to build a bridge, both she and Adam knew something had to give. They were in trouble and their precious bond was in danger of being damaged or broken forever.

Things finally came to a head after a tearful weekend during which Jamie was holed up in his own apartment after a blazing row about holiday plans. What had started out as a vague suggestion had erupted into a verbal attack on Adam after Daisy appeared hesitant and, according to Jamie, overly concerned about her pathetic and annoying lodger. Tradition dictated that every summer and Christmas, Daisy and Adam returned to France, so when Jamie suggested a romantic fortnight in the Algarve that July and Daisy didn't jump at the idea, stating that her parents would be disappointed not to see her *and* Adam would have to go alone, all hell broke loose.

Although Adam did point out to an inconsolable Daisy that perhaps Jamie was showing his true colours and she should take note of his short fuse, his words were falling on partially deaf ears and until she saw it for herself he was wasting his time. What saddened Adam the most was to hear Daisy sobbing and hiccupping that she couldn't choose and it was unfair of Jamie to expect her to cut her best friend out. Surely they could find an amicable solution where nobody was excluded.

One thing Adam did know for sure was that he couldn't remain in the apartment and as far as Jamie was concerned, even being next door would be too close for comfort, so maybe it was time for a complete change, to untie the knot that bound them together and ultimately, set Daisy free.

Just a few weeks later they met in their favourite tapas bar after work and here, without the aid of Dutch courage and wanting to remain in complete control of his feelings, Adam made a shock announcement. Taking a huge intake of breath he told Daisy he was leaving Manchester to start a new job working aboard a cruise ship. He had secured the position as a host on a luxury liner currently docked in Southampton but owing to the nature of his new career, he would be at sea for much of the year.

For a second Daisy was astounded, then began laughing hysterically, presuming it was some kind of joke, before bursting into floods of tears when she noticed Adam's dead-pan expression. Daisy was a very loud crier, much to the consternation of the other customers and Adam who had hoped that a neutral environment would avoid a scene. Despite fervent hand-patting and soothing shushing, Daisy was in pieces. The tears eventually dried up and quickly evolved into anger towards Jamie, who she now blamed for pushing Adam away. She was going to dump him immediately as there was no way he was getting away with this; she couldn't lose her best friend, it wasn't fair.

Knowing it was time to gain more of the moral high ground and in a genuine bid to soften the blow, Adam painted a wonderful picture of a new stage in their lives and by the time he'd finished, sort of believed it himself.

They had been inseparable for seven years and nothing and nobody could ever take that time away from them. Their love for each other was rock solid and that was the best foundation to move on from. The last thing he wanted was for Jamie to cause a permanent rift so before things got out of hand, it was time to take action and preserve their friendship. This could only be achieved by going away.

Adam insisted that he was looking forward to having an adventure, seeing the world and making new friends but obviously none would be as perfect or special as her. And he loved the sea. From the very first time he had taken the boat with her to France Adam had been drawn to the outside decks and would sit for ages staring towards the horizon, mesmerised by the waves. Daisy would complain that it was too cold and her hair got tangled in the wind so she'd leave him alone, lost in his thoughts while she took refuge in the cafe. His new job was perfect, combining his love of the sea and travelling to far-flung places and therefore she shouldn't worry.

Daisy was having none of it. They had chosen to remain in Manchester together and now he was abandoning her. And how would he manage without her for back-up? There would be randy guests and amorous colleagues to fend off, and Daisy pointed out that he wasn't a skinny student with a scruffy rock-star hairdo – not anymore. Adam had grown into a tall and very handsome man who attracted attention from both sexes and just the thought of him all dressed up in his ship uniform setting hearts a flutter brought on a panic attack.

"Daisy, stop it, right now. I have to do this, don't you see? It's time I stood on my own two feet and learned to look after myself. I've relied on you for too long and perhaps you need a bit of freedom to be yourself without me hanging about all the time. I swear on my life I will be in touch constantly and I'll visit, I promise. I can stay in a hotel or with Kiki and Carol, or maybe Tommy, I'll play it by ear. But I think you need some space, see if it's going to work with Jamie. I don't want to be the reason you guys split up and as much as I think he's a jerk, it's your life and I know you like him a lot so please, let's give it a go."

"I'm just so annoyed with Jamie. I don't feel like I can forgive him for pushing you away and I can't even imagine not having you around, I feel poorly just thinking about it. I actually think I'm going to vom all over the table! This is so unfair Adam, on both of us."

"Or maybe it's fate, or a test, so come on, cheer up. We've survived this long so a few months here and there aren't going to kill us. Our Ryan manages it so I'm sure two tough nuts like you and me will walk it." Adam was exhausted from the effort of persuasion but just when he was running out of steam, he spotted a shift in mood. "Was that a smile I saw or are you really going to throw up? I thought the days of holding your hair back were long gone." Adam was scraping the barrel so when he saw Daisy's shoulders relax and the twitch of her lips, he hoped he was getting through.

Daisy scowled. "It was a grimace not a smile! Oh Adam, I'm going to miss you so much. My head is scrambled and I could've done without you mentioning Ryan, or did you do that on purpose just to make me compare him to Jamie?"

"You got me...guilty as charged, but joking aside please keep your eye on things with Jamie. We obviously see two different people and while I accept that love is blind, I'm not. I don't want you making a huge mistake or getting hurt otherwise I might have to come back and sort him out...or maybe get our Ryan to do it for me." At this remark Adam had the decency to hold his hands up and silently admit he was stirring the pot, laughing as Daisy threw a cocktail stick at him.

"Right, that's enough! Bloody hell Adam, it's bad enough Jamie taking the huff over you, never mind him finding out I've still got the hots for your brother, that's all I need."

Adam clapped his hands in delight. "Ah, there it is at last. A confession!"

"Sod off, it was a slip of the tongue." Daisy looked away, avoiding eye contact, but Adam was on a roll.

"Yeah, right! Well, I've still not given up hope that one day he'll dump Chas and come back for you. And I'm heartened to hear you use the present tense, and no way was it a slip of the tongue, you can't kid a kidder!" Adam covered his face as Daisy flicked an olive and a slice of lemon in his direction, laughing as he begged for mercy.

"I've told you to stop mentioning Charlotte the Harlot so now, as punishment, you're buying me dinner. I'm starving so let's get a giant dish of paella to share and then we can make some plans. I'm not letting you go anywhere without swearing an oath in blood that you'll come back, like they do in films. We need to slice our thumbs and push them together so our blood merges, come on, don't be soft, I'll go first." Daisy picked up her knife and shuffled her chair closer to Adam, who pretended to faint then slump on the tabletop, so ignoring him she called over the waiter.

As she waited for Adam to recover from his pretend faint, Daisy gazed at the top of his head, wistfully remembering days when life was much simpler and not so bloody depressing, which was how she felt right now. His dark unruly curls had been tamed by a shortish haircut, and as usual his now broader shoulders were encased in the leather jacket that Ryan bought him, all those years ago. Pushing that name from her thoughts Daisy reached over and ruffled the hair of the beautiful man opposite, her beloved friend, whose heart was still as fragile as the day she met him.

She had to think of a way to protect Adam from afar, just in case his kindness or lack of guile was misinterpreted and he ended up being gossiped about or misunderstood. And mashed up amongst her sadness and worries over Adam was that familiar fluttering in her heart, a flickering flame that was ignited deep within her soul. It was impossible to ignore and only ever happened when she heard that name – Ryan.

Chapter 18

Bad Timing
Marham, Norfolk 2009

On 4 June 2009, six Tornado jets and three VC10 transport aircraft landed at RAF Marham to an emotional homecoming ceremony, and amongst the many young men and women who waited patiently as their troop carrier taxied off the runway, was Ryan. Operation Telic was over and along with his comrades eager to be reunited with their families, Ryan couldn't wait to see his brother who he knew would be impatiently watching the huge plane from inside the bunting-festooned hangar.

*

When he'd heard the news that they were pulling out early, Ryan's immediate thoughts were of home and passing the surprise information onto his brother and Daisy, moments before he checked himself, reminded that she was no longer part of their equation. It was a sobering thought that had a painful sting in its tale because Ryan wished now that he had listened to intuition, not been guided by his nether regions and selfish nature when he chose Charlotte over Daisy.

Ryan held his hands up to his huge mistake. And as much as it rankled at the time, he'd taken the snide remarks and teasing from his mates on the chin because all of what they said was true. Not only was Charlotte possessive, she was blatantly ambitious and it soon transpired that Ryan was included in her plans, fully expecting him to tread the same career path as she – one which led to a future together.

When Charlotte took umbrage to his resistance at meeting her parents, the ensuing epic tantrum didn't particularly distress him.

He'd already come to the conclusion that their work/life balance required far too much effort and was, as Dan had predicted, suffocating. It was her announcement mid-tour that she'd applied for a transfer to the south coast, closer to her family and friends, that caused a slight ripple in their relationship when it transpired that her plans included Ryan. And when he bluntly refused, all hell broke loose.

Owing to being stuck on a base within a base, protected by barbed wire fencing and heavily armed sentries, escape was tricky to say the least. He was caught up in a toxic relationship where it was Charlotte's way or the highway. Ryan chose the latter. Later, once Dan stopped laughing, he did suggest that letting her down gently might have been the easier option all round, perhaps pretending to mull over the proposition first.

That had been three weeks ago and during this period Ryan had plenty of alone time to ponder his mistakes, book a holiday to Greece with his mates and allow his mind to wander home, to Adam and Daisy. Yes, he had been bitten on the arse where Charlotte was concerned and definitely needed his own space for a while, but once he got back into the swing of things on the base in England, maybe he could get back on track with his personal life too.

Ryan's head was full of ideas as he packed his ops bag and cleared his room in Qatar. He was owed loads of leave and his bank account was extremely healthy so perhaps a winter holiday with Adam would be nice, his treat. And come to think of it, Daisy had promised him freedom and according to Adam she harboured no ill feelings so maybe they could all hang out together, in Manchester. Ryan enjoyed the contrast between the Norfolk countryside and city life and if he was lucky, given time, perhaps he could rekindle the flame with Daisy. It was worth a shot.

*

The lads agreed that those with wives and children should disembark first therefore Ryan was one of the last off the plane and as he made his way down the steps, scanned the crowd, looking for his brother. He spotted him immediately, right at the edge of the swarm of camouflaged bodies, a sea of desert khaki. Adam's tall frame allowed his long, wildly waving arms to be seen above the other bodies yet midst the euphoria, just for a second Ryan experienced a sense of disappointment at Daisy's absence, before brushing it away, waving back in a more understated kind of way.

By the time Ryan had descended the steps, Adam was within reach and the brothers were locked in a manly, back-thumping embrace, unashamed by their show of affection and relief. And as they made their way into the hangar, Ryan left the Middle East and Charlotte behind, buoyed by the warmth of Adam's company and hopeful of the future, and since a recent heart-to-heart, one in which he was determined to change his ways.

Dan was the person Ryan trusted most amongst his colleagues and someone he'd opened up to about his childhood. After listening to Ryan's tale, Dan gave him sound advice: to stop being scared of failure and live a little. Shit happened, life went on, and seeing as he'd survived the wrath of Charlotte he could survive anything. Not all women were like her *or* his mother and somewhere out there he'd find 'the one', he just had to choose wisely in future. Which is why after lonely nights in the block where he relived events of the past, comparing it to the successes of himself and Adam, Ryan drew up a new plan. He resolved to be less selfish and allow a hint of colour into his life. He'd had his fill of monotone so would attempt to deconstruct his barriers and take a chance, on Daisy if she would have him.

Life in Ryan's brave and imaginary new world didn't last long, just a few hours really, enough time to enjoy a quiet meal in the pub and for Adam to pluck up the courage to tell his travel weary brother all the latest news from Manchester. And while on the outside Ryan did his utmost not to look shocked or disturbed, inside he was stunned, right to the core.

Next, Adam explained the circumstances that led to his decision to strike out on his own. Ryan was left verging on despair, an alien emotion that left him swamped, his new-found resolve disappearing by the second into a muddy hole. While Adam attempted to put a positive spin on everything, Ryan was sucked deeper into a quagmire filled with anger towards Daisy for not preventing such a drastic situation and more or less betraying Adam for another man. This was sullied further by hate towards Jamie.

Nobody treated his brother like that and Ryan had to curb the desire to drive over to Manchester and teach the arsehole a lesson. And on top of that, the thing that caused Ryan's blood to boil, poisoning his heart with bitter frustration, was that Jamie had stolen Daisy from under their noses, just when he was about to make everything right and fulfil Adam's whimsical notion. Now, he was losing the two people he cared for most in the world – one to the sea and one to another man.

As he lay in bed that night, staring at the ceiling, listening to the snores of his sleeping brother, Ryan faced up to his mistake. He had left it all too late. There was no way he could alter the past, any of it. And despite everything, personal sacrifice, hard work, self-imposed rules in pursuit of a better life and living by his ridiculous code of conduct, he had made a mess of it. He couldn't control the future and had been a fool to think that it would wait for him to catch up, and even more arrogant to assume that Daisy would always be there for him.

So what now, what was left? This was the question that, despite burning eyeballs and drooping lids, refused to allow Ryan any sleep. Soon, Adam would be on the other side of the world; the tables had turned because now, Ryan was the one left waiting for his sibling to come home on leave. And worse, if the rumours were true, a new campaign was to be fought on another front, meaning more months away on operation making homecomings a logistical nightmare. Then to heap misery onto the prospect of their impending separation, the one person that linked them all together, who could be relied on to step into the breach and turn a crappy situation around and fill your world with light and love, had found someone else. The chain had been broken and it was all his fault.

Ryan bashed the pillow with his fist then turned on his side, desperate to get comfy, willing sleep to curtail his endless torment. Deep down he already knew the answer to his problems, it was obvious really. Dan had meant well with his advice but maybe Ryan's new leaf and outlook on life was merely wishful thinking, a fantasy. When it came down to it he was safer in the world he'd become accustomed to. All he had to do was revert to type, stick to his code and carry on regardless. Work was his saviour and the lads on the squadron a surrogate family so for now, it would have to do.

Pulling the duvet over his shoulder Ryan yawned, comforted slightly that he'd taken control and could see a way forward, the notion permitting some rest. Drifting into oblivion, Ryan accepted his fate – it was just a case of very bad timing and even if he did succumb to the creeping chill of loneliness, he would ignore it. He didn't care if his heart froze over. It numbed the pain and anaesthetised a brain that insisted on reminding him of another favourite Olive saying: you never know what you've got Ryan, not until it's gone.

Five years later

Chapter 19

A life on the ocean waves
Somewhere in the Caribbean, New Year's Eve 2014

Adam had been away from home *and* Daisy for four years, six months and eleven days precisely, and during that time he'd suffered severe homesickness, crippling bouts of depression, hideous seasickness, five doses of Delhi Belly and agonising yet self-inflicted sunburn. Add this to unwanted advances and regular infatuations from both sexes, including a handful of randy divorcees, three widows and a rather persistent widower. But in the end and despite frequent urges to abandon ship, he'd come out the other side a stronger and definitely wiser man.

New Year always made Adam slightly maudlin in a reflective type of way. Over the years he had spent many nights like this, celebrating under jet black skies set ablaze with fireworks amidst the sound of cheering revellers. And no matter how much Champagne flowed through his veins and despite the frivolity of his shipmates and passengers, Adam always experienced the sensation of being utterly alone. The lure of a campsite nestled in the Loire and a house that he knew without doubt would have a chimney billowing smoke, the tiles on the roof covered with glistening frost and inside, someone he still loved dearly and longed to be with, even after all these years.

Although he could look back and laugh about it now, it hadn't been easy and the separation from Daisy had almost killed him. He knew what it was to be one of the broken-hearted, dumped or worse, bereaved. That's exactly how Adam felt for much of his first eighteen months in his new job. He missed Ryan too but had become used to their separation, always filling the gaps between visits with letters and phone calls.

*

Once he left Manchester those gaps stretched, becoming wide chasms meaning that jolly postcards and information-packed emails had to suffice. But what he couldn't get used to and the merest thought of it made him rage inside, was being on the outside. Knowing that not only had Jamie taken his place in Daisy's heart, he'd infiltrated Pamela and Bill's home. It was sheer torture.

To make it worse, that bloody black dog had reared its ugly head and for a while snapped at his heels, waiting to pounce. Although he had never fully succumbed or admitted to its presence, Adam had endured many a battle with the hound and relied heavily on Daisy to pull him from its slathering jaws. While she often hinted that maybe he was suffering from a touch of depression, he would rather die than admit to what he saw as another failing, an accompaniment to his secret flaw. Keeping a lid on his inner turmoil was Adam's forte.

Over the years his thirst for knowledge on many subjects had led him to the Internet, which was a great source of information and at times, comfort. Here, not only had he discovered self-help sites and chatty forums where he could anonymously receive counselling and advice about his unwanted pet, Adam had also found others, just like him, those with a label that described their state of what he could only describe as 'in limbo'.

Still, whilst he festered, self-medicated, healed and grieved alone, thousands of miles away from his friends and family, Adam had kept his pulse on the goings on in Daisy's life and his source of vital information, the one person who could be relied upon to revel in any hint of misfortune and pass on every single nugget of gossip, was Fliss.

Daisy was constantly in touch of course – some form of communication passed between them on a more or less daily basis. However, due to the animosity that had built up between himself and Jamie not only were their communiqués kept secret, details of her own turbulent relationship were omitted from conversation wherever possible. That's where Fliss came in.

Her snippets were often second-hand and arrived at after she'd bored the pants off him with tales of suburbia and the joys of motherhood. The interesting stuff she passed on came via Shalini or Kiki and Carol. Daisy fastidiously steered clear of Fliss whenever possible, but on those occasions where their group of friends gathered for celebrations, Adam was provided with not just a running commentary but photographic evidence as well.

He'd sighed over a crowd scene at a summer garden party where Daisy was amongst the guests, looking so miserable and lost – was it his imagination or wishful thinking? Or the one of Jamie, caught in the background, sitting alone at a large table; while everyone danced the night away, he was on his phone and minding the handbags. And a group photo where Adam focused on the couple just to the right. One was wearing a tense expression, the other a fake smile, immortalising a snapshot of the truth or a whiff of discord. Maybe he zoomed in and read too much into what he saw, yet Adam's instinct told him he was on the money.

He didn't directly ask Fliss to be his spy, just counted on the fact she'd be unable to resist the temptation to not only dish the dirt, but rub his nose in playing second fiddle to Jamie. Still, Adam embraced the bitch in Fliss through gritted teeth, rising above the undercurrent of her jealous and cruel nature knowing it was merely a means to an end. He had to be ready and waiting if and when Daisy's relationship faltered and according to the evidence, it was inevitable.

By all accounts there had been two occasions when Daisy left Jamie following bouts of what could only be described as unreasonable behaviour. It seemed he was unpredictable and volatile, more so when fuelled by alcohol. Then there was their 'no show' for the christening of Fliss's baby boy. Daisy had mentioned the gift and new dress she'd bought for the event, so what happened there? Then months later at Jimmy's birthday party, Jamie left early and alone after descending into a huge strop because Daisy wasn't paying him enough attention. The consensus of opinion amongst their friends denounced Jamie as a bad apple, controlling and becoming increasingly prone to petulant behaviour and what's more, despite her hopes, Daisy was kidding herself if she thought he would ever propose.

It therefore came as a walloping great slap to Adam's smug assumptions when he heard that Jamie had in fact bent the knee, but following an email from Fliss his rose pink vision of the perfect moment was drained of colour once she gleefully divulged the circumstances of said proposal. It seemed that Daisy had suspected Jamie of cheating and after a huge confrontation that led to another night in Shalini's spare room, along with threats never to return, Jamie talked Daisy round and just to prove her and his critics wrong, proposed.

On hearing the news Adam suffered such despair that he considered asking for compassionate leave, quite prepared to invent some dreadful event that required his presence at home. Contrary to his initial feelings, he soon came round to thinking that being trapped inside a huge steel tank that floated on an endless ocean had its benefits because due to confinement and location, he was forced to contemplate the situation sensibly.

Calm eventually descended but not before he'd exhausted his vocabulary of expletives and insults during long, irate and threatening messages to Jamie, and in contrast, sincere, pleading ones to Daisy. He wisely deleted them all when it slowly dawned that this was precisely the reason he had left home in the first place – to preserve their friendship and allow Daisy to make her own mind up about Jamie. And maybe, given a bit more time she would see him for what he was, so why interfere now?

He wasn't prepared to be fake though, respecting her too much to pretend he was pleased at her choice of husband-to-be and he wasn't a hypocrite either (spying on Daisy via her worst enemy didn't count, it was for the common good). Instead, he sent a jokey, light-hearted message, minimal in its content and more or less bare of joy and glad tidings. Adam told Daisy he was happy that she was happy, wished her well for her future of wedded drudgery and regardless of her marital status, would always be there for his best girl, no matter what.

Since then, Daisy's life back in Manchester and his aboard the Pacific Princess had carried on regardless. While the best girl struggled through a life devoted to appeasing a narcissist, the best boy spent much of his avoiding the unwanted attentions of guests and crew members alike. He sometimes imagined his life aboard ship as a sped-up scene from a Carry On film, dressed in his smart white uniform being chased around the decks by a hoard of randy pensioners and sex-starved divorcees.

On a more serious note, whilst the bad days were behind him and on the whole life was good, it had been difficult at first. Adam hadn't relished the transitional period after he left Manchester. His safety blanket was thousands of miles away and he had to learn to live without Daisy's protective shield. Despite her physical absence she was still there in spirit, perhaps a figment of their combined imagination and a continuation of the falsehood they had built Adam's life upon and around. To perpetuate the lie that had so far prevented any undue attention with regards to Adam's sexuality, or lack of it, Daisy had collated an album of photographs, which to the onlooker gave the impression of two young people very much in love.

*

She had presented it just moments before he left Manchester, forbidding him to open it in her presence, admitting that to look upon the contents just one more time would kill her all over again. After spending a whole morning at the printers followed by an afternoon of nausea- inducing weeping and wailing, Daisy had put together a visual fantasy, a photographic smokescreen that would convince anyone that Adam was in a long-term relationship with his very understanding girlfriend back home. His cover story was their desire to buy a home of their own, which required self-sacrifice to save for a deposit, thus the need for Adam's long periods apart from his beloved Daisy.

When Adam finally plucked up the courage to open the album he too cried for hours over the photographs inside. Image upon image of a young couple, lazing by the beach, dining with the in-laws-to-be, opening Christmas presents by the fire, lost in a maze at Chatsworth, covered in mud at Glastonbury, pink and blue birthday cakes, laughing faces attached to bodies locked in an embrace.

Obviously there was a huge chunk of their story missing; their younger years, crazy carefree uni days were omitted so it would appear they had met and fallen in love later – Adam was free to invent any scenario he wished. But what made him cry the hardest was the missing chunk at the end – the final part of their story. Because of Jamie there would be no more photos like this, no continuation album. Adam was stranded on the edge of everything, the awkward subject in a conversation, the unwelcome guest at the wedding, the cuckoo in the nest. That middle section of his life, bound by faux leather to form a solid mass of memories, only served to remind him of his present circumstances; he was disjointed, dislocated and defunct.

Amidst his desolation and panic Adam had heard the soft padding of paws, creeping along the corridor, waiting patiently outside his door. Adept at beating off the hound, Adam clung on to the notion that this was just Daisy trying to protect him from afar, a token of her love, not a subtle hint that the final page in the album was the end of them – time to move on.

No, it couldn't be over, he wouldn't let it, but Adam had no idea how to alter the course of their destiny, which now seemed to be precarious in the least. They say that worry is a natural way for the brain to process information and once this potentially self-destructive period is over, a glimmer of hope is admitted, lifting your spirits. And it was true.

From the dying embers of his ravaged heart, Adam remembered something. Daisy had made him a promise and if he knew one thing for certain, it was that she would never break it. They had found a way before so all he had to do was wait patiently and pray that Jamie would mess up. And there was something else, or someone, who forced him to splash water on his face before stepping outside his cabin to start another shift, and that was Ryan.

*

During their reunion weekend in Norfolk after Ryan returned from Iraq, Adam had unveiled his plans for a new life on the ocean waves. At first Ryan was dubious and slightly incredulous and took some convincing of Adam's desire to go boldly where nobody ever expected him to go. But once he realised that his brother was serious, Ryan had launched a spiteful attack on Daisy – accusing her of casting Adam aside in favour of the first bloke that came along – for using him like a puppet and playing with his emotions. Ryan's opinion of Daisy worsened with each eventuality, insisting she should've put Jamie in his place and stood by Adam, not waved him off at the train station before running back to lover boy.

To disprove Ryan's point, Adam related the farewell scene, which was hideously distressing because Daisy had to be literally prised from his body otherwise he would've missed the train. In Adam's opinion this and the fact that Daisy had holed up with Shalini for the whole weekend, completely inconsolable and riddled with self-loathing and regret, proved Ryan wrong. But Adam didn't leave it there. He couldn't allow Daisy to take the blame or incur the wrath of his irate and spurned brother. While most troubles could be laid at the feet of Jamie, Adam apportioned some of the blame to Ryan who he denounced as selfish and borderline cold-hearted, along with being a fool for letting Daisy slip through his fingers and thus leaving all of them wide open to misery.

To Adam's surprise, Ryan accepted the uncharacteristic outburst and accurate indictment, admitting he had made a complete hash of things. But they couldn't change the past and ultimately both were left with only one option in a Daisy-less world – they had to move on.

*

And this is exactly what they had done. One brother continued on the path he most enjoyed, that of a military and single life, and ever since their heart-to-heart had completed numerous overseas tours and kept women at arm's length. Ryan had been posted to Italy when the Arab spring took hold and the crisis in Libya called for an international response, followed by more tours of the Middle East, his current temporary home being Kandahar Airfield in Afghanistan.

Adam immersed himself in his life of masquerade, making the most of work and having fun. When he had leave everyone believed he was heading to Manchester and his beloved Daisy when in truth his compass pointed in the direction of France. It was clear that neither Bill nor Pamela were enamoured by Jamie but felt duty-bound to respect their daughter's choice of partner, and whilst they supported Daisy from afar, remained loyal and devoted to Adam.

On rare occasions, Adam took courage in both hands and returned to Manchester where he snatched precious moments alone with Daisy, away from the watchful, petulant stare of Jamie who still resented his presence even when camouflaged amongst their friends. Whilst the atmosphere was uncomfortable and restrictive, both Daisy and Adam accepted that taking the path of least resistance was the only way to preserve their friendship, no matter how much it rankled.

Adam's patience and vigilance finally paid off when, after a particularly eventful afternoon compèring the talent show, he returned to his room and spotted the numerous texts and missed calls from Daisy. To his eternal shame, as he tapped the screen and called her back, Adam prayed she wasn't going to announce happy news, like an impending wedding or birth.

When he did discover the reason for her call, despite hearing the words he'd so fervently wished for, Adam was awash with guilt because at the other end of the line, thousands of miles away and out of reach, his best girl forever was in pieces.

Chapter 20

Adam

A glimmer of hope

To Adam's own surprise, once he'd heard of Daisy's cruel uncoupling and unhappy predicament, his first instinct wasn't to hand in his notice and follow her to France – it was to stay put and see how things unfolded, biding his time from afar. Once Daisy was in the care of Pamela and Bill she would be fine. It had occurred to him there was always the possibility that history could repeat itself so he wasn't going to risk everything, not yet anyway. Adam was also aware that if he ran to Daisy's aid or went the whole hog and relocated again, Ryan would go spare and accuse him of being a fool for traipsing after her.

Instead, Adam set himself a twelve-month target, during which time he would continue to support Daisy as best he could without burning his own bridges. Maybe she'd get bored of the country life and return to Manchester once her wounds had healed, and although he did miss city life and his friends, he had no desire to head north.

Adam had grown accustomed to his job and shipmates and the lifestyle suited him. He was at the centre of the all the fun aboard a cruise ship, which docked at some of the most beautiful places on earth. It always seemed to be sunny, he ate well, got paid for socialising and if the fancy took him, harmless flirting with the wealthy guests who tipped well. He had seen sights he'd only dreamed of (in the architectural and scenic sense), although there had been a few incidents on-board involving naked body parts of amorous passengers that he would never unsee. He'd also met some wonderful people amongst the hundreds of travellers and made new and rather brilliant friends.

His partner in crime and closest friend aboard the Pacific Princess was his co-host Allison and together they spent many a happy hour being just that, along with earning their wage organising activities, receptions, surprise birthday parties, weddings and once, a funeral. There was a new challenge every day and although some passengers could be demanding and relentless, they had so much fun. Allison was the only person with whom he had contemplated sharing his secret, yet just the thought sent shivers of cold dread through his body, horrified by the thought that she might not understand or accidentally betray his confidence. It was easily done in a moment of inebriation and he couldn't take the risk. Another reason he kept his own counsel was that to Adam, sharing with Allison was tantamount to betraying Daisy. It was their secret, an intrinsic link and although he wasn't superstitious, Adam wasn't prepared to jinx it.

Everyone believed his story about his beautiful and patient girlfriend in Manchester so why tempt fate? Even Allison joked that he was never off the phone and would wear his fingers to the bone from texting. The photos of them on his cabin wall merely added to the illusion. Over time, Adam had built himself a reputation on-board for being one of the lads, game for a laugh with a great sense of humour to boot. He was also someone his female friends could confide in or ask advice, as could his gay colleagues who found him approachable and understanding.

Allison was fascinated by Adam, describing him as a vibrant technicolour social butterfly, or a chameleon. Someone who hovered between sexes, a superhuman creature who was absorbed into the life or mind of whoever he chose to befriend. He was considerate and patient with their more elderly passengers, kind in the extreme, yet retained the ability to stare down or rise above the most obnoxious of guests. Adam adeptly spotted the lone traveller who had taken courage in both hands to embark on a solo cruise but now, faltered at the edge of the dining room, or was too shy to join in the quiz. Once taken under Adam's wing they would thrive, being introduced and guided for the duration of their stay.

One of his most endearing metamorphoses occurred when he was around children. Adam was a natural in the company of the little ones, making them laugh hysterically or comforting them if they were sad, wiping away tears and, with a box of face paints, could literally place a smile on all of their faces. One of Allison's frequent comments, meant kindly and said in praise, was how lucky Daisy was to have Adam in her life and what a wonderful father he would make one day. And while Adam always responded with a roll of the eyes or a joke about shackles and chains, inside, her words stung like hell.

To fend off any hint of gloom or homesickness Adam simply focused on the lighter aspects of life at sea and related many a hilarious and peculiar tale during his letters and phone calls home. When Daisy's first Christmas without Jamie arrived, Adam called in favours and wangled leave, turning up in person just days before, much to the joy of everyone. It was like a second homecoming; first their daughter had unexpectedly returned to the fold and then, even for a short time, their adopted son.

Whenever Adam thought back to that Christmas visit he was gripped by overwhelming and conflicting emotions because it was the last time he had seen Bill alive. Shortly after, three months in fact, Adam's mate and mentor, driving instructor and confidant, the dad he'd wished for passed away and was gone from all their lives.

Adam wished he'd seen the signs, read more into the words he'd shared with Bill while he searched for a special bottle of wine in the depths of his dimly lit cave. It was an unexpected heart-to-heart that took place in his cave, well away from the ears of Pam and Daisy.

"I'm glad you came back son…it's been a real tonic having you both under the same roof, now that bloody arsehole Jamie has finally done us all a favour and buggered off. I know the whole business upset our Daisy but I think it was for the best, don't you?" Bill was wiping dust off labels, squinting as he searched for a vintage bottle of red that Pamela insisted they'd opened years ago.

Adam was picking a cobweb out of his hair. "Yeah, if I'm honest I think it was. Not that Daisy would see it like that but she's getting there. I think she's doing well to be fair and told me she's looking forward to the new season. I just wish I could be a bit more help. I'll chop some more wood before I leave next week, and if there's anything else you need just say and I'll get cracking." Adam moved a cardboard box that was full of corks and stacked it on top of a similar one containing empty bottles. "Bill, have you got any idea at all where this wine is? It could be anywhere. You've not exactly got the best system going here. I bet Pam's right and you have opened it." Adam was now checking the higher shelves while Bill did the lower ones.

"Well there is something you could do for me now you mention it, but its got nowt to do with logs…it's more of a promise. I need you to do me a little favour." Bill kept his eyes on the bottles while Adam stopped, resting against the wooden framework of the racks.

"Sure, ask away, as long as it's not going to get me in lumber with Pam. She's already told me off for online betting – I knew that horse had three legs but you wouldn't listen and now we're both in the dog house." Adam continued with his task, determined to be the winner in the treasure hunt.

Bill tutted. "Bloody hell, it was only a fiver! You'd think I'd gambled our life savings the way she goes on, so next time, be a bit more discreet – you can be right gormless sometimes. I want to put a tenner on the football tomorrow so keep out of her way otherwise she'll hide my card and then we'll have to use yours."

Adam laughed at the put down and the idea of Bill being punished. "You are so scared of Pam, you big girl! Anyway, you still haven't told me about this favour."

"Oh that, yes, well I want you to promise that if anything happens to me, you know when I peg it, that you'll look after Pam and Daisy for me, keep an eye on them like, and make sure they don't struggle with the site. They'll be okay for money. I've sorted all that but this place needs a man about and I hope I can rely on you. It will give me peace of mind." Bill continued in his task but Adam was frozen to the spot, horrified that Bill would even mention death and leaving them.

"Hey mate, don't be saying stuff like that. You're not going anywhere and it's Christmas so you're not allowed to talk about depressing things, this is supposed to be a happy time." Adam was grasping at something positive to say, desperate to change the subject but Bill wasn't having any of it and turned to face him, wiping dusty hands on his best trousers as he spoke.

"Aye lad, I know it's a bit maudlin but now and then these things need saying and I'd rather get it off my chest. I was going to drop you a line but you saved me a stamp and the bother by turning up. So what do you say, can I leave you in charge? You're the next best thing to a son and I doubt I'll see any grandkids so I'm passing the buck to you. Just keep an eye on them both, that's all I ask." Bill held Adam's gaze, trying to ignore the startled look in the lad's eyes.

Adam's reply came from the heart. "Yes, of course you can. I won't let you down, I promise…but I'm not ready to take over yet or cut that top bloody field by myself so don't go anywhere for a while, okay?" Adam was freaked out by Bill's random request, and not only that, the dim light bulb was accentuating shadows under his eyes, highlighting folds of skin that hung looser on his once full and ruddy face. He hadn't noticed before.

Having said his piece and in receipt of a promise Bill turned away and resumed his search, concentrating on the row of wine before him as he replied to Adam's own request.

"I'll do my best son…I'll do my best, ah, here it is, I knew we hadn't opened it, come on, let's get back and show Nelly Know-All up there that I'm right for once. And can you grab that box? There's some bits and bobs I've been meaning to sort out, just stick it in the cupboard under stairs while she's not looking." Bill was already making his way up the wooden stairs as Adam attempted to pull himself together, heaving the cardboard box upwards before following his friend, eager to get out of the gloom and into the light.

Adam left before New Year. It was a busy time aboard ship yet his heart was heavy as he said his farewells. In his rucksack were treasures, given to him by Bill the previous evening after one of his notorious short and sweet speeches, followed by a firm pat on the back and a clearing of his hoarse throat.

"Here you are lad, I want you to have these. I know you're fond of old stuff so I thought you might like some of my relics for your collection, anything you don't want just cob 'em in the bin. I won't mind." Bill held out a scrunched up carrier bag, which Adam took, untying the handles, a curious expression on his face.

The contents were a haphazard array of mementos from Bill's past: a pair of brown, leather motorbike gloves, and wrapped in kitchen roll was a commemorative china mug from King George's Coronation, faded and worn but in perfect condition, along with a rather racy set of black and white playing cards from the fifties, the topless ladies inside deserving of another quick peek and a cheeky wink from Bill. There was his grandad's silver pocket watch, which needed repairing, an envelope containing paper money, defunct notes in various denominations from all over the world and finally, a tin can containing postcards of the Beatles, dog-eared black and white images of the Fab Four. Bill said he collected them with his Esso petrol stamps and even though they weren't worth much he knew Adam loved the group as much as he did.

Adam couldn't speak as he held the treasures in his hands; to him, they were more than souvenirs, these were heirlooms, and Bill had passed them to him. There was one final keepsake reserved for Ryan, again wrapped in protective kitchen roll: a campaign flag from Suez and a half-pint Coronation tankard with ER painted on the glass.

"Will you give this to your Ryan? I think he'll like it seeing as he swore to protect Queen and country. I'd have given it to him myself but it looks like him and our Daisy have had some kind of falling out so I'll leave it with you." Bill looked rather pleased that his bequests had such an effect on Adam, but then again he knew he'd appreciate them and why.

Taking a breath, Adam pulled himself together and began to replace each object carefully inside the bag. "He'll be made up, thanks Bill. You don't know how much it means that you've given us these. I'll treasure them forever and so will our Ryan. I'll leave them in my room here if that's okay, with all my other stuff? I don't want to lose anything so I'll put them with my gran's jewellery, they'll be safer here."

"Whatever you think's best, son. And you know you'll always have a place with us. This is your home now, just remember that." Bill drew the conversation to a close, wandering off towards the kitchen in search of Pam and his dinner.

And still Adam didn't see the truth or hear what Bill was trying to say, or did he? Maybe he'd just blocked it out, forbidding the underlying message to enter his brain, refusing to believe that Bill was saying goodbye. It would be something that haunted Adam, the lost opportunity to comfort or reassure a dying man. Maybe there were other things he'd wanted to say. What if he was scared and needed a confidant? He could've taken compassionate leave and been there at the end, supported Daisy and Pam, or held Bill's hand. Anything rather than wearing blinkers and ear protectors, taking the coward's way out.

Bill's death left everyone in shock, even Ryan who for once proved he did have a heart and returned to France for the funeral. Whilst the whole affair was deeply distressing, one good thing came out of it: Daisy and Ryan were reunited if only for a short time, during which they managed to patch things up. Amidst such sorrow it was good to hear them laugh and tease one another about their unfortunate choice of partners and bad timing, even the 'Dear Daisy' letter and jokey promises of revenge for breaking her heart.

But time as always was against them and all too soon, before the flame could be truly reignited, Ryan waved goodbye once again. Brief as it was, the interlude provided Adam with a hint of hope and a platform on which to rebuild.

Back on-board, Adam's emails to Daisy and Ryan were more or less duplicated when relating anecdotes of everyday life – copy and paste was invaluable – but once the funny stuff was over he concentrated on them separately, showing interest in their lives while digging for information.

Apparently Ryan's new philosophy was to live each day as though it was his last, look forward not back and whilst he assured Adam that he was happy to be friends with Daisy, he had no intention of pursuing a relationship with her or anyone. Maybe the photos Ryan posted on Facebook of him and pretty young women were all part of his arsenal, weapons to punish Daisy for meeting Jamie at the wrong time. Whatever it was, Adam did his best to pave a way, never giving up on his dream, the master plan.

Daisy in the meantime focused on Pamela and the campsite, full of ideas and busy as a bee on speed, determined not to let her dad down or be made a fool of by a man, ever again. Her letters were full of news from the village, her old friends and the goings on at Campanule, amusing holiday anecdotes, along with gentle hints that the place wasn't the same without Adam by her side.

With each message, phone call and month that passed, Adam felt his resolve weakening and the pull of the beautiful countryside and his best girl became harder to resist. There had been no serious relationships, not even a hint, apart from the time Cassandre enrolled Daisy on a dating website, which lasted all of two weeks. And Adam was aware of something else, a very loud ticking clock, but not the one that Daisy frequently referred to in her jokes about turning into an old maid, the spinster of the village. It was the one in his head that caused him the most anxiety and lately, a clanging alarm bell had started to ring.

Ever since Bill had died, Adam had glimpsed that black dog, lingering on the perimeter, his imaginary foe waiting to pounce. Resorting to self-help, he would open his drawer, the one that amongst other talismans held the first scarf that Pam had knitted him and Bill's leather gloves. When he placed the soft wool against his face, inhaling the hint of wood smoke that lingered amongst the fibres, it told of hours by the fire in a room he knew so well, Pam's needles clicking away. And when he slipped his hand inside the gloves that Bill had worn, skin and sweat impregnated into the leather, the vibrations of a younger man, speeding along on his motorbike and racing towards his future, seeped into Adam's pores.

Taking stock of his own life, Adam compared it to the full and productive one that Bill had lived, a man who had clung on, desperate not to leave his loved ones behind, desiring just one thing – more time. This was something that Adam presumed he had plenty of and whilst he hadn't squandered any of it, was increasingly aware of his own mortality, and that bloody ticking clock.

And so it was that when the novelty of a life on the ocean waves began to feel like toil and the ports of call became too familiar – sleeping all day rather than exploring – and the voices of demanding passengers began to grate and the walls of his cabin seemed to be closing in, Adam knew it was time to jump ship.

He had given Ryan every chance to change his ways, Lord knows he'd tried to counsel, hint and cajole, yet his brother seemed hell bent on punishing himself for everyone else's mistakes, so Adam gave up. As for Daisy, he'd allowed her plenty of rope, even though he'd kept hold of the end, but she'd shown no signs of tying herself permanently to another man and had more or less given up on any dreams of personal happiness. And whilst he'd thrown in the towel where Ryan was concerned, he wasn't going to do the same with Daisy.

Gradually and with caution, Adam altered his perspective on the future, drawing on lessons from the past and now, in possession of a wiser head and braver heart, had decided the time was right. After fulfilling what remained of his contract he would hand in his notice, put his Manchester affairs in order and then, the rest was up to Daisy.

*

Regarding his reflection in the mirror, Adam straightened his tie and brushed down his uniform before heading up on deck.

Signal permitting he would ring Daisy and then join in with the celebrations on-board, bidding goodbye to an old year and life. This was the last time he would see in the New Year with a wistful heart because the one that beat inside his chest was now giddy with anticipation. He was in possession of a carefully rewritten blueprint, a virtual map and right at the centre, the point at which all roads met, was drawn a heart. Inside, written in bold were two names: Daisy and Adam.

Chapter 21

France, New Year's Eve 2015

Daisy absolutely hated 31 December, dreaded it in fact. There was nothing joyous or uplifting about heralding another year or saying goodbye to the old one. As far as she was concerned it was just another day spent struggling to blot out the past and while she had no desire to erase the good things life had bestowed, tainted memories still hurtled around her head. To even contemplate the future seemed futile and foolhardy, even on a night like this.

Outside the Atlantic wind was howling, rampaging across the Loire countryside and bringing with it the sheets of pounding rain whipped up from the sea. Daisy listened as twigs

clattered against the windows and onto the roof, knowing that in the morning the campsite would be strewn with fallen branches and a full day of clearing up was on the cards. As the fire roared and the logs crackled, Daisy pulled the blanket further over her shoulders and allowed the flames to occupy her eyes. Her ears were already busy, listening out for falling slates or creaking floorboards.

Upstairs, Pamela was sleeping, or at least Daisy hoped she was because the notion of her mum crying into her pillow was too much to bear. This was the second New Year without her dad and Daisy was resigned to the fact that his loss wasn't something they would ever get over. Those who had already experienced bereavement assured Daisy that given time it would get easier. How she longed for that day to arrive, for some respite from the pain she felt inside. Of course her mother was no stranger to loss and had survived the death of her own parents so Daisy had proof that it was possible. And compared to those dreadful days right after Bill died, they were definitely making progress.

She'd heard all the well-meant platitudes – life goes on, Bill would want you to be happy, continue what he started, make him proud, don't give up, your mum needs you to be strong –and although she'd tried to act on every single one, during endless nights like these it all seemed too much, just impossible. Yet despite their grief Daisy thought that she and her mum had done bloody well to keep going and not cave in. How they'd opened the site at the beginning of the new season was beyond her. Bill's death was still raw, an open wound, but somehow they managed to sound breezy and business-like, taking bookings over the phone or smiling at the guests when they checked in.

All of it was made more possible by their loyal team and wonderful friends who'd rallied round, and when he could get away, Adam pitched in too. He remained virtually by her side, his constant texts were a lifeline, his voice a sedative and to see his face on Skype was the equivalent to a triple gin and tonic.

There could be no good thing to come out of her father's death, of that Daisy was sure; however, the thawing of Ryan's cold and distant attitude towards her brought relief if nothing else and amidst such misery, his support at the funeral was appreciated.

*

She didn't expect him to come and neither had she asked yet it felt right, to have him stand with them in church, the four of them at the front, a family unit minus one. There had been no time or inclination to talk of personal matters and Daisy suspected that Ryan wouldn't encourage a deep and meaningful discussion about their failed relationships, or welcome an opportunity to rekindle theirs either. Instead they joked and brushed off the past – a comedic reprieve was easier than facing their mistakes seriously.

Ryan had gone through the motions, saying and doing all the right things but Daisy felt he had closed himself off, an emotional shut down. Maybe his attendance was merely the right thing to do, in return for her contribution to Olive's funeral all those years ago. There was something though, she could feel it, see it in those dark, brooding eyes that he thought were adept at hiding his soul. His presence still filled up the room and the touch of his skin as they washed and dried the dishes opened up a window to the past, a brief flicker of passion, and Daisy wanted to drown in that moment. It was the antidote to pain, anaesthetic to dull her weeping, painful heart.

Before he left, Adam gave Ryan the gift that Bill had entrusted to him. Daisy was there when he opened it and on seeing his reaction, the tremble of his lips and eyes that swam with tears, she gained a moment's worth of knowledge, a glimpse inside his soul and proof that Ryan was human after all. During their farewell hug as his arms wrapped around her body, Daisy closed her eyes and was transported back to the day they first met. He was still that same young man, she knew it. Somewhere deep inside was the Ryan she used to know; all she had to do was find him again.

At least they had been able to resume their long-distance correspondence, tentatively at first via a 'thank you' text message and then friendship on Facebook, which with hindsight may have been a mistake. These days, Daisy had little of interest to post about. Ryan on the other hand seemed to be enjoying his single life and going by the odd photo here and there, the company of very pretty women. As much as Daisy had tried to adopt 'friend mode' by liking his posts then adding a jokey comment underneath, just seeing his face or reading his name on her news feed was enough to instigate a violent battle between her heart and her head.

In her low moments she had lain in bed, writing an imaginary letter to Ryan, baring her soul, giving him one last chance and asking him to reciprocate, laying down workable terms for a mutually beneficial relationship, prepared to renew her promise not to tie him down or vow devotion. When shafts of morning light cascaded through her bedroom window, a new day bringing clarity to a rested brain, she would berate herself for being pathetic and lacking in pride, reminding herself of the cruel lesson she had learned from Jamie and to be wary of giving her heart once again.

But what Daisy didn't admit, believing that her subconscious mind could keep secrets from its cerebral and more sensible cortex, was that her heart had been lost to Ryan long ago. And no matter how hard she tried, she just couldn't get it back.

*

Daisy checked her watch. Another hour to go then she could try to sleep but not before she'd heard from Adam who, despite being off the coast of Jamaica and six hours behind, had promised to ring her at midnight. Daisy needed to hear his voice so badly and was glad she'd already had a good cry. Every single tear had been shed making it easier to convince him she was doing okay. Breaking down would only stress him out.

It was her own fault, a clear cut case of rubbing salt into wounds by spending hours looking through photo albums and flicking across images on her phone, tormenting herself really. Trawling through the past had given her nothing but pain yet she still insisted on doing so. It made the future seem bleak, without the three men who had made the world a better place to be – her dad, Ryan and Adam. Those days had been just perfect, in whatever combination – all of them together at the campsite or the moments they'd spent separately, magical times.

Inés and Cassandre would be furious if they knew she'd been wallowing again, especially after they had invited her out for the evening to prevent just that. Both insisted that Pamela would be fine and wanted her to have fun, not sit sobbing into her hanky. Her friends had been so wonderful, opening their arms when a hug was required and their homes when Daisy was in need of company and the distraction of noisy families. But it was a no-win situation because amidst their solace, seeing her friends settled and secure with a family around their feet served only to remind Daisy that time was running out. Which was why, once her prolonged period of mourning appeared to be coming to an end and aware of Daisy's 'ticking clock syndrome', Cassandre and Inès set about remedying the situation. Needless to say, it didn't go well.

*

They began by attempting to dredge up eligible men from what could only be described as meagre pickings then gave up after admitting that the countryside wasn't abundant with singletons, none that Daisy would fancy, anyway. Next, Inès signed her up for Internet dating, which if nothing else provided them with the most fun they'd had in ages, howling with laughter at Daisy's computer-generated pairings, none of whom she intended corresponding with, let alone meeting. Verging on desperation (an emotion that was also beginning to resonate with Daisy) they wore her down and she agreed to a date with the best of the bunch, a recently divorced university lecturer who, on paper, seemed interesting and harmless enough.

Precisely forty-five minutes after she arrived at the wine bar, Daisy was back at home, hiding under her duvet and in a foul mood. When the elderly, suited gentleman with a slight limp approached her table she presumed he would continue to the vacant one adjacent, until he stretched out his hand to introduce himself. Once the shock wave receded, draining the colour from Daisy's face, it was quickly replaced by a tsunami of rage and what she could only describe as shame that her life had descended to this – devoid of alternatives, she had driven for miles to meet a stranger. The image caused tears to prick her eyes. And that he had the audacity to saunter up to her table, nonchalant in his belief that she wouldn't notice or comment on his deception irked her greatly and a sense of entrapment unleashed the devil in her.

At least twenty years older than the photo on the website, the grey-haired, slightly tatty-looking faker before her definitely wasn't the man she'd been cajoled into meeting. Before he even had time to begin what Daisy suspected would be a frequently used monologue, she was on her feet, handbag slung over her arm, and after telling him and the whole room what she thought about deceitful old men who lured young women on dates, she flounced off, her cheeks burning as she stomped onto the pavement and towards her car.

After Daisy reported said pervy fibber to the dating site, she summarily deleted her account then rang her interfering friends and related her embarrassing version of events. Despite Daisy's indignant anger, neither took her insistence that they refrain from matchmaking seriously whilst their hysterical laughter could be heard in the next village. And to prove a point, in the months that followed, at supposedly casual dinners or impromptu apéros, Daisy found herself seated next to a variety of eager yet unsuitable men where she could only sigh, accepting that rather than desist, her friends would persist.

It was during an al fresco dinner on a warmish spring evening that she was caught off guard when a good-looking, fair-haired latecomer appeared in the garden and was hastily introduced as Denis. Of all the ineligible men of late, this one seemed okay. He was an electrician (potentially handy around the campsite), had never been married (baggage-free) and had his own home on the outskirts of Rennes (not in need of lodgings).

Looks-wise he was shortish but not so much she'd suffer a stiff neck, and Daisy surmised he might be rather vain due to him repeatedly fiddling with his groomed hair, but at least he paid attention to personal hygiene going by the haze of aftershave that enveloped him.

Denis was attentive, genuinely interested in Daisy's job, making suitably sad faces in all the right places and eventually, much to the delight of her watchful and smug friends, they arranged a date. He was going to pick her up at seven and take her to dinner at the Italian restaurant in town but by eight thirty the following Saturday, Daisy had entered the hallowed halls of the 'stood up'.

Ripping out the pins that held her curly hairdo in place she kicked off her shoes in temper, unzipping her new dress as she stomped up the stairs, cursing men and her pathetic taste in them. Pamela meanwhile hid in the kitchen and opened a bottle of wine, bunging a dish of frozen lasagne in the microwave, then on reflection decided that egg and chips might be a more tactful choice.

Daisy refused to discuss Denis ever again while Cassandre and Inès were forbidden to enrol or rope her into anything that involved the opposite sex for the rest of their lives – if they wanted to have a life, that was. In truth they'd already decided to retire from matchmaking after discovering that Denis was a bit of a chancer who had been chucked out by his wife, the mother of his four children.

It also transpired that Denis had conducted affairs with Matilde from the boulangerie whilst courting recently divorced Arielle from the bar in the next village. No doubt the daughter of a campsite owner whet his appetite, as did Gina, the widow who bought the vineyard and employed him to rewire her home. Despite being twelve years his senior, Denis soon had his feet under Gina's table after putting the spark back into her life, in more ways than one.

Yes, there'd been a few flirty looks from men who should know better, seeing as their kids were swimming in the pool while the wife had her nose in a book. Or the grandad who lost control of his tongue *and* his mind after a few G&Ts, leerily suggesting a ramble in the forest after dark. All were treated to withering looks and the brush off, as was the leather-clad biker and the chap who came to drain the septic tank. The only comforting thought in a long time was 'at least they tried', otherwise Daisy's self-esteem would have rested at the bottom of the empty smelly pit on the other side of the field.

Daisy was still attractive, she hadn't let herself go and living mostly outdoors gave her a golden glow, but that was on the outside. Inside she was decidedly dull. It occurred to her that this might be how Adam felt – one of her links was missing. Perhaps it was lying somewhere on the camping meadow or on one of the woodland tracks, but wherever it was Daisy had no inclination to find it.

Pamela egged her on, not wanting Daisy to be lonely but one look at her heartbroken mum only affirmed Daisy's commitment to going it alone. Love was a risk because no matter how much effort you put in or how perfect it was, in the end, it could be taken away with the click of God's finger or the wink of a flirtatious eye. Daisy had watched her mum struggle on, the inner glow had definitely dimmed and it hurt so much to see her like that so maybe it was easier to remain single and in the long run, save the pain.

There were only two men in Daisy's life now. One would never forsake her and in those selfish, contrary moments she prayed for his swift return. The other, Daisy feared was lost forever, intent on his one-man mission, too stubborn and set in his ways to take a chance on real love but then again, so was she.

Resolved to focusing on the campsite, Daisy invested some money from the sale of her flat and then got on with building up the business, dabbling in online marketing and during the winter months sprucing up the grounds and recreation areas. Daisy hoped it would give Pam a boost too, working together to keep Bill's dream alive, a reason for them both to get out of bed each morning and put one foot in front of the other. In all honesty, it seemed her only option.

*

A shrill sound made Daisy jump. She'd almost succumbed to the hypnotic flames, luring her into sleep, but after waiting for so long and afraid that Adam might lose signal, she flung back the blanket and grabbed her phone, pressing it to her ear as she accepted the call. Despite her belief that every last tear was spent and her conviction to keep the conversation light and positive, just hearing his familiar voice, imagining him standing on the deck of a ship that was too far away, defeated her. Daisy could bear it no longer.

She had kept her promises for years and years. She'd foolishly set one brother free but this one, her best boy, she needed in her life, here in France. With Adam by her side she would survive anything. They'd get by together. Daisy just knew it. Once the tears subsided and the hiccupping ceased, she didn't hesitate to make a demand of her own, it was only fair. So before they lost the signal and he had chance to speak, Daisy just blurted it all out and asked Adam to come home.

Chapter 22

The secret and mysterious plan
France, September 2016

Daisy was hyperventilating by the time she reached her phone and just about managed to swipe the screen before Adam disconnected, again. She had spotted the six missed calls just as the lorry pulled into the forecourt where despite her curiosity, she reminded herself there was a million and one things to do so gossiping would have to wait.

Top of the list was to guide the driver to the newly prepared pitch where the process of installing a new caravan could begin, but once she'd handed over responsibility to Sasha, Daisy hot-footed it back to the office and hearing the persistent ringtone, yanked the phone from the charger. As she sucked in huge gulps of air and placed her hand over a thudding heart, Daisy listened patiently to Adam as he babbled on.

"Where have you been? I've rung about twenty-five times and I tried the house phone too. Where's your mum? It's like the bloody Marie Celeste there! Is everything okay, I was starting to get a bit worried?" Adam was still prone to over-exaggeration, which Daisy ignored.

"She's gone to the chiropractor, her back's playing up again, and we've just had a new caravan delivered, which is why I couldn't answer the phone. You have totally rubbish timing as usual and I *did* tell you I'd be busy today. Do you ever listen to what I say?"

"Oh yeah, I remember now, soz."

"Anyway, what's up, are you skiving or in dock?" Daisy always pictured Adam at work, set against a tropical backdrop or sailing across azure seas towards some exotic destination.

"I'm on the loo actually. I've got a bad case of the trots and I swear I'm in so much agony Daise, my arse is completely numb because I've been glued to the sodding toilet seat all day *and* I've got cramp in my legs but I daren't move, it just sets me off again." The sound of the toilet flushing caused Daisy to grimace, stifling her amusement at Adam's predicament.

"Bloody hell, Adam. Too much information! What have you eaten this time, or is it a stomach bug? In fact don't tell me, I've not had my lunch yet and I'm starving. Is that all you wanted to tell me, that you've got a runny bottom?" Daisy sniggered and heard the loud tut at the other end, just before Adam revealed the reason for his call.

"No, it's far more important than my bowel movements. I've had an amazing idea and I need to tell you all about it. I can't get it out of my mind and I swear I'm going to burst, and I mean my head, not the other end."

"Go on then, I'm all ears. Does it involve me or is this a solo venture?"

"It's both."

"Okay, so am I supposed to guess or do you just want to string this out for the duration of your illness?"

"No! You'll never guess in a million years but I'm not going to tell you over the phone. I need to explain it all face to face so you know I'm serious and I can gauge your reaction."

"Well, why didn't you just FaceTime me now? Ugh, on second thoughts forget that, just ring back tonight instead."

"No, it's too mega for a fuzzy conversation that keeps freezing every two minutes. That's why I want you to meet me in Manchester for my special birthday party, I'll explain then, so you need to book your flights and I'll pay for the hotel room. Will your mum be okay holding the fort for the weekend? I can't imagine you being too busy at this time of year."

"Hold on a minute, can we back up a bit? It's not till November and what's special about being thirty-three? And when did you decide you were having a party, and why can't you just come here and celebrate? Mum would love to see you and you know how I feel about Manchester."

"Because going to Manchester is all part of the big plan. I need to make some arrangements and set the ball rolling, you'll understand once I've explained but it's just easier all round if you meet me there. I've only got a few days' leave and I need to pack loads in so won't have time to fly to France. And thirty-three is special. It's two matching numbers and this phenomenal phenomenon only happens nine times in your life…unless you get to 111, but that's three, and highly unlikely I suppose."

"Adam, just shut up! What's going on, are you ill, oh God, you are, aren't you? I bet you've got some dreadful disease and you need to say goodbye. Adam, please tell me you're not dying."

"Calm down woman! No I'm not dying so stop interrupting because I'm wandering off the point. I'm perfectly well apart from bloody shellfish poisoning. I've come up with a fantastic idea that will take a bit of planning but in the long run it ticks all the boxes."

"What boxes?"

"I'll tell you in Manchester. I'm not saying any more until I see the whites of your eyes but it has something to do with your meltdown at New Year and the fact that you begged me to come home." Adam heard a squeak of delight at the other end.

"Are you jacking it in and coming here, you are, aren't you?" Daisy was jumping up and down with excitement, convinced she was on the money.

"Like I said, I'll make my mind up when I've seen you. It's a big decision and I need to know it's the right thing to do, so will you meet me? Then we can have a proper talk, face to face and serious."

"Okay…but I don't understand why you can't just tell me now."

"Daisy! Stop being difficult and impatient, I'm not talking about it again unless it's in Manchester, okay?"

"Okay Mr Narky, you're always grumpy when you don't feel well, but I promise I won't ask again."

"Thank God for that, now, what's the latest on the dating scene, have you had any interesting propositions?"

"No! I told you I'm off men for good but I have got a bit of juicy gossip. You remember Denis, the no-show?"

"Oh yeah, the one who's a bit of a social climber and stood you up for that old, rich bird who owned a chateau?"

"Yes that one. And it was a vineyard but thanks for rubbing it in. Anyway, it turns out she caught him in bed with her cleaning lady and now he's living in a caravan in his friend's garden! Serves him right the sleazebag."

"Well I'm glad you didn't end up with him, or any of the other no-hopers Cassandre tries to set you up with."

"What do you mean you're glad? I was quite hopeful when Denis turned up. You know there's not a lot on offer around here especially if you require a non-alcoholic boyfriend with a full set of teeth. It looks like I'm permanently on the bloody spinster list, and anyway, I'm resigned to life on the reject pile. Men are just too much hard work and I really can't be bothered anymore, no matter how much Cassandre nags me."

"Look, forget all that dating nonsense, like I said I have a plan and if you are up for it your days of trawling the streets of Le Forêt looking for single French men will be over, trust me."

"Ha, that's never going to happen! *You* said Glastonbury and bungee jumping would be fun, and I'm not even thinking about that sodding rollercoaster we went on, or facing my fears at the reptile house. There was nothing fun about being attached to a piece of elastic and throwing myself off a crane, neither was wetting myself or the soggy indignity of being unclipped afterwards! And fainting in front of a boa constrictor is not up there on my list of happy memories either, so no, where *your* fantastic ideas are concerned I'm understandably wary."

"Okay, I'll hold my hands up to a few errors of judgement but this is pure gold and I swear I've thought long and hard. It's a biggie so please trust me one more time and meet me in Manchester. I know you swore you'd never go back but this will probably be the last time for me, so we can say goodbye together."

"That does *not* fill me with confidence! Why will it be the last time? You really are freaking me out now."

"Sorry, sorry, I'm not selling this very well despite thinking about it non-stop for the past nine months, but I swear on Liam Gallagher's life that I am not ill or dying and my secret and mysterious plan is a nice one."

"Okay, as long as you promise and this isn't some kind of ploy to get me there so you can tell me something awful. I couldn't bear it if you left me, you know that don't you?"

"Yes, I know, and I promise you it's nothing bad…apart from one teeny-weeny detail, but you've already said you'll come now so you can't back out."

"For God's sake, Adam! What teeny-weeny detail have you purposely omitted in order to dupe me into a trip I had no intention of making? Come on. Spit it out smart-arse."

"Don't freak out."

"Just tell me," Daisy's voice sounded resigned, a sense of foreboding creeping in.

"Well…it just kind of slipped out during a quick Facebook chat and I was running out of things to say so I sort of mentioned I might be coming back to Manchester for my birthday and you know what she's like – before I knew it she'd offered and I didn't know how to get out of it." Adam was rambling.

"Get out of what, who are you talking about? Oh for crying out loud…ADAM! Please tell me you're not talking about Fliss!"

"Yes! I'm really sorry. Please don't change your mind."

"You are a total dickhead, you know that don't you?"

"Guilty as charged, but at least we won't have to clean up the mess and we can stagger back to the hotel after stuffing our faces with those yummy nibbly things she always makes *and* she's offered to bake me a birthday cake. A chocolate one! She's inviting the rest of the gang and it'll be nice to see them all. It's been ages, even longer for you and it's just drinks, things on sticks and my cake, then we can split. I've already told her I want to go into town and hit the clubs so we'll be at hers for two hours, max."

"Shut up Adam."

"Okay."

"Right, just because it's you and I'm intrigued *and* slightly scared at the same time, I'll book the flights tonight and send you the details but I swear, this idea of yours better be bloody good otherwise you are in deeper shit than you are right now. Got it?"

"Got it."

"I'm going now. I can feel a migraine coming on so I need to do some yoga and meditation."

"You don't know how to meditate or do yoga, you get cramp when you sit cross-legged."

"I think it's time I learned, what with your mystery plan and the thought of spending an evening with Mrs Perfect and her ever-expanding brood, I need all the help I can get."

"I really am sorry about Fliss, I just didn't think."

"You never do!"

"Harsh but true! Love you Daisy, text me with your flight details and if you're there before me just let yourself into the room. I'll book somewhere posh to make up for my loose lips, I know just the place."

"It's okay, I've forgiven you already, and I can deal with Fliss, don't worry. Love you too Adam. I'll see you in a couple of weeks, and I hope your bottom heals up soon. Take care and be good."

"You too. I miss you Daisy. You're still my best girl forever. Love you loads."

"I miss you too Adam. And you're still my best boy, just about! Bye for now, love you."

When the line went dead Adam sighed with relief, yet at the same time was annoyed by his stupid mistake. He could've kicked himself when he let slip to Fliss about returning to Manchester, he should've known she'd jump at the chance to take over but it was done now. He knew how much she irritated Daisy and why, but at least they'd get to see all their old mates in one go, maybe for the last time.

The muted and thus far non-violent feud between Daisy and Fliss had been rumbling on for years, remaining smothered in the presence of their friends when they met up in various formations for birthdays, summer barbeques, two weddings and four christenings, Fliss and her cherubic babies hogging the limelight at three of them. Fliss hadn't changed and probably never would, remaining oblivious to just how overbearing and controlling she could be in general and in Daisy's case, downright insensitive. Then again she'd proved to be an unwitting ally while his loyalty remained with Daisy who preferred to show the world a tough outer shell, one that she vowed Fliss would never crack, no matter how hard she tried.

However, if his excellent plan came to fruition he could eliminate at least two of Daisy's troubles. Adam was prepared to sacrifice all of his old friends for Daisy so after distancing themselves from Fliss and their ties in Manchester, they could start a brand new life in the land of happily ever after. Together forever.

Chapter 23

Party time
Manchester, November 2016

Lighting a match was just one of those skills, albeit basic, that had always eluded Daisy. Her already-tested stress levels had now reached breaking point because instead of illuminating a birthday cake, she had burnt fingers, and a pile of snapped and blackened matchsticks littered the tabletop. Why hadn't Fliss bought number candles because even Daisy could manage to light a wax 'thirty-three'?

As per usual Fliss, Managing Director of Control Freak Central, had insisted on individual candles, which would look superb on the cake *she* had made, with her very own perfectly manicured and dainty hands. The irritant in question had then flounced off to pour Prosecco for the toast, leaving Daisy to set herself on fire. Everything, and Daisy really meant *everything*, about Felicity Freak Show irritated the hell out of her. The list was endless and had been added to over the years, ever since she had invaded their group and latched on with super-glue-infused suckers.

Fliss was just one of those people who effortlessly sailed through life, gaining the best grades, looking marvellous in charity shop grunge and attracting the hottest blokes on campus. She had fun ideas and was credited with being a kind and understanding friend, spookily on hand in any crisis. Fliss didn't mind holding your hair while you threw up in the toilet or listened to you weeping for hours when your boyfriend turned out to be a complete and utter shit, or lent you her best clothes when yours were trapped inside the communal washing machine on a Bank Holiday weekend. Daisy wasn't being a two-faced hypocrite because she never asked for one-to-one counselling or the loan of a gorgeous vintage blouse, or to be reminded, as you jettisoned the contents of the salad bar into the pub toilet, that it's time to curb your excessive and frankly unladylike drinking habits.

It's just that Fliss had always been there, foisting her opinions and homemade chilli onto anyone who hadn't the gumption to tell her to stick it, and apart from Daisy and eventually Adam, everyone thought she was bloody marvellous. Daisy could never fathom why they didn't see what she did – a toxic, opinionated, interfering, glaringly false, calculating control freak! During their uni days, in all subjects other than Adam, Daisy accepted defeat to her adversary and eventually learned to suffer Fliss. Adam regularly smoothed her ruffled feathers by pointing out that Fliss was insecure so tried too hard to fit in and maybe, given time, she and Daisy could be good friends, and that any unpleasantness could result in their friends taking sides and drifting apart. As the years rolled by, despite the interloper's veiled obsession with Adam, Daisy's paranoia had proved unfounded and during momentary flashes of maturity, she'd managed to accept Fliss for who she was – a limpet stuck to their rock and nothing, not even a hammer and chisel, would ever remove her.

Daisy had used up all the matches so began rummaging through the kitchen drawers, sighing with relief when her eyes rested on the mini blowtorch, smiling wickedly as she set fire to thirty-three candles, her face warming in the golden glow as melting wax dribbled slowly onto the cake. On hearing the clip-clopping of heels Daisy swiftly banished the image of Fliss, her shiny blonde hair smouldering under the blue flame of a blowtorch.

"Oh, you've managed it, clever girl, and doesn't it look magnificent even if I do say so myself? Now, you go on in front of me and hold open the door then switch off the light as we enter the dining room. Niall knows to start the birthday song as soon as he sees you and everyone should have a glass of bubbly by now. Adam's going to love this! It's his favourite – chocolate fudge." Fliss had entered the kitchen as she did most rooms, with an excited whoosh and enveloped in whatever heavenly fragrance her husband had plucked from duty free as he jetted in from some high-powered business meeting.

Doing as she was instructed, Daisy allowed Fliss her moment of glory and set off in the direction of the dining room, at least then she'd be able to drown her sorrows, which since clapping eyes on Fliss had only multiplied. Yes, it did cross Daisy's mind to let the kitchen door slam into the glowing chocolate creation – she'd seen it done countless times on You've Been Framed and could picture it smeared all over the beautiful Victorian floor tiles. Or perhaps splattered up the wallpaper that cost over a hundred pounds per roll – Fliss left no brag-worthy detail unannounced, especially where Niall's salary was concerned.

As Daisy pushed open the door to the dining room and flicked off the light, she heard the haltingly embarrassed strains of the birthday song and once Fliss and the cake were safely in the room, diverted towards the food and drink-laden table from where she swiped a glass and bottle of uncorked bubbly. Daisy sneered at the feast Fliss had laid out, obviously intent on making a night of it. So much for a few nibbles and cake!

As everyone loosened up and threw caution to the wind, singing the last line with gusto, Daisy made her way to the conservatory and flopped into one of the comfy sofas, popping the cork in unison with the cheers as Adam blew out his inferno, closely followed by a round of applause. He'd be loving all the fuss surrounded by their oldest friends and wouldn't even mind that she wasn't leading the singing. Adam didn't need her glued to his side. He never had and never would, just knowing she was in the room, seeing her face in the crowd when he turned around was enough and the feeling was mutual. Daisy also knew he'd come and find her eventually, at the end of the night when he needed her counsel or an arm to link as they trudged home, just like he always had and always would.

Pouring the clear, bubbly liquid into her glass Daisy took a long unladylike swig and allowed her anxiety to ease slightly. Perhaps it was not having to look at or hear Fliss, or maybe knowing that Adam was close by, in the same room and city for a change, the one person in the world who could make her problems and customary scowl simply vanish. Well almost, he wasn't a miracle worker but the closest thing to perfect as you could get. Adam was unique, Daisy loved him unconditionally, and for almost fifteen years he had loved her back, in his own very special way. That was the only reason she had acquiesced and made the journey back to Manchester.

Even arriving at the airport was traumatic, a minefield of memories – her old place of work and where she set eyes upon Ryan for the first time. And then, as the taxi trundled towards the city, her heart became clogged with such conflicting emotions. It was as though her life here was fragmenting into sections of joy and despair, beginnings and endings, ordained chance meetings and desperate farewells. By the time the taxi pulled up outside the hotel Daisy was weighted down by it all, the past stuck to her skin while her head fought ferociously to maintain order, dredge up something, anything positive. The solution in the end was obvious – Adam.

Chapter 24

Shadows from the past
Manchester, November 2016

Adam was now quite drunk and to be fair so were Jim and Tommy, which was possibly the reason their wives had simultaneously dragged them off home before either could agree to heading into town. Shalini was working the following day and had to be up early for her shift so had ruled herself out, which left Kiki and Carol, who were currently upstairs with Fliss being shown around the freshly painted nursery. Daisy had politely declined the offer of a guided tour despite at least two attempts by Fliss to cajole her into moving from the sofa. The uncomfortable and somewhat deafening silence as everyone cringed at Fliss's insensitivity only angered Daisy more, forcibly refraining from telling the hostess-with-the-mostest to fuck off.

Knowing when enough was enough, Daisy pulled out her phone and rang for a cab. She didn't care if they headed towards a club or the hotel, all she wanted was to get as far away from Fliss and her huge baby bump as possible. Shalini as always was kind and sensitive, placing a gentle hand over Daisy's as the entourage left the room. Words were unnecessary yet the touch of Shalini's fingers as they wrapped around hers, offering support and understanding, only agitated deeply buried memories. Unwanted shadows from the past lingered, revisiting the day before her twenty-ninth birthday, one filled with so many emotions – anger, despair, loss and shock.

*

It had been a simple comment – made not long after Jamie had spotted Adam's indulgent birthday gift of a china dinner service – that ignited within her fiancé a tirade of bitter, accusatory words, borne from seemingly suppressed frustration that he could no longer contain. Daisy had watched him simmer for twenty-four hours and heard the sarcasm in his voice when he presented her with a spa weekend voucher, apologising that it wasn't up to Adam's standards. As they dressed for her birthday dinner and in a nervous attempt to draw Jamie out of his strop, Daisy expressed excitement that by the time she hit thirty they would be married and hopefully have a baby on the way. This diversionary tactic immediately backfired and simultaneously her birthday dinner, hopes and dreams simply crashed and burned. She lit a fuse and once the white spark fizzed inside Jamie, nothing could put it out.

During his vicious and damning condemnation, he hissed that he felt trapped, forced into a proposal that he had no intention whatsoever of honouring, or of becoming a father, especially with her. Daisy could only weep as his venomous words spat poison into her wounded heart while her sobbing irritated him even more. Such humiliation was then compounded by the frank and seemingly guilt-free confession that her creep-show relationship with her hanger-on friend made him sick, all of which was made worse by her pathetic obsession with marriage and starting a family. And the final lash of the whip came with a confession. In Jamie's opinion, all of this, Daisy's oppression, had driven him into the arms of another and let's face it, who could blame him?

In contrast to his previously smothered feelings on marriage and parenthood, Jamie had no such reticence when it came to laying blame and was forthright in his reasons to end their relationship. Daisy could only weep and beg as she watched him drag clothes from hangers, hurling them onto the bed before stuffing his belongings into a suitcase. It was done, over.

In the absence of Adam, Shalini stepped in, remaining with Daisy throughout the weekend, whispering wise words of comfort and hope, insisting there was no need to feel foolish. But that is exactly how Daisy felt after announcing to the world that she was going to be married and then repeatedly telling anyone who'd listen that they intended starting a family straight away. It was something she longed for most in life and was determined to achieve well before she hit her forties. Perhaps Jamie was right and it had become an obsession.

To compound Daisy's suffering and despite Shalini's valiant attempts to fend her off, on hearing the news via jungle drums, Fliss arrived bearing a shiny bag of birthday gifts, a giant box of tissues and a bottle of posh gin. Throwing herself into the role of agony aunt and saviour, Fliss denounced Jamie as Satan's twin and someone she (and by all accounts their whole group of friends) had never really liked or trusted. Every faux word of sympathy stung. Hearing that the man she loved was secretly disliked by her peers and regarded with suspicion and derision did nothing to comfort Daisy, it only compounded her humiliation. As did the notion that Fliss was revelling in every minute of her pathetic predicament.

After days of silence, to add final insult to injury and simultaneously extinguishing any hope that he would return shamefaced and apologetic, Daisy came home from work to find an empty apartment stripped bare of all his belongings, any evidence that he existed wiped clean.

At this pitifully low point, Daisy had truly believed her life couldn't get any worse yet within a matter of months it would descend further into misery when another loved one made an unexpected departure. After a hastily planned trip to France to seek solace in the arms of her parents, it became clear that they too had been keeping secrets. One look at her father told Daisy that the mild illness described by her mother was anything but. After very little thought and with an immense amount of ease, Daisy handed in her notice, sold her apartment next door to Adam's and moved back to France, permanently. But despite her haste and erudite observations, by the end of the year, her dad was gone.

*

Footsteps on the stairs and the dulcet tones of Fliss alerted Daisy, who quickly proceeded to gather her things, one of them being Adam. The hostess realised immediately that the party was coming to a close, which sent a flash of anger across her face, controlled swiftly by the robot within and replaced by a well-practiced look of doe-eyed disappointment.

"Oh no, are you leaving so soon? There's tons of food left and we haven't had coffee yet. I've made some delicious biscotti especially, shall I pop the machine on, it won't take long?"

Daisy was impervious to the rather obvious guilt tactics so answered briskly, not caring if she offended Fliss or made the others cringe.

"No, we're fine thanks Fliss, but if you fancy tagging along I can order another cab, that's if your ankles can manage a shimmy on the dance floor, they're looking a bit on the swollen side." The thunderous look from Fliss silently answered Daisy's question but she was on a roll so decided to get her money's worth. "Never mind, but can we steal Niall? I'm sure he'd love to let his hair down and escape domestic bliss for just one night." Daisy turned and waited for a reply, knowing full well that Niall would be going absolutely nowhere, with or without his wife.

"No, its fine, you guys head off, I'll give Fliss a hand here. Why don't you sit down darling, Daisy's right, you do look worn out?" And with that Niall began guiding his flustered wife to the sofa as their guests hastily collected bags and coats where, after thanking Fliss profusely for a wonderful party, they began to filter towards the door.

When Adam finally extricated himself he found Daisy waiting outside, perched on the garden wall as she watched for the taxi. He was carrying a huge carrier bag and a white cardboard box, which she presumed contained the remainder of his chocolate cake.

"Well you're going to look like a right pillock if you walk into a club carrying that lot! Why didn't you leave it there so her little darlings can finish it off, and what's in the bag?"

"Because she's got a sulk on and insisted I took it. I swear she was literally shaking with rage. Poor Niall's going to cop for it now.

I suppose we could dump this lot at the hotel then head back out, what do you think, and where's Kiki and Carol?"

"Oh, they took the first cab, they're too tired to go clubbing but promised to meet up for coffee before we leave. Look, here's ours now. Give me the cake before it ends up on the pavement, and stop swaying! No more drinking for you old man, I think you've had quite enough for one night."

"You might be right. I can see two of you. I reckon Fliss spiked my drink…she still wants to have her wicked way with me, the randy cow! But it proves I've still got it even though I'm nearly forty." Adam jiggled his hips in a very unsexy kind of way forcing Daisy to snort sarcastically.

"Got what exactly? And you are nowhere near forty you bloody drama queen, now get in the cab. We can drop this lot off first then we're going to Chinatown. I want something proper to eat, and you need to sober up." Once they'd piled into the taxi Daisy rested the box on the seat between her and Adam and while he gave the driver directions, she glanced towards Fliss's impressive townhouse. And there she was, lurking in the shadows, a solitary figure behind the glass, arms folded, watching intently as they drove away.

Lying on the bed, too full to move, Daisy gazed out across the illuminated Manchester landscape, the large windows affording her a magnificent view of a city she once called her second home. As promised Adam had booked them into a lovely boutique hotel, very modern and quite upmarket. The Hilton stood to the left, one of Manchester's most recognisable landmarks. The tower provided a focal point as you entered the city and could even be seen as you approached the airport by plane.

After donating the leftover party food to the taxi-driver who was more than happy to take it off their hands, they treated themselves to a huge Chinese banquet after which both Daisy and Adam agreed they were too full for dancing so decided to make the most of their swish hotel room. While Adam soaked in the bath, luxuriating in the complimentary toiletries, Daisy forced herself to relax, determined not to allow bad memories to spoil their time together. It was easier said than done and inevitably her mind wandered across town, towards the Northern Quarter and the apartment and life she once shared with Jamie.

Maybe they were doomed from the beginning because of all her boyfriends, casual or otherwise, Jamie found her relationship with Adam hardest to deal with. Or was it just another excuse amongst many to blame for his sudden departure. Yes, it had sometimes been difficult, juggling her closeness with Adam while keeping a new romance alive and on track, defending him and their superglue bond.

Daisy smiled as she listened to Adam singing – if that's what you could call it – and tried to ignore the images that were being recycled by her brain, snapshots of the past and a time she had consigned to the trash bin of life. Daisy knew that coming back would be a mistake and she shouldn't have let Adam coerce her into this trip. Not only that, he had steadfastly refused to discuss his grand plan, insisting they got the party over with first. For some reason Adam felt that when he finally got round to it a clear head was required, along with her undivided attention.

Heaving herself off the bed Daisy made her way to the long window and leant against the glass, looking down at the people below, wondering if they were happy and had someone to head home to or like her, were floundering on the edge of Nowhere Land.

In some ways it seemed like yesterday, when she more or less ran away from Manchester, packed her bags and left a huge part of her life behind without so much as a backward glance. Her mum had insisted that it had been fate, sending Daisy home just in time so she could spend precious months with her dad before saying goodbye.

When she thought back to that day, closing the door to her apartment for the last time, a place that held so many memories and where she'd spent a happy chunk of her life with Adam, the awful pain that had invaded her heart flooded back. Her only salvation was that her brain had switched to self-preservation mode, allowing her limbs just enough functionality to pack her car and make the long drive to Portsmouth alone.

*

As Daisy joined the M6 heading south, the rattling sound of her most treasured possessions that were rammed into the boot or piled on the back seat served as a reminder of the home she'd left behind and how after all those years, her life amounted to no more than a tin can on wheels stuffed with 'things'. Although they were obscuring most of the rear window, Daisy couldn't bear to leave her worldly goods behind, mainly because so much of it linked her to Adam and to a lesser degree, Ryan. Anything that connected her to Jamie lay discarded on the shelves of the local charity shop.

Relieved to have left the A roads for the smooth tarmac of the motorway, Daisy felt less worried about the fragile items becoming damaged, particularly her dinner set. This was by far the most valuable of her belongings and ironically, had probably been the catalyst for Jamie's pathetic tantrum and the bitter end of her relationship with him.

Adam pulled out all the stops with his gift. It was delivered by courier and emblazoned with the words 'fragile' and 'this way up' stamped all over the box. Daisy had only just set it on the table and was quizzically examining the delivery note when the phone rang and at the other end was Adam, who insisted she open it there and then. He was thousands of miles away but nevertheless Daisy could picture the expectant look on his face, hear the breathless anticipation in his voice and she wished more than anything he could be there.

After rushing to the drawer for a knife and then slicing open the lid, she carefully pulled back the tissue and bubble wrap to reveal her gift. Inside was a fine bone china Royal Stafford, 1950s vintage dinner service.

Daisy gasped as with trembling hands she removed one of the delicate cups, recognising instantly the Violets Pompadour design.

"Oh Adam...what have you done?"

"Do you like it? It's just like the one we saw at Chatsworth House, I compared it with photos we took that day so now when I get home you can make me a posh cream tea and we can pretend we're royalty. Hey, why don't we hire some old-fashioned clothes and then take a photo for posterity? We could Photoshop it and make it look sepia, that'd be a right laugh."

Daisy was having trouble seeing and speaking, tears were blurring her vision and a huge lump was blocking her throat but eventually managed to force out a reply.

"Adam it's perfect, where did you find it? This must have cost a fortune and I'm never ever going to use it, it's far too precious. I can't believe you've done this, you're totally mad, do you know that?"

"You are worth every penny and you'd better bloody use it! Don't you dare put it in a cabinet, it's for eating off not dusting, so make sure you slap a piece of birthday cake on it at the weekend, or else!"

"Okay I promise, and I'll send you a photo. I miss you so much Adam. I wish you were here, nothing's the same without you, especially my birthday. Please come home soon."

"Stop being mard and put the kettle on, I've got to go now but I'll imagine you sipping Earl Grey out of your teacup while I call afternoon Bingo...some guys have all the fun, eh?"

"Will do. But try and ring me tomorrow? I'll be here all day then we're going out at around seven so call before then." Daisy felt immediately awkward. The mere hint of her fiancé was guaranteed to ruin any conversation and as expected Adam took the opportunity to end the call swiftly.

"I'll do my best but if I don't get through will you say hi to the gang for me and have a brilliant time at your birthday meal. Love you loads Daisy, you're still my best girl forever."

"Love you too Adam, and you're still my best boy, you know that. Now take care and thank you for my perfect surprise."

Daisy's heart was already on the descent because those three simple words sometimes made their situation seem so unfair and in a way, widened the distance between them.

The sad and weird thing was that even though her fiancé was supposed to be her best boy forever, the title actually belonged to Adam and always would. Saying it seemed disloyal and Jamie would have a fit if he heard. Even the mention of Adam's name caused a dip in mood, a fact that irritated Daisy so much. So it was no surprise that when Jamie saw her dinner set, a gift that wiped the floor with his, he settled into a mammoth sulk. The rest was history.

Once the shock and awe of her uncoupling had worn off and Daisy settled into her old life in France, despite her misgivings about how her future would unfold it had all worked out well and Adam was returned to his rightful status, by her side. Whenever he had shore leave he flew to France and spent his time with Daisy, helping out on the campsite or simply enjoying the peace and quiet of the countryside, and obviously, his best friend.

Maybe her mum had been right and some things were meant to be, but what a cruel heart fate possessed, giving and taking at will with no regard for feelings or at the very least, offering an explanation to its warped thought process. But life went on, it had to, although Daisy's world was a hell of a lot easier to bear when Adam was right at the centre of it.

*

The sound of a siren down below and then Adam, launching into another dreadful rendition of an unrecognisable tune, snapped Daisy from her reminiscing while fresh images of her mum, home alone, prompted her to pick up the phone and check in, hoping that focusing on the present would banish murmurs of the past.

It would do no good to go over old ground. The most important thing that remained intact, a direct result of her years in Manchester, was Adam. Of that she was positive. This city was ingrained within her. The place she had met Ryan, the other brother and a man she would have loved given half the chance but instead, wasted precious time on someone who didn't deserve her. And apart from missing out on spending more time with the father she adored, Daisy had no regrets. Destiny had drawn her north, across the sea to an unfamiliar place where waiting in a corridor, all those years ago, was a beautiful young man, her best boy. And she wouldn't change that, not for anything.

Chapter 25

Another roof
Manchester, November 2016

D aisy could always tell when Adam was nervous because he fiddled with whatever inanimate object he could get his hands on, focusing on it to avoid eye contact while he rambled on about the first thing that came to mind. In this instance he was twirling the bowl of hors d'oeuvres around and around whilst boring her stiff with Manchester City's latest injury concerns over Aguero and Kompany. The appearance of the waiter delivering their drinks provided a welcome interruption, and determined not to let Adam steer himself back to football, Daisy prepared to boldly broach the subject he'd artfully avoided all day.

They'd woken late and met up with Lester who after flying in especially to see them, was jetting out to Courchevel for a spot of skiing, straight after buying them lunch at a lovely Italian restaurant just off Deansgate. Lester remained their most colourful university friend who blew in and out of their lives amidst a whirlwind of county gossip and scandalous liaisons, mostly involving himself. His haphazard yet refreshingly relaxed outlook on life never failed to take their minds off their own mundane existences, enthralled by the world of a wadded merchant banker and Lord of the Realm. Once he'd air kissed them both goodbye and zoomed off in a taxi, Adam suggested a shopping spree and after walking for what seemed like miles around the city centre, they finally returned and changed for dinner.

Daisy now found herself on the roof terrace of their hotel from where the vantage point afforded panoramic views of Manchester and beyond, and a rather salubrious but calming environment in which to spill the beans. Unbeknown to Daisy, Adam had purposely chosen a hotel with an open rooftop, somewhere that resembled the place where he once made another startling announcement to his best friend. They were both much older now and too wimpy for freezing to death under a duvet in the open air so he was glad of the warmth from the fire pit and the comfortable sofas on which they lounged.

"Do you remember that night on the roof of our halls, when we watched the stars from under my duvet? I can still taste those cheese butties. There's something about Dairylea slices, you just can't beat them." Adam looked wistful until Daisy chipped in.

"Of course I do, I think my nose got frostbite and my bum was completely numb, and my legs ached for days afterwards. Why do you ask, has rooftop camping got something to do with your surprise?"

Adam raised one eyebrow, trying to look mysterious. "Sort of. That night changed everything for me. It was like a new start, finding an ally and getting a few things off my chest. And now it's like we've come full circle and ended up here in Manchester, back at the beginning, so I thought it was a good place to move on from. We can start again. Form another circle, or maybe this time a triangle."

"Okay, now you've lost me. Have you been converted on one of your voyages because all this sounds a bit Zen and I have no idea what you are getting at? So come on, just spit it out, and what the hell has your faithful triangle got to do with all this?"

Adam looked up to be met by the same kind and understanding eyes he had stared into all those years ago. "Sorry, I've probably over rehearsed what I'm going to say and now it sounds a bit shit but I had to get it right in my head because it's so important, another life-changing speech I suppose." Once again Daisy remained silent and held out her hand before closing her fingers around his, signalling that it was okay, she was ready to listen. All he had to do was speak.

"Okay, here goes…do not interrupt! I mean it – ferme la bouche!" Adam gave a stern look as Daisy made a zipping motion across her lips with her free hand, still amused by his propensity to overdramatise.

"Right…time to be serious. After our chat at New Year I did a lot of thinking, in fact I'd been toying with the idea of jacking my job in even before you mentioned it. But I had to be sure that it was the right thing for both of us and you weren't just having a meltdown that you'd regret the next day, or worse, you'd meet someone and then change your mind. That's been my greatest concern really, that I'd look a right fool if you fell in love again." Adam's heart was pounding in his chest so he welcomed Daisy's forbidden interruption. It gave him time to calm the palpitations.

"I know I was in a bit of a state that night but I meant every word I said. Still, you're right. It wasn't fair of me to spring that on you and I get that you needed to think it over, and then there was your contract, only you can decide if you want to renew it. This is your life and I want you to be happy." When Daisy realised she'd butted in she held up the palm of her hand, silently signalling her apology to which Adam exhaled loudly and rolled his eyes.

"I'd more or less made my mind up anyway but I was chuffed to bits that we were on the same wavelength…see what I did there? Sea, waves…no, okay. Anyway, I've made my decision, as well as a few others but I'll come to them later in my speech." Adam took a gulp of his beer and allowed Daisy another interjection; he knew she wouldn't be able to remain silent or resist the temptation to tease him.

"Ooh, sounds mysterious, come on, spill…and by the way I've got used to a life of celibacy, in fact I'm officially an old maid."

"I don't think you're quite there yet, you'll be wearing black tights and a headscarf next, and what part of don't interrupt can't you understand, now shut it! Bloody hell Daise, I'm bricking it here and need to get this over with, okay?"

"Sorry, okay, I'll be quiet." Daisy zipped her mouth again and this time threw away an imaginary key, causing Adam to sigh, shaking his head wearily.

"I've realised that now you've sacked Manchester there's no reason for me to come back here anymore. I love it in France, it's my second home and even though this place will always be special to me I think it's time I let go, just like you have. I want to put down new roots, which is why I'm going to sell the apartment and maybe buy a place in Le Forêt. I've already made a few appointments here and should get the ball rolling before I go back to Southampton, that's if you give me the thumbs up. There you go, that's the first part over with but before I get to part two, you have permission to speak." Adam exhaled, relieved to have strung together a sensible sentence and allowed his pounding heart some respite while Daisy spoke.

Daisy clapped her hands together, fizzing with excitement. "Of course I've not changed my mind you idiot! I feel the same as I did on New Year's Eve, I just realised I was a bit full on with all that sobbing and feeling sorry for myself. It's a fantastic idea and Mum will be made up but there's no need for you to buy anything. You've already got your own room at ours so it's no big deal. Just stick the money in the bank and then if we spot something in the village or nearby you could buy it and rent it out, just like you've done here. I'm so chuffed Adam, I swear to God I feel like I'm going to burst." Adam's mysterious comments about this being the last time he'd be in Manchester were beginning to make sense, until something occurred to her.

"But you could've told me all this on the phone so why was it so important that you told me face to face?" Daisy leant forward, her arms rested on her knees, curious.

Adam took a sip of his drink and then clasped his fingers tightly together to stop them shaking. "Because there's much more to my plan and it involves three things: the money I make from the apartment and you. Oh, and a dog!"

"A dog?"

"Yep!"

Daisy took a quick sip of her drink then concentrated on Adam's face, focusing on his very wide and nervous looking eyes. "Okay, go on, I'm intrigued."

"Right, here goes…again. I want to use some of my money to invest in the campsite. I know your dad always wanted to build log cabins on the field by the lake, do you remember that time we paced it out and then lost count and had to start over and over again? He never got round to it and I've no idea how much it would all cost but I thought we could make his dreams come true and maybe I could live in one, retire by the waterside when I'm old and grey. But for now I'm more concerned with the next few years and helping you achieve your dream, too. And I'd yes, I'd like a dog. I wished so hard for one when I was a kid and then when I was finally able to buy one of my own, being a grown up with a job and an evil landlord that forbids animals, it kind of got in the way. Would you and your mum mind if I bought one?" Right at that moment Adam thought he was going to explode. Maybe holding his breath wasn't helping but all this meant so much – it was his future.

"Wow, Adam! I don't know what to say, and of course you can have a dog, I'm sure Mum would love one too. As for the cabins, it's a kind and generous offer but are you sure you want to tie yourself down like that, and what if something happened in the future? We probably wouldn't be able to buy you out and it might cause problems, and what do you mean about my dream, you're talking in riddles again?"

Adam turned sideways and grabbed Daisy's hands, enfolding them in his, squeezing tightly. This caused her to frown, her forehead scrunching as she waited warily for the puzzle to be solved.

"Daisy, I have no intention of going anywhere once I've sold up. I'm going to hand in my notice at work and come and live with you and your mum. Apart from Ryan I have no one, and he always seems so far away so when I think about the future, the picture in my head has you in it. It always has."

"Well that's fine by me Adam, you know that – a promise is a promise." Daisy could feel tears pricking her eyes. And as a trillion happy thoughts zapped through her mind one simple truth stood out. It had been so obvious, a foregone conclusion maybe. Adam was right, the circle was complete, their lives in Manchester were over and it was time to start again, honouring the promise she made on another rooftop all those years ago. But as for a triangle and her dreams, she was still a bit perplexed, but it was all about to make perfect sense, just a few seconds after she heard Adam take a deep breath.

"And now for the biggy…this might be the part where you totally freak out and change your mind so just go with the flow, okay?"

"Okay…"

"To complete my perfect vision and make your dream come true in the process I want us to have a baby together, you and me." Adam was transfixed, gauging Daisy's reaction, which right then was one of stunned silence so before the anaesthetic of his words wore off he decided to plough on and top up the dose.

"Look, I know how much it bothers you, that you're running out of time and suitable villagers to bed, so I'm offering to give you what you want, a child, someone we can both love and care for together, our baby." Adam thought his cheeks were going to pop. He could feel them burning and it wasn't from the heat of the fire pit. And from the look on Daisy's face, just like the last time he'd spilled the beans, he could tell she was speechless, totally astounded.

Chapter 26

What drives Miss Daisy

Apart from the waltzers and the horse carousel with its lovely music, Daisy hated fairground rides as opposed to Adam who absolutely loved them – the scarier the better. Following a coach trip to Alton Towers, Daisy vowed never to return after spending most of the day minding bags and coats while everyone else had a great time. Adam finally persuaded her to go on the Oblivion ride, assuring Daisy that she'd love it and if not, he would go on the kiddies teacups as punishment. So, mindful of wasting the entrance fee she decided to give it a go.

Needless to say Daisy hated every second of being strapped into the implement of torture and despite Adam's words of encouragement almost died of fright when she was plunged into the darkness. The velocity at which they travelled, filling her lungs with air, along with the shock of the descent caused her to gasp for breath as tears stung her eyes. And yes, despite his protestations Adam did keep his part of the deal and took a lovely spin in the teacups, watched with amusement by some five-year-olds and their suspicious parents.

Now, the lung-filling gasp of shock, in that moment of terminal velocity when her heart almost stopped, was being replayed right there on the rooftop as Adam's words filtered through to her brain.

"Adam…are you serious, is this a wind up?" Daisy held her hand against her chest, acutely aware of her heart thumping away inside.

"Do you really think I'd tease you about something as serious as this?" Adam's voice was soft and sincere to which Daisy inhaled, covering her flushed cheeks with the palms of her hands before speaking in a low and incredulous voice.

"Oh my God! You really mean it, don't you?"

"Yep, every single word and believe me I've thought the whole thing through, right down to the last detail and apart from the bit where you almost passed out from shock, my grand plan is perfect in every way."

"But Adam…how can we have a baby, what would people say, how would we explain to everyone, like my mum for a start? I just don't understand how you think it will work, especially the most important bit, you know, actually getting pregnant." Daisy rolled her eyes and looked in the direction of Adam's groin, causing him to laugh, easing the tension a notch.

"Don't go overthinking everything as usual. It's totally doable. Look, just let me explain it all the way through and once you've heard me out you can ask as many questions as you like, okay?"

"Bloody hell Adam, how can I not overthink this? My head is spinning, but okay, I'll listen…and I'm definitely getting a feeling of déjà vu here. There's something about rooftops that brings out the chatty man in you so go on, get it off your chest. And I'll try not to interrupt, but I still can't believe we are having this conversation, it's too weird."

"Just promise you'll have an open mind. This is really important Daisy, for both of us, and I'm deadly serious. It's life-changing stuff and certainly not something I could say over the phone." Adam heard Daisy fortify herself with a large intake of breath before she spoke.

"I promise."

Adam leaned forward, deep in thought, looking straight into her wary eyes. His expression had taken on an intensity that Daisy had witnessed many times before. He was normally so easy-going yet equally susceptible, beleaguered by deep and meaningful topics, so his idea required her full and serious attention. The first thing she did was to remove the bowl of nuts because he had resumed his fiddling and swirling, which was distracting. Daisy wanted him to get on with it so once she prized it from his fingers, Adam took this and her raised eyebrows as a signal to speak.

*

The idea had come to him more or less as soon as he saw the announcement on Facebook that Fliss and Niall were expecting their third child, not that he intended to include this fact in his summary to Daisy as any reference to her bête noire would tarnish the whole idea. Nevertheless, it was the spark that ignited the flame and once it began to glow there was no stopping it. Adam's plan became an inferno that consumed every waking moment. He'd already decided to move to France, that was a no-brainer, and so long as Daisy remained single, having a baby was simply an extension to his original idea.

Daisy had made no secret of the fact that she wanted to start a family and despite it being clear to Adam and all of their friends that Jamie wasn't marriage *or* daddy material, she carried on regardless, determined to change his mind. Daisy wasn't going to waste almost four years of her life by dumping him whenever they hit a bad patch, adamant that far too much effort had gone into the relationship. Daisy had been overly conscious that her days as a twenty-something were nearing an end. Henceforth she formulated a timetable of events, which meant by her thirtieth birthday she would be married or, failing that, in a comfortable co-habiting relationship with a baby on the horizon.

While Shalini and the other girls (Fliss was never privy to these conversations) assured her that there was plenty of time, Daisy countered that it was different for them. They weren't prepared to give up their wonderful careers and lifestyles just yet and while she respected their ambitious plans, they should respect hers. And this entailed having a baby well before she was forty. And one vital point Daisy withheld from the group, wary of exposing the green-eyed bitch inside, was that Fliss seemed to churn out babies on a regular basis. This alone made her ever more aware that time was of the essence and failure wasn't an option.

Adam knew exactly what drove Daisy. They'd had many truthful conversations concerning the topic of Daisy's ticking body clock, her insistence on getting pregnant to Jamie rather than start a quest for another suitable partner. Daisy also pointed out that men played by a different set of rules. Women had to reproduce within a window of opportunity, while they still had fresh and fertile eggs and a body that was capable of carrying a baby, whereas men could go on and on indefinitely. Their sperm bank had flexible opening hours. Adam did point out that it was a risky business, more or less wearing someone down until they resignedly agreed. It didn't bode well, remaining with a partner who preferred life just as it was and who might resent the intrusion of a baby. Adam also thought it sad that Jamie didn't realise what he'd got, ungrateful even.

Once the subject was closed and Daisy's attention drifted elsewhere, Adam was left drowning beneath a wave of despair, the conversation forcing him to face a certain truth of his own. The spectre of a lonely, childless old man still hovering on the edge of everything came back to haunt him. As far as he was concerned being a husband, let alone a parent, was eternally out of reach and the best he could hope for would be the role of an uncle. He couldn't even be a godfather to Daisy's much-wanted child as he still didn't believe in all that churchy stuff, regardless of her gentle ministering. Along with his meat-eating preferences, Adams reluctance to accept anything spiritual into his life was something that Daisy had tried to influence over the years. She was a firm believer in heaven and the afterlife, utterly convinced of it in fact, whereas he preferred to keep a firm hold of reality, which is precisely why he'd decided to intervene and alter the course of events.

No matter how hard Daisy tried to convince him otherwise, encouraging Adam to be more open, take a chance on love or at least engage with others who were asexual and perhaps forge a life with someone who understood, he always stood firm. There was only one love in his life and that was Daisy – final, end of story.

Adam had spent too long as an understudy, patiently waiting in the wings for Ryan to sort himself out and then for Daisy to throw in the towel and admit defeat where finding true love was concerned. The time was right. He had played the long game, given everyone a chance to grab happiness while he floundered, drowning in the blackness that sometimes seeped inside his head. He was no longer prepared to leave the remainder of his life in the hands of a fickle fate or even the residents of heaven above. Adam was taking control – it was now or never.

Chapter 27

Our boy
France 2017

Daisy's cheeks were hurting, but in a good way – the after-effects of smiling too much, if it's possible to overdo a natural reaction to feeling immense and unbridled happiness. The cause of her joy was the grainy black and white image that stood on the mantelpiece of their kitchen. A similar photo lay on her bedside table; Adam had one in his room too and the pocket of his denim jacket, plus a photocopy in his wallet. On the flip side, written in his swirly handwriting were the words: My boy.

They'd both agreed that they wanted to know the sex of their baby so at the twenty-week scan, as the cool gel was squirted onto Daisy's nicely rounded stomach, the parents-to-be were eager to hear the news. Adam was holding Daisy's hand so tightly she had to tell him to stop, while their eyes never left the screen, waiting for the image to appear. They had both shed happy tears the first time they saw their little blob, concentrating hard on the tiny heart beating away, desperate to make sense of the swirling mass that was their baby.

On the way home from the clinic they had both talked non-stop, making plans about decorating the spare room whilst willing the tractor in front to move out of the way so they could get home and tell Grandma Pam the news.

They had come so far since that evening on the roof when Adam revealed his secret and mysterious plan. At first, once the shock wore off, Daisy's brain was invaded by scrambled thoughts. So many questions and doubts vied for attention yet one by one, Adam brushed them all away.

*

After retreating to the sanctity of their hotel room he produced his iPad and calmly showed Daisy all the articles he had saved regarding conception and artificial insemination, the words alone causing her to blush immediately. Yet slowly, Adam's practical and extremely serious approach to all aspects of the subject began to reassure her. His research and attention to detail allowed them both to take one step back as he tactfully explained the process and envisioned the future.

"I know it's all a bit clinical and totally unromantic but we can buy everything we need off the Internet. There's no easy way to say any of it so we should just be sensible and adult then we won't feel embarrassed or uncomfortable. All we will be doing is omitting the part where the chemistry takes place simultaneously – I do my bit and then a few seconds later you do the rest." Adam flicked on the kettle, unperturbed by the enormity of their discussion.

"Well, put like that it is *the* most unromantic way of creating a baby but in our circumstances I agree it's the best way to look at it. Otherwise it's all going to feel weird."

"Exactly, and I want the creation of our child to be special, as special as we can make it anyway. Before all that occurs we need to get you in prime condition and also work out when the best time to conceive will be. I've got some printouts of healthy diets in my bag and we'll order an ovulation kit, that way we won't have to keep trying. And you never know we might get lucky first time but if not, there's no rush."

Adam, whilst appearing busy fiddling with the sachets of Nescafé, was monitoring Daisy's every nuance, petrified that if he went too far and said the wrong thing he would freak her out or cause offence; it was like walking a tightrope. "Am I going too fast? Just say if you think I'm being pushy or insensitive. You look like you're in shock so please be honest and tell me what you're thinking. Go on, say what's in your head right now."

"What if it doesn't work?"

"It will. I just know it."

"Ah…so after all these years you've just discovered your psychic ability? But face facts Adam, lots of people try and are disappointed so why are we so special?"

"Fair enough. I agree I can't promise it will work but let's at least give it a go. We have as much chance of having a baby as the next person. I know that's not theoretically correct but you know what I'm getting at. Next question, go on, I can see you are full of doubts so just say it then we can work things out."

"What about Mum? What the hell will she say, or even think? And then there's Ryan, can you imagine what he's going to say about all this? It will freak him out, I just know it."

"I've already thought it all through and we should start off by telling them that I'm moving to France. Once that's out of the way and I'm settled in we can either tell them about our intentions or keep schtum until you're pregnant, whatever you feel most comfortable with."

"I don't know what's best…and we've spent the last fifteen years fielding off accusations and insinuations from outsiders but Mum and Ryan always stood by us, defended our friendship and believed that's all it was, all it is. So how will they react when we announce we're having a baby? They'll think we've been lying or kidding ourselves…stuff like that. And what about our sleeping arrangements, before and after? Mum's not daft. She'll wonder how we managed to conceive a baby from separate rooms and surely you don't want us to pretend to be together – that's just too weird and I couldn't deal with the deception."

"Which is precisely why we're going to tell your mum *and* Ryan the truth, about me. I agree there's no way that we can deceive them, and you know what? I'm tired of living this lie. It's served me well over the years and I couldn't have managed without you as my staunch ally and whilst I don't want the world knowing my business, it's time that I was honest if only with our family."

"Are you sure? I know Mum will understand and I've always believed you judged Ryan too harshly. You should have told him years ago Adam, he'll accept it. I know he will. But what about other people, what will we tell our friends?"

"A version of the truth. You wanted a baby and so did I. That's why we decided to have one together, simple. Two best friends, living under the same roof as Grandma Pam and bringing up their child in a beautiful place surrounded by people who love him or her, that's our story. There's no need for them to know about me, and loads of men donate sperm to strangers so why not to the person you love most in the world? It only has to be complicated if we make it and after living my lie I think a bit of honesty will be refreshing. There's loads of alternative scenarios if you prefer: we had a drunken one-night stand, or we could've been secret lovers for years enjoying the fruits of an open relationship, maybe we both realised after all this time we were made for each other, but my favourite is that you were sex-starved and desperate so pounced on me."

Daisy whacked him with a pillow, laughing at his final version.

"But seriously, none of those will give us peace of mind and our child's life will be built on lies and I don't want that Daise."

"I'm totally with you on that. Lies breed more lies and it's no way to start a new chapter, so we agree, honesty is the best policy if only with mum and Ryan, which leads me to my final question. What will we tell our baby? I don't want it to grow up in a fake family, one where you and I play-act. Yes we will be Mummy and Daddy, but not man and wife. We will have to find a way to explain when the time is right and in a way that's not confusing or causes our child to feel different. If anyone knows what it's like to feel stigmatised, you do." Daisy grabbed Adam's hand knowing his past was always difficult to talk about.

"Believe me I've thought the same thing but my situation was different. I was ashamed of my parents for their failings, and their inadequacies stuck to me and Ryan like glue, but our child will have the best family a kid could have. They won't want for anything especially love. That's what matters the most, the rest we will face one step at a time and anyway, family units are made up differently these days: two mummies or daddies, two daddies and a mummy who gave birth to them, step-parents, half-siblings, lots of combinations. I really don't think it's as big an issue as we might think."

Daisy was feeling brighter now, a bubble of excitement slowly building. "You're right! We will deal with it step by step and we've come this far together so the future will be a piece of cake."

"But there's something else, one thing you've not mentioned and we need to face up to it."

"What? Now you've got *me* worried."

"I know you are adamant that your dating days are over–" Daisy opened her mouth to interrupt but Adam held up his hand and silenced her with a stern look. "Let me finish, this is important and needs addressing. One day, could be years from now, your Prince Charming might come riding into camp with his backpack and one-man tent and if he does, I will step aside and let you get on with your life. It will be no different than if two people split up and Mummy gets a new man. But I want you to promise that I will remain in my child's life, hands on, every day, not shuffled off while Stepdaddy takes over. That's why I mentioned living in one of the cabins. I'd want to be there, close by and see my child grow. That's my only ask."

Grabbing both of his hands then squeezing tightly with hers, Daisy made another promise. "Oh Adam, I swear on my life that I'd never push you away or treat you like that, surely you should know that by now. I kept my promise to you all those years ago and I'll never break it. Please say you believe me otherwise this mad idea can't even begin. We have to have total trust in one another, just like always."

Adam let out a deep sigh. "I do trust you Daisy, but maybe it's other blokes that make me wary. Look what happened with Jamie. Call me selfish, obsessive and paranoid, whatever you like, but what scares me to death is not just the thought of losing you, but being alone. So imagine having everything, right there in the palm of my hand, my soul mate and my child, for it to be taken away. I think it would kill me, I really do."

"Well it will never happen, especially because I've given up hope of someone half-decent pitching up at Campanule and I certainly won't go looking for love because I'll have everything and everyone I need under one roof."

"Are you sure you're sure?"

"Yes, I'm sure! Now let's chill out, I'm bloody exhausted from all this thinking...I'm surprised you've not made yourself ill, worrying and planning and trawling the Internet for your bits and bobs. I'd love to see your browsing history!"

Adam managed a smile. Daisy was right, he was weary and overwrought. "Yep, you can safely say that I've had my money's worth from the ship's Wi-Fi and the photocopier. I bet they'd dock my wages if they knew how much ink I've used these past few months."

Daisy plumped up the pillows on the bed while Adam moved his stack of printouts and searched for his charger. Once he'd plugged things in and flicked off his trainers, he settled down beside Daisy and wrapped her in his arms. They soon drifted into contented silence, both had heads full of so many things and as much as they could have talked all night, sleep quickly claimed them. Here, thoughts shot off at tangents, transforming into disjointed dreams, conjuring images, nudging memories from their hiding places, swirling hints of happiness mixed with shadows from the past.

While their minds played tricks and their hearts kept time, both Adam and Daisy were unaware of being joined by an invisible essence – the patient spirit of new life, hovering on the periphery of a perfectly formed triangle.

Chapter 28

Pamela
Joining up the dots
September, France 2017

Pamela was on the early shift and seeing as the site was quieter, able to enjoy a few moments of peace, watching the mist rise as the birds heralded the start of a new day, one which would see Adam leave for England and a very momentous rendezvous with his brother. It was also a trip that without a doubt would result in Daisy pacing the floor and worrying herself stupid over the outcome.

Pushing these thoughts away, determined to make the most of her solitude, Pam focused on the sun, which was making its first appearance over the tops of the highest trees in the forest. Smiling, she waited for its gentle morning rays to warm her skin as she drank her coffee and listened to the sing-song of hungry birds hunting for breakfast. Pam loved September maybe as much as she loved March but for diametrically opposed reasons. Both months signalled a change in pace, cogs in a wheel creaking into action or slowing down, a simple mechanism giving her life order and purpose.

The beginning of the season brought a sense of expectancy, the natural rebirth associated with spring complimented by the man-made smell of fresh paint and the visual satisfaction of a spruced up campsite, ready and waiting for new arrivals and the buzz of a busy summer. By the time autumn arrived such feelings of vigour were definitely waning as a quieter existence and even the onset of a cold winter were both tempting and eagerly awaited. This year though, everything would be different because by Christmas there would be a new member of the family. Her grandson would finally be here and Pam thought her heart would literally pop, just at the idea of it. It had been a crazy few months, a whirlwind of change that began in January when she found Adam and Daisy waiting at the kitchen table, their default setting for grand announcements. As she pulled back a chair, puzzled and slightly nervous as she sat, Pam had no idea of how life was about to change, for all of them.

*

Obviously it had been a huge shock when she heard the news she was going to be a grandma, especially under the circumstances. She'd only just got used to Adam's decision to move to France, not that she minded, in fact Pam had been pleased as Punch when he and Daisy pitched their idea. It had brought a tear to her eye, knowing that Bill's plans would come to fruition and later that night while her mind was alive with thoughts of the future and memories from the past, sleep evaded her so she headed to the office. Here, after rummaging around in the filing cabinet Pam pulled out a battered A4 envelope that contained hand-drawn maps and a site plan, notes and ideas that were her husband's dreams. Naturally Adam pored over the details, promising to honour Bill's vision and follow the pencil diagrams, coveting a piece of history smudged by his mentor's fingerprints and a circular tea stain.

Pam found Adam's presence comforting. It was reassuring to have a man about the place, not that they couldn't manage without one because the male members of staff had more than stepped into the breach, but it sort of felt right; the natural order of things had been restored.

The dog, however, was another matter and while Adam slipped into his role of project manager for the cabins, he was also required to be chief pooper-scooper and his canine companion was fully trained and prevented from running amok on the site. Not just that, the naming of his first pet turned into a task of epic proportions because as with everything Adam did, an immense amount of thought went into giving the dog a name. Lists were made, names crossed off, opinions sought, names put back on again until finally he came up with a shortlist of three.

Dylan, after one of Adam's music idols; Puke, from one of his favourite books by Gerald Durrell; and then the outright winner, Basil, which Pam presumed was a nod to Mr Fawlty but the choice went deeper than that. Mrs Basil was the dinner lady at Adam's primary school who took him under her wing and made lunchtimes more bearable for a shy little boy. In the canteen, Mrs Basil always made sure Adam was first in the queue for seconds, and later in the big playground, she would hold his hand while she patrolled the yard or mend cut knees when he fell over. Every now and then he would find a 10p mix in his school bag, a Kit Kat or a bag of crisps. He knew it was Mrs Basil and apart from being grateful for the extra nourishment, Adam appreciated more the gift of human kindness. On the last day of term before he left for secondary school, whilst some of his friends shed a tear at leaving primary life behind them, after being enfolded in a lunchtime bear hug and a hearing a whispered goodbye, Adam's tears were for Mrs Basil.

At first, Pam wasn't sure if she had made the right decision but it was hard to deny Adam anything, especially after she heard the story behind Basil's name and saw the look on his face when he brought home the giddy, chocolate-eyed crossbreed from the rescue centre. Basil's puppy stage just had to be endured, as did the chewed kitchen cabinets and puddles on the floor tiles. They said he was part terrier with a hint of the unknown, but whatever he was, Adam *and* Daisy adored him and even Pam had to admit, once the messy stage was over with, so did she.

But it was during a second heart-to-heart, involving just Pam and Daisy, that her world was turned upside down then set straight again, a conversation in which Daisy explained quite frankly the true nature of her relationship with Adam and how he chose to live his life. Compared to welcoming a new business partner and a daft dog into their lives, this revelation had come as the greatest shock, not because Pam thought there was anything unusual about the way Adam was – it took all types to make a world and she was a firm believer in 'live and let live' – it was more that the poor lad had kept it to himself all these years. And she so wished he had been more open with her and Bill. For a start it would have saved them both a lot of wasted time speculating about Adam and Daisy, more so when Ryan came into the equation. They had both presumed and worried slightly that his presence would complicate matters.

Oh yes, they'd whispered and watched surreptitiously although neither would have objected to Daisy and Adam eventually becoming more than best friends, but most of the time they were just curious and a bit baffled. And then later, lying awake at night, listening to the sound of laughter from the kitchen below, Daisy, Adam and Ryan sharing some joke, Pam and Bill had ruminated on the curious nature of their easy-going and somewhat liberal friendship. Neither could fathom Adam's lack of jealousy or his ability to turn a blind eye to what had clearly been a developing mutual attraction between Daisy and Ryan.

Now, it all made sense and rather than it easing her heart, it actually made Pam sad. In his rather innocent quest for a family life borne quite simply from the fear of replicating his parents or ending up alone, Adam more than likely viewed Daisy and Ryan's coupling as a perfect solution, sort of a lifetime guarantee. But while Pam saw the logic in Adam's plan it also crossed her mind that perhaps underneath his libertine persona (albeit for totally understandable reasons) lurked a more calculating chap. And while she agreed that for Adam it would have been very convenient, having his brother and best friend joined in matrimony or whatever, life and true love rarely fell easily into step. Despite their simmering affection for each other, Ryan and Daisy were like passing ships and seemed fated to always glide on by, no matter how diligently Adam stationed himself at the helm.

Now, benefiting from both truth and hindsight, Pam was able to piece together what she viewed as Adam's arduous journey through life where, to his credit, he appeared to have regrouped and recalculated. And it was this, the sheer effort of Adam's somewhat contrived idea that made Pam question her daughter's role in their decision, needing to be convinced that becoming pregnant wasn't out of pity for Adam or as a result of pressure, or even misplaced guilt. Again, meticulous attention to detail, this time on the part of Daisy, had been paid to pre-empting a long list of doubts and questions, each of which was answered sensibly and with genuine appreciation for a mother's concern.

Requesting space to mull everything over and condense what was basically information overload, Pamela took a walk in the woods. Here, she talked it all through with Bill as she sat by his memorial, as usual conducting a one-sided conversation. It always helped to say things out loud, imagining him sitting by her side, rolling his eyes and tutting, or more often than not pretending to pay attention when he was actually more interested in whatever was on the telly. But there was one thing she needed to get off her chest, a feeling of unease that she couldn't shake and it needed airtime. Even admitting it to herself felt bad, which was why it remained unsaid to Daisy, perhaps in case it meant one day eating words or getting scorched feet from a burning bridge.

As the tale had unfolded before her, interspersed with great logic and deep feeling on Daisy's part, Pam had a felt the creep of something less earnest in the part of Adam. Was it guile, or a hint of entrapment? Had her daughter been somehow managed? Once the box of disquieting thoughts had been opened memories came tumbling out, swirling in her head, faint images, snippets of conversations or amusing anecdotes that in the past had been put down to Adam's quirks and obsessions.

Setting Ryan aside, where Daisy's flirtations and relationships were concerned Adam had appeared to turn a blind eye and given her space, yet in truth could be likened to a hovering spectre, a watchful guardian who on occasion had thrown a spanner in the works, albeit in a humorous and supposedly innocent manner.

Adam knew Daisy inside out and whilst in the love stakes he'd been usurped by Jamie, on all other matters he reigned supreme. Pam had thought it touching, rather endearing, and was somewhat comforted by his dedication and steadfastness. But now the soft harmonious waves that had previously cushioned her daughter's life appeared at a tangent, sharp contrasts were bringing everything into focus. Pam saw things with a new and clearer perspective.

Daisy had intended to pursue a career in France, make the most of being bilingual yet had chosen to remain with Adam, and then came the apartments, side by side, sort of tying them down. And now there was a final knot, the baby. Had Adam choreographed Daisy's life, not just now, maybe all along?

Pam laid her head against the bark of the Grandad Tree, eyes closed, lost in thought. Oh how she wished Bill was here or there was someone else she could talk to but even her friends in the village would have trouble with this, and where would she begin? This wasn't a simple case, an everyday conundrum that could be solved over a glass of rosé and an éclair. This was life-changing stuff and she had to get it right. Her bottom was getting damp from the leaves underneath and the late February chill had begun to seep and chill her bones, so raising herself slowly, allowing creaky knees to straighten and recover, Pam set off around the lake.

As she took the well-trodden dirt path around the cold grey water, surrounded by barren trees that yearned for an end to the cloudless, monotone skies above, Pam shrugged off the shroud of gloom and instead savoured the silence. With the onset of spring her surroundings would be daubed with colour, blue horizons and a palette of nature's finest hues, and the dormant campsite would be filled with noise from holidaymakers old and new.

Thinking of their guests and some of the incidents she had witnessed reminded Pam that whilst she felt the weight of a very new world resting on her shoulders, now and then troubles came your way. It was part of life and rarely was anyone perfect, families in particular.

They'd had their fair share of 'domestics' over the years, eager campers who hoped that their longed-for fortnight break would be just what everyone needed to cement some cracks, forge bonds, teach them patience. There'd been couples fighting on the terrace, airing their dirty laundry and venting a year's worth of pent-up frustration when being stuck in a confined space for days on end became too much. Bill had intervened in happy hour punch-ups when flirting got out of hand and then there were the loved-up teenagers who'd sloped off, causing warring parents to launch search parties. One set zoomed off at sunset in a panicked attempt to curb a budding romance, their tearful daughter sobbing in the back seat while the others endured hate-filled silence and vengeful stares from their left-behind lover boy.

Yes, they all rolled up in shiny cars towing their trailers and mobile homes, looking like the image of perfection. Energetic cycling couples who thought they were on the same page but weren't, one longing for a lazy all-inclusive fortnight, not burning calves and blisters. Groups of families who would never holiday together ever again, and fathers who longed to be back at work, well away from their squabbling demanding kids. Mothers who laughed at their own foolishness in imagining they'd get some rest…it all went on under canvas or tin so why should Pam think her life would be any different?

She wouldn't be the first mother who felt unhappy over the choices of her child and now found herself in the same catch-twenty-two situation that many parents had faced before her. Should she lay down the gauntlet and face rejection or remain silent, supportive yet reserved?

It took time, three-quarters around the lake in fact, before gloom lifted and the clouds that obscured clear thought began to part and Pam was able to see a way forward, one that would deliver equilibrium.

Although the circumstances were unconventional, Daisy and Adam's plan, if nothing else, made sense. In truth, she would rather Daisy have her much-wanted baby with someone as lovely as Adam than find herself pregnant following some dalliance with a totally unsuitable man who would become embroiled in their lives. The worst-case scenario was that as Daisy frequently prophesised, she would end up on the shelf, so knowing how much being a mother meant, Pamela was unable to deny her only child this chance of happiness. And after taking his situation into account, Adam too.

They did have deep feelings for each other, an intense loyalty, a seemingly unbreakable connection and total respect. And how they laughed together and shared so many interests and happy memories, all the important things that went into a relationship. Together, Daisy and Adam had almost everything a mother would want for her daughter. So who was she to deny them this chance? How could she stand in the way of what could only be described as a different kind of love?

But she would keep an eye on things once the baby arrived and look for signs, make sure that Daisy's life wasn't being choreographed, that she had free will and if it presented itself, a more conventional kind of love. Pam loved Adam dearly. He was a member of their family and would always be treated as such so now, understanding what made him tick would allow her to judge situations wisely and act accordingly. She would always care and want the best for him but Daisy came first.

They were both waiting in the kitchen when Pam returned, Adam fidgeting nervously with the table mats whilst Daisy tapped the side of her mug. Just the sight of them, together as always, two young people whose lives were entwined not tangled, pure and uncomplicated, reminded Pam that while some things weren't meant to be, others like Daisy and Adam, were. When she entered the room both looked up, their eyes wide with anticipation and anxiety, a pivotal moment diffused by one simple gesture.

"So, it looks like you're going to make me a granny at last! I think that calls for a group hug, come here you two, stop looking so worried, it's all going to be okay. In fact, it's going to be bloody marvellous."

*

Hearing the familiar sound of Basil barking in joyous anticipation of an early morning walk with his master, Pamela sighed, knowing that quiet time was over and what promised to be a warm but potentially stressful day was about to begin. Collecting her mug and plate she made her way inside the office and towards the door that connected to their home, resigned to her first task, that of calming both Daisy and Adam. The former was riddled with anxiety and the latter bursting at the seams to see Ryan.

And while Pamela could only offer support, if she was honest with herself there really was no way of knowing how Ryan would take the news. In fact, she had a sneaking suspicion that as far as their plan went he was the weakest link and here, they had made an error of judgement.

For all intents, he and Daisy had moved on. Their affair was a thing of the past but Pamela wasn't totally convinced. She'd spotted the wistful look and that moment of contemplation as Daisy paused when she dusted the mantelpiece, slowly wiping the frame of her graduation day photo. Pam knew it was Ryan's face she gazed upon, not Bill's as there were plenty of him scattered about the place. What if, despite Daisy's protestations and Ryan's turbulent love life, the flame hadn't been truly extinguished for one or both of them?

In her somewhat out-of-touch opinion of what appeared to be the more casual way of conducting relationships these days, she thought it odd that Ryan had kept his distance where Daisy was concerned. Had he been 'over it' then why not come and visit? Reading between the lines of snippets of information, Pam also surmised he was irritated by his brother's emigration to France, or could he be jealous? Maybe he was just as confused as she and Bill had been so kept his true feelings hidden, unsure of where he stood. Whatever it was, Pam had a sneaking suspicion that when it came down to it, despite Adam's joy and his eagerness to join up the dots, when he heard the 'baby news' Ryan wasn't going to be pleased, not at all.

Chapter 29

Daisy and Ryan
France, September 2017

Daisy felt sick, something she had become resigned to over the past few months; however, this was a different type of nausea, like waiting in line at a job interview or those seconds before you open the envelope containing your exam results, but much, much worse. She was dreading being parted from Adam, mostly due to raging hormones playing havoc, causing random bouts of weepiness and uncharacteristic clinginess. But worse, Daisy was increasingly worried that a huge bucket of ice-cold water was about to be thrown over their happiness. As far as she was concerned Ryan was an important detail and someone they had misjudged in their meticulously thought-out plan.

*

Once Adam had been given the thumbs up from Pamela, the next person he wanted to speak to was Ryan. But instead of enthusiasm, Adam was thrown off kilter by his brother's cautious and muted response. Whilst not quite vetoing the idea, Ryan managed to pick holes, envisaging only pitfalls where upping sticks and settling in France was concerned, let alone investing in the business. The only person unsurprised by his attitude was Pamela, who right at the outset had hinted that where matters of the heart were concerned nothing was ever straightforward and perhaps there was a tinge of the green-eyed monster in Ryan's reaction.

With the ball rolling, Daisy became determined that nothing would ruin their plans so brushed away her mother's observations and stuck firmly to the mantra that had kept her heart protected for years. She was over Ryan, moved on and all grown up and if he had a problem with that, then tough! He was the one who ruined everything, not her. She had been patient; he had been greedy. All three of them had led their own lives and Ryan in particular had made an art form of being absent, allowing his roving eye, thirst for adventure and desire for freedom to be his spirit guide. Therefore he had no right to cast aspersions on Adam's choices *or* interfere with his future.

But there was something else that really rankled and it wasn't just the fact that her mother was far too perceptive, irritatingly so. Right from the moment Adam had revealed his bizarre yet perfect dream and no matter how much she denied the fact, somewhere, maybe sequestered in the tiniest crack in her heart or lurking in a hidden room deep within her consciousness, was Ryan.

As had frequently been the case, Adam told his brother about the impending move to France via a long-distance phone call to The Falklands when, due to the time difference and Ryan's shifts, there was only time to outline the basics. Maybe being caught slightly off guard resulted in Ryan being surprised yet accepting of Adam's decision, but the email which arrived a day later, pointing out financial hazards and other thinly veiled concerns proved he'd had time to mull it over and full approval wasn't in the bag just yet.

It seemed clear that Ryan was irked at the idea of Adam leaving his career, apartment and friends behind to follow in the wake of Daisy who at any time could shack up with some guy, thus leaving Adam high and dry. The tone of the 'brotherly advice' was polite and measured, albeit to the point, avoiding a war of words by assuring Adam that schedule permitting he would *try* to visit, sending hellos and best wishes to Daisy and Pamela. Still, he'd managed in a few paragraphs to take the shine off Adam's news and as far as Daisy was concerned, tarnished what remained of her nicer memories, and it hurt. The damage was done.

Which is why, as soon as Daisy's second trimester had safely passed and the end of the holiday season arrived, Adam felt it was time he made arrangements with Ryan to meet up and tell him face to face the other news, that he would soon be an uncle.

Using the excuse of his upcoming birthday, which coincided with Ryan's leave and a stag night in Cambridge, Adam booked a flight and eagerly awaited the rendezvous. Any qualms Ryan had could be discussed over the weekend and once his fears were allayed, they could all get on with being a family.

It was something Adam wanted to do alone and for that Daisy was relieved. In her turbulent emotional state she had no way of knowing how she would react at the merest hint of derision from Ryan, let alone seeing him in the flesh. No, it was better this way. In the meantime she would have to trust that Adam's unbridled excitement would rub off on the decent and honourable guy she had fallen in love with all those years ago. She prayed so hard that the boy who put his little brother first and then spent much of his life protecting would surface just when he was needed the most and give them both his blessing.

*

Ryan was suffering with the hangover from hell and Satan was definitely making full use of his pitchfork to prod the inner sanctum of a very tender brain. After a session of self-inflicted injury Ryan had collapsed into his bed at the Holiday Inn and lay comatose for much of the morning. He'd been woken by the maid who, on spotting his semi-clad state, gave him a jaded 'seen it all before' look and closed the door behind her. Scrabbling about for his phone, which he finally located inside his shoe, Ryan managed to focus on the time, relieved to see that he had at least five hours to sober up before Adam arrived. Crawling on his stomach to the other side of the bed, he undid the bottle of water and thirstily swallowed almost all of it.

This was the last thing he needed, to feel rough *and* have to pretend to be pleased about his brother's wonderful new life because no matter how hard he tried to get his head around it all, Ryan just couldn't shake off the feeling that it was all going to end in tears. It just didn't make sense. Not only that, Adam had insisted that he wanted to go for an early birthday curry, just the two of them – no crazy night with the lads or one of Ryan's women friends tagging along. It seemed that there was serious stuff to discuss that required his undivided attention. Maybe once they'd had time to talk through whatever Adam's latest piece of news was (Ryan dreaded to think) his opinion would change but for now, the jury was out.

Hauling himself off the bed Ryan headed for the shower – a long soak under a jet of steaming water might help clear his head. No matter what happened he needed to think straight, not say or do anything that might alienate Adam or hurt his feelings. They had survived so much separation in their lives yet managed to remain close, so now, just when Ryan was approaching a transitional period in his life it was imperative he didn't fall out with his brother. His military service was coming to an end, which meant a few important decisions of his own, and one of them had included Adam, a pipedream that had since been firmly crossed off the list.

Enveloped in body-cleansing steam, Ryan closed his eyes and allowed the jetted water to pummel his face and skin, his thoughts focused on what could have been and his own plans for the future. One of Ryan's ex-squadron mates had set up a scuba diving school in Greece and was looking for investment so after a couple of visits, checking everything out and noting that the business plan was viable, he'd more or less made his decision. In all likelihood the following summer and maybe the rest of his life would be spent in Crete. The idea was to buy a small yacht, something they could use to run fishing and diving trips. Ryan had suggested they employ someone experienced with customers and hosting events while they focused on the diving and naturally, Adam fitted the bill.

Ryan intended floating the idea via an email but was pipped to the post by an exuberant call from Adam. As his heart deflated slowly, the rosy image of them spending their days in the sun and building a life together simply faded away. Yes he was bitter and annoyed, not just at his own procrastination but at Daisy too.

Not only had she lured Adam to France, she was the ghost who wouldn't be banished, a chink in his armour and he couldn't deal with the frustration that just hearing her name, let alone picturing her face, induced in him.

It had taken a while but with age came wisdom, albeit too much too late. He hated to admit if only to himself that he'd been self-obsessed and missed his chance with Daisy. Jamie had snuck in, that was a fact, but despite his many failings Ryan sometimes felt that they were destined to be thwarted at every turn. And while he had to accept that he'd probably blown his chances with Daisy, as the end of his service career loomed and the uncertainty of life on the outside seemed slightly daunting, he had found new hope in his brother.

In Ryan's own deluded fantasy world Adam could be the key to everything and once he was on board with the Crete idea, then maybe, just maybe, Daisy might follow suit. Hazy images of Grecian seas and golden beaches, a fleet of yachts and a thriving business that they all could share had occupied his mind during many a long shift. Now, not only had that little scenario crashed and burned, *she* was completely responsible for ruining things for him and Adam.

Turning off the shower, Ryan grabbed a towel and still dripping, made his way back to the bed then flung his damp body onto twisted sheets. Staring up at the stark, white ceiling he allowed his mind to wander, realising the slow creep back to sobriety – whilst slightly less painful – wasn't such a good thing. As the throbbing ebbed, irritants he'd stored in the far recesses of his mind, stuffed like socks in the bottom of a rucksack began tumbling out, spilling into the open. Ryan knew he had two options: either sort them into some kind of order or cram them back in and turn out the light. Closing his eyes, a soft thud kept time at his temples. Instead of housekeeping Ryan chose sleep, an easier, safer bet.

Thirty minutes later he admitted defeat. Peace eluded him, his brain refusing to play fair, producing images of his crazy, curious brother and by his side a freckle-faced beauty. The Daisy of his mind was the total opposite of Adam – uncomplicated and open, patient and annoyingly perfect in every way, the lost love that no one ever lived up to. The girl he sought out amongst faces in clubs across the world, drawn to, mesmerised by anyone who fitted the bill before choosing the complete opposite to spend the night with. Nobody ever made him feel the way Daisy did, and not just in the sack, it was more than that, *she* was more than that. He still had all of her letters and the daft gifts she'd posted to wherever he was stationed. Funny postcards, tickets from trips to the cinema, even a boarding card from one of their weekend trysts – tokens and memories that reminded him that there was a time when he actually felt something. Just once, he'd fallen in love.

How could he have cocked it up so badly? Putting his career first then allowing Charlotte to more or less take over his life and ultimately, being pipped at the post by Jamie. He'd considered chasing after her when she went to France but from what Adam said her heart was broken, badly damaged and in need of repair. So he left it alone and not long after found himself in the dry and desolate desert of Las Vegas, a special posting he volunteered for. Ryan could read his own behaviour like a predictable book: any sign of trouble he would extricate himself and jump feet first into a new challenge. And then another tour, this time to the bottom of the world, the frozen landscape of the Falklands put paid to any ideas of rekindling his relationship with Daisy. It was easier that way, safe.

Ryan could feel his eyes closing, maybe one more hour of kip would do him good and now his stomach had settled he might keep down some painkillers. Heaving himself upwards he located some paracetamol in his rucksack and after washing them down, settled back against the pillows. God he was tired, not just from lack of sleep and air travel but of being alone in hotel rooms and the air base, and missing his brother and that warm sense of belonging that he'd always felt whenever he'd visited Pamela and Bill. This final thought jolted him slightly. An unexpected moment of clarity that made him feel slightly vulnerable and uncomfortable, as did the next.

Maybe he'd been too quick to judge Adam. What right had he to deny his own brother that same sense of being part of something? Yes, by following Daisy, Adam had most likely put the kibosh on Ryan's brotherly enterprise but in truth neither had a malicious bone in them so how could he be angry? And really, Ryan had no right to criticise or condemn. After all, he'd done whatever he wanted for years so while that thought began to settle, not quite as hard to deal with as expected, another surfaced.

What if Adam gravitating back to Daisy was the best thing for all of them? Perhaps it *would* pull them all closer together, give Ryan a golden, last-chance opportunity to see how the land lay before he made firm plans and headed for the Greek islands. Was there still hope, could he and Daisy give it one more go? As the paracetamol began to work, Ryan felt something akin to optimism and yes, a flicker of excitement, which teased a faint smile to his lips.

Turning on his side Ryan laughed and gently shook his cotton-wool head, telling himself he was going soft and if he wasn't careful he'd end up like Adam, away with the fairies. And it was thinking of his brother and some of the bizarre things he'd thought and said over the years that triggered a faded memory of a forgotten conversation, many moons ago.

The two of them were hunched over a table. Adam was firing off questions while Ryan battled through another hangover and his brother's deep interrogation while they ate a full English breakfast in a greasy spoon cafe in the heart of Manchester. Adam was cross because of that dreadful girl, Fliss, before his attention had focused on Daisy, wanting to know how Ryan felt about her, matchmaking for all he was worth. It was then he had mentioned a triangle and how perfect it would be if they could all be together, him, Ryan and Daisy.

Fancy remembering that after all these years. And even weirder, was how things can eventually turn out, come full circle and find a way of straightening out the zigzag lines that crackle through your head, confusing your heart and interfering with the natural order, sending you in the wrong direction, missing what's important.

Ryan yawned and told himself to get some sleep. The lads had warned him that hitting forty sent you daft – maybe they were right. Pulling the thin sheets over his bare shoulders, Ryan forced his brain to take a break. There was time to sort it all out when Adam arrived and when he did, he would apologise for the tone of his email, offer his brother whatever support he needed and invite himself to France for Christmas. Yes, that would be a good starting point. It was a special time of year and the place where it all began for him and Daisy. And if there was any glimmer of a second chance, Ryan swore an oath to himself that this time, he wouldn't screw it up.

Chapter 30

Adam and Daisy
Time to say goodbye

Adam could only remember ever seeing Daisy cry like that once before – at Piccadilly Station when he'd had to prise himself from her grasp so he could board the train for Southampton and then start his life aboard ship. Pamela put it all down to hormones and anxiety over Ryan's reaction to their news, but whatever it was Adam had been unsettled by her distress and almost called off his trip. At the last minute Daisy pulled herself together and summoned a brave face as she waved him off. He watched through the rear window of Rémi's boneshaker as it drove away from the campsite and then out of the gate, both waving until they were out of sight.

He consigned this image to his bank of memories. Strawberry waves blowing across her sun-freckled face, one hand attempting to tame them so that she could see, her other hand held high, moving slowly in a sad au revoir. He never tired of looking at his best girl who with the sun behind her, was framed in blinding, yellow light, as ethereal as the day he first saw her – his throwback spirit who'd been sent to save him.

After a traumatic farewell and a journey that could only be adequately likened to a white-knuckle ride, Adam was now enjoying the relative calm of the departure lounge. Rémi, who Adam swore was at least one hundred and fifty years old, had volunteered to escort him to Nantes. The trouble was that along with looking like someone from a post-war drama in his buttoned-up shirt and tweedy jacket, sporting hobnail boots that were welded to his feet, Rémi still drove as though it was 1953 and there were only five cars in the whole of the department, his being one of them.

He didn't indicate at all, not even at roundabouts, which added to the stress of missing the turning, twice if they were lucky. Instead of paying due attention to other road users he treated the whole journey as a sightseeing experience, pointing out landmarks and the winding river below, making the bridge crossing particularly hair-raising. And despite Adam hardly speaking French (it was a work in progress), rattled on in his mother tongue for the duration, laughing at his own jokes while frequently scratching his woolly hat and armpits, causing Adam to lean as far away as possible just in case Rémi had nits or fleas, or both.

Feeling lucky to be alive they arrived at the terminal in one piece and once the security rigmarole was complete Adam found himself a quiet seat in Departures. He occupied himself by watching the dispassionate faces of his fellow travellers; their bored expressions were preferable to that of a disconsolate, tear-streaked Daisy. He had already phoned home and listened as she apologised for making such a huge fuss, extracting promises that he would phone the second he landed, got in a taxi, arrived at the hotel and finally, had spoken to Ryan. Only then would she be able to relax.

Oaths made and Daisy appeased, Adam settled into people watching, focusing in particular on the young couple with their daughter, maybe two years old and enjoying a game of chase with her dad, toddling around the lounge, occasionally bumping into a suitcase or tripping over the feet of a passenger. Watching the scene made Adam's heart swell, a mixture of anticipation and pride in the knowledge that soon he was about to enter the ranks of parenthood. He too would bear the title of Father and have his own child to chase and care for.

Dad – that word sounded so good, it would belong to him, spoken by his baby boy, someone who would intrinsically bind him forever to Daisy. And really, from the very beginning, she was all he'd ever wanted. The creation of their child was the most wonderful bonus, a perfect dream come true and the culmination of his well-laid plans.

*

After they made their pact, Daisy flew back to France while he remained in Manchester and took care of financial matters, placing his flat on the market and all of his belongings in storage. Their Manchester friends were supportive and unsurprised when they heard about his move, while the baby plan remained a secret. He worked his notice and after saying goodbye to his shipmates, arrived in France just in time for Christmas then, over New Year, he and Daisy laid some of their cards on the table.

Had Pam turned down his offer to invest in the campsite, Adam had a contingency that entailed buying a couple of properties close by that he would rent out. Daisy assured him that living on site wouldn't present a problem but they had to accept Pamela's decision regarding investment, maybe it was too soon after losing Bill. Despite their concerns Pam was thrilled and the fruition of Bill's dreams seemed to revitalise her. The later revelation was somewhat more tenuously received.

When it came to the nitty-gritty, Daisy and Adam kept the finer details to themselves, although Pam was tactfully made aware of how her grandchild would be artificially conceived. Once the talking was done and Pam's blessing given, Daisy threw herself into preparing her body for pregnancy, taking supplements and eating healthily whilst monitoring her monthly cycle so, by early March, the chart deemed it the optimum time to try for a baby.

In the absence of a conventional conception, Daisy and Adam still wanted it to be special, something they could remember in as romantic a way as possible. Their child would be as precious as their love for one another no matter how both might be perceived, which is why Adam booked a weekend retreat, a secluded cottage perched high above the sea on the cliffs at Carnac.

This was another of Adam's fascinations, the mythology and mystique surrounding the origins of the Neolithic stones, the unproven theories adding to the ethereal sight. Were they erected by the pre-Celtic dwellers of Brittany in honour of their ancestors or perhaps astronomical aids? Maybe it was a lunar observatory or a seasonal calendar so farmers knew when to plant their crops.

Did priests use them to foretell eclipses? Adam's favourite theory was that Merlin himself turned a Roman legion into stone and even though he still had no proof that magic (not card tricks but proper wizard spells) even existed, it allowed his imagination flight. Whatever the stones were, Adam soaked up the atmosphere of Carnac, invigorated by the wind that blew in from Atlantic while embracing the sea air and spectacle of the waves crashing onto the rocks below.

On the morning of their momentous day, Adam and Daisy had walked along the blustery beach, wrapped up warm against the elements as March hadn't yet turned on the heating. The seaweed-strewn sand was dark-golden and compact underneath their feet as they made their way arm in arm along the shore, at times lost in thought and others, daring to make tentative plans before quelling their respective anticipation, both mindful of tempting fate.

"What do you think the gang in Manchester will think, you know, if it works?" Adam was examining a shell, which he tossed away, a crack deeming it inferior.

Daisy was keeping her eye on the shoreline, not wanting to get her Ugg boots wet. "To be honest I don't really care one way or another but I think most of them will be pleased for us, apart from the obvious nut-job."

Adam snorted. "Yep, she's going to get a zillion gossip-miles out of it, but don't you think you're being a bit hard on the others? They've done nothing wrong and they've been our mates forever." Stopping, he inspected a perfect razor clam, which he brushed off and slipped into his pocket.

"Sorry, I don't know what's wrong with me. Maybe I'm just getting a bit tetchy in my old age. But you know how I feel about Manchester. I left it behind and now everyone here comes first. I don't even bother with Facebook anymore, I just look now and then out of politeness and so I don't offend them. Once it's all in the open I have no problem with them coming over, it would be lovely to show off our baby and you're right, they're part of our lives so it's mean to cut them out entirely. But until I'm well on my way let's keep them at arm's length, our secret, like you agreed."

Adam could hear the tension in Daisy's voice, which told him she was either gearing herself up to a meltdown or protecting herself against disappointment. "Are you scared Daisy? You know, about having a baby inside you and then it having to come out? If you are worried about any of it we can talk it through, all you have to do is tell me. I feel a bit shit that it's going to hurt and I can't share any of that pain…I think women are really brave and I honestly don't know if I could do it." Adam had watched documentaries on every stage of pregnancy and childbirth and wasn't afraid to admit the latter stages made his eyes water.

"Well I'm not thinking about that just yet and I don't intend watching any of those videos you've bookmarked for me, for now I'd prefer it to remain a mystery. I'll face up to it nearer the time and anyway, we shouldn't get ahead of ourselves. It might take a few goes, which probably means we'll end up visiting the whole of France in the process. What's next on the Grand Conception Tour – Lourdes?" Daisy nudged Adam who was laughing, mainly at himself. He had a huge list of places he wanted to visit now he was a French resident with amazing places right on his doorstep.

"Well there's no harm in making the most of our situation and combining baby-making with a bit of sightseeing, it will broaden our horizons and turn us into wise and well-travelled parents. But being serious, are you scared Daisy? You could get hypnotised and there's bound to be some holistic approach we could try, in fact there's a centre near here that does all that type of stuff. They put warm stones on your head and massage your feet, or it might be the other way round, I'll have another look."

"Adam! Will you stop – right now! Yes I am bloody bricking it if you must know so just change the subject before I chicken out and change my mind, and for the record I am NOT being sodding hypnotised, got it?" Daisy was laughing but Adam knew she meant it and when to back off.

Adam was in front of Daisy, walking backwards in order to get her full attention. "Okay, okay, I get it. Let's talk about names instead? Can we at least make a list, once we know if we're pregnant? I know what I want if it's a boy and there's loads of options for a girl…have you had any ideas?"

"Of course I have but I'd rather wait, and just to shut you up I promise that once we know for sure you can make a hundred lists, it's what you do best! And I already know what name you'd choose for a boy, I'd put my last euro on it." Daisy tapped the side of her nose and gave him a knowing look.

"Bet you don't."

"Bet I do!"

"Go on then, smart arse…what is it?"

"Nope, I'm not saying, you'll just have to wait and then I'll prove to you I'm psychic."

"And a very good guesser who knows me too well."

"Yes, and that! Now if you've finished giving me the third degree I want to go into town and get some lunch, I'm starving."

Adam began to jog backwards, his pockets heavy with seashells. "Come on then, I'll race you to the pathway, you'd best make the most of being able to run before you turn into a big fatty." Adam sprinted away before Daisy could slap him, both of them laughing as she whacked him with the end of her scarf as he weaved his way across the sand, slowing down just enough so she could almost grab his jacket before speeding off, his best girl in hot pursuit.

Much later, while Daisy waited patiently in a candlelit bedroom, she had watched the sunset paint the horizon lavender and pink, mesmerised by the ochre flames that danced inside the wood burner as the soundtrack to their life played on Adam's phone.

He'd compiled a list of music, signposts that marked important moments and crazy times, right from the day they met to the present. With each track came a memory, a subconscious snapshot captured forever. Sometimes in full colour, others in arty black and white, posing in front of Manchester landmarks and accompanied by three minutes of music to create a sensory time capsule, a pod containing their history.

Two young people walking home in the rain from a gig or setting fire to the cooker in the halls, picnics on the roof and windy voyages across a choppy Channel, the first night in their apartment surrounded by pizza boxes, being sick as dogs after drinking too much vodka, crying in the cinema at the end of The Notebook, crying with laughter over an episode of Friends; their album of the mind was full, page after page of Daisy and Adam. He had only included music that conjured happy memories, positive vibes and an aura of peace, adamant that their baby would begin its life in an environment cushioned by the sound of love.

They had both felt rather sheepish about telling Pam that they were going away for the weekend, although it was obvious why, but it would have felt wrong, sneaking upstairs with their mini-chemistry kit while the granny-to-be watched telly downstairs. And they had a fit of nervous giggles when the package arrived from Amazon and they unwrapped it on Daisy's bed, both grimacing at the syringes and collection pots, resorting to humour and teasing to dispel the rather clinical nature of what they were about to do, which was precisely why Adam decided to regain control of the situation – the conception of his child was epic and such creation had to take place in the antithesis of a laboratory.

And there was something else that guided him, a curious sensation that he'd never experienced before, not quite yearned for but always hoped to feel – the ability to connect with something other than the tangible. Apart from the sensation of great peace and a connection to nature that Adam felt when he spent time in the forest at home; the impending creation of life had somehow touched his soul. This miraculous microscopic science astounded Adam. After waiting patiently, dormant and still, cells from two separate bodies began swimming, joining, splitting, growing, forming – it simply blew his mind and left him consumed with an overwhelming passion, or was it compassion? Whatever it was had a profound effect and after giving it much thought, Adam could only describe it as some kind of spiritual awakening.

Yes, he had become mildly obsessed with the foetal images on his laptop screen, reading tirelessly about each stage, making sure Daisy took her folic acid, preparing her body so that even before it was born their baby would have the best home in which to grow. And despite the biology and chemistry that went into the whole incredible process, Adam was increasingly in awe of one simple fact. They were creators giving life to a beautiful new soul and whether he had glimpsed some kind of higher meaning or gained a deep, Zen-like respect, it made Adam feel weird, different, and he liked it. In fact, he felt kind of reborn himself.

Still, no matter how much music they played or money was spent on a cosy cliff top cottage and a shopping bag full of scented candles, the fact remained that Adam still had to perform before Daisy could do her bit. As he left her alone in the flickering, glowing bedroom to do the deed in the privacy of the one next door, just for a second he considered the alternative before dismissing it out of hand. What they had was pure and must remain untarnished by what would undoubtedly be a huge, embarrassing mistake. And anyway, he knew he was up to the task, he'd been practising, just in case.

Adam returned bearing his gift, which he passed over silently, kissing Daisy gently on the forehead before leaving the room to offer similar privacy. When he heard her calling his name he found Daisy lying underneath the covers, her hips clearly elevated with a cushion, looking rather pleased, quite serene. Pulling the covers back and patting the mattress, Daisy signalled that he should join her so obeying, Adam climbed into bed and pulled the duvet over his body.

They lay together side by side, holding hands in the darkened room, the candles burning low, watching the sky turn black as the moon and stars illuminated the Atlantique below. Warmed by the fire they listened to their life on a loop, remembering the past and imagining the future, one praying, the other wishing that new life was already being created deep inside Daisy's body.

They repeated the process two more times, following the online advice and taking full of advantage of Daisy's window of ovulation opportunity. As they drove home at the end of their retreat, both were silent, pensive yet hopeful. Five days after she missed her period, unable to wait any longer, Adam and Daisy took a trip into town to buy a testing kit. Even passing it to the cashier filled him with the fear of failure; swiftly banished by a heart swamped with such expectation. Neither spoke all the way home, not even when they made their way upstairs to the bathroom or while Adam waited outside. When Daisy opened the door and sat by his side on the landing, their hearts were going mental because this was it, the moment of truth.

"Remember what we agreed. If it's negative then we just try again, okay?" Daisy sounded more confident than she looked.

"I know. There's no need to get all stressed – and no tears either, we just have to stay positive. Loads of people try over and over. Thirty seconds to go. I feel a bit sick, do you?" Adam watched the numbers decrease on his timer, keeping pace with his heart.

Daisy swallowed nervously, holding the white stick face down. "No, but either way I think I'm going to cry, I can't help it. Shall I turn it over yet?"

Adam was concentrating hard. "No not yet."

"Okay. God this is the longest three minutes of my life! I think I need another wee, or should I save it in case we need to double check?"

Adam shook his head. "Just cross your legs and don't dribble on the carpet." He focused on his timer.

"I'm getting the nervous giggles, I can feel them coming Adam. I think I might really wee." Daisy stifled the urge to laugh whereas Adam was deadly serious.

"Just hold on, we've only got ten seconds to go, and don't turn it over till I say. Shall I video it, the big moment? Shit, we should've videoed it from the start, not you weeing on the stick but from when you came out of the loo. I can't believe I forgot, bugger! I know – shall I get your phone?" Adam made to get up but Daisy grabbed his arm.

"Adam its fine, stop panicking and what if it's negative? That would be totally shit and depressing, anyway it must be time now, look my hand is shaking, actually I think I'm going to throw up... yep, it's either that or a heart attack." Daisy held her chest with her free hand, trying to quell whatever was happening inside.

The drama was interrupted when the timer on Adam's phone began to bleep causing Daisy to catch her breath. Both were stunned into wide-eyed silence before Adam came back to earth and switched it off, just as Daisy had a belated idea.

"Why don't you film it now, go on, turn your camera on. We can delete it if it's negative." Adam sensed that Daisy was stalling, delaying the moment of truth, her nerves causing uncertainty, logic a swinging pendulum – up one minute, down the next.

Pointing his phone in the direction of Daisy's hand Adam noticed a slight screen tremor, which he ignored, focusing instead on the white stick of plastic.

"Here goes." Daisy and Adam clasped their spare hands together while one filmed and the other flipped the stick so the window was uppermost and readable.

"Oh my God." Daisy was stunned, her voice a whisper.

"Say it out loud Daisy, go on, read it so there's no mistake."

"Enceinte."

"That means pregnant, right?"

"Yes, it means I'm pregnant. I'm really pregnant. Oh my God Adam, we did it. I can't believe it. We're going to have a baby!"

It was at that point the cameraman lost control of his device and all that could be seen on the rest of the footage was the crack in the landing ceiling and a big cobweb hanging from the lampshade. The soundtrack was basically whoops and laughter, Adam asking Daisy if she was definitely sure then suggesting they do another test, just to check. The furore was then interrupted by the sound of Pam coming home from the supermarket, shouting upstairs if anyone wanted a cuppa.

Filming resumed shortly afterwards when Adam retrieved his phone and Daisy, clutching the plastic stick, pounded down the stairs, their hurry interspersed with orders to take care, slow down and don't trip. At first Pamela wasn't too pleased about being filmed because she had bobble-hat hair and was wearing her unflattering plastic raincoat, then she spotted the white stick and the penny dropped. Caution was immediately thrown to the wind and the moment caught for posterity with a selfie – Granny Pam, Mummy and Daddy, on the happiest day of Adam's life.

*

Feeling a lump forming in his throat and the hint of a tear at the corner of his eye, Adam shuffled in his seat, composing himself, the memories of that day still as fresh as they were seven months earlier. And now, after a long, hot summer in which Daisy blossomed and he threw himself into running the site, it was finally time to relate every joyous moment of his wonderful news to Ryan.

It wasn't going to be the easiest of chats because accompanying the baby announcement would be a revelation and however awkward, he was finally able and ready to tell his brother everything. Adam was a man now, he was going to be a father, the best dad a child could wish for and owing to this he felt elevated to a status of not superiority, but maybe it brought him level with his brother, someone everyone viewed as normal, an alpha male.

In his before-life of being the oddball brother, the one who people speculated over, surmised wrongly and probably judged unfairly, Adam wouldn't have had the confidence or resolve to even begin to explain what being 'him' meant. There had been no way of knowing how Ryan would've reacted and worst-case scenario, affected the love the elder had for the younger. It was actually the unknown that struck most fear, things unsaid, thoughts that Ryan may have carried in his head and kept to himself. Would his brother feel pity or scorn? Attributing Adam's nature to the failings of their parents, assuming he was the defective result of a faulty gene, forced to make excuses about his weird brother? To contemplate that his only living relative, Adam's rock, would feel even an ounce of shame or irritation at being saddled by a freaky sibling, well, that would've killed him.

The really shocking yet equally liberating thing was that now, Adam just didn't care. Becoming a father-to-be and the part-owner of a thriving business with plans for the future made him feel untouchable. He'd laid the foundations of a new life, which were cemented into the heart of a real family. And planning his forever, however unconventional, with the woman he loved with every fibre of his body, well, that made Adam feel invincible, superhuman. No mere mortal, not even his brother, could ruin that for him.

Was he nervous about his heart-to-heart? In truth he was. Adam wanted to get it just right and falling short of writing a script, he more or less knew the conversation off by heart. He was going to start at the beginning and once he had answered any of Ryan's questions, he would move onto how he felt about Daisy because, really, she was the key, the centre of everything.

He had to make Ryan understand that theirs was a different kind of love but by no means inferior to that any other couple experienced, regardless of its gender combination. And while there was a missing element to their relationship, it by no means diminished their admiration, respect or adoration for one another. In fact, apart from the obvious, when you looked at their situation as a whole they had it all, which was why they were having a child together, before it was too late.

Adam knew this would be the biggie, the obstacle that Ryan might have the most trouble with so without drawing him a diagram, he intended to make it quite clear how their baby was conceived. In truth, it was none of Ryan's business because he'd had his chance with Daisy. She might've had a child with anyone and he would have had to deal with it.

Once the bomb was dropped Adam would say he hoped, no, expected Ryan to be part of his nephew's life. He had been the absent brother for too long and now his military life was coming to an end there should be no more excuses and disappearing acts.

Ryan had to step up, join in and instead of grieving the lack of family life when they were younger just embrace what's right in front of his eyes.

Adam had become accustomed to Ryan's absences, accepting it was a means to an end, forever grateful for his brother's support, both financial and emotional. They had endured being apart, striding out into the world, a period of independence and growing up. Ryan had made a huge success of his career and set himself up for the future, laden with credentials and a couple of properties that he'd never even lived in, plus a healthy bank account. But now it was high time he stopped running away.

In fantastical moments Adam further embellished his dream for the future, adding a stick-man drawing to the one of him, Daisy, their boy and Pam, oh and Basil. But in recent months Adam had begun to colour it in, his mood becoming bolder as the picture took shape. What if, given time, Ryan too could be part of the business? As tiny shoots of an idea began to burst into life, Adam allowed these seedlings to flourish and unable to contain his enthusiasm, he committed them to paper. A plan for an adventure centre, a place where youngsters could experience the outdoors, canoe on the lake, cycle along the forest tracks, sleep under the stars or in the log cabins, and who better to lead the way? Adam's very own intrepid traveller, outdoor-man himself, the alpha-male and all rounder – Ryan.

Just as he had feared ending his days alone, Adam now recognised that his brother was heading in that very direction so it was time to drag him into the fold, experience real life with his family. It was this notion of Ryan being included that stirred within Adam a previously absent emotion. Maybe approaching fatherhood had left him open to a gamut of unexplored inner depths but whatever it was, he was succumbing to the strangest awakenings, considering his own mortality, seeing responsibility through the eyes of his old friend Bill.

Adam now understood why he'd set so much store on leaving things in order, looking after Pam and Daisy, seeking clandestine assurances from Adam. It was this example that prompted Adam's visit to the notaires and the subsequent putting in order of his own life, taking care of business. There was only one person he would trust with his family, who he would share them with, and that was his brother.

But it wasn't just the spectre of his demise that had troubled Adam, it was the worst of his traits that came back to haunt him – a nagging hint of jealousy that sometimes ballooned and rampaged through his mind, completely out of control, and green had never been his colour.

Having settled his mind on a life in France, Adam embarked upon a meticulous thought process where any pitfalls and humps were thoroughly examined and ticked off, even Pam's potential reticence, yet there was just one aspect of his master plan that remained beyond his control. Once everything was within his grasp and after the wheel of fortune was set in motion, Adam became increasingly aware of all he stood to lose. For now though, he could console himself that Daisy had the impending birth to occupy her so her mind was focused. Not just that, she needed him now more than ever because as their baby grew, so did her fears.

Adam knew from their many chats following antenatal appointments and parenting classes that she was truly terrified of labour and had made Adam swear that she'd be given everything on offer to reduce her pain. While on the surface she appeared carefree, Daisy often got herself into a state about all sorts – snakes, fairground rides, gypsy curses, Ebola, a butter shortage, Donald Trump. The list of random fears that rarely affected her life went on and on.

In comparison, what scared the crap out of Adam was that once the baby years were out of the way and their son was toddling towards the school gate, maybe Daisy would be less absorbed, latent hormones rekindled, inclined then to search for satisfaction of the sexual kind. After all, although *he* didn't have such urges, Daisy did.

Pushing these troubling interlopers from his mind as they sullied his current state of utopia, Adam reminded himself of her promise that he would never be pushed out or away, from her life or that of their son. The fact that she had remained true to her word since the beginning was comforting, so the recent renewal of her vow would just have to do. Then there was the law – he would be on the birth certificate, his name in black and white, never mind the DNA, an invisible irremovable hallmark. Adam was part of the campsite too and Pam looked upon him as a son, so how could he ever be cast aside? No, his worries whilst understandable were for now unfounded; he had done well, so many ticks in the box.

Noticing that people around him were collecting their baggage and heading towards the gate, Adam glanced at the screen in the departure hall, which told him his flight was boarding so he picked up his rucksack and joined the queue. After showing his passport and boarding pass he headed down the steps, across the tarmac and towards the plane. Placing one hand on his chest he felt the familiar crinkle – the inside pocket of his jacket held a photograph of his boy. Adam wanted it close to his heart during the journey and ever since the nurse handed it to him at the clinic, looked at it frequently, still in awe of the little alien that he had made with Daisy.

Once he was seated by the window Adam left the other passengers to their faffing and bag stuffing, the sound of overhead lockers slamming shut distracting him slightly from texting. The first message was to Daisy: I'm on the plane. Hope you are okay. Get some rest. Miss you already. I'll text when we land. Love you lots ♥

The second was to Ryan: On my way. Can't wait to see you, mate. It's been too long and I miss my big bro. Will txt when I'm in the taxi ☺

Adam waited until the last minute for a reply before obeying the rules and switching off his phone, deciding to enjoy take-off then maybe sleep during the flight. It was probably going to be a long night, talking things through with Ryan.

As the plane roared down the runway and jettisoned its bird-like frame towards the sky, Adam placed his hand on his heart, smiled and closed his eyes, drifting into a fitful sleep. He was accompanied in flight by voices selling drinks and snacks, images of Daisy and a black and white alien, his family home in France and somewhere miles up ahead, his brother.

Chapter 31

Daisy

Unable to sleep or relax even, Daisy had driven to Cassandre's who, sensing trouble, had enlisted the moral support of Inès and together attempted to lift their friend's spirits and clear her head. They had been brilliant, right from the beginning. When she and Adam announced their baby news, the relief they felt at their acceptance of the situation emboldened them, made them feel braver than they were. Telling Daisy's closest and oldest friends had been a test, a way to gauge how others may take the news, their friends in Manchester for a start.

There were no lies or secrets where the French community were concerned. It was common knowledge that Adam was the donor and they were going to bring up the baby together. It had been refreshing and surprising that even in a small and devoutly Catholic village made up of mostly elderly residents, their news was greeted with delight – and some gratitude for a snippet of rather unusual gossip. Their English friends remained in the dark. Daisy and Adam had asked that no hints or announcements were made on social media, not until Ryan had been informed.

Now, as the big reveal loomed, Daisy felt cast adrift and out of the loop so sought comfort and reassurance from her girls, all the time watching the clock and checking her phone. She knew Adam had landed and the last message, from the taxi, told her not to worry and he'd ring her once he'd spoken to Ryan. His battery was on its last legs so he'd charge it as soon as he checked in. All she could do now was wait.

"Come on Daisy, it's going to be okay. I am positive that Ryan will be happy for you both, very shocked at first but he will understand. He's a nice guy underneath his macho image and wanderlust ways. I always had a good feeling about him. He was a bit deep but seemed kind and sort of dependable so there's no reason to think he has changed." Cassandre was chopping lemons, which she placed into the large jug of ice-cold water. The Indian summer and Daisy's flushed face called for refreshment of the non-alcoholic kind.

"I know, I know. I've gone over it in my head a thousand times but he's always been prone to being blunt and his opinion could go either way. It won't affect this little guy but it will spoil things for Adam and might ruin our happiness." Daisy ran her hands over her bump, deep in thought.

"And this is why Adam flew to England. They must discuss any awkward feelings before the baby comes, otherwise it will be uncomfortable when he visits his nephew. But I think the hardest part will be getting over your affair, that may bring problems." Inès never minced her words.

Daisy felt her cheeks redden. "I am over him and the feelings mutual. That's not going to be an issue." Suspecting her face resembled a tomato and knowing her friend's knack for seeing through a fib, Daisy averted her eyes, thus missing the silent look that passed between Cassandre and Inès.

"Well, that's good news…and it's not like you ever had a big argument or said nasty words to each other so you can start again, a blank page, just good friends. No kissy kissy or sexy looks." Inès raised her eyebrow and waited for Daisy's response to thinly veiled sarcasm.

"Exactly! Nothing like that is on the cards…*nothing* at all. We just sort of drifted apart once I met you-know-who and I didn't see him again until Dad died. And the funeral wasn't the time or the place for a heart-to-heart, or anything really. After that, well, he just seemed to fade away. We pass the odd comment on Facebook and like each other's photos, that kind of thing, but if I'm honest got a bit fed up of seeing him with other women and lately I've kept my head down where social media is concerned, for obvious reasons."

Cassandre spread her arms dramatically and sided with Daisy. "See, there's nothing to worry about. You both have to behave like adults, shit happens. We have sex, it was very nice or a horrible waste of time, and then we move on. It's as simple as that! How do you think I feel every time I go to the boulangerie and Victor passes me a baguette? We both know exactly what we got up to in his father's barn on his sixteenth birthday, and then there's Louis at the déchetterie – I blush just thinking of him – and Alexis, the doctor's son. I swear that grumpy old man looks at me funny whenever I go to the surgery, and what about Mathis, and Ruben! I talk to his wife all the time outside school, and remember–"

Inès didn't have the time or patience for a stroll down memory lane with the scarlet woman of Le Forêt. "Yes, yes Cassandre, I think we get the message. But not everyone is as libéral as you, maybe Daisy still has feelings for Ryan. It's not a crime and let's face it, he is *really* hot."

Cassandre gasped in mock shock causing Inès to defend herself.

"What? Don't look at me like that! There's still a bit of life in this happily married woman, we all have our fantasies." Inès winked at Daisy who took the teasing in her stride yet at the same time, couldn't quite shrug off the truth.

"Okay, cards on the table…I do still think of him now and then and wonder what might have been but it's not like I weep into my pillow every night. Like Cassandre says, he's a part of my past and most of the time I can honestly say I'm over him, until his name is mentioned or I see a photo then I go a bit gaga, but it wears off. I'm not putting my life on hold for him or anyone ever again, that's gospel." Daisy took a sip of the lemony drink, her watered down confession had in some part unburdened her, but worry remained.

"Daisy, stop looking at the clock! You will go mad wondering what is happening hundreds of miles away so just leave it to the boys and whatever the outcome, we will deal with it. No point making yourself sick and fed up. My sister-in-law was horrible when I was having Lola. I swear that woman made me want to commit murder, interfering and stirring the pan." Cassandre folded her arms, indignant.

Inès, however, rolled her eyes. "Cassandre is being over-dramatic as usual but for once is correct. And I think you should say stirring the pot, not the pan, am I correct Daisy?"

Daisy nodded towards Cassandre whose faux pas had injected some humour into the conversation as Inès continued, looking smug. "You must be patient and by bedtime everyone will be happy, and then we can all be excited for Christmas and our new arrival. It will be such a wonderful time for all of us." Inès leant over and covered Daisy's hands with hers, eliciting a smile from her pink-cheeked friend.

"Okay, okay. I give in. Enough of my troubles. Now, can I come with you to collect the kids from school, I might even invite myself for dinner? Mum's having apéros with her book club so I'll go mad if I'm home alone."

"Perfect, and you can help Lola with her homework, she is a complete nightmare and thinks of any excuse to wriggle out of it. She will behave for you, the contrary little monster." Cassandre gathered up their glasses and the jug, pleased to have an ally for later.

As they scraped back chairs and headed for the door, Daisy was convinced that a walk through the village and an hour or two in the company of a bolshy eight-year-old was just what she needed to take her mind off things. So checking her phone one more time, she placed it in her pocket and followed her friends outside, eager for the day to be over.

It was gone eight when Daisy drove through the gates of Campanule and swung her car around the back of the house, parking next to Pamela's before collecting her bag and a carton of apples from Cassandre's tree. She was going to make crumble for when Adam returned. There was always a glut of fruit freebies at harvest time and the perfect opportunity to stock up the freezer for winter.

Opening the back door Daisy placed the carton on the kitchen table and went in search of her mum – it was strangely quiet – expecting the sound of Pam watching one of her soaps but instead, as she neared the lounge she was sure she could hear sobbing. Rushing forward she faltered at the door, listening in silence before slowly pushing it open. With each centimetre of movement came a creeping sense of dread. Pamela was sitting in her armchair, a tissue pushed to her face, shoulders rising and falling quickly with every sob, oblivious to Daisy's presence and lost in her own bubble of grief.

"Mum, what's wrong?" It was all Daisy could muster, a strained whisper but enough to cause Pamela to start, her reddened, tear-soaked eyes focusing on her daughter and in that moment, transformed further by despair.

Standing quickly Pam reached out then stepped closer, tentatively approaching Daisy whose hands remained by her side, trembling, the involuntary vibrations beginning to course through her body.

"Oh Daisy, oh Daisy I'm so sorry, please sit down, just sit down. I need to tell you something, I'm so sorry my love." Pamela was flustered, almost panicked.

But Daisy didn't want to hear it, whatever it was, so she stepped backwards, placing both hands over her ears, blocking out Pamela's voice, retreating from the room while her mouth moved silently, the word 'no' repeated over and over.

When she bumped into the wall, missing the opening, the thud and sharp corners of the doorframe jolting, stinging, it gave Pamela seconds to approach and take Daisy's hands in hers, and once they were clutched to her own breast, their eyes locked together. Only then did she speak, hating each and every one of the most dreadful, painful words.

"Daisy you have to listen to me, and you have to be very brave and calm, breath slowly, that's it, good girl, take your time." Pamela attempted to steer Daisy towards the sofa but she resisted, frozen to the spot.

"Just say it. Just tell me." Daisy could barely be heard, however there was steeliness to her tone.

"It's Adam." Pamela's voice cracked. "There was an accident on the motorway. The taxi was involved in a pile-up and there was nothing they could do…Oh Daisy, he's gone. I'm so sorry but our Adam is gone." Pamela was sobbing again. The pain in her heart was as unbearable as the look on her daughter's face. It was as though Daisy's features dissolved, her body following suit, becoming limp, sliding down the wall and forming an inert heap on the carpet. And then came the screaming.

How many hours had passed since the dreadful news, Pamela couldn't recall. The day had stretched on forever, the evening bringing with it no respite from the horror they were forced to face. It was all a blur, constant noise, wailing, such terrible sobbing, and anger. Then Cassandre and Inès arrived. Next came the doctor. There were so many questions, no answers, only imaginings of some tangled horror and a race to the hospital where they tried in vain to save their precious Adam.

Pamela just wanted it to stop and then rewind back to that morning. For Rémi's van to break down or the flight to be cancelled or for Adam to get into another taxi. She would hug him for longer, say something more meaningful than 'don't forget my Paxo'. What a waste of precious minutes, their last moments. So many thoughts raced. If she had a wish it would be for the obvious but that wasn't going to happen, so instead perhaps she could ask for all the pain that was consuming her daughter – the loss, despair, heartbreak – to be absorbed into her own body. Pamela would willingly take every ounce of it, suffer for the rest of her days, anything was better than seeing Daisy like that.

How would they ever get over this? And then there was the baby. Pam's eyes wandered to the photograph on the mantelpiece but it hurt too much to linger, and anyhow, she couldn't see it properly. Another flood of tears sprang forth only to be interrupted by Inès, tapping gently on the door.

"I'm sorry Pamela, to intrude, but Daisy has woken up and she wants her phone so she can ring Ryan again, she insists. We tried to persuade her to wait until morning but she's adamant so I think we should let her try, otherwise she will become more distressed." Inès looked awful, drained and very pale.

"You're right, best let her get it over with. It might help them both, though God knows how. Here, you take it up and I'll make us some warm drinks and then you need to get home to your husband, you look exhausted." In truth Pamela wanted them to stay because then she could hide in the lounge and not face her poor Daisy.

"It's fine Pamela. I'll stay as long as I'm needed, Cassandre too. And please, if you need anything just say, I know this is terrible for you too." When Inès saw Pamela nod then look away quickly she took the phone and retreated from the room silently, leaving the sobbing woman to her grief.

Daisy was propped up against a mass of pillows, phone in hand, alone in her bedroom. The girls had gone downstairs while she made the call. They had left without much persuasion, glad of a break, needing some time away from their friend's despair. Daisy was still hoping that this was a hideous dream and soon she would wake up, thoroughly traumatised but gloriously relieved. Or maybe she was delirious and had been poisoned by lemon water or Cassandre's cooking and once the toxins left her body she would wake to find herself tangled in sweaty sheets, the fever abated. Whatever she was experiencing certainly didn't feel real because her body was numb, each movement she made was slow, her thoughts dull and one step behind, which made even the pressing of a button on her phone seem difficult. And while she waited for the ringtone, the only other sound was her laboured breathing, quite ghostly and accompanied by an unwanted sensation – that of a thumping heart, reminding her she was still alive when all she wanted was to be dead, and with Adam.

It was 1am and there was a chance that Ryan would be asleep, perhaps he'd cried himself into a pain-free state. She so wished it had worked for her. He answered after the eleventh ring, Daisy counted each one, expecting it to go to voicemail.

"Daisy." He began to cry.

"Ryan...Ryan, I'm so sorry." Then so did she.

It took a while for it to stop, their outpouring of tears but eventually, between deep breaths, they took control and were able to speak, string together a sentence, but whatever they said sounded wrong, crass and morbid.

"Have you seen him?"

"Yes, at the hospital, I got there as quick as I could but it was too late. He looked like he was asleep. I held his hand. They let me stay for a bit then I had to go. I didn't want to leave him on his own Daisy but I had to...I feel so bad. I've been thinking of going back and begging them to let me sit with him, I don't know what to do."

"Sssh...please don't cry, Ryan. I can't bear hearing you like this. I wish I was there with you. I hate the thought of you being on your own. And don't beat yourself up. You tried to get there and they probably wouldn't have let you see him straight away."

"But I wanted to speak to him Daisy, let him know I was there, that he wasn't on his own with strangers. I should have been there when he went. They should have let me in."

More crying. It was the most dreadful, soul-wrenching thing Daisy had ever heard, made a thousand times worse by separation and knowing he was alone. The urge to hold him was profound, her body actually ached – could she feel his pain or was it her own? When the sound slowly abated Daisy spoke softly, desperate to get through.

"Look, I'll come over. I'll help you. And I want to see him, I need to say goodbye. We can go together. Is that okay?"

"Yes, I'd like that. When can you come? I'll drive over and get you, no, that's stupid, I should wait here. Sorry, I'm not thinking straight."

"It's okay I understand, I can't think properly either. There's so much I want to ask you but I'm too scared. I just want to remember him how he was but I need to know the facts too, does that make sense?"

"Course it does, but now's not the time, it will just upset you more, and me too. I can't bear to even think about it but it won't go away either."

"Look, I'll go downstairs and talk to Mum, make some arrangements then I'll ring you back later. There'll be stuff to sort out and you need to rest. I'll send you a text in case you are sleeping then ring me when you get up. There's lots of options for getting there so I'll just choose the quickest, okay?"

"Yeah, okay, you're right. But you need to rest too. Thanks for ringing Daisy, I've been lying here wondering what to do, how you were and if I should call but I felt sort of numb, like I was paralysed with shock."

"Me too…and I keep praying it's a dream."

"Oh God I wish it was Daisy, I'd give anything for that to be true." When he began to cry Ryan set Daisy off so they rode the wave of grief together, somehow managing not to drown.

Daisy spoke first, trying hard to be the brave, sensible one. "Now try and close your eyes and I'll get off and book something. Okay?"

"Okay."

"Oh and by the way, have you got Adam's phone?"

"Yes, it's here, they gave me a bag with his stuff in, why?"

"Well there's a page in his notes, it's a list of stuff he wanted should the worst happen."

"Are you kidding me?"

"You know what Adam is like…" the words stuck in her throat, almost choking her, but she carried on. "He wrote things down, all sorts of random things that sprung into his mind. He liked everything in order and said it kept his head straight so you'd better check it in case there's anything we need to know, or do. You'll need to charge it, he told me it was almost flat, just before, you know…"

"Oh God, this is all too much Daisy. I can't believe we are having this conversation." The sound of sobbing at both ends filled their ears until minutes later, when it eased, they agreed to get off the phone. It was doing no good talking.

"I'll text you soon, bye for now Ryan. Try to be strong. I'll be there soon, I promise."

"Okay, bye Daisy. And will you give my love to Pam?" As soon as he heard her say yes, his voice cracked and he was gone, the bleeping sound filling the room.

Sliding off the bed Daisy stood and immediately had to steady herself, slightly dizzy and lightheaded. She needed to eat and make plans, then get to Ryan as soon as she could. There was so much to do, to explain. During their conversation, amidst the pain, Daisy had found some strength. It was nothing short of a miracle compared with how she had felt just before but by reaching out to Ryan, she had managed to survive a few more minutes.

And this was no dream, she wasn't going to wake up and shake her head at foolish imaginings. It was real. Opening her bedroom door Daisy made her way down the stairs, weary already, grasping onto the banister and a faint sense of purpose, encouraging her to put one foot in front of the other. Ryan needed her.

Chapter 32

A kick in the teeth

Ryan managed to sleep but only for a couple of hours. He couldn't even remember closing his eyes. He just lay on the bed and allowed grief and exhaustion to do the rest. Picking up his phone he saw it was 4.30am. Heaving a leaden body off the bed, turning on the bedside light he stared at the blue, plastic carrier bag that contained Adam's denim jacket and converse trainers. The rest were at the hospital, streaked in blood, cut open by the staff in A&E. Grabbing the bag he shook the contents onto the bed and then scrunched up the plastic, stuffing any reminders of the hospital room in the bin. He was looking for Adam's phone. Daisy said it would need charging before he could read whatever crazy notes were stored there. Ryan dreaded it.

Sitting down on the bed he felt the outside pockets of the jacket, nothing, but maybe it was on the inside so just to be sure he flipped the denim open and patted the fabric. There was no sign of either his phone or wallet, apart from what appeared to be a photo, just peeping out of the left pocket. Ryan slid it out. It took a few seconds to register what he was looking at because there, in black and white, was the very clear image of a baby and when he flipped it over, in Adam's spidery handwriting was written two words: My boy.

"My boy…what the fuck?" As air was sucked from his chest Ryan held the photo closer, scrutinising the handwriting and the image of a baby. Surely it couldn't be Adam's baby. Nah, it was impossible. He didn't even have a girlfriend, or did he? He'd got someone pregnant at work, or one of the guests, was that why he resigned so quickly? But why hadn't he said, when had it happened? Then the light dawned – this was what Adam wanted to talk about, his baby. He'd been buzzing about something.

Ryan had heard it in his voice. *'No it's a mistake. It's got to be a practical joke. Yeah, that's what it'll be, one of Adam's pranks. But if it wasn't, why hadn't Daisy said something earlier? Wrong time you dickhead! I should ring her now and ask her what's going on. No, she'll be sleeping, let her rest.'* Ryan silently talked himself through the shock and his options.

Throwing the photo down onto the bed he stood and began pacing the room, ravaged by questions, nervous energy kicking in. Unsure of what to do with his shaking hands, he clasped them together in a praying motion. One minute his arms were wrapped around his body, the next behind his head, palms encapsulating his skull, protecting his brain, which was about to explode. Ryan paced, then he sat. He looked at the photo then stood again, pacing, thinking, breathing deeply.

His eyes fell on Adam's rucksack – the phone, he needed to charge it. Grabbing it from the floor Ryan threw it on the bed and unclipped the catches then tipped everything onto the duvet, the phone and charger revealing themselves immediately amongst Adam's clean t-shirts and underwear. It was plugged in within seconds. Ryan waited for it to come to life. The red battery sign fluctuated as electricity began to pulse then the home screen appeared, displaying a picture of Adam and Basil.

Ryan groaned. It was agony, sheer mind-blowing, stomach-churning pain, just looking at the perfect, laughing face of his precious brother hugging a scruffy dog. Scrolling sideways he prayed there wasn't a code; he was in luck. It seemed that Adam was happy for his phone to be unsecured, open, nothing to hide here folks…or was there? There had to be a clue somewhere, maybe in his contacts or the notes that Daisy mentioned, or what about texts? The mother of this baby might be in touch so he'd start there, and although it felt like he was invading Adam's space, plundering his privacy, Ryan just had to look.

Running his eyes over the inbox of messages there was absolutely nothing that alerted him, no new female names, just Pam, Daisy, surely not Cassandre or Inès, Allison, the girl from the ship, but a quick peep uncovered nothing. The rest of the names were male, leaving Ryan more perplexed. Then it occurred to him that Daisy would probably know all about it so there might be reference to something, either baby or girlfriend related, in one of her messages. But was it wrong to poke his nose into their correspondence, they might have discussed Ryan, and what was it their gran used to say about eavesdroppers? Well this was sort of the same but in print, like earwigging at a door.

It took only a second to make up his mind. He'd be asking her later anyway so it was best to get some of the story beforehand, help him set his head straight before he spoke to Daisy. Tapping her name, a whole screen of messages opened up, back and forth, so he began to scroll through, searching in reverse. There was nothing innocuous or helpful in the first few pages, just Daisy stressing about the journey and making Adam swear oaths to keep in touch, so Ryan continued, convinced that somewhere there would be a reference to the baby. If not he would check the notes instead, and then the photo album. There had to be a photo, something that would explain. When he came to Saturday, four days earlier, Ryan found his answer.

DAISY: On your way back from the tip can you get me some ketchup crisps, two big bags!!

ADAM: No, they are bad for you, eat tomato butties instead!

DAISY: Pleaaaaase. I ♥ them.

ADAM: You'll get fat!

DAISY: I'm already fat!

ADAM: You'll be a dobber!

DAISY: I don't care. They're not for me they are for the bump – he says he ♥ them too so just get the bloody crisps!!!!!

ADAM: Ok you psycho. See you soon Daisy Dumpling ♥

Time actually stopped, as did Ryan's heart, just for a beat and then it resumed but at a rapid pace, his face flushed hot, eyes refusing to believe what he was reading. He was stunned, really and truly stunned, like after being slapped. That's what it was, a hard slap, like hitting the water, a belly-flopping crack that stings like hell after. And Ryan was stung alright. Whatever sorrow he'd felt during the past twelve hours dissipated and was swiftly replaced by a whole new range of feelings: hurt, anger and intense humiliation.

Yet despite being engulfed by such negative emotions, he had to carry on. The wound was open and he had to cut deeper. The truth might poison him but he simply had to know, needing to clearly see the deceit, read the lies and discover the truth.

Moving to the photo album, Ryan opened the first most obvious file on the screen, the one that said 'Our boy'. One tap. That's all it took to close the case and seal Ryan's heart because there, thanks to the wonder of high definition, he found image upon image of Adam and Daisy, and their bump.

It was 6pm and both Daisy and Pamela were in a heightened state of delayed shock combined with deep anxiety, not helped one bit by fatigue, grief and frustration. Ryan had gone off grid.

He wasn't answering his phone, which rang out at first so she thought he might be in the shower or sleeping, meaning he'd switched it to silent, but now it was turned off.

Just to be sure Daisy rang the hotel with the intention of leaving a message, perhaps he'd gone to the restaurant, but she was wrong again – he'd checked out. Eleven hours of nothing followed. Where was he? Had he done something stupid? No, not Ryan. Pam suggested he might be on his way to them, a thought that brightened Daisy for a while but with each passing hour it became more unlikely because unless he was walking from Norfolk, he'd have arrived by now. Daisy couldn't think straight, she couldn't even remember much of their conversation – lots of crying but not much else other than her promise to go to him as soon as possible.

"Do you think we should phone the base, love, check if he's there? Surely there must be some way of getting a message to him.

He might have lost his phone. I bet his head's all over the place. Yes, that will be it. He'll have left in a rush and it's probably under the bed in his hotel room or maybe in his car, or the battery might be flat. We just need to keep calm and wait."

Daisy was so frustrated and slightly annoyed. "But Mum, he knows that I was going to go over there. I said I'd let him know when I was arriving so what the hell is he playing at? He's either out of his mind with grief or gone on a bender and to be honest I think it's the last option. He'll be blocking it all out and getting wasted."

"That's a bit harsh love and I'll be a bit disappointed in him if that's the case, never mind leaving you in the lurch. I'll go and make some tea and toast then we'll try again. And why don't you look on Facebook, see if he's posted anything on there? If it comes down to it you'll have to contact his friends, or the base."

"Okay, I'll look now but Mum, no toast, I couldn't keep it down."

"Just try half a slice, for me and the baby." Pamela saw Daisy nod before heading towards the kitchen. Tea and toast was her default remedy for most things, even disappearing bloody airmen.

It didn't take long for Daisy to discover zilch on Ryan's Facebook page. He hadn't posted about Adam so she could only presume that apart from those in France, everyone else was in the dark or respecting Ryan's privacy. Trying his phone again to find it was still switched off, Daisy curled up on the sofa and buried her head in a cushion, desperate for sleep yet far too wired, Ryan-related scenarios shooting through her mind.

It was then that a thought occurred. She remembered mentioning Adam's phone, saying it would need charging, so even if Ryan's was on the blink then he could have used Adam's in an emergency, just to make contact. It was picturing Ryan, all alone in some soulless hotel room during the early hours of the morning, searching through Adam's phone for a list of his final requests that caused the truth to hit home.

'Oh dear God, oh what have I done? Oh no, no, no. You stupid, stupid woman! The photos, he's seen them, and in the notes there will be bloody all sorts. Emails from the clinic, appointment times, everything.' Daisy sat bolt upright, a million panicked thoughts racing, her hands covering burning cheeks, not knowing what the hell to do next. *'That's why he hasn't rung, he knows, he's worked it out. Oh God please help me, what shall I do, what shall I do?'*

"Mum, Mum, come here, Mum!" Daisy was on her feet heading towards the kitchen, meeting a worried-looking Pamela halfway. "Oh Mum, what have I done? He knows, Ryan knows about the baby and he hates me, he hates us both, what am I going to do? I need to explain, I need to explain for Adam…" The hysteria came in waves and Pamela rode each one with Daisy, while in the calmer moments managed to ring Cassandre and asked her to come back.

Once she arrived, Pamela took matters into her own hands and found the number of the base at Marham then put a call through to the switchboard, explaining that there had been a death in the family and they needed to speak to Ryan urgently. She didn't give a fig about protocol or that he might be annoyed that she'd rang his place of work. All Pam cared about was her child, and the unborn one she was carrying inside her.

Daisy's phone rang forty minutes later and when it did, Pam and Cassandre left the room, knowing that the conversation to be had was deeply personal on so many levels. Daisy was so terrified that for a brief moment she considered not answering but that was cowardly and she owed it to Adam to set the record straight.

Ryan took control immediately, his tone the complete opposite to the last time they spoke. It was hard and measured, almost business-like.

"You wanted to speak to me?"

"Yes, of course I do. You were supposed to ring me back. Didn't you get my text about plane times?"

"Yes I got it."

Cold dread was washing over Daisy. Ryan's ice-cold voice told her he knew yet she ploughed on, waiting for him to show his hand. "So where have you been, why didn't you get in touch? I've been waiting for hours."

Again, a harsh reply: "I've been busy, making arrangements."

Daisy was aware of the exasperation in her voice. "But that's what I'm going to do when I get there, help you sort things out."

"There's no need. The squadron chaplain is looking after it all for me so there was no point replying *or* for you to come over. I'll be fine by myself, it's all in hand."

This was all wrong, too rushed. What the hell was he playing at? "But what have you arranged, surely you can't have fixed the funeral date already, people need to be informed, have you even told any of his friends?"

"Adam will be cremated, just as he wished and the service will be held here in the village. I'm going to post on Facebook tomorrow and if any of his friends want to attend the service they can but I'd rather you stay away."

"What? What did you just say?" Daisy thought she was going to faint.

"I said I'd rather you stayed away. I don't want you here. In fact, I don't ever want to see you again. Is that clear enough?"

"Ryan, stop this, stop it right now! What the hell is the matter with you, why are you being like this?" It was a bloody stupid question yet still Daisy held back, afraid to raise the subject of her baby.

"Why am I being like what? I don't owe you any explanations Daisy. Adam is my brother and I will see to things my way. Like I said, I don't want to see you and neither do I need your help."

"That's enough! And you do owe me an explanation and I have the right to be involved and you bloody well know why! So go on Ryan, have the balls to say it – let's see if you are man enough to be honest. I'm waiting, come on, let's get this over with." Daisy was literally trembling with rage.

Ryan let rip, unable to contain his anger. "How fucking *dare* you talk to me about being honest when the pair of you have been lying for years? Going behind my back and telling everyone you were just good friends when it's bollocks, it's all been bollocks!"

"You know nothing about it Ryan, which is precisely why Adam came to see you, he wanted to explain face to face, and yes, it's something he should have done years ago but I respected his decision so kept his secrets. So don't you dare judge either of us until you know the truth."

"Truth – do you even know what that is Daisy? Looks to me like you've been living a lie for years." Ryan's snort of derision only served to incense Daisy further.

"Oh I know the truth alright so while we're flinging insults perhaps if you hadn't been running off wherever the fancy took you and spent a bit more time with Adam instead of your tarts then he wouldn't have needed to get on that fucking plane and end up dead in the back of a taxi!" Daisy's hand shot to her mouth, unable to believe she'd actually said such dreadful words that could never be taken back, the horror of them resulting in not only a gasp from herself but Ryan too.

"You evil bitch…that's not true and you know it! I had my job and Adam had his so if anyone is responsible for Adam's death it's *you*!"

"*Me*…NO! How can you even think that?" Daisy felt bile rise in her throat, the air in her lungs seemed trapped and her chest was tight.

"Yes, you! I've had all day to think about it and it's so obvious now, laughable really if it wasn't so fucking pathetic and sad. You treated Adam like your puppet for years. Daisy's very own lapdog at her beck and call, well, in between shagging whoever came along and then when you finally found someone stupid enough to stick with you, Adam was surplus to requirements and got shuffled off overseas. And don't say that's not what happened because it's exactly how it was." Ryan hadn't raised his voice once. He didn't need to because his cruel words were enough, yet still Daisy persisted.

"No Ryan, you *have* to listen. You are so unbelievably wrong on every single count. I've stood by Adam, ever since we met. In fact I put loads of things on hold. I changed my plans and stayed in Manchester and even neglected relationships simply because I didn't want him to be pushed out. He decided to leave and I begged him to stay, I swear I did so where the hell is all this coming from? You can't suddenly twist the past to suit you because you're grieving. Stop taking it out on me. I get that you need someone to blame but it's not fair to accuse me and I shouldn't have blamed you either. I'm sorry for that so please, can we calm down and talk like adults, like old friends?" Daisy felt weak, the fighting spirit was ebbing away. It was all too much and so unnecessary.

"Friends, is that what you want to be Daisy? Well friends don't lie to each other or have secrets or get pregnant by their best friends. They don't coerce their mates into giving up a career or selling their property, which then miraculously gets invested in their business. What was it Daisy, were you skint or bored and needed your lapdog back, or had you been through all the blokes in the village so thought you'd resort to good old Adam?"

"For God's sake Ryan, what is wrong with you? This was Adam's idea and he planned all of it from the word go, even the baby, you have to believe me, please let me explain. Look, I'll ring you tomorrow when you've calmed down and then perhaps I can make you understand. This is getting us nowhere, screaming at each other and slinging insults. You've really hurt me with the things you said but I forgive you, it's just shock talking, that's all."

"Are you not listening to me? I don't want your forgiveness Daisy. I want nothing from you whatsoever...you've made a fool of me and you've made a fool of my brother but it ends right here and now, tonight!"

"You're not making sense, why have I made a fool of you? And I certainly haven't made a fool of Adam. I made him happy, he made me happy. I'm giving him a son, a child we both thought we'd never have, how can that be wrong?"

"It's just sick, all of it."

"No it's not! This baby is innocent in all of this and deserves a family and now his daddy is gone, don't you see how sad that is? I'm carrying your nephew, Adam's son, his little boy. And he wanted you to be part of his life so I'm begging you, please, don't be like this Ryan. If not for me or Adam, for this baby."

"Don't even try emotional blackmail, it won't work. That baby is *nothing* to me. I can't be part of his life while you're in it. And the other really fucked-up part about all of this is that a few hours ago I was actually contemplating coming back to see Adam and maybe give you and I another chance, and all that time you were at it with my brother...so what does that make me Daisy? A complete fool, a joke? But you know what's the really, really sick part? Had you not kept Adam on the end of your rope and lured him back to France then he would still be alive right now, he'd be out there, somewhere on the ocean and having fun, not like you said, lying dead in the back of a taxi. You are responsible for taking away my only family and I will never be able to forgive you. Now listen to me very carefully while I repeat what I said earlier. I never want to see or hear from you again. Stay away from me *and* my brother's funeral. You're not wanted, now *or* in the future, do you understand?"

Ryan wasn't sure whether he'd got through to Daisy because the last he heard from her was uncontrollable sobbing and her whispering his name over and over, begging, then there was a thud, total silence, and the line went dead.

Chapter 33

Rituals
France, December 2017

Pam was on guard duty and from her station behind the office window watched for signs of Daisy emerging from the woods. She had been gone for almost two hours and whilst Pam worried about her being alone out there, she knew exactly what her daughter was doing amongst the trees she regarded as old friends, her silent comrades. Daisy was looking for Adam.

It had become a daily ritual, as had sitting for hours in his room, playing records or lying on his bed, often crying herself to sleep. Other times poring over photograph albums and the images on her phone. The doctor had assured Pamela that a daily constitutional was good for Daisy, breathing in fresh air and taking some exercise. He saw too many mothers-to-be who spent their pregnancy in a more sedentary state, watching television and eating their way through each month, which wasn't helping them or the baby.

Daisy on the other hand was the opposite and seemed consumed by her grief, like it was eating her alive. Pamela could do nothing other than watch her daughter shrivel. That's the only way she could describe it, like she was shrinking, her body mass withering away just like her broken heart.

And it wasn't all about Adam, no, Ryan was equally responsible for her current state and had it not been for the promises Pamela had made to Daisy then she would have tore a strip off him either by message or phone. Actually, she was so incensed that she would have quite happily hopped on a plane and flayed him alive for the distress his cruel words had inflicted.

It was early December and as was usually the way, with the days and weeks that passed Pamela's anger had receded slightly but no matter which way she looked at it – Ryan's hurt and shock taken into consideration – he owed Daisy an apology, on both bloody knees. His behaviour had affected them all, not least his insistence that Daisy stayed away from the funeral. Pamela and some of the French also wanted to say their goodbyes but were prevented from doing so, not just because they would have felt uncomfortable attending but out of loyalty to Daisy.

Even thinking back to that time exhausted Pamela. How she'd had the strength to get up each morning she had no idea, or allowed herself to sleep at night. Facing Daisy, finding the right words, which more often than not were wrong, and then tiptoeing through the interminable hours that stretched before them had been debilitating. And when she tried to switch off, desperate to sleep and rest weary bones and mind, Pam reverted to the toddler years, one ear on alert, listening out for Daisy crying out in her sleep.

The girls had done their best to help in so many ways, especially when Daisy forbade any intervention. They'd played devil's advocate only to have their heads bitten off in the process.

"Daisy, please let one of us contact Ryan. We can explain everything on your behalf and once he knows the truth he will stop hurting. He is confused and angry and simply looking for someone to blame."

"No! I told you…leave him. By now he will have told everyone about us and slagged me off to the lot of them so let them think what they want. I'm not going and that's that!"

"But Daisy, love, you have the right to say goodbye to your best friend, the father of your baby, no matter what Ryan said the other night. He wasn't in his right mind and neither were you. Things just got out of hand because you are both grieving so please, if you don't want to speak to him let one of us make contact."

"Why won't you listen to me? What's the point of sitting in a church staring at a box knowing Adam is inside it and then, they are going to burn him! That's what will happen...why would you want to see that? It's sick." They all heard the fear and building hysteria in Daisy's voice.

"Is that what you are scared of, seeing the coffin? It's very normal to have these fears and I was the same at my grandmother's funeral, literally shaking in my shoes but I got through it, and we will be by your side, we will help you." Inès spoke kindly as did Cassandre next.

"And you will want to take part, say some words for Adam. He would want that and everyone will expect you to be there, to pay your last respects."

"You are not hearing me are you? There's no point in words or songs or prayers because none of it matters. It won't bring him back or make it all better and stop everyone from looking at me like I'm the freak-show, murdering bitch who lured Adam to his death. The lying slapper who conned them all. How can you expect me to face them, never mind Ryan? So will you all please leave me alone and stop harassing me. I will not change my mind and I swear if any of you contact Ryan I will never speak to you again. Do you hear me? I will pack my bags and leave. I mean it, I will go!"

"Okay okay, we understand. But what are we going to say to your friends? Your phone is full of texts and voicemails, as is the answering machine in the office. I can't fob them off forever." Pam was on the verge of tears herself, reminded of the terrible twos and a little girl with a monstrous temper.

"Well you'll just have to try! Tell them I'm too grief stricken to talk, or I'm ill or dead. I don't give a fuck, I really don't."

Pamela gasped, she was hurt and shocked and so, so tired. "Daisy! That's a terrible thing to say."

"Well this is a terrible situation Mother, in fact it's shit and it's not going to get better so you might as well get used to it, okay? Adam is gone. Ryan hates me and everyone else will too, so let's just learn to live with it." Daisy crossed her arms and rested them on her bump, her foot tapping angrily.

Inès was the bravest, so she asked the next question. "So, do these rules apply to Ryan, too? If he rings will you speak to him, give him chance to say he's sorry?"

Daisy snorted her derision. "Ryan won't apologise, he's happy to blame me for everything because it absolves him in the process, so if that makes it easier for him, fine! Leave him to it. I'm going to remember Adam in my own way. I don't need Ryan or any of them. I have my baby, that's all that matters now, and Basil."

"And your mum, and us. We are hurting too Daisy so don't push us away." Cassandre sounded hurt.

"Yes, I'm sorry, I know. But don't push me either, let me do this my way. I need you to support me not tell me what to do or interfere. Will you do that?" Daisy glared, waiting.

All three nodded solemnly, knowing when they were beaten, forced to respect Daisy's wishes and feelings. While she'd raged through most of the past few minutes, her tone was softer now, fatigued almost.

Yet Inès still needed confirmation of one point, to avoid doubt and another bout of histrionics. "But you didn't answer my question. Will you speak to Ryan if he rings?" There was a pause, all three unsurprised by Daisy's answer.

"Yes, if he rings I'll speak to him. Now I'm going for a lie down, and you should get off home. The kids will wonder where you are and so will your husbands. I don't want them hating me, too."

Daisy pushed back her chair and stood, her dull, red-rimmed eyes dry, like they'd ran out of tears, avoiding contact with those seated around the kitchen table. Once the sound of her footsteps receded and they heard the door of her bedroom close they all sighed. Pam held her head in her hands while Cassandre and Inès shook theirs, all resigned to a simple fact. They had made a promise and would have to stick to it so all they could hope for now was that Ryan would do the decent thing and get in touch. Each of the women had prayed fervently (Cassandre for the first time in many years), privately convinced that once time had healed and before it was too late he would pick up the phone. They were all wrong.

Pamela fended off all enquiries from the Manchester crowd, insisting that Daisy was far too ill and distressed to speak and for this reason would not be making the trip to Norfolk for the funeral. One, the girl named Fliss, was most persistent and really did push her luck. After sympathising with the depths of Daisy's despair she enquired as to the nature of her illness – which Pamela had already decided would be glandular fever – then the ins and outs of the symptoms. Next she suggested sending flowers and perhaps, after the funeral, she could visit if that would help, or recuperation in Manchester amongst their friends who were all very concerned. Pam politely refused and couldn't wait to get the nosey parker off the phone.

Thankfully, after running all this by Cassandre, Pam was made aware that to even mention the name 'Fliss' would stoke up hell's fire and consequently the message was torn from the pad and the call never took place. Although she had been annoying at the time, reminding Pam of one of those cold callers selling PPI, two very interesting things had come out of the conversation. Firstly, that Ryan hadn't dispelled the reason for Daisy's inability to attend the funeral and the other was that for now, he had made no mention of the baby because according to Cassandre, had this Fliss person got wind, it would be headline news for sure.

Pamela couldn't decide whether she was offended or relieved that her grandson had been denied, but maybe until the dust settled it was for the best. There was no way to prevent the cards from arriving, and neither could she force Daisy to open them, which was why they remained in the kitchen drawer and the flowers sent by the persistent one lay rotting on the compost heap. Yet amidst her capitulation, Pam did assert some authority and free will, mainly because it was an area they hadn't discussed.

So, as she wasn't breaking any promises and feeling the urge to defy Ryan, a large and elaborate wreath was sent directly to the church from Daisy, Pamela and friends in France, daring him almost to refuse them. Pamela stipulated the colour scheme and which flowers were to be included – a visual message for Ryan and everyone attending. Their fate remained a mystery but maybe he allowed them, if only to perpetuate the falsehood of Daisy's absence. It hadn't been too hard to locate the venue, Pamela simply Googled all the churches in the area and rang each and every one until finally she hit the jackpot. She didn't even mention it to the girls, that way they were exempt from a telling off should the subject ever arise.

No matter how hard Pamela prayed and wished in those days, then hours as the clock counted down to Adam's funeral, Ryan didn't get in touch and Daisy dug her heels in further. Facts had to be faced and Pamela was resigned to weathering whatever lay ahead, and she dreaded it, she really did. It was far easier to bear one's own grief than watch suffering in those you loved. How she missed Bill and having him there to lean on, but she had to get through it alone, keep going for Daisy and the little one. That was all that mattered now.

*

Spotting movement in the distance Pam exhaled. Daisy was making her way back along the path, bundled up against the late November chill, her head protected by a woollen hat, her hair blowing freely in the wind. Deep down, Pamela was selfishly grateful for Daisy's absences, not the long and lonely woodland walks, more the squirreling herself in Adam's room. Was that bad, for a mother to crave respite from worry, close her eyes and forget their troubles? After all, her child was thirty-four, not a newborn who refused to sleep. Somehow, between them, they had forged a harmonious existence, marking time, moving forward, and waiting.

Daisy was approaching the office looking, thought Pamela, quite purposeful. Basil was close behind, keeping up with her brisker-than-usual step whilst carrying another stick for his collection. Basil's allegiance was now to his mistress who he faithfully accompanied on her quest for his old master.

From the back Daisy didn't look like she was nine months pregnant, only when she turned did you see the neat baby bump protruding from her fragile frame, her pale skin tight across her drawn face, green eyes saucer-like and sad. And whilst they'd reached an impasse where her obsessive behaviour was concerned, Pamela had managed to get through regarding nutrition and caring for herself and, as a direct consequence, her unborn son. Insisting she had no appetite Daisy agreed to eat the three small but healthy meals that were placed before her each day, picking like a desolate sparrow.

Pam watched like a hawk, her sad child who lived in a bubble of grief and remained hell bent on inhabiting a world that revolved around Adam, waiting for a sign and to finally look upon the face of his son, which she was convinced would be the embodiment, the spitting image and living, breathing replica of his father.

Daisy knew her mum was watching from the office window, supposedly doing paperwork when it was obvious she was keeping lookout. *'Poor mum,'* thought Daisy. *'But it's okay, I've worked it all out,'* she told herself and the silhouette of Pamela as she marched on. Her eagerness to get home and set in motion her plan made Daisy fleet of foot – she'd finally realised what was wrong. It was so obvious and now a resolution was in sight, it was going to be okay. All she had to do was make contact, the first move, be brave and bold so that she could free everyone from this state of all-consuming sorrow.

*

At first the suffocating concern drove her mad, forcing unscheduled retreats upstairs or outside when really she would have preferred just to sit and appreciate her mum's company, take comfort from having her near, but in silence. It was as though they had entered a new world, one where those surrounding her were being punished for something she, Daisy, had done. And then, to make it a million times worse they were forced to repeat their purgatory over and over again, like that annoying film Groundhog Day. The sadness clung to you, like a sticky invisible fog, lingering in every room, hovering above every sentence. Then there was the thinking. It was a plague that infested your brain. The what-ifs, replaying of last conversations, hearing the same platitudes time and time again, hollow promises of reprieve from a crime she hadn't even committed. And when it all became too much, short-tempered retorts were followed by apologies, hugs and undeserved forgiveness.

After the bleak days of waiting to be summoned or forgiven had passed, the day of the funeral came and went without incident. It was just like any other in the Land of Loss. Real life wasn't like a spooky film or creepy book. Photographs didn't tumble from the shelves. A cool breeze wasn't felt in the room, no white feathers floating down from above. Adam failed to visit her in her dreams or appear to any of them, anywhere. He really was gone and somewhere in the midst of the confusion, maybe in order for the brain to make some sense of it all, the rituals began.

Initially it was a form of retreat and a way to break the cycle of grief and recriminations, but in doing so Daisy embarked quite by accident on another circle of torment with ritual number one. Locked inside her head and Adam's room she drowned out the silence that was his absence by listening to music, the familiar lyrics diluting questions on a loop. Daisy chose randomly from their collection of records, hers or Adam's, it didn't matter because their tastes entwined. As she pulled one disc after another from the boxes, Daisy sought solace in comforting sounds, filling the room with an essence of her best boy, lyrics mingling with his scent. Resting her head on the pillow where his had lain or lying numb and inert beneath the bed sheets, searching for a trace of aftershave on his shirts, maybe a hint of wood smoke as her face became submerged in the softness of his jumper.

The irony of the songs she listened to wasn't lost as hot tears flowed, each one had a meaning and only Kirsty truly understood Daisy's pain, it was all there in the words of New England, all about a girl who waited beside the telephone, hoping and praying for someone to pull her through.

This led to ritual number two – keeping her phone by her side at all times. It had to be fully charged, ringer on loud, and for most of the day she sat staring at the screen, waiting for it to come alive. And no matter how much she willed it, just like the song, Ryan never made the call, while pride and hurt and a stomach-churning fear prevented Daisy from doing the same.

Ritual number three – Daisy wouldn't give up on the notion that she'd have a visitation, maybe he was waiting for her in the woods or on the pontoon by the lake, playing his music and drinking beer. So regardless of the weather she went to look and listen for him. Every single day. Starting with the site marked out for the cabins, then along the lakeside path and slowly into the woods, checking the memorials they'd made for her dad and Olive, expecting them to have been altered, a pebble sign left in the earth. Sitting inside the Grandad Tree she waited patiently. Sometimes the frustration became too much and she called his name, screamed it, begging him to show himself or let her know he was okay, just like he promised. Poor Basil shot off into the undergrowth, disturbed by her despair before trotting back to make sure she was okay. There they would remain, her arms around Adam's dog, taking comfort from his soft steamy fur. It was all she had so she clung on tight.

Ritual number four – in the evenings she watched the soaps, Coronation Street and Emmerdale. He would want to know what was going on with Paddy and Rona, and his favourite, Cain. And he'd be shouting at the screen, hoping Phelan would be caught and Eileen would wise up. She imagined watching with Adam; surely he was there by her side, sitting on the sofa, drinking tea and dunking biscuits. Once the titles played Daisy would kiss Pamela goodnight and head upstairs to his room and here, she would look at photographs, turning each page slowly, smiling at the tattered images stuck under worn polythene and in the background, their music played.

And it was whilst Daisy had been partaking in one of her daily rituals that she had her epiphany. As she flicked twigs and stray leaves from within the heart of stones that marked Olive's resting place, a simple thought occurred. It was December now and their baby's birth was imminent so perhaps Adam was waiting for that, saving his celestial energy for a trip down to earth. Daisy had read all about how much effort it took for spirits to make contact so it was imperative that earthlings were diligent and watched out for signs, but so far nothing had arrived. Then she hit upon another theory – maybe, just maybe Adam was cross with her, with all of them for falling out so was being stubborn, refusing to make an appearance until they'd sorted themselves out. But it was as she smoothed the earth that lay above the casket containing Olive's ashes, and thinking back to the day they'd placed it there that the light dawned, and finally everything made sense.

Daisy's hand came to a stop as she stared at the damp earth between her fingers, remembering how pleased Adam had been when she had suggested this place for Olive's ashes and how her dad had carved the cross that stood at the foot of the tree. And there it was, the blindingly obvious missing link. Previously, any thought of this kind had been reprehensible, an image she had flushed from her mind because the disposal of Adam was too terrible to contemplate but now, this hideous yet necessary fact of life made sense.

If Adam had left final instructions, with Ryan or the notaire, or even on his phone, then Daisy knew without a doubt that here, right next to Olive and Bill would be his choice of resting place and until then, he wouldn't settle *or* send her a sign. Adam was waiting to come home to France, to be with Olive and Bill therefore Daisy had to arrange it, make it happen before their baby arrived. Calling Basil from his snuffling amongst the undergrowth, using the tree trunk for leverage she lifted herself from the cold ground and once she was straight, her knees and spine unlocked, they set off at pace towards the house, Daisy's heart racing with each step.

"Come on Baz, we've got things to do…we need to get your dad home. Yes, that's right, he's coming back to us, I promise." Daisy looked down at her dog, his big brown eyes focused on hers as she said his name, understanding from his mistress's voice that something good was happening – maybe it meant he was going to get a bone. Whatever it was he snatched up his latest find, sticking close by, tail wagging furiously because after a long time of sensing sadness Basil was at last picking up on a good vibe.

When they reached the office door, Daisy ignored her mother's attempts at looking engrossed and interrupted her pretence.

"Mum, I know what I have to do!"

"Really love, about what exactly?"

"Adam, obviously!"

"Oh right…and what is it, this thing you have to do?"

"I'm going to bring Adam home, well not me personally but I need to get in touch with Ryan and ask him, no, I'm going to tell him to bring Adam's ashes here so we can lay him to rest beside Olive and Dad." Daisy paused for breath then continued. "And then, as soon as he arrives I'm going to explain everything, just like Adam wanted. If I pull my finger out he could be here before the baby comes…what do you think?"

"Well, it all seems like a very simple idea but what if Ryan says no, or refuses to speak to you, then you'll get yourself in a state again and it's not good for you Daisy. We've been through all this."

"Mum, stop being a Debbie Downer, and I won't get in a state I promise but I've got to try. Don't you see this is what Adam has been waiting for – he wants to come home and for us all to be friends again. And this is the way to make it happen. I can't believe I didn't see it before." Exhausted from her brisk walk and frankly talking without breathing much, Daisy flopped into the chair opposite Pamela who was quietly cautious.

"I do see that Daisy I just don't want you getting your hopes up and I mean it, if Ryan is horrible to you one more time he will have me to deal with, Adam or no Adam, do you understand?" Daisy nodded, too shattered to object. "You and that baby are my priority right now so he's on his final warning, it's his last chance." Pamela reached over and grasped Daisy's cold hands, rubbing warmth and strength into them.

"Yes mum, I get it, I swear. Right, I'm going upstairs to send an email, and then I'll contact him on Facebook and by phone, just to be a hundred percent sure he's got the message." Daisy was standing again, eager to get on.

Pamela remained cautious. "Well that seems sensible, he might react badly if you just ring him up, you know, have a knee-jerk reaction and upset you again."

Daisy's wide eyes were bright, excited. "That's what I thought and if I'm honest I haven't got the guts to just ring him out of the blue. I think this way is best and an email will give him space and time to think things through but honestly Mum, do you really think he will refuse? Surely he will want to carry out Adam's wishes. I'd bet my life on him wanting to be with Olive, and dad. What do you think?"

"I agree, but did Adam not mention it to you? I'm surprised because he was always so open about things, well, mostly. But I'm sure you're right, here would be the logical place otherwise what else will Ryan do with them?"

"Exactly! And no, it was something he didn't discuss, everything else under the sun but not that. Maybe it's because we had all of our lives ahead of us and it was the last thing he wanted to talk about, especially when he was going to be a dad."

"Right, well you get yourself upstairs and think carefully before you press send. I'll be right here if you need me, and Daisy, it might be an idea to pass on my regards just so he knows I'm not cross with him, well, not as cross as I was at the time."

"Okay, will do. And will you give Basil one of his dog chews and chuck that stick outside when he's not looking – he's got loads now. He takes after Adam collecting things."

"Course I will. Come on Baz, let's get you a nice treat and we'll make Mum a cup of tea while we're in the kitchen. It's nice to see her looking so perky…come on boy, and bring your stick."

They all made their way through to the house where Daisy headed straight upstairs leaving Pamela watching from below, silently praying her daughter wouldn't have her heart and hopes squashed but most of all that this time, Ryan would listen and do the decent thing. Daisy was right – it was time that Adam came home.

Chapter 34

Ryan and Adam
Marham Norfolk, December 2017

Ryan had experienced great difficulty with the steps to his accommodation block because they just wouldn't stay still, which made it hard to get up two flights of stairs, never mind find his room, which was somewhere along the corridor that seemed narrower than usual, causing him to bounce from wall to wall. Still, he'd managed to keep hold of his pizza, albeit upside down and no doubt the pepperoni and extra cheese was stuck to the lid. Recalling, through a haze of alcohol, that his room was the one next to the window, he headed towards the end of the blue carpet where he congratulated himself on locating the correct door number. Getting his key out of his pocket was another matter and during the extraction process he managed to scatter loose change and drop his pizza box on the floor, right side up this time, which Ryan saw as another great achievement.

Once the door swung open, slamming loudly against the wall and eliciting shouts from his neighbours to keep the noise down, he retrieved the soggy box, leaving the coins for the cleaning lady. Kicking the door shut Ryan staggered towards his unmade bed and flopped onto the mattress. Flicking off his shoes and pulling down his jeans he left them in a crumpled pile on the floor, adding to similar discarded items of clothing and an assortment of takeaway cartons and beer cans. 'Christ, what a shit hole,' Ryan muttered as he dragged the duvet over his body and reached for his pizza, lifting the lid on a pile of unappetising mush, forcing him to close it and throw the box on the floor.

Maybe he'd set a world record. Being smashed for three days running at the same time as trashing your room was quite an achievement. Ryan's self-destruct mission began as soon as the troop carrier landed at Brize en route from the Falklands, a place where despite the wind and rain, he would have preferred to stay. The irony of this wasn't lost because soon his service career would be over, a few months in fact and then, he wouldn't have his job or the RAF to hide behind, he would have to lay down his shield for good.

As the ceiling swirled Ryan sighed, closing his eyes and asking himself the same question he'd pondered every drunken night that week: 'What the fuck are you doing to yourself?'

The answer was easy and he even knew the cause – Daisy and those bloody messages.

*

The first one came by text while he was at work, sorting through paperwork as jets roared overhead. His heart had quite literally lurched when he saw her name on the screen, staring at the word Daisy for ages before even contemplating reading the message, which he regretted instantly. It wasn't even because it was from her or that the contents made him angry. It simply told him what he already knew and had been avoiding, more or less forcing his hand. It read:

Dear Ryan, PLEASE don't delete this message. It is very important and about Adam. I know you were angry with me last time we spoke and I understand why but there are things we need to discuss and arrange, like what to do with his belongings and most of all, his ashes. I don't know if he left instructions with you but if he didn't, I was hoping you would allow them to be buried alongside your gran. I think Adam would have wanted that. Also, Adam was on his way to tell you about the baby but there were other things he desperately needed to explain and now it falls to me to pass on that message so please, will you come to France and give me the chance to put things right? The baby is due on the 19th of December and it would mean so much to have sorted things out before he arrives. Adam wanted you to be part of his son's life so please bear that in mind before you reply.

I have respected your wishes and stayed away from the funeral but now we need to talk. You might not want to be friends anymore but out of respect for Adam please could we try. Mum says hello and to tell you that you are always welcome here. I will leave things there and wait to hear from you. Take care. Love, Daisy x

Ryan didn't delete the message, in fact he'd read it about a hundred times, acknowledging if nothing else Daisy's determination when he received an identical one via email and Facebook Messenger. But while he was physically defiant, refraining from typing any message in response via all media, psychologically he went into meltdown. Ryan just couldn't deal with the situation and as had become his way, instead of facing up to his responsibilities and mistakes he turned to drink and drowned out the lot.

Turning over onto his side Ryan's eyes fell on the box that stood beside his television – an oak casket containing Adam's ashes that he'd collected from the funeral director. Daisy was right and as she'd expected, not only had his brother left detailed instructions contained in various files on his phone, he'd tied up all loose ends with his solicitor in England, and prudently, made sure that French laws were also adhered to.

*

In the days that preceded the funeral, Ryan was set on autopilot, merely marking time. Following a brief and preliminary conversation, apart from some minor bequests, Ryan knew that the bulk of Adam's estate was left to his unborn son, consisting of his pension, the funds from the sale of the Manchester apartment and his bank balance (it seemed Adam had been quite a saver), plus a rather hefty insurance policy from which Daisy had been given an allowance so that she and their child would be cared for.

While he listened to the solicitor, Ryan felt immensely proud of his little brother, the man who had made sure his child was provided for financially and in that instant, another crack opened up in his broken heart. Just thinking of this unknown baby, a tiny stranger who would grow up not knowing someone as wonderful as Adam, made material things seem worthless and family all the more important.

As for more personal matters, like what to do with his belongings, the files on Adam's phone had made Ryan weep. He'd still not been through all of them simply because it was unbearable and unless absolutely necessary, tantamount to raiding Adam's soul. Yet Ryan had been grateful for something to follow, a kind of route map that led him through various stages, arranging the funeral being the first. The note was both specific and liberating but at the same time came with a sting in the tail, serving to remind him that Daisy should have been a part of it all, and his castigation was both cruel and uncalled for. Still, Ryan stubbornly forged ahead, blinded by confusion and hurt.

Adam wasn't fussed where or how his funeral service was carried out. If it made Daisy happier to have a religious ceremony then that was fine, he knew Ryan wasn't of faith so this decision should be left to her. He didn't want any hymns, preferring the music that had accompanied him through life was played as he was dispatched. Somehow, from the hundreds of songs on Adam's playlist he had chosen three. Ryan knew they sent out a powerful message, yet still he ignored it. His final stipulation was written in bold and here, there was to be no negotiation or deviation because for his resting place, just as Daisy had suspected, Adam wanted to be in France, beside his gran.

Ryan had been relieved and grateful for the help he was given by work who offered any assistance he required, as did the lads from the squadron who volunteered to be coffin bearers. The strength he derived from having Dan's arm around his shoulder and knowing his oldest mates were just behind him as they proceeded towards the altar, made it possible to put one foot in front of the other, and being flanked on either side by them during the service helped him remain upright. He steadfastly avoided looking at the photo on top of the coffin and the wreath of flowers that had arrived from France, white and yellow blooms dotted with daisies.

The congregation sobbed openly as Adam went in to Oasis. They sang about living forever, followed in the interlude by Bob Dylan who reminded them that times were changing and the final one, as the curtains closed and Ryan blinked away tears, by Kirsty MacColl, giving thanks for the days, those endless, sacred days that they would remember all their lives. The Manchester crew surmised it was in honour of Daisy and Adam's friendship, his absent soul mate, whereas Ryan told himself that they were just lyrics, simple words, nothing else.

From the second he'd opened his eyes that morning, all Ryan could think about was getting through the day, having it all done and over with. The only way he could face the next few hours was by formulating a code of conduct. He would not make a fool of himself by losing it in the church, he'd be polite and understanding of the other mourners' grief, remember to thank the vicar and above all, not think about what was happening to Adam's coffin behind those dark purple curtains. Next was to ensure the mourners were fed and watered after making the long trip to Norfolk, stoically accept their condolences but avoid conversation or a stroll down memory lane. And then he was going to run, as far away from this horror story as possible.

To some extent he managed just that, shielding himself behind his colleagues, preferring the others to talk amongst themselves and discuss Adam as they wished, as long as they didn't expect him to join in. But what Ryan actually wanted to avoid was hearing or speaking the name Daisy. He wasn't going to lie for her and neither was he going to divulge the real reason for her absence. It was none of their bloody business. And he almost achieved his aim, in some part owing to the allowances made for the bereaved. It seemed you could get away with anything – reticence, detachment, that cold blank look or a faraway gaze, rudeness even. Everyone put it down to grief and left you alone, respected your need for privacy, all except for one person, the limpet that refused to let go – Fliss.

It had been bad enough fending off her messages since news of the accident filtered through and Ryan was grateful that the only way she could contact him was via Facebook, having blocked her number many years before. He had no intention of discussing the funeral arrangements, the reason for Adam's visit to the UK or for that matter Daisy's illness, which he gleaned from her message was glandular fever (for that snippet he was grateful), and neither did he need her help, not for anything. Fliss had kept her distance for much of the day, speaking only briefly during formalities at the church but as the wake was drawing to a close, she chose to make her move.

There was nowhere to run so Ryan accepted his fate. After assuring Fliss he was fine and disentangling himself from her grasp, stepping backwards to retain his personal space, he forcibly quelled a wave of irritation when amidst a fresh flood of tears she hoisted herself onto a stool, obviously going nowhere soon. It was telling how quickly she gathered herself, more eager to talk than sob and began by pointing to the table where the Manchester crowd were seated, singling out an unfamiliar woman named Allison, apparently one of Adam's old colleagues.

"That's Adam's friend from the ship, she's been telling us all about his antics on board and how much everyone adored him, you should come over and listen. I'll grab you another drink and find you a seat then you can hear how wonderful he was."

"No, it's fine. I said hello to her earlier and I already know how wonderful my brother was so I don't need to listen to second-hand stories about him." Ryan hoped she'd take a hint. There was a pause while Fliss gathered her wits and clearly, chose to ignore the slight.

"Now don't be shy, you can't hide from us all day and the bar doesn't need propping up so come on, Adam would've wanted you to spend some time with us and share our memories." Ryan opened his mouth to protest but she was like a machine gun, rattling on and on. "It's just a pity Daisy couldn't make the effort and be here. I must say we are all a bit shocked and disappointed in her. None of us has heard one word from France and I know this may sound harsh, Ryan, but Adam was our friend too and it wouldn't have killed her to get in touch. Surely glandular fever isn't that debilitating and she could at least send a text. And what about her mother, or the French lot, why haven't they shown their faces?" Fliss had a habit of staring an answer out of you, her glare locked on, ready to fire the next missile.

Ryan steeled himself, replying in a flat, disinterested tone. "I think it's highly contagious and lasts for a few weeks, maybe they don't want to infect everyone. Anyway, thanks for coming but I need to excuse myself, call of nature." Ryan could feel his hackles rising and had to get away but Fliss ploughed on, ignoring him completely and resting her hand firmly on his arm.

"Well that doesn't excuse her ignorance but if you ask me, she's been funny ever since she went home and it wouldn't surprise me if that's why Adam was less chatty once Daisy got her claws into him. That one took being best friends to another level, although according to Allison over there, they were more than that. Everyone on the ship thought Daisy and Adam were an item and the only reason he was at sea was so they could buy a house together. Don't you think that seems a bit odd? Still, I didn't contradict, it would feel wrong somehow, like Adam was fibbing but then again, *I've* been saying it for years but nobody believed me. Anyway, enough speculating, what's done is done. Now, what are you drinking?" Fliss was as succinct as ever. She'd made her point and twisted the knife as only she could, completely unfazed by Ryan's glare and the tick of his jaw, his whitening pallor providing further confirmation that she'd hit a nerve.

"I said no thank you and for the record, my brother's private affairs have got nothing to do with you so for once in your bitter, twisted life will you just butt out and quit slinging mud." Ryan turned away but could see Fliss through the corner of his eye, mouth open, hand on chest and when she didn't retreat, he went in for the kill, hugely irritated by her continued and obstinate presence.

"Oh, and while I'm at it stop having a go at Daisy because it really used to piss Adam off, big time! In fact he only put up with you because of the others – if it hadn't been for them he'd have told you where to go a long time ago. Now sod off and ruin someone else's day!" Ryan glared at Fliss, defying her to continue.

"Ryan, I know you are upset but please don't take it out on me, I was only making conversation, really, there's no need for nastiness." Fliss was on the verge of fake tears, which Ryan ignored and he turned away, literally biting his tongue.

Focusing on the optics behind the bar he contemplated a chaser or two after his pint, which he picked up and drained, slamming the glass pot down onto the counter. Startled by the thud and seeing his raised hand attracting the barman as a sign of dismissal, Fliss admitted defeat and slid from her stool before flouncing off towards her husband and their friends. Sensing movement on his other side, Ryan glanced to see Dan who, true to form, had been watching his friend down pint after pint, winding himself up, preparing to explode. Knowing the moment of extraction had arrived and damage limitation was required, Dan had moved in.

"I think it's time we got on our way. The lads fancy a curry so we're going to treat you to a Tandoori. I might even throw in a few more pints if you behave yourself." Dan waited for the words to sink in as Ryan placed his hands on the bar and inhaled, staring down at his shoes, composing himself before nodding silently.

Dan patted him on the back, his steadying hand resting where it was. "Do you want to say anything, you know, make a quick toast or say goodbye? I can do it for you if you want?" Dan was a stickler for protocol but his mate's feelings came first.

"No, let's just go. This place is doing my head in, it all is. I just need to get out of here."

"Right, it's your call, c'mon, let's be having you. Kev's ordered a taxi and it should be here any minute." Without a backward glance they moved off, gathering their colleagues on the way before heading straight out the door.

Yes, you really could get away with anything when you were grieving, like being ignorant and rude. But the one thing you couldn't get away with was hiding from the truth or the pain caused by raw and stinging hurt, and facing up to your mistakes as you unravelled the confusion that tied knots in your brain. As Ryan jumped into the taxi he knew only too well that eventually, once he'd stopped running away he'd have to undo every last one of them.

*

Turning off the bedside lamp, Ryan yawned. He was exhausted and very drunk, a familiar state that usually aided a peaceful sleep, allowed him respite. He was glad to feel his eyes droop, his limbs relax and the swirling roof disappear, swallowed swiftly by blackness. His dreams were random and untroubled, disjointed snippets of workday moments, flat lines of nothing then bizarre scenes, jumbled images of something he'd seen on television, a cereal advert and a catchy song, then whistling, bloody annoying whistling that went on and on, waking him from his slumber.

When Ryan opened his eyes, focusing slowly on the person responsible for the tuneless sound, one that had woken him a hundred times before when they shared a box room at their gran's, the sight of Adam, rummaging through unopened mail was no real surprise. That was until Ryan remembered he was dead.

"Adam! What the...how come...you shouldn't be...what's going on, how did you get here?" Ryan was hitching himself slowly upright, incredulous at the sight before him because Adam looked just the same, wearing his uniform t-shirt and faded jeans and what looked like brand new Converse trainers, in City blue.

"Well, nice to see you too, bro!" Adam threw down the letters and made towards the bed, grinning as he spoke.

"Yeah, I mean it's great to see you mate but it's just a bit of a shock, you know seeing as you're supposed to be..." Ryan couldn't bring himself to say it just in case Adam didn't know, like in that film where the ghosts don't realise the truth. In fact, what the hell was this – a dream or was he really talking to a dead person?

"Dead? Yep, I'm toast alright, see what I did there?" Adam chuckled, pointing to the box of ashes by the telly. "But never mind that, budge up because me and thee need to have a bit of a chat and I don't have much time." Adam flung himself onto the bed and made himself comfortable, repositioning a pillow behind his back before leaning against the wall.

"What do you mean you don't have time, where are you going? There's loads I need to ask you, like are you ok, are you happy, and where exactly have you been, what's it like, you know, up there?" Ryan signalled upwards with his finger but despite his earnest questions Adam just smiled, like he was privy to some private joke, or secret, clearly unwilling to answer.

Realising he was talking too fast and maybe asking too much Ryan flopped backwards onto the pillow, the bizarre quality of the scene sinking in. "Shit, this is fucking weird!" Ryan rubbed his eyes, half expecting Adam to have disappeared when he opened them but no, he was still there, and laughing.

"Mate, I'm fine, I promise it's all good but I haven't got time to talk about that, I need you to listen to what I have to say. It's really mega important so concentrate, okay?" Adam looked serious now, his tone less jovial, his eyes seemed to bore into Ryan's, like he could see inside his head.

"Okay, fire away, I'm all ears." Ryan could feel Adam's legs through the duvet, resting against his feet, so real, so close.

"For a start you need to open your mail, get yourself organised and clean this shit hole, and you can knock this drinking lark on the head. It won't solve anything and you don't want to end up like those two arseholes we got lumbered with."

"Yeah, yeah, I'll hold my hands up to being a slob and you're right about the beer but I'm nothing like them, never will be. You know that."

"Well make sure you stay that way cos being sick in the cleaner's mop bucket isn't on. The poor woman was disgusted when she found it, you scruff!" Adam puffed out his cheeks in mock-vomit mode.

"How the hell did you know about that?" Ryan's voice became high pitched then noticed Adam's raised eyebrows and instantly twigged.

"And that's not all…I've seen what you get up to with all those merry American widows when the cruise ships dock in Port Stanley – you randy sod!" Adam was laughing his head off, at Ryan's shocked face more than anything.

"Seriously…is nothing sacred? I'm being spied on by the bloody ghost police now!" Ryan was totally freaked out, glancing over to the pile of letters then swiftly back to Adam, still worried he might disappear but he was right there, waving off the question.

"Never mind about that…just open your bloody post then go a little crazy but without the beer, okay?"

Ryan scrunched his eyes, baffled by the cryptic comment then focused back on Adam who was clicking his fingers, attracting his attention.

"Right, now this is the biggy so concentrate because I can't stay much longer." Adam leant forward, slightly agitated and quite stern, which Ryan sensed. So whilst being fixed to the spot by Adam's mesmerising eyes, he simply nodded in agreement.

"I want you to stop all this nonsense with Daisy and go back to France, as soon as you can, like pronto! The baby will be here soon and there's some stuff you need to know before he arrives so get your finger out and stop being a mard arse. I mean it Ryan! Daisy needs you, she's scared and sad, her heart is broken too." Adam held his brother's gaze and Ryan was instantly awash with shame.

It was obvious that Adam knew all about his behaviour and now more than ever he wished he could take it back, but if all this was important enough to warrant a visitation, why not just explain, here and now? "I know, I know, I've been a total arsehole. And I'm sorry for the way I reacted but come on, can't you see that it was just a massive shock, it all was. I feel truly shit about the way

I spoke to Daisy and I will apologise, but I don't understand why there's such a big mystery, what's going on?"

"Mate, I'd love to sit here and explain but it will take too long and I need to start at the beginning…and that's a long, long time ago but trust me, Daisy knows it all and that's why she's the best person for the job so please, just go."

"Okay, okay I get it. Bloody hell you haven't changed, have you? Once you set your mind to something you never let go. But just for the record I'd already made up my mind to get in touch with Daisy. I have to deliver those…seeing as you've gone all European on me." Ryan nodded in the direction of the ashes, his obvious unease causing Adam to laugh out loud.

"Oh those…I was looking earlier. I made a right big pile of dust. Who'd have thought it, eh?"

"It's not funny Adam, they freak me out."

"Really mate, don't let it trouble you. Just look at them as treasure, millions of carbon molecules and photons, my imprint that I left behind. I reckon there's scientific magic going on inside that box, a bit of chemistry and physics zapping away, living on."

"What the hell are you going on about now?" Ryan scratched his bristled chin, a reminder of his self-neglect.

"I'm trying to tell you that there's more to everything than flesh and bones, ashes and dirt so if I'm not bothered then you shouldn't be either, but it's brought me very nicely to my next point."

"Go on, amaze me." Ryan sighed, remembering when Adam wanted to get out of washing the pots or sweeping leaves in Gran's garden, he would negotiate terms for hours until he got his way.

"Once you've done the honours with the treasure you have to promise to look after my son, *your* nephew. He's our blood, Ryan. I don't want him growing up without a dad or worse, some random no-hoper who wanders into his and Daisy's life. Apart from you being a pisshead, if I could choose a role model, someone for him to look up to and learn from, it's you. So be his hero and his mate, the best uncle in the world. Promise me you'll be part of his life and not keep buggering off for months at a time to the other side of the world. We both wanted a proper dad and missed out on loads of stuff when we were growing up, you know it's true. I can't bear the thought of our boy going through that and you're the only person I trust to look after them both. Can you do that, for me?" The air was still and oppressive, like before a tropical storm and there was something else. Adam's voice seemed different, more distant, like he was fading away and the thought panicked Ryan.

"Hey, you're not going are you? Adam mate, don't go, stay a bit longer, we need to talk some more, I don't want to lose you again." The room was beginning to look strange, a bit blurry.

"I have to go soon but I'm never far away Ryan, just remember that. Now hurry up, do I have your word?"

"Yes, I promise. I swear I won't let you down." Ryan was desperate to make Adam believe him because he could feel him slipping away, like a boat on rippling water, moving slowly out of reach.

The image of Adam appeared softer now, his eyes large and round like deep brown pools reflecting love, calming Ryan who was overcome by a sense of great peace, the sheer emotion of the moment bringing tears, which he wiped away fiercely, desperate to keep sight of his brother. Adam was fading fast, almost diluted, but his voice was still clear.

"Nice one bro. Now you take care. I love you mate. Be good to yourself and be happy, I really want you to be happy okay?"

Ryan simply nodded, unable to speak, mouthing that he loved him too, but Adam had one more request, almost inaudible, a whisper in the night, a murmur.

"And there's one last thing I need you to do…" As Adam's words flowed, so did his spirit, further and further away until he was out of sight. Ryan's eyes became heavy once again and he too drifted off, lulled by soothing words and an all-consuming memory, the tranquil face of his brother.

The alarm clock bleeped insistently, urging Ryan from the deepest sleep and as he dragged himself into the daylight, yawning and scratching his head, he noticed something else. He felt light, sort of unburdened and dare he say it, happy. Although it was the last thing he expected or deserved, whatever he'd been carrying around for the past two months seemed easier to bear, like there was hope. Sitting up quickly, his head a thudding reminder of the previous night's excesses, he scanned the room for Adam, not really expecting him to be there but just in case.

Ryan knew it had been a dream but one he remembered every word of. He could still feel that sense of whatever brought Adam to him, an essence, love perhaps, and he would keep it with him always, a talisman.

His gaze then fell on the pile of letters so throwing back the duvet he strode across the room and began sifting through the envelopes, discarding junk mail until one in particular caught his eye. Ripping the paper and pulling out the contents he saw first the solicitor's letter and attached to it, a cheque. His breath caught and his hands began to tremble as he swallowed down the lump in his throat. Deciphering the message through blurred eyes, it told him of Adam's bequest, barely able to believe the words. The money was payback for helping him through university, a lump sum to do with as he so pleased, go crazy or save it for a rainy day.

Leaning against the cabinet for strength, his free hand clasped over his mouth, Ryan assembled all the mad thoughts that vied for attention as euphoria coursed through his veins. Go a little crazy. No, it couldn't be, could it? Ryan sat down on the bed and went over everything, walking step by step through his insane dream. He looked down at the letter and read it again, then scanned the detritus of his room and remembered being violently sick in the cleaner's bucket. Had the solicitor mentioned Adam's bequest when they spoke on the phone? He'd blocked so much out it was hard to remember the days before and after the funeral.

But facts were irrelevant, Ryan knew that now, there was more to life and this feeling that coursed through his veins proved it. Without one single moment's worth of hesitation he sprang into action, his heart pounding in time with a headache that he ignored – there was too much to do, no time to be ill.

Two hours later Ryan locked the door of his spotlessly clean room then flung a bulging holdall over his shoulder before picking up the box containing Adam's ashes. He was going to France, to see Daisy and be there to welcome his nephew into the world. No more running away. Almost marching along the corridor and taking the stairs at a run, Ryan burst outside into a frosty December morning. After throwing his bag in the boot and placing Adam's ashes on the passenger seat, he turned the key. He was taking his brother home.

Chapter 35

He's here.
France, December 2017

Daisy opened her eyes, wakened by the creaking of her bedroom door. The alarm clock told her it was 2.15pm and she'd been sleeping for hours, something of a miracle when you were plagued by an aching back and what her mum assured her were practice contractions. She'd also given in to fatigue and any hope of seeing Ryan's car coming along the track, or even receiving a reply to her message. Daisy was so tired of it all, the waiting and hoping. She couldn't even be bothered to second-guess him anymore. After another long, uncomfortable night propped up in the armchair staring into the night, she'd climbed into bed, pulling the duvet over her head, blocking out the first strands of grey morning light.

The creaking signalled the arrival of her mum, no doubt checking up or hoping to coax her downstairs and sure enough, just as Daisy emerged from beneath the covers, Pam's head peeped cautiously around the door.

"Ah, you're awake sleepyhead. I've been up and down these stairs I don't know how many times but you were out for the count." Pam closed the door then headed towards the bed, sitting herself down before taking her daughter's hand, smiling at her tousled-haired, pale-faced girl.

"Sorry Mum, I didn't mean to sleep for this long. Has Basil been good?" It was at this point she heard him barking somewhere outside, no doubt chasing leaves. Hearing his excited woofs made her smile.

"Basil's fine love, don't fret about him. I'm just glad you got some proper rest. Now, how about coming downstairs for something to eat? You must be starving." Pam gently brushed a stray curl from Daisy's face, biding her time, waiting for the right moment.

"I wouldn't mind some toast and a big mug of tea." Daisy smiled at her mum, listening to Basil barking. "He'll end up getting filthy again. You know what he's like when he thinks no one's watching him and I bet there's mud everywhere, it rained loads last night." Daisy yawned and stretched as she spoke.

"He'll be okay. Someone volunteered to take him for a quick walk while I came to check on you."

"Oh good, is Rémi here? I need to ask him if he'd check the door to the storeroom, it keeps banging in the wind, did you hear it last night? It was driving me flaming mad."

"No I didn't, and it isn't Rémi out there with Basil."

"Oh, is Cassandre here?"

"No love, it's Ryan. He arrived about an hour ago." Pam left her words to sink in, keeping hold of Daisy's hand as she watched her daughter's face pale further before flushing, eye's wide with shock.

"He's here, he came?"

"Yes love. Now don't go getting all flustered, just take your time and keep calm. We've had a nice chat and I made him a brew, he wouldn't eat anything though. He's a bit nervous to be honest."

Daisy gripped her mum's hand. "Mum, what am I going to say? After all this time wishing he'd come, now he's here I'm scared. I don't know if I can face him…or where to begin."

"Well, for a start you need to make yourself look presentable, you're a bit crumpled and boggy-eyed at the moment, but when you're ready just come down and say hello. Remember he's the one come cap in hand so just take things a bit at a time."

"What has he said to you, I hope you didn't shout at him?"

"Of course I haven't, in fact the first thing he said when I opened the door was, 'I'm sorry, Pam,' so I just gave him a big hug. There was no need to go on and on, he's been through enough. Now stop asking questions and get a move on, the poor lad is itching to see you so don't make him wait much longer, he's been on the road since dawn."

"Right, I'll be as quick as I can, and I don't want any toast now, I feel a bit sick."

Pamela was having none of it. "Daisy! You are having something, in fact I'll warm some soup. You both need to eat and I won't take no for an answer. Right, I'll see you downstairs. Chop chop!"

Standing, she helped Daisy to her feet then pointed in the direction of the en suite. Basil's barks were drawing closer so after straightening the bed covers Pam left Daisy to her nervous preparations, feeling for her daughter who had set so much store on making peace with Ryan. As she headed downstairs, slightly anxious herself about the meeting to come, Pamela knew it was one of those occasions where someone had to be the grown up, keep calm and take control and today, that role fell to her.

*

Daisy made her way cautiously down the stairs. The aroma of soup was doing nothing for her nausea, agitated further by the kaleidoscope of butterflies that'd taken up residence inside her stomach. Outside the kitchen door, hidden from view, she listened as her mum chatted about the weather forecast (one of her favourite topics) and on hearing his voice, asking about snow, tears threatened. Accepting she couldn't put it off any longer Daisy took a fortifying breath, deep and long then with all the courage she could muster, stepped forward. The movement caught Ryan's eye causing him to stand immediately, the noise of wood on tiles startling Basil who, spotting his mistress, leapt from his basket to welcome her into the room.

Suddenly self-conscious because her bump seemed larger than ever before and flaunted her perceived betrayal, Daisy was glad of Basil's interruption. Fussing him gave her a moment to gather herself – the force of her feelings on seeing Ryan had taken her by surprise. Through the corner of her eye she saw him move, navigating his way around Pam and her soup pan and soon they were only inches away. Approaching tentatively, Ryan spoke first.

"I'm sorry, Daisy, for taking so long and for everything I said. I just want to start again if you'll let me, if you can forgive me. I was wrong and just need a second chance to make it up to you. I'm glad you asked me to come because I was too much of a coward to make the decision myself." Ryan swallowed, his heart hammered while his eyes focused on hers and when she smiled, he knew in an instant it was going to be okay.

Daisy didn't speak, she couldn't. All she wanted was to be held. One step forward was all it took, and her simple wish was granted.

Pam was busying herself laying the table. After the tears and forgiveness and Basil's confused barking, she had ushered Daisy and Ryan into the lounge as it was obvious neither were in any fit state to eat soup. They needed to clear the air first so hopefully while she sliced bread and kept an eye on the pan, they were doing just that.

Daisy and Ryan sat side by side on the sofa, hand in hand, merely a gesture of comfort yet it still felt good. The wood burner churned out heat while Basil kept a watchful eye on them both from his spot on the rug. It was strange, slightly surreal. After a period of wretchedness it was cathartic to sit in silence. Venting intense emotion required a subsequent break, thus allowing the dignified regaining of composure before the talking can begin, the unravelling of whatever caused such anguish.

Daisy could hear Pam clattering around in the kitchen. "Poor Mum, I don't think she's ever going to get rid of that soup. She's been trying to force feed me for days. At least now she's got another victim to palm it off on." Daisy turned sideways so she could see Ryan properly, keeping hold of his hand, which completely enveloped hers.

Ryan smiled. "She's been really kind ever since I turned up. I was scared to death when I knocked on the door but as soon as she saw me it was like I'd never been away. It was the biggest relief, I can tell you. I thought she'd rip my head off for the way I spoke to you."

"Mum's a big softie really and understands. She just wants us to get it all sorted."

"Well I just wish I'd come sooner. But I need to know, do you really forgive me Daisy? I said some awful things to you. I think I just lost my mind and was so consumed by anger at everything. I wasn't thinking straight, that's my only defence, which is still really poor." Ryan twisted his body so he too faced Daisy, her pale skin coloured only by two red dots high on her cheekbones, and she looked tired, a bit weary. He knew that feeling well.

Daisy faced Ryan and smiled. "I promise, I forgive you. You were confused and didn't know about me and Adam, the truth I mean." Daisy spoke softly, gearing up to what she had to tell him. They had all waited too long and she needed to get it over with, set Ryan straight.

"So what is it, the truth? I know Adam was on his way to tell me something and I presumed once I found the photo that it was about the baby, but there's something else, isn't there?" Ryan couldn't get the weird dream out of his head, the essence of it still lingered; something about it clung to him and wouldn't let go – Adam insisting that Daisy would explain. Not that he was going to mention it right now. It wasn't the right moment and anyway, she'd probably think he'd lost the plot.

"Yes, there is. And it's not so much about me, it's more to do with Adam and once I've explained you'll understand this." Daisy laid her free hand on her bump, stroking her jumper and the firm dome beneath. "I'll have to go back to the beginning, when we first met in Manchester because that's when it all began really, me and Adam, our story I suppose."

"Okay, go on, is it going to take long because Pam's soup might burn then all hell will break loose?" Ryan laughed and shifted in his seat, resorting to flippancy because he was really nervous, unsure now what he was going to hear and whether he would like it.

Daisy, sensing he was wary, shook her head and smiled, rearranging a cushion behind her back, ignoring the sharp practice contractions that had returned. "Mum and her soup pan will be fine, don't worry. So, as I said, it all started when we were at uni. God, that seems like such a long time ago but I can remember everything like it was yesterday, see his face in the queue, feel the leather of his jacket as he stood by my side." Recognising the threat of more tears as her eyes misted, Daisy shook away the image and pulled herself together. "Right, so this is what happened, this is how it all began..."

Ryan couldn't stop crying. No matter what Daisy did or said – brought a glass of water, passed tissues – he just wouldn't stop. It was as though her words, the truth about Adam had raised a barrier, opened a tsunami gate and now there was no way to push it shut so all she could do was wait. She couldn't hold his hand because both were covering his face so instead she rubbed his back while his shoulders heaved. Doing his bit to help, Basil came over and laid his head on Ryan's lap, staring dolefully upwards, wondering what the hell was going on. After a time, the sobbing slowed and eventually, Ryan was able to compose himself, regain order and then speak.

"Why didn't he tell me Daisy? Why couldn't he be honest with me? I wouldn't have cared, I don't care now so why would I then? I just want him back so I can tell him. I love him so much and now he's gone and it's too late."

"And he loved you too, you were his hero and that's why he didn't want anything to break your bond or taint how you saw him. That really mattered to Adam, and he was just as scared that if anyone else found out they might let it slip. Look, you and Adam told me all about your parents and it was pretty clear that neither of you wanted to be like them, in fact you made a point of making each other proud, like you were both hell bent on deleting any genetic blips. In Adam's head and no matter how many times I told him otherwise, he saw his truth as a chink in his armour, a flaw, and he wouldn't risk telling you. He overthought everything, could build the smallest worry into a mountain overnight and on top of all that Adam had to deal with who he was, so he hid it. I became his ally, his camouflage I suppose. Like a safety blanket in case anyone became suspicious or malicious and believe me there are some horrible, intolerant people out there and Adam was far too sensitive to deal with that crap."

"But wasn't he lonely? Didn't he ever feel left out? It's just so sad. I can't bear to think of him feeling that way. I'm gutted Daisy, that's the only way I can describe how I feel. And it actually hurts, right here." Ryan touched his chest, indicating the site of his pain.

Daisy inhaled, desperate to say the right thing. "Ryan, it's going to take you a while to get your head around all of this, it's not something you can deal with or understand in an afternoon. It was a shock for me but I sort of learned as we went along. I got to know his moods and could spot a mile off when he was feeling insecure or floundering, which wasn't often, I promise. But you have to cling on to this one fact because it's the truth – Adam was happy with just you and me at the centre of his life. We were enough. It's as simple as that. To know he had you in his world, his big brother, the one who saw him through uni, was always just a call away, the name that made him grin when he got mail, the person who gave him an anchor."

"And then there was you." Ryan was slowly starting to get it.

"That's right. I made a promise on that roof and I kept it as best I could but I swear, it wasn't a chore, I did it simply because I loved him so much and he loved me. Just in a different way than most people do. We were like two halves of the same person. We got each other. Most people didn't get us, though. They thought we were weird, making snide remarks behind our backs, jumping to conclusions, calling me names. We didn't care about them, but Adam *did* care about you and what you thought. I know you'd have understood but he wouldn't be swayed and I did try, I swear. But in the end I had to respect his wishes."

"It all seems so obvious now, when I look back. And that's why he always tried to push us together, it was the perfect solution wasn't it? He saw the bigger picture yet I was too pig-headed and selfish. I hate myself right now Daisy, I really do."

"Well don't! Just because Adam had a master plan didn't mean we all had to follow it. Life's like that Ryan and it doesn't always work out exactly how we want, look at what happened to me with Jamie – don't you think I'd change that if I could?" Daisy allowed herself a breather when she saw Ryan nod. Persuasion was exhausting.

"I did think that was a bit weird to be honest, Adam never bringing home a girlfriend or meeting one of the conquests he mentioned now and then, which is why I suspected he might be gay. It was the only explanation I could think of and not just that, it puzzled me why he wasn't jealous of the two of us. He was happy to step aside." Ryan sagged into the back of the sofa, sighing loudly. "Oh mate, why couldn't you be gay like so many other people? You could have been happy, got married, the whole bloody shebang. Trust you to be different!" Ryan was staring ahead, talking to the photograph on the mantelpiece. Graduation day. Adam laughing into the camera yet behind those eyes there was something else, hidden away, and it was just so sad.

Daisy could see Ryan sinking back into guilt so tried to haul him out. "But don't you see? He was happy. He had loads of friends and was a really popular guy. Adam was wise and clever, and financially astute. He was like my personal advisor and kept me in check where shoes and clothes were concerned. Lord knows I'd be bankrupt by now if he hadn't been strict and made me budget!" Daisy was glad to see she'd raised a smile so kept momentum, stayed positive.

"And he travelled the world and saw so many amazing places, wait till you see his room, it's like the British Museum up there, it takes ages to dust. And then there was football and music, I swear that record collection was part of him, an extension of his personality."

Ryan rolled his eyes, laughing at last. "How many boxes has he got now?"

"Seven! All catalogued and in order, he even took over mine because it annoyed him that I left them all over the place. So don't you see? Adam is made up of so many parts, he could simply do without, you know, being with someone. It wasn't something he missed or craved and even though it caused him bother, he just filled that gap with other stuff. And after all his angst he did so well. Please don't see his life as a failure or be sad for him. Yes, he made a mistake and should have told you but no matter what, he thrived, he smiled and laughed and made plans. Adam dealt with how he was in his own way. Maybe it toughened him up because keeping control took a lot of effort. He knew what he wanted and always seemed to get it – like having a family." Daisy affirmed her belief by patting the bump.

"He almost had it all, didn't he?" Ryan's voice was no more than a whisper. His question, a simple statement of fact, served only to break Daisy's resolve and after trying so hard to avoid it, talking of Adam in the past tense hit home, reality and pain kicking in. As tears flowed, Daisy took comfort in Ryan's arms as they sank once again into restorative silence, condensing words, gathering reserves of strength.

Time passed and their solitude was eventually interrupted by footsteps and then tapping on the door, followed by Pamela, her cheery face masking wary eyes.

"I just thought I'd see how you were getting along and if you needed anything. Shall I make you a cuppa, or would you like something to eat?" At this Basil's ears pricked up, hopeful that he too was included in the invitation.

"Yes, okay Mother! We surrender and will eat your flipping soup. How much did you actually make? It's lasting forever. Can't you put some in the freezer or down the grid? I promise not to tell the soup police." As Daisy spoke she felt Ryan stand, offering his hand before hauling her upwards, grinning as she rolled her eyes.

Pam tutted. "I'm not wasting good soup and for your information there's already some in the freezer, now less of the sarcasm, I'll go and dish it up." Bustling out of the room, satisfied that her intervention was timely, Pamela chanced a smile. They'd been talking for ages and from the look of them they both needed a break, in fact everyone did.

Content that she had fed and watered her flock, Pam had gone for a nap. The tension of the day had taken its toll. Basil was once again by his new friend's side, his head resting on Ryan's lap where he enjoyed being stroked, reminded of someone else and the firm touch of his missing master.

"Looks like you've made a new mate. Do you think he knows who you are, like he can sense the connection between you and Adam?" Daisy was fetching the biscuit tin, suddenly hungry again, a sensation she had almost forgotten.

"He might do. Dogs are supposed to be sensitive to stuff like that. Do you think he misses Adam?"

"Definitely! At first he waited at the door for him and whined constantly to be let outside then he'd shoot off as though he was trying to sniff him out. It broke my heart because I couldn't explain." Once again Daisy blinked back tears that were never far away. It was so hard to hold it together but she had to otherwise they'd spend all night crying when all she wanted was to talk about Adam and never stop.

Easing herself onto the chair Daisy passed Ryan the tin. "Tell me about the funeral, did it go okay? Did everyone turn up?" At this Ryan coloured and Daisy instantly regretted asking but before she could apologise, he got there first.

"Oh God, there's another thing I regret. I'm so sorry for stopping you from coming. I hate myself. It was cruel and a massive mistake because on the day I wanted you by my side, it felt so wrong without you and Pam." Ryan couldn't look up, saving Daisy from her own shame.

"Well I need to make a confession about that…and you'll probably think I'm a selfish cow when I tell you but in the end I was glad you told me to stay away. Not at the time, I was really shocked and hurt but as the days passed I realised I was more upset about us falling out than not going to the funeral."

Ryan looked up, surprise etched on his face. "Really! Why?"

"I was too scared, and a coward, so when it came down to it you did me a favour because I don't think I could've coped with it. How could I say goodbye to him again, see his coffin or watch those curtains close? You gave me a get-out and I was thankful for it, *so* bloody relieved in fact. I dug my heels in and made everyone swear not to contact you or plead my case. I think Mum guessed. She said on the morning of Dad's funeral she wished for a really good excuse to stay at home or a super power to fast forward to the end of the day. But in the end brave, decent people like you and Mum pull themselves together and get on with it. I'm just selfish and disrespectful."

"No you're not and if it makes you feel better, that's exactly how I felt. I swear Daisy, all I wanted to do was get the whole day over with, follow Adam's wishes and then scarper. I just went through the motions and did what was expected. In some ways I felt detached from it all and thinking about it now, maybe if you'd been there I might have crumbled and let you take the burden. Looks like we're both a pair of wimps after all." Ryan smiled, reaching over to wipe away a stray tear that was making its way down Daisy's face.

"Yep, out of all of us it looks like Adam was the tough guy, so go on, tell me all about it. I can deal with it from the safety of the kitchen table, and while you're up put the kettle on, I think this requires another cup of tea." Daisy winked at Ryan who sighed and then did as he was told.

One packet of biscuits later, Ryan had finished relating the hideous day and although he hated every moment, owed it to Daisy. After listening passively to a potted account of the service, of which she approved yet remained glad to have missed, Daisy's interest was piqued at the mention of how their friends perceived her absence and the reaction of one person in particular, Fliss.

"That woman really boils my blood! She keeps ringing but we let it go to answerphone. I don't care if I never speak to her again. She's a nosey cow and only out to make trouble, but it's the others that bother me. I can't ignore them forever and the baby will be here soon. We were going to tell everyone once Adam had spoken to you but now I've lost my confidence, I don't think I could cope with all the questions. I bet they all hate me for being an ignorant bitch and I really can't blame them." This nagging doubt had plagued Daisy for weeks. It all seemed so simple when Adam was in control. Nothing could dampen his elation whereas now the plan was ruined. But Ryan had the answer.

"We'll face them together. Once the baby is here we can announce his birth to everyone, shout it from the rooftops. Post a million pictures on Facebook or wherever. Let them gossip all they want, who cares? I'm going to make sure everyone knows how proud I am of my nephew, and you are of your son. We'll soon see who your real friends are, and Adam's. So don't worry, I've got your back and won't let anyone upset you or disrespect my brother, either." Ryan saw relief flood through Daisy, she even had more colour in her cheeks.

"It's a deal, thanks Ryan. And I know all this has been a shock so if there's anything at all you want to ask me, if something springs to mind just say. It's just so good to have you here, which reminds me, how long can you stay?"

"For as long as you need me. I rang work and put in some leave. I'm owed loads because I've been overseas so much, I just need to keep them in the loop. Will it be okay to stay here, I don't want to intrude?"

"Of course, and you're not intruding. I want you around especially when this one arrives. I'm not letting you go that easily." There was a moment when their eyes met and then it was gone,

Basil interrupting by pushing his empty bowl around the floor, dropping the hint.

As Daisy sighed and heaved herself upright, she remembered something. "So what changed your mind? I'd just about given up and then you appear out of the blue." Daisy pulled a packet of dog bones from the cupboard and passed one to Basil who shot off, delighted.

"Ah well, that's another story and you might think I've lost the plot if I tell you." Ryan wasn't sure how or where to begin.

"Why would I think that? Go on, tell me." Daisy was back in her seat and waiting.

"Promise not to laugh…"

"I promise, I think."

"I had a really weird dream, just last night. But it was so real and sort of uplifting and I swear I could hear and see him just like I can see you right now."

Daisy's eyes were wide. "Who…Adam?"

"Yes, Adam. He came to talk to me in a dream. I don't believe in all that spirit stuff but I'm telling you it was like he was there, in my room, and I could actually feel him when he sat on my bed."

"Seriously?" Daisy felt strange and slightly numb, like time had stopped and the only thing that told her she was still functioning was her giddy heart.

Ryan nodded, relieved that she hadn't laughed at him. "I swear, I wouldn't joke about something like that."

Daisy was transfixed. "I'm a bit jealous now, even of a dream because I've been waiting for one for so long, and I looked everywhere for a sign, anything, just so I'd know he was okay. We made a promise you see, years ago, and I wondered if he'd forgot. So tell me, what did he say, in your dream, what did he look like, was he okay?" Daisy wanted to cry, she could feel it building along with the expectation of hearing about Adam, making her hands tremble, so she grabbed Ryan's, his fingers closing around hers.

"Daisy don't take it too seriously, it was just a dream, okay? Maybe it was my subconscious or very guilty conscience prodding me to do the right thing. And I'd had a skin-full so my brain was more or less pickled. You mustn't set too much store on it. I reckon it was a combination of things, coincidences or my head making sense of problems I couldn't face when I was awake and sober. Not only that, I desperately wanted to see him again, too."

"Or, he could have specifically chosen you, the one person who doesn't stand for bullshit and sees things in black and white. If I'd gone to see Gypsy Rose Lee at the end of the pier, or Cassandre told me she'd dreamt of him I'd take what they said with a pinch of salt, but not you. You're probably the only person I'd know wasn't being dramatic or trying to make me feel better so perhaps that's why he appeared to you. What if it wasn't a dream? You said yourself it felt real." Daisy had already convinced herself that it was Adam, not a dream.

"It was, but like I said I was very drunk and the last thing I want to do is upset you, again." Ryan was being glib and regretting the mention of his bloody dream because Daisy was hanging on to every word.

"Okay, I'll be open minded, I promise. So go on, what did he say, was he okay?" Daisy was determined to extract the story so a small fib was allowed.

"He looked fine, just the same, but he had new Converse, they caught my eye straight away. They were pale blue, City blue, and there was something about his eyes, too. They were so brown and huge like they were hypnotising me, and I know this all sounds totally mad but it was like I was in a bubble because the edges of the room were sort of fuzzy." Ryan shook his head but Daisy just told him to go on.

"He was looking through my letters and then came to sit on the bed. He did that thing he used to do, you know, throw himself backwards onto the mattress from a great height, then he crossed his legs and basically started bossing me about." When he saw Daisy's eyes filling with tears he tried to call a halt to the telling of his mad dream. "Look, if it's going to upset you we can leave it for another day."

But Daisy insisted, desperate to imagine Adam being alive and bossy. "No, I really want to know, I might not look it but I'm happy. Please carry on, what did he say?"

By the time Ryan repeated the dream Daisy was in floods of tears and had gone through half the kitchen roll but no matter how many times he tried to stop, she insisted on hearing more.

"Hey don't cry, it was a good dream, he looked so well, happy even."

"I know, I know, I just can't help it. I'm sorry, go on."

"It was like he was giving me cryptic clues, typical Adam and when I woke up the next morning I opened my mail and there it was, a letter from the solicitor with a cheque and a message telling me to go crazy, just like he told me. It just hit me there and then that I had to do what he said. I needed to come here and sort things out so I just got my shit together and set off."

Daisy blew her nose and took a deep breath, overwrought but happy. "Thanks for telling me, it's given me comfort and whether you believe it or not I think he did come to see you. I bet he wanted to show off his new trainers." Both of them smiled before Daisy caught a strange look. Ryan was considering something.

Daisy had absorbed every single word and not laughed at him once, so now she was calmer there was one last thing he'd remembered, probably the weirdest bit of all and the final part of the dream. "And there was something else, just before he faded away…"

Daisy pushed a stray lock of hair behind her ear then gave Ryan her fullest attention. He was also aware that her grip on his hand tightened, then tightened some more until it was becoming quite painful, as was the look on her face.

"Ryan…" Daisy took a deep breath. "Ryan, I think it's happening."

"What's happening, are you okay, you've gone a funny colour?"

"The baby, I think it's really coming, these pains are different, but it can't be. It's a week early and I'm not ready." Letting go of his hands she tried to stand, panic etched on her face, which looked hot and clammy. "I'll just walk around, it usually helps then they go away. Go away, go away, go away." Daisy repeated the words over and over as she pushed back the chair and began to pace the kitchen, joined hastily by Ryan who held her hand and shuffled along by her side.

"Shit, they really hurt, please make them stop Ryan. Something's wrong. I'm scared, I'm not ready."

"Don't be scared, I'll stay with you, are you supposed to breathe or something? Do that panty thing?" Ryan began to puff air from his lips like he'd seen women do on the telly; the withering look from Daisy told him to stop. "I know! I'll get your mum…just stay there, I'll be right back. Don't panic…stay calm." Ryan tentatively released her hand and ignored the wide-eyed look of fear on Daisy's face as he shot off, calling Pam's name in a loud but measured voice.

Daisy held onto the back of the chair, watched by Basil from his basket. Praying she'd be spared another contraction, Daisy tried the panty thing and for a moment thought she was off the hook until a strange sensation down below was followed by the trickling of water onto the kitchen tiles. Hearing the noise caused Basil to prick up his ears then pad cautiously over to investigate before looking up at Daisy, most impressed by her big puddle then hoping he wouldn't get the blame. And as if by magic, once the trickling ceased another contraction took hold, causing Daisy to wince then cry out for her mum. It was really happening and there was no doubt about it. Adam's baby was on his way.

The hospital had fallen silent. Gone were the daytime sounds of hustle and urgency, swishing curtains, murmured voices, pacing footsteps, clanking trolleys. While night nurses kept watch on sleeping mothers and babes, the pace seemed gentler, keeping time with the hum of strip lights, the only disturbance in an otherwise serene and perfect world.

Daisy and Ryan were cocooned in a private room inside the maternity hospital, the glow from the bedside lamp casting a warm light onto the face of the sleeping boy, Adam's son. Pam had gone home, list in hand and eager to ring round half the village to spread the news once she'd had some kip and the hour was more civilised. It was 3am and despite the exertion and drama, neither felt the need for sleep, both entranced by the baby Daisy held in her arms.

"I can't stop looking at him. He really is perfect isn't he?" Ryan was in awe of his nephew.

"Yep, one million percent gorgeous, and look at his hair, I can't believe he has so much. We'll have to look through that box of photos at home and see if you and Adam had the same. Here, do you want another hold while I drink my tea, otherwise this one will go cold too."

Not needing to be asked twice Ryan leant forward, the awkwardness he'd felt when Pam passed him over earlier a distant memory, the shock of witnessing a real-life birth reverberating through his body. And he was so proud of Daisy who had been terrified yet once in the throes of labour became gradually braver, the deliverance of her baby overriding fear.

Of everything he'd seen and done – breathtaking clifftop moments before abseiling into a void, the roar of wind as you surfed across the ocean, fresh snow under skis on a downhill stretch, the stomach-churning thrill of a jet as you were catapulted into the sky – all were eclipsed when, on either side of Daisy, holding her hands tightly, he and Pam cheered and wept as Liam entered their world.

"Did Adam choose his name?" Ryan stroked the baby's hair as he spoke.

"Oh yes, but I knew that's what he'd pick, I even wrote it down just to prove I could read his mind. I suppose it should be Noel. Loads of babies are given the name over Christmas, it's a French tradition but Adam insisted on Liam. I'm just glad his musical idol wasn't called Ozzy or Prince…or Elvis, can you imagine shouting that across the campsite? Elvis, your tea's ready!" Daisy sipped her drink, watching Ryan study the tiny fingers of his nephew.

As he laughed at the idea of baby Elvis, a memory pinged into his head but then thought better of it, but Daisy had caught the look.

"What? Don't you like the name…obviously he's going to have Adam's too?"

"No, it's not that, I love his name and we'll make sure he listens to all of the other Liam's songs, it's just that you reminded me of something Adam made me promise. Knowing him he probably planned it all this way."

"Why, what have you remembered?" Daisy replaced her cup and immediately focused on Ryan as goosebumps appeared on her arms and neck. The air in the room had changed, maybe she'd sucked it all in.

"You know earlier, when I was telling you about my dream but this one decided to interrupt me mid-story?" Ryan looked down, then up at Daisy's moonbeam eyes, her head nodding, encouraging him onward. "Well just before Adam began to fade he asked me to give you a message. I had to listen and repeat it exactly. He said you'd know what it meant." Ryan's mouth had gone dry because he knew, just from the look on Daisy's face, awash with tears, that this was what she'd been waiting for, all this time.

He reached out his hand, she held on.

"Adam said that you were right about the angels. They do wear sparkly dresses in every amazing colour of the rainbow." Hearing Daisy catch a sob, her free hand covering her mouth as tears pumped from her eyes, Ryan continued, determined to get it right.

"And Elvis doesn't work in a chip shop. He runs a burger bar in heaven."

*

Epilogue

Three years later
France

Daisy watched as Liam ran ahead in hot pursuit of Basil who refused to relinquish his popped ball, another one for the bin. Her son's blue football shirt stood out amongst the woodland greens, curly brown locks bouncing as he ran amongst the trees, trying in vain to outwit their daft dog.

They were on their way to meet Ryan who would be closing up the boathouse after a day on the lake teaching children how to canoe and windsurf. As they broke through the clearing, a hint of woodsmoke drifted from the cabins that were dotted amongst the trees, reminding Daisy that winter was on its way, the summer months a fading memory.

Nowadays they were busy all year round after slowly expanding the business, the cabins proving a popular choice with those looking for a rustic, Christmas escape. They also had a steady flow of local people eager to use the new sailing facilities and recently, a surfing club had been formed. They were inundated with bookings from schools and colleges wanting to attend Ryan's outward bound courses, the notes that Adam left behind the inspiration behind it all. They now had a three-man team who taught outdoor skills, leading adventurous and timid youngsters alike on hiking expeditions, teaching them rock climbing and map reading or wild camping under the stars.

Daisy had never been in any doubt that once Ryan returned he would stay, not out of duty but for love. After so long apart, both desperate to right any wrongs and defy whatever plans destiny had for them, Daisy and Ryan wanted only to be together, neither prepared to waste another day. Just as there had been no plan for her and Adam, Ryan and Daisy took things one day at a time, making it up as they went along. And so far they'd done a damn fine job of being happy, which started with telling the world about Liam.

*

Once mother and baby were home and everyone caught their breath, Ryan and Daisy announced his arrival, proudly introducing Adam's son, a beautiful boy he shared with Daisy. The carefully composed message briefly explained Adam and Daisy's desire to be parents and bestow upon each other the most precious gift. It was accompanied by a collage of photos showing Daisy and Adam with their baby bump, a black and white alien, Granny Pam with bobble-hat hair, and a sleeping infant swaddled in the arms of his mum with his proud uncle by his side. It was sent to all of their friends then later posted on Facebook, just in case they'd missed anyone. The good guys now understood why Daisy was too distraught and fragile to attend Adam's funeral or make contact, and neither did they pry, accepting and respecting their friends' private decision.

At the end of March, just before the site opened for the season, three-month-old Liam met his daddy's friends for the first time when they all came to stay for Adam's memorial. It was held in the forest underneath the boughs of the Grandad Tree on a sunny spring day. Here amongst the shedding of tears, shared stories, music and laughter, they celebrated Adam's life and this time, Daisy was there to hold Ryan's hand. They were brave, together. It was a joyous day, filled with love and memories where turns were taken to hold the baby who, with a mop of dark hair, reminded them so much of his daddy.

Jim and Tommy raided the City superstore, vowing that Liam would be dressed in blue for life, and Lester bought him a star that was named after Adam – they even had a solar map so they could point it out. Kiki and Carol brought their own little girls, while Shalini came hand in hand with her handsome doctor friend. Even Allison made it, overjoyed at last to meet Daisy and her son.

The only person absent was Fliss. She wasn't invited and everyone knew why. There would be no more excuses or blind eyes. Adam's memorial was sacred and neither Ryan nor Daisy wished it to be tainted by those of a malicious nature, it was as simple as that. A new chapter was about to be written and as Liam grew, with an open invitation extended to the good guys, he would only be surrounded by those who knew and loved his daddy best.

*

Daisy loved seeing Campanule so alive and thriving. It was hard work and the admin side alone kept her and Pam occupied, not to mention Liam who never seemed to stop. He was a mini-whirlwind, on the go from the second he woke and even when his tired, action-man limbs gave in, his enquiring mind had a reserve of battery power. Pamela said he was the image of both Adam and Ryan, a tiny pea from a three-pea pod and it was sometimes hard to see where the similarities between them ended.

Liam adored Daddy Ryan, hero-worshipped him in fact and followed him around like unfaithful Basil, who had quickly dumped Daisy in favour of the man who reminded him of his first master. Liam knew all about Daddy Adam whose photo was on the cupboard in his bedroom, right next to the treasures he was allowed to touch, as long as he was very careful. At night his mummy played music that came out of the magic circles she kept in boxes. They were Daddy Adam's and he'd left them for Liam when he went to live in heaven with the angels.

Daisy knew that as he grew, Liam would ask more questions, which she would answer one by one, truthfully and with care, but for now her son was happy with his lot, untroubled by loss. The thing they were most worried about was how to tell Liam that the bump in Mummy's tummy was a girl, *not* the baby brother he'd insisted on. Ryan on the other hand was ecstatic and couldn't wait, assuring Daisy that Liam would be just as happy with a new bike, and anyway they could get him a baby brother the next time, or the time after that!

As they reached the lakeside path Daisy told Liam to slow down – he always wanted to be the first to reach Ryan but Basil repeatedly pipped him to the post. Spotting Ryan at the shore Daisy waved, his attention now drawn to his family and the little boy who raced towards him. Soon Liam was hoisted on Ryan's shoulders while Basil barked eagerly for attention, demanding his ball was thrown into the lake.

As they wandered home through the forest, hand in hand, looking for nature's treasures, when the breeze caught Daisy's hair or leaves fluttered and scattered, the thought did cross her mind that Adam was there too. Just like on hazy days, as she looked across the lake and heard the sound of laughter, listening for his voice amongst the crowd, a whisper on the wind. Daisy remained vigilant but she was no longer desperate, her life hinging on a sign. Keeping his side of a promise they made so many years ago, as they lay on the pontoon watching stars, Adam got a message through. She'd, received it loud and clear and knew that he was okay, more than likely busy doing other things. He could be anywhere and everywhere. Fishing with her dad or having a day at the seaside with Olive in between popping back for visits, keeping an eye on his family before shooting off on a star.

Daisy imagined him in all his favourite places. On the stands at the Etihad watching his team win the league, perhaps he was part of the pitch invasion, running around like crazy with the other fans. He'd have been to Glastonbury for a dance and a spaced-out chat with Turnip or maybe he was overseas, learning the secrets of the pyramids or the stones at Carnac. But wherever he was Daisy imagined him happy, at peace with himself, all his questions answered, content that down here on earth, everything was as it should be, just like he planned.

Sometimes though, the truth that he was gone crept up and swallowed her whole. A piece of her heart remained wounded, impossible to heal. But Daisy would never lose Adam. He was part of her and their son, ingrained in her past and future. They were surrounded by the treasures he'd left behind, things they could touch and hold, look upon or hear, and be reminded. Liam was the greatest treasure of all.

One day, she would see Adam again, of that Daisy had no doubt. Until then he would forever be her best boy, her soul mate, her missing half. And should anyone question her belief in him, or if they didn't understand what they had, it didn't bother her. Daisy just didn't care. It only meant one thing, a simple truth that she told herself time and time again, whispering the words to her favourite photo of Adam when she was alone – they don't know about us, and they've never heard of love.

The End

Acknowledgements

I do hope you enjoyed the story of Daisy and Adam. I loved writing it, especially because during my research I had an excuse to listen to the songs of one of my favourite singers, an inspirational lady in life and lyrics.

This brings me nicely to some other wonderful women, the team at Bombshell Books who believed in my book and supported me throughout the publishing process. Thank you from the bottom of my heart to Betsy, Sumaira, Alexina, Sarah and Heather. And Fred, who made sense of music copyright law and gave me great advice. A huge thank you goes to Lydia, my editor, who along with polishing my work allowed me to express myself freely and bring my characters to life in the way I imagined them.

My writing journey would not be complete unless accompanied by my friends and followers, the fabulous people who read my books and lend their support in so many ways. Thanks to every one of you, including Karen Fell for choosing Basil's name and Allison Ferraris for sharing her experiences and adventures aboard ship.

I am forever indebted to Angela Rose, my wise friend who has loyally supported me from the beginning of my writing journey. I must also thank Anne Boland, Noelle Clinton, Nicki Murphy and Tina Jackson for your Beta reading skills but most of all, your friendship,

As always the final words are for my family, you are the best. Love you all x

Printed in Great
Britain
by Amazon